The

Jeff Dawson is a journalist and author. He has been a long-standing contributor to *The Sunday Times* Culture section, writing regular A-list interview-led arts features (interviewees including the likes of Robert De Niro, George Clooney, Dustin Hoffman, Hugh Grant, Angelina Jolie, Jerry Seinfeld and Nicole Kidman). He is also a former US Editor of *Empire* magazine.

Jeff is the author of three non-fiction books – *Tarantino/Quentin Tarantino: The Cinema of Cool*, *Back Home: England And The 1970 World Cup*, which *The Time* rated 'Truly outstanding', and *Dead Reckoning: The Dunedin Star Disaster*, the latter nominated for the Mountbatten Maritime Prize.

Also by Jeff Dawson

An Ingo Finch Mystery

No Ordinary Killing
The Cold North Sea
Hell Gate

THE COLD NORTH SEA

JEFF DAWSON

CANELO

First published in the United Kingdom in 2018 by Canelo

This edition published in the United Kingdom in 2021 by

Canelo
31 Helen Road
Oxford OX2 0DF
United Kingdom

A CIP catalogue record for this book is available from the British Library.

Print ISBN 978 1 78863 562 2
Ebook ISBN 978 1 78863 191 4

Printed and bound in Great Britain by Clays Ltd, Elcograf S.p.A.

For Clare, Mack and Mae

Based on a historical event

Part One

Chapter One

The North Sea – October 21st, 1904

Joseph Smith watched the deckhands run the line out from the starboard boom. In the last throes of daylight it snaked across the water – till the steam capstan took up the slack and, with a *crack*, it whipped taut.

The trawler kicked and the screw shaft whined. Bulging with a ton of herring, the twin nets would place even greater strain upon the rattling boiler. When they'd hauled them in earlier, Joseph feared they'd be dragged under, the stern barely a foot above the waves.

Joseph… *Joe*… waded shin-deep through the squirming mass of slippery silver and positioned himself well clear. He felt the watchful stare of the bosun. The sudden flex of a rough hemp rope could shear off fingers – even a limb, he'd been warned. Against a turning boat or swinging outrigger, it could crush a man dead against the gunwale.

Glad he had survived this much on his maiden voyage, Joe reached into his oilskin and pulled out his smokes. Fourteen years old but he felt like a man. He stroked his chin and fancied there were bristles to rasp. The bosun rolled his eyes. Beside him in the *Crane*'s wheelhouse, Captain Smith, Joe's father, was squinting through the telescope. He had placed his boy in the bosun's care.

The speed picked up and the Gamecock fleet went about its business, dragging the depths, harvesting the fathoms. A day out from Hull, the boats were well over the Dogger Bank now – shallow ground but fertile. Darkness fell and the fog crept about them, the sea relatively calm, just a gentle swell. Though as every hand had cautioned Joe, it could change in an instant as the Arctic weather funnelled down from the north or the winds swung from a benign wet westerly to the savage dry stab from the east.

The bosun had asked Joe to observe the fleet's 'Admiral'. He was up ahead in a converted smack, a sailing boat with a steam engine implanted. The Admiral had been sending up rockets to indicate his tack – red for port, green for starboard. He'd then hung a blue lantern from the foremast, the signal to shoot the trawl. The *Crane* had done the same. One by one a string of azure pearls wound through the mist, forty beads in total spread over three square miles.

In autumn the weather was cold but tolerable. This was nothing, the old salts would add – veterans of long hauls to the Faroes and Iceland. One, a smiling white-beard, regaled Joe with tales of deadly squalls and fifty-foot waves and chipping the ice off the rigging. Not what it used to be – those days when you caught your fish, came home and flogged your wares on the quayside.

The Gamecock, a 'box fleet', was a different proposition – sitting there for five weeks, heaving in fish, having others do its bidding. A company cutter had been up before sundown for the first day's catch; another would arrive at dawn.

The cutters were refrigerated, packed with ice. They would ferry the fish directly to London then return with supplies. No romance in that, it was tutted – just a factory process, and with too many opportunities for a swindle. The coalers would be back and forth, too. And then the mission ships, selling tobacco and woollens, providing also, on request – not that many men did – something to read.

Joe, nominally the 'cook' but essentially a skivvy, went below to the tiny galley, made tea and toted mugs to the bridge. He moved on to two of the hands and the second engineer. The others were hot-bunking between watches, all of them cultivating an infernal stink.

Nets cast, the blood-splattered deck crew got back to gutting and rinsing the several hundredweight of fish slithering around them. Herring was the fleet's chief prize. They had spawned on the Dogger and were moving *en masse* towards the Skagerrak. Knives were ground, fish bellies were slit, gulls screeched and swooped. The fish were sorted into boxes (hence 'box fleet') – herring, cod, some pollock, the rest thrown back to churn in the wake.

Back on watch, Joe counted the lights. To the east and south were other fishing boats, probably Dutch or Danish; sometimes, off Scotland, they'd run into Norwegians, they said. Two points off the starboard bow, maybe three miles distant, came the shapes of bigger vessels travelling south and Joe shouted it up to the bridge. They were lit fore and aft. Not fishermen – probably Royal Navy, the bosun mused. The Home Fleet had been out on manoeuvres.

They had encountered the navy before, Joe was told. Sometimes a destroyer or frigate would dispatch a launch and buy up some stock for cash, a sum to be split between the crew in the absence of the company cutter ('Not a word to anyone, lad').

These ships, however, were moving with purpose. They were on course to pass close by and, at their current speed, would throw up quite a wash. Definitely warships – you could see the guns now. But not British. The Royal Navy always kept a good line, said the bosun. This lot were irregular, the lead ship steaming ahead while the others strained to keep up. And now their lights were going out…

The skipper grabbed his loudhailer and yelled something to the *Mino*, the nearest trawler on the port side. She was too far away to hear. The bosun sounded the steam horn and the call was echoed throughout the fishing fleet – a signal to the warships, indicating their presence. The men paused in their gutting. The lead vessel, now less than a mile away, was at least slowing. The others in its party appeared to catch up, beginning to fan out.

The first ship was huge, looming through the mist, the thick air muffling its sound – a great silhouetted wall of turrets and muzzles and giant stacks belching smoke. It was a cruiser, possibly even a battleship, someone said. But *definitely* not British. You could just make out the unusual script on its bows.

The Hull boats tooted again – this time a welcome. Some trawlermen waved. But there was nothing in response. The skipper shrugged, the bosun muttered. He looked down at the deckhands and motioned for them to get on with their business.

WHOOSH!

With a tremendous squeal, a rocket went up. It made Joe jump. Way above, a red star burst and drifted down. Acrid smoke rolled across the water. It was not from the Admiral this time. It had come from the first warship. It was steering exceptionally close.

There were shouts now in a foreign tongue. Joe threw his hands to his eyes as searchlight shutters were clacked open and an intense beam of light swept the *Crane*'s deck. It hurt to look, too dazzling. You could hear the whirr of a motor – a gun turret…? A barked, guttural order…

And then…

In a ferocious whirl of phosphorescent white and a crack like thunder, a plume of spray shot twenty feet into the air. It was as if the sea itself were now crashing down upon them, hundreds of pounds of water pulled earthwards. They flinched and turned their backs. There were bellows and yells as the searchlights swept and, to a metallic rattle of breeches and magazines, deck cannon began the methodical *pom-pom-pom* of raking the nearest fishing boats from stem to stern.

The bosun ducked and curled into a ball. In the wheelhouse, shrapnel and splinters were flying in a demonic blizzard. He pressed his hands to his ears to stave the din. Through a crack in the boards he looked out. The *Crane*'s bows had gone; water was gushing in, swirling in a torrent.

To the port side the *Mino* lay shattered, cleaved through its main deck. Men were flailing in the water, being sucked under by heavy oilskins. The *Moulmein*, too, had been badly hit, its funnel gone, the superstructure shredded. Some men waved fish in the air, protesting innocence, as if they were white flags.

It was quiet for a moment and then more chaos... The lead vessels were rotating their guns. Though this time they were turning *away* to fire, inexplicably, on the tail of their own line, a mile or more to the rear. There were great orange flashes as the guns of the stragglers returned the favour.

Stray shells screeched overhead in an incessant banshee wail, the lead warship, the battleship, the apparent prized new target. They smashed into the water some hundred yards or so behind the *Crane*, kicking up jagged teeth of foam. On the foremast of the battleship, towering above the water, a blue lamp was hastily illuminated – not unlike the fishermen's. It was a signal of sorts. Soon the shelling ceased.

The bosun coughed on cordite, wafted smoke from his eyes and yelled with all his might a great animal rage of defiance. On the rail of the warship sailors leaned over, quizzical but unmoved, casually observing the carnage as one might contemplate a sunset. One of the men flipped a cigarette into the water. The bosun recognised the uniform... the hooped blue and white undershirt beneath the V of the tunic, the tally ribbons trailing from the cap.

The engines surged and the lead warship moved on, offering no succour, no lifebelts, no concern for the great flotsam wash now sweeping the floundering survivors. Its accomplices began scattering. The Hull boats had had no chance to flee, weighed down by their nets. A nearby trawler, the *Gull*, had cut its lines to motor over, its deckhands reaching out. The *Crane* was tilting, fast going under.

In the wheelhouse, the bosun lay the body of the skipper down and jumped back to the deck, praying the man's son hadn't seen. But Joe was transfixed by the prone third mate, gutting knife still in hand, a great ragged hole where his face used to be. The bosun wrested off his oilskin and lay it over him. His name was Leggett, he said.

To a desperate call from Rea, the chief engineer, a dazed Joe waded down into the darkness to try and work the pump. The skipper's lad was brave, knew the bosun. He *had* seen what had happened. The two emerged a minute later, their labours to no avail. Joe helped round up the others. They were abandoning ship.

There were over thirty warships, someone was shouting – of the ones they could see; probably more out there in the fog. They needed to get out of there. A parting warship tooted its foghorn as if in friendly farewell. It was that, for the bosun, which really twisted the knife.

Chapter Two

Finch shrugged off his overcoat and planted himself in the safe remove of a window seat. He regarded his ale. It was an object of devotion – the tawny hue, the beads of sweat, the overflow of soft, sudsy head. He waited for it to settle, an essential part of the pre-noon ritual. Then, and *only* then, did he take the first sacred sip, letting the alcohol infuse the sweet spot budding behind the eyes – source of 'the bliss' as he had come to call it (which alternated with 'the dagger').

He rested an elbow on the windowsill. The thin light of autumn strained behind low, grey cloud. On the roof opposite, a jackdaw flapped over crumbling tiles. It was so quiet within the pub – just the ambient crackle from the inglenook – you could hear the bird squawk.

The road formed a narrow cut between looming, gabled buildings. A section of Watling Street, the thoroughfare had once channelled the Claudian legions. Later, as the coaching route between London and the north, it became studded with inns. After that had come the railways, decline. And now…

The thing announced its presence long before you could see it – a distant rasp that rose with proximity then swelled, via punctuating splutters, into a metallic cacophony. And then it came, hurtling along the cobbles, bouncing over ruts, before shifting down through the gears to a pedestrian pootle. In what seemed an act of supreme impertinence, it slow-rolled to idle right outside the window, a mechanical hum that resonated round the bar room and shook a horse brass off the wall.

'Good God!' blurted a man with a white walrus moustache. He set down his port, craning his neck.

The automobile was bright yellow – a Spyker, Finch recognised. It had green leather upholstery and a beaming wide-eyed female passenger, her broad-brimmed hat tied down with a chiffon scarf. The driver was trussed up in tweeds, goggles and a preposterous pair of flared leather gauntlets.

He yanked the handbrake lever, big enough for a railway signal box, then hopped over the running board to raise a flap on the bonnet and go through – what seemed to Finch – the theatrics of *faux*-checking something or other. Seconds later he issued a thumbs-up, climbed back on board and opened the throttle. The contraption went grinding off again, accompanied by a fairground shriek from the lady friend and an unnecessary double honk of the horn.

The blessed silence resumed. Finch sighed, lit a Navy Cut, drew deep and exhaled a billowing lungful. He studied the wisps as they curled beneath the low, blackened beams, mingling with the creeping fug of woodsmoke.

On an empty table lay a copy of *The Times*. He nodded to the man with the walrus moustache, who gestured that the paper was free. Finch unfolded it, smacked out a crumple and sent some ash tumbling down his waistcoat. The news contained the usual catalogue of Great Power posturing: Germans sabre-rattling over Morocco; Germans sabre-rattling over just about everything... The Anglo-French *Entente*, '*Cordiale*' as they were calling it, ink not yet dry, was already being tested.

And now this business with the Russians...

'Of course, it'll be *war*,' piped White Walrus.

The stand-off was into its third week – that grisly incident in the North Sea where the Russian battle fleet had fired upon those poor trawlers from Hull.

The man raised his walking stick, stabbing at the paper.

'Mark my words, sir... You mark my words.'

Already embroiled in a brutal conflict with Japan, scrapping over territory in Korea and Manchuria, Russia had dispatched its Baltic squadron on the long haul to the Far East. It was why those warships had been chugging across the North Sea that night. The latest excuse being proffered by Russia's foreign minister for its bombardment of the Hull fishermen was that the Imperial Navy had simply mistaken the vessels for Japanese torpedo boats.

'*No matter that the theatre of war is round the other side of the globe?*' challenged today's incredulous *Times* editorial. Or, pondered Finch, that torpedo boats, the latest naval wonder weapon, could operate at only short range from home, hardly 10,000 miles.

Ralph, the giant barman, paused for a moment from wiping glasses.

'How about it, Dr Finch? Battleships, cruisers, destroyers, all spooked by a hundredweight of halibut?'

There was a muted splutter around the room.

'If you want my opinion…' added White Walrus.

'I'll ask for it,' muttered Finch and rustled his newspaper, hoisting it high.

Finch groaned. The public appetite for war seemed never to dim. The press relished every moment. Britain had put on a show by closing the Suez Canal – the Russian fleet would now have to divert around the entire continent of Africa. But the fact that the diplomats were burning the midnight oil, working to construe Russia's explanation as a plausible scenario, suggested to him that no one in Whitehall seriously wanted a dust-up with Russia. Not when the *real* enemy lay elsewhere. For Russia, its spat with the Japanese was already proving a military disaster – an old and decadent empire humiliated by a vibrant and modernising one. Let its fleet get chastised there.

A business item drew a wry smile from Finch and memory of a distant voice: '*Buy stock in Frigidaire*' – advice he evidently should have heeded. His mind slipped into the past and he felt ill again. No, not ill… *detached*. Not really present. He took another restorative sip of ale, another puff on his cigarette…

A man was slumped at the bar. His belly strained at his buttons. He raised his head.

'Should give the bastard a damn good pasting.'

'The Tsar?' echoed White Walrus. 'Hear! Hear!'

'I mean the driver of that bloody car.'

The ripple of chuckles masked the creak of the door. A smallish, thin man in a worn jacket, scarf and flat cap darted nervously to the bar and enquired something of Ralph, who stroked a wild sideburn and nodded in Finch's direction. The man made his way over, tentative, catching his thigh on the armrest of a stray, empty chair.

'Dr Finch… Dr Ingo Finch?' he ventured.

Finch huffed and nodded, sanctity now well and truly violated. The man removed his flat cap and kneaded it in the manner of a supplicant. He kept his voice down.

'Sorry t'trouble you, sir, but someone say I might find you n'here.'

The man cast his eyes around the room, glanced out into the street, then settled on Finch again.

'You know, my surgery's a two-minute walk,' Finch offered. 'You might want to drop in there, speak to my receptionist…'

'It's nothin' like that, sir.'

His accent was rural, Finch noted. Not of these parts. East Anglia. Not the twang of Suffolk, but the full-on, near impenetrable sing-song of Norfolk. It took concentration.

'I see.'

Finch whispered the next bit, trying to affect some tact.

'…In which case, if you'd like to send along the *young lady* in question…'

'No, sir. No. No, no, *no*.'

Flustered, he cast an eye behind him, then looked to the street again.

Asked Finch: 'Then, Mr…?'

'Sorry… *Pickersgill*.'

He said it like 'Pick'sgill'.

'Beg your pardon?'

'Pick-ers-gill. Sidney Pickersgill.'

'Then, Mr Pickersgill, you'd best have a seat.'

Finch gestured to a chair. Pickersgill scraped it back. He sat, hunched forward, eyes darting still.

'Drink?' asked Finch.

'What?'

'You want a drink?'

'Oh… No thank you, sir. I don't.'

Finch sipped his ale. The froth clung to his moustache.

'Good for you. Bugger on the liver… In which case, I don't suppose…'

He offered him a Navy Cut.

'No, sir. Thank you.'

Finch struck a lucifer and lit another.

'So what ails you, Mr Pickersgill?'

'Nothin', sir.'

Finch shook out the match.

'Let me rephrase. What *vexes* you?'

'Vexes?'

'Please… Your demeanour. It doesn't take a student of behavioural psychology to deduce that something is troubling you.'

'Behaviour-what, sir?'

'Never mind. I mean… You asked to see me. Here I am.'

Finch nodded to Ralph. Ralph brought over a glass of water. Pickersgill thanked him.

He was an outdoorsman, Finch supposed. The weathered face and grey hair probably added ten years to his appearance, making him, what, fifty, fifty-five? His hands were cleanish but the palms like leather, the cracks deep and lined; no end of scrubbing could erase the etched-in dirt. It was the same with the blunted nails.

'You don't rec'nise me, sir. I dint expect you to,' he went on. 'But I come a long way t'find you. Endthorpe. Norfolk coast.'

Finch stuck a mental feather in his own imaginary cap.

'Been several days I spend movin' around the eastern counties. Had to sleep rough…'

'Rough?'

'Not through choice, sir.'

Finch glanced at his wristwatch – Zeiss, German.

'Look… I haven't got all day. I think you'd better begin at the beginning…'

The man composed himself.

'South Africa, Dr Finch. Like you, I was in South Africa.'

'There were quite a lot of us down there. Half a million.'

'The push on Pretoria. You tended to me, God bless you, sir. Took a bullet to the wrist…'

He pivoted his left hand back and forth, as if to demonstrate that Finch's battlefield ministrations had done their trick. Finch concluded he must be younger than he thought.

'The war ended two and a half years ago, Mr Pickersgill…'

Finch raised his glass.

'…I've been doing everything in my power to erase it from memory.'

He took another demonstrative sip.

'Still a way to go.'

'But, sir—'

'Look, if I assisted you in anyway, I'm glad to see you in fine fettle. If you spent any time in the Cape, you'll have seen some hellish things and I pity us both the memory, but I hope you don't think it rude when I tell you I treated literally thousands of men. Some days… the Modder River… Magersfontein… Kimberley… the Medical Corps field stations, we were tending to up to three hundred men a night. Later, God forbid, women and children…'

Finch set his pint glass down again.

'You were fortunate you copped a bullet. Our biggest killer was typhoid.'

'The good Lord, he sent some things t'try us, make no mistake. I was with the Norfolks, sir, 2nd Battalion. First dose of action at Paardburg. Then… with General Roberts… all the way through the Transvaal. Stayed on for the surrender and annexation. Then the guerrilla—'

'Mr Pickersgill, I feel you must get to your point.'

Pickersgill's eyes flitted to the window again and back to the door. His hands started shaking.

'What *is* it? Spit it out, man. For God's sake.'

He had greenish, intense eyes. Around them his face creased with pain.

'Sir, I'm so sorry t'burden you, but I'm in trouble.'

'Trouble?'

'Tent no other way t'describe it, sir.'

'Then if it's not a medical matter...?'

The man cleared his throat.

'The reason I had to see you, sir, was because... with the army and everything... I heard you were involved with, you know...'

He whispered it with urgency.

'*...military intelligence...*'

Finch said nothing for a moment. Then he stood emphatically, drained his glass in one go and slammed it down.

'Mr Pickersgill. Good day to you, sir.'

The drunk at the bar stirred again.

'Bloody Tsar... Kaiser too...'

'Cold steel...' added someone else. 'One for the Crimea.'

Finch turned to the room as he left – the sad gaggle of cock-crow drinkers and their purpled faces who gargled cheap booze for breakfast and from whom he kidded himself to be a man apart...

'And *you*!... *All* of you! Every bloody day! Will you cease talking about war as if it were some damned bloody football match!'

Called out Ralph: 'I say, steady on, Dr Finch.'

Another horse brass fell as Finch slammed the door.

Chapter Three

There was something deeply erotic about watching Maude get dressed, a sort of reverse re-enactment of what had passed the night before – not that Finch's recollection of it extended beyond the hazy. He enjoyed the fussiness of the underwear, the studious threading of the high bootlaces and the pernickety smoothing down of the dress. Then came the re-pinning of the hair and the frustration with the dangling strands of auburn that refused to be tamed.

Here was a woman, so confident most of the time, but who now oozed an emotion that ran counter to the norm: *guilt*.

She exited with an unsmiling 'See you', trying not to bang her head on a low beam. He heard the flush of the indoor water closet and a sloshing in the basin. The ritual was well-worn – park the bicycle out of sight, leave at dawn, home via a back route and a mumbled excuse to her landlady – or curious neighbour – that she hadn't been able to sleep ('No, really') and had got up early to take a pre-breakfast constitutional.

The bike seemed the perfect instrument of her shame. Maude had told him of one elderly lady who had berated her in public for riding such a contraption – the unladylike manner of its mounting, the vulgarity of the saddle.

The stairs creaked and he heard mumblings. Maude had bumped into his own housekeeper, though this was not a problem. Mrs Pereira-Armitage was a diminutive woman – Portuguese he had thought, but Brazilian he soon discovered – who had come to England via a naval marriage. She was long widowed and took vicarious pleasure in the romance of others.

For her there was no such thing as shame. Love – '*amor*' – was something to be cherished, celebrated… *practised*.

There were two things she disliked about England, she once told Finch, in a rare moment when he had plied her with sherry: the damp cold of winter and the fact that love – '*amor*' – was denigrated, suppressed, treated as a sign of moral weakness.

This house was once hers but, when her husband died, she had lost it to her brother-in-law in a contested will. The man put the house on the market. When Finch bought the place, after South Africa, he had seen no reason to kick Mrs Pereira-Armitage out. Save for a reallocation of the rooms, she – 'Mrs P-A' – had stayed on as a sort of default housekeeper, an arrangement that suited both of them just fine.

He heard the back door close and the creak of the bike on the garden path.

Finch lay in bed for a while, staring at the ceiling. When he rose, the accursed 'dagger' made its presence felt. He gulped water from the jug on the nightstand, stretched his aching body, opened the window, and stood naked in the chill morning air, the sill high enough to cover his modesty. He leaned out, looked back and forth up the road, and let nature birth him into a brand new day.

There was a fine mist that clung, the smell of damp, fetid autumn and the seasonal ache in his knee to go with it. Woodsmoke began to waft. The languid, familiar clip-clop echoed down the lane. Soon he would hear the scrape and clank of milk churns. And he thought for a moment of the scrape and clank of the drayman.

The milk cart was accompanied by a plaintive warbled whistle. The milkman, a sour-faced man whom Finch knew personally to loathe his job, could quaver a melody with the tenderness of a Viennese choirboy. Everywhere, it seemed, the two selves were in conflict – the public versus the private. And Finch was no different.

After a hearty repast of bacon and fresh farm eggs, served up by Mrs P-A, Finch drank a whole pot of rooibos tea, threw on his overcoat, grabbed his Homburg and set out on the walk through town, the dagger still throwing him random, mischievous stabs.

The willows hung bare over the river where it forded the road by the watermill. The great abbey stood silent. Though a rural town – a 'city' by ecclesiastical design – St Albans' proximity to London, and the presence of the railway line, had made it a growing attraction. New homes were being built, developments spreading across the farmland. The rash of Ladysmith and Kimberley and Mafeking Roads proliferating across the country bothered Finch. Did the dead deserve nothing better than a nameplate bolted to a street-corner wall?

As Finch's gait deteriorated to its usual limp, he was passed by bowler-hatted gentlemen striding purposefully to the station. He had heard them referred to as 'commuters', a word that conjured the conversion of a death sentence – maybe it was the same thing.

Outside the town hall there were people handing out flyers, excoriating the Russians and demanding that justice be done on behalf of the Hull fishermen – '*our boys*'. There was a march this weekend in Trafalgar Square. Finch kept his hands in his pockets and pushed on.

He entered his practice at just after half past eight, the ground floor of a newish semi-detached domestic building that had been subdivided for businesses. He bid good morning to his secretary, Daphne, who expressed her frustration that Finch was both late and hadn't warned her of the advent of a patient who had been here since eight… and that the system would be much more efficient if he could just inform her of any privately arranged appointments.

He apologised, but in truth had completely forgotten.

'Good morning, Mrs Ashby,' he said, affecting cheer, as he swung open the door, pulled off his hat and coat and hung them on the back of it.

'Doctor… I'm so pleased to see you… You know, my…'

'A fine morning,' he cut across.

'Dreadfully gloomy.'

The dagger prodded. It was being particularly sadistic.

'Did Daphne… Miss Wilson… get you some tea, Mrs Ashby?'

'She did, Dr Finch…'

Mrs Ashby pointed to a cup. Daphne had used the fine bone china.

'As I was just saying…'

Finch put his palm up politely. He went around and sat down. His sprung chair squeaked. Mrs Ashby was in her seventies with an evident fondness for jewels and fur. A no-doubt expensive pelt of some pale tundra weasel was draped across her shoulders, its beady eyes staring at nothing in particular.

'I'm sorry. Please go on, Mrs Ashby…'

'It's this cough, Doctor.'

'A-*ha*.'

'And a pain in my elbow. Both my elbows actually.'

'I see.'

'And my knees.'

'Your knees?'

The knees were new.

'Last week it was your stomach…' said Finch.

He flipped through the file Daphne had placed on his blotter.

'The week before that, your ears…'

'You mean my eyes.'

'No, I mean your ears, Mrs Ashby. The time before *that* was your eyes.'

'I see.'

'Well then, that's good, I mean… If you can *see*…'

She raised her spectacles, the lorgnette kind mounted on a gold stick, and examined him, not quite sure if he were ridiculing her.

Finch came out from behind his desk and went through the charade of placing a spatula in her mouth and making her say '*Aaaaaah*'. She smelled of rose water. She wore too much powder. It clung to the hairs on her chin. He flipped with feigned purpose through his medical compendium.

'My dear Mrs Ashby,' he said. 'I believe, with this combination of symptoms, there is only one drug which will do. It is with good fortune that I anticipated your condition and had it delivered forthwith all the way from the famous Bayer factory in Leverkusen.'

She cooed at his attentiveness. He scribbled furiously on a chit, then handed it to her. He rubbed his throbbing forehead.

'Take two drops of this, four times a day. Have Daphne… Miss Wilson… check this for you. We'll have an errand boy run it over to the chemist.'

Mrs Ashby read it out, slowly and studiously.

'Acetyl chloride combined with sodium sali—'

'Sodium salicylate.'

'…producing acetylsal—'

'Acetylsalicylic acid… The very thing, Mrs Ashby. The very thing.'

She immediately perked up.

'Oh thank you, Doctor. *Thank* you.'

'My pleasure.'

'It's so exciting, isn't it? I mean, what with *this*… and the *war*.'

She pulled a town hall flyer from her handbag and waved it.

'The Russians, Dr Finch. The *Russians*.'

She gurgled with joy.

'Good day to you, Mrs Ashby.'

He plastered on a fake grin and showed her out.

Door shut, he sat down again, reached into his desk and wrestled out a half-drunk bottle of single malt – Talisker. He pulled the cork quietly and took a swig… then another. The dagger was gently withdrawn. He heard the newly enlivened Mrs Ashby chat with Daphne, then the front door close. Sure that she had gone, he took a third sip for luck and went back out to reception. Daphne held the prescription.

'Acetyl chloride combined with sodium salicylate?' she read off.

'Aspirin, Daphne. *Aspirin*.'

She gave a strained chuckle. But her eyes were red. She had been crying. Had Mrs Ashby seen?

'Why, Daphne...'

She dabbed at them with a linen handkerchief.

'I'm sorry, sir. It's no use.'

'No use. What's of no use?'

She was silent for a moment, awkward about saying it.

'I can't work here any more, sir.'

'But Daphne...'

'I'm sorry, sir... Dr Finch... I mean, I love this place...'

'But?'

'But every day...'

She hesitated. He sighed. They might as well hand him a blindfold and cigarette.

'Please, go on...'

'It's just that you're late, you go missing after lunch, sometimes you don't show up at all... We're losing patients hand over fist... and all the while I'm sitting here, having to cover, having to make up stories, get you out of trouble, *lie* for you...'

'Anything else?'

She shook her head.

He perched on the edge of her desk, affecting casual ease. There was nothing she said with which he didn't agree. Absolutely nothing. She just hadn't added 'drunk'.

'Daphne, I'm so sorry. I appreciate everything that you do, believe me. I realise I can be somewhat... *mercurial*. If there's anything I—'

'I'm sorry, sir, but I've already found another job...'

'Oh.'

She looked down, embarrassed.

'Is it the money? Then a small raise, maybe. I'm sure we can—'

'...One of the hotels in town. I'll stay on, work my notice, obviously...'

-

With Wednesday a half-day and no more patients, Finch shut up shop before noon, let Daphne off early, and walked down to the elementary school, trying hard not to get too despondent. Kids were already pouring out of the red-brick schoolhouse into the tight little playground. Two boys whizzed past firing imaginary guns, arguing about whose turn it was to be 'the Russians', which neither wanted to be.

There were small, excitable girls hanging off Maude's skirts. Finch stood back but they had already seen him… *and* the bunch of gladioli. They teased their mistress about her 'gentleman sweetheart'. She blushed. Dispatched to their mothers outside the railings, Maude made her way over.

'Miss Carter,' he said.

'Why, Dr Finch,' she smirked and took his arm.

They walked off up the street. People nodded 'Good afternoon'.

'You know if someday I were to marry, I would have to resign my position,' Maude said.

'Meaning?'

'Meaning nothing, Ingo. Meaning nothing.'

Finch steered a course past the pub, doing his darnedest to avoid its pull. He could see Ralph through the window, wiping glasses.

It was a glorious day, Maude declared, and quoted Keats. He felt her romanticising of the season touching but erroneous. This greying autumn already had one foot in winter. But he appeased her desire for rural air and, half an hour later, they were on their pushbikes, bundled up, pedalling hard through the great country estate along a handsome avenue lined with poplars. They passed a farm with its prize Aberdeen herd mooing around the cattle shed, a farmhand thrusting a pitchfork into a mound of straw. Other than that, they were the only ones around.

Finch made heavy work of the steep hill up to the old Elizabethan ruin, once the home of Sir Francis Bacon, labouring on the heavy black cast-iron contraption he had purchased on the strength of it being a gentleman's sporting accessory. Maude got there first. Only the front wall, the porch and a window frame remained of what was once a stately home, its banqueting hall the envy of Tudor England, Finch had read. Maude sat on the front step, the stone worn concave from ancient visitors.

'You know, Good Queen Bess was supposed to have stayed here,' said Finch. 'Shakespeare too...'

He pointed to an imaginary upper floor.

'...They say he wrote *Twelfth Night* in—'

'You tell me that every time we come here.'

He sat down next to Maude and produced a hip flask. He offered it to her first. She rolled her eyes but took a sip. She declined a Navy Cut, but when he lit one for himself she prised it from his fingers and took a drag.

'Ingo?'

He hated his name.

'What?'

He took back the flask and swigged.

'I was serious back there.'

'What do you mean?'

She passed the cigarette back.

'Outside the school gates.'

'Oh.'

'I'll be twenty-seven years old soon. If I don't...'

She was right in every way, he knew. The second woman of the day to have got the measure of him.

'It's just... why *me*?... You could have anyone,' he said, examining the glowing ash.

'I don't want "anyone".'

He stood up again. She grew sterner. She shivered. Nerves or cold, he couldn't tell.

'This is life, Ingo – the real thing, not a rehearsal. If you have a desire for a family... kids...'

He swigged again.

'Your birthday,' he said.

'Don't change the subject.'

'Next week.'

'Thursday.'

'Then this weekend… Saturday… I'll take you up to London. We'll make a day of it. The Stieglitz photographic exhibition. Dinner in the evening…'

'*Why* Ingo?'

'Why?'

'Yes *why*…?' Her voice was raised now. 'So you can sleep with me when you get home. Use smoke and mirrors to conjure away all questions about the future?'

He affected that it was all just light-hearted, just banter.

'Why not just concentrate on *today*? Look at all this…'

He swung his arm around the sweep of the vista – the rolling hills, the knolls of trees, the road curling down to the old, half-buried Roman amphitheatre and the grand abbey beyond.

'It was *you* who was just talking about Saturday.'

He stretched out his hands; she took them. He pulled her to her feet. He passed her the flask. She took another sip.

'Come on,' he said. 'It'll be my treat.'

Minutes later they were freewheeling down the hill, Maude forgoing her usual scream of delight as they hurtled at a ridiculous speed, Finch taking his feet off the pedals in a poor demonstration of his daring. And then he heard it, despite the rushing wind: the automotive drone that shifted through the gears and rose in pitch as it got nearer. Louder, *louder*…

As they rounded the fence by a large wooden barn, the machine met them head-on, and only a last-minute swerve by both parties and a furious screech of brakes kept Finch and Maude upright, not plunging off into the ditch. They stopped and turned as the driver of the yellow Spyker waved and parped his horn, shifting down to take on the hill.

Maude swore with the force and creativity of a navvy.

'And that's why I like you, Maude.'

'*Like* me?'

She sighed and wrangled her skirts. Then she set off again.

'You're a bastard,' she called out.

'I know,' he said.

It was getting chilly, the wind whipping up from the east. In catharsis, Maude pedalled like the devil. Finch struggled to keep up, the pain in his knee now compensating for the lack of one in his head. They rode on for half a mile and then…

She gave a yelp.

'What?' he called ahead.

'A flat. I've got a flat… A puncture.'

She slowed down and got off. She crouched to examine the wheel.

'Two flats…'

Finch was catching up, about to dismount when…

Bang!

…his own front tyre burst. He wobbled, pulled his brakes and hopped off.

'But these were brand new pneumatics,' he protested. 'Dunlops. It doesn't make…'

'Nor does this,' she said.

With her kid-gloved hands she was brandishing a shiny new brass tack, about a quarter of an inch long with a round, flat head. He could see the glinting cap of another poking from the tread of his own front tyre. There were several studding her rear wheel.

He grunted, 'What the…?'

Behind them there were tacks strewn right across the road.

A rustle in the hedgerow made them both turn. A small, slight man burst forth, trailing sprigs of hawthorn.

'*Pickersgill?*'

'I'm sorry, sir… Dr Finch…'

He turned to Maude and touched his peak.

'…Miss.'

'*You* did this?' snarled Finch. 'The tacks?'

'It was the only way.'

'Jesus Christ, man. What the hell are you playing at?'

'You *know* him?' asked Maude.

'It seems so. Regrettably,' said Finch.

Pickersgill came forward, arms out. He was dressed in the same attire: the cap, the muffler, the threadbare jacket patched at the elbows, the worry etched into his face.

'I try t'find you today, Dr Finch, as the Good Lord's my witness. Come to your practice like you say. Only you be closed…'

'Out of my way, Pickersgill.'

Finch pushed his bike forward. Pickersgill blocked him. He clasped his hands together, pleading, almost in prayer.

'Please, sir. You *have* t'listen to me. There are people out a-do me *harm*.'

A brusque Maude shoved her bike forward and began wheeling it in earnest.

'Come on, Ingo.'

'Please, sir!'

'I think you've done enough damage here, Pickersgill.'

Pickersgill turned and looked down the lane, the direction in which Maude was headed. He was suddenly startled, spooked by something.

'Wait!'

'What?'

'Did y'see him?'

'See *who*?' asked Finch.

Pickersgill darted back into the hedge.

Finch pushed on to catch up with Maude. They would have to walk the rest of the way.

Chapter Four

The noise from the Coronet receded: the rough laughter, the bawdy shanties, the overbearing trill of the wheezing accordion. Outside the sea air was rich, sobering – though not as much as the man would have liked. He was now painfully aware of his own frailty, his human limitations, the very act of walking a challenge.

He had never known money like it and understood now he should have been more careful. He had bought people drinks… people he didn't even know… his fists so stuffed with coins he'd been dropping pennies and didn't even care. And what did it gain him?… Companionship? Respect? *Hardly*. They had taken his generosity, and yet some still mocked him. Most poured scorn.

There had been specific warnings given about his sudden good fortune – something beyond his frame of reference. Discretion was its price, he'd been told. Absolute. He would be wise to heed it. But he had tossed aside those patronising cautions.

Why the hell was it *their* business? He'd done his job. He'd been paid for his service. He could do as he damn well pleased and hang the consequences. Yes, and if they scoffed at him, belittled him when he bought them ale, it was *his* privilege… and *his* alone.

Out there in the blackness the lights winked – the crab boats going about their work. Their flickers danced like glow-worms, till he managed to regain his focus and bring them under control.

The wind was picking up. He pulled close his jacket but struggled with the buttons. The tide had begun to recede. He could tell by the sound of the stones – he could still gauge *that* at least – the deep roar and grind of the incoming wave followed by the slow dragging hiss of the retreat.

But now again, out here, in the dark, there was the *menace*. He knew it lurked. It had been there ever since that night – that night that they'd put out to sea. The menace waited. The menace loitered. It bided its time… It had claimed the others, he was sure of it. And with a sickening barbarity. It had been absolutely no coincidence.

Between the seafront lamp-posts, bunting fluttered. The bandstand was empty. Up onto the esplanade and a sheet of newspaper flapped across the empty street, like a skate across the seabed.

At the Grand Hotel life resumed. Around its entrance, gigs and buggies clopped past – gentlemen, ladies, their servants, off to or from God knows where. Through the open windows of the ballroom, a man finished warbling to the plink of a piano. There was polite clapping, the clink of glasses, the waft of cigar smoke.

He could not feel it directly, the source of his angst – the dark presence out there – but he knew it would be close… and could strike at any moment. He had glimpsed it that night at the foot of the cliffs… Again by the fishermen's slope. He thought he had seen the menace… briefly… on the hump of the railway bridge, silhouetted in the gaslight, shrouded in steam as a train passed underneath.

He needed to get home.

The shortcut took him across the scrubland behind the Grand. There were bins and rubbish. You could hear the scrabble of rats. At the far end two men, kitchen staff, mooched around, smoking. They laughed at some joke then went back inside. Silence again.

The ground was patchy gravel with clumps of thistles and dandelions sprouting. The man tripped on a stray brick and wobbled. He was worse than he thought. He tried to steady himself but tumbled like a toddler, stinging and grazing the heels of his palms as he put his hands out to break the fall, taking a painful whack to his knees in the process.

He lay on his back and stared up at the stars. He hugged his shins. Above him a seagull squawked. It seemed to be mocking him, too.

There were stables. He heard the rustle of straw and the scrape of hooves. Unsure again, he eased himself up, staggered, and then clung to the rear wall, his back pressed in hard while he regained his breath. His heart thumped so violently he could feel it in his throat.

He reached into his jacket for his tobacco and papers and rolled himself a cigarette. But he dared not light it. Three, four minutes... he would be behind his own front door. He could do it then. The worst that could happen to him there was a scolding from the wife.

The wind dipped and he heard people... back in the ballroom. There was further genteel applause. Someone making a speech. He didn't know why but he found himself suddenly smiling at the absurdity of his own ludicrous lot. And then it swelled – swelled from within into an unrestrained, unburdening guffaw.

Mocked by a seagull!

He went ahead and lit his match. Fuck everybody. He drew deep, wiped his tears and concentrated on the mechanics of walking – back onto the lane and that final gaslit stretch. The path was bathed in an amber glow. He was almost in the clear.

He fumbled for his pocket watch, saw the time and wondered how much trouble he was in. Then he snapped it shut, accidentally jerked the chain out of his buttonhole and the watch clanged to the ground. He bent down... swayed down... and picked it up. It was scratched, a little dented, but he put it to his ear and heard it tick.

There was a scuffle behind him and he turned. Just a cat. It shot across the road.

But as he eased himself round to resume his march, he looked up. He felt sick to his stomach, cold to his innards, his lame knees buckling.

It had found him at last.

He opened his mouth and screamed – a plea to the men from the kitchen... to *anyone*. But the fear strangled his throat. On the wind his voice cracked... and was lost...

Chapter Five

On Saturday Finch rose late and mooched around the house, readying himself for his day out with Maude. Mrs P-A was away for the weekend visiting friends, so he lounged in the sitting room in his underwear, read *The Times*, cranked the gramophone and put on a record disc… Offenbach – *Orpheus in the Underworld.*

His enthusiasm for the day's excursion was tainted by knowledge that, where Maude was concerned, there remained questions to which he owed answers. He toyed with the idea of an early one in the pub, but instead made a pot of rooibos tea, the supply of which he had arranged via an importer in St James', adding a tot of Talisker for good measure.

The Victor gramophone could achieve a reasonable volume. Last summer, when he had the windows open, the neighbours had complained – shocked to find that a doctor ('of all people!') could behave with such irresponsibility. (If only they knew, thought Finch. If only they knew.) He turned the sound knob and let the scratchy *oompah* of the cancan chorus carry him away.

Upstairs in the bathroom, while the stirring rhythm wafted up, he hummed as he clipped his moustache and pondered the grey that was now sprouting in it. He then lathered his face with his badger brush and went to work with the cutthroat razor.

He didn't hear the door at first, but when the rap of the brass knocker came again, he threw on his dressing gown, draped a towel over his shoulder and went downstairs, wandering through the sitting room with its low beams, packed bookshelves and crackling fireplace. He rechecked his watch. He wasn't due to pick up Maude for another half an hour, though it was not unlike her to be spontaneous. He thought for a moment of *Romeo and Juliet* and the 'lovers ever running before the clock'. No… it was *The Merchant of Venice.*

He opened the front door but there was no one there. He stepped out onto the terracotta tiles of the porch, cold on bare feet.

'Maude?'

As he turned to go back in, a figure stepped out from behind the high screen of myrtle.

Finch sighed.

'Jesus Christ, Pickersgill. Is hiding in bushes a speciality?'

The man was looking around, going through his usual paranoid routine.

'Again, I'm sorry, sir, but you're really all I've got. My only hope.'

'You keep saying that, but I don't know what the hell it is you're talking about. All I know is you owe me two sets of bicycle tyres. And not the cheap ones either – premium Dunlops.'

Pickersgill looked mournful. He was wet and shivering. It had rained hard during the night, shredded leaves and twigs lay scattered over the small front lawn. A pot on the doorstep in which Finch left notes for the whistling, miserable milkman, was brimming with water.

The man began coughing. Finch cursed to himself.

'Look, you'd better come in, dry out…'

He rechecked his watch.

'…But I've got to leave in twenty minutes. You understand?'

'Yes, sir.'

He held the door open and ushered Pickersgill inside. He smelled of earth and dampness and with a hint now of the unwashed.

'Thank you most kindly,' he said.

'No overcoat?'

'No, sir.'

The door opened pretty much straight into the sitting room. Finch directed him towards the coal fire.

'Where the hell have you been?'

Finch took a poker to the grate.

'Sleepin' rough, like I say, sir.'

He hung the poker back in the holder, alongside the dustpan, the brush and some implement for which he'd never figured out the purpose.

'Good God, man, what on earth for?'

Pickersgill said nothing. He just pulled off his jacket, his home-knitted green pullover and collarless shirt, and stood there in his undershirt, braces dangling, flapping the wet clothing before the fire. Finch eyed him up and down. He was scrawny, not an ounce of fat. He turned down the volume on the gramophone. There was a blanket on the settee, an old throw. He handed it to Pickersgill, who dropped his wet things on the hearth and bunched it tight around his shoulders.

'You hungry?'

The coughing returned. It was a phlegm-tinged hacking that went on for some time. Pickersgill grabbed a greying handkerchief from his pocket and clutched it to his mouth.

'I am, sir. Yes.'

'Will you please cut out the "sirs"? It's most irritating. There's some fresh bread and butter there…'

He pointed through to the kitchen.

'…and some bacon on the side. Cooked. Just about warm. Help yourself. I've just got to go upstairs and…'

He gestured to his own lathered face.

'Thank you, sir…' Pickersgill checked himself. 'Thank you.'

'Make yourself a fresh pot of tea. Pour me a cup while you're at it.'

Finch finished shaving, pomaded his hair, donned his finest suit – taupe – and came back down. Pickersgill was in the kitchen, perched on a stool in his full-length underwear, tucking into a bacon sandwich.

'Rooibos tea,' the man remarked, lofting a cup with a rare attempt at a smile. 'Haven't had this since the war. Dint know you could get it here.'

'You have to know where to look.'

'Thank you,' said Pickersgill again. 'God bless you.'

The shivering had abated, but there was still the odd tremor. Finch grabbed his whisky bottle.

'Care for a tot?'

'No, thank you.'

'Brandy?'

'I don't.'

'Of course. I forgot.'

Finch glanced at his watch again.

'Like I said, we're on a ticking clock here.'

It didn't take long for the agitation to return.

'Come on, man. *Out* with it.'

Pickersgill led Finch back into the sitting room where he had placed his jacket on the back of a chair. He reached to an inside pocket.

'First I must show you *this*...'

He pulled out a small, battered, black leather-bound book.

Finch sighed.

'Please God *no*, Pickersgill...'

It had a gold-embossed cross on the front – a Bible, slightly damp round the edges.

'Trust me, you're wasting your time. Your Good Lord gave up on me long, long ago.'

'No, sir. S'nothin' like that.'

'No "sirs". Remember?'

Pickersgill slipped out a newspaper cutting that lay folded within. He handed it to Finch. It was half a page ripped from an edition of the *Eastern Daily Press*. Its date was from two days ago – *since* their meeting in the pub, noted Finch. And you couldn't get the paper locally.

'See there?'

Pickersgill pointed.

'Can't see a damn thing.'

Finch moved towards the light of the front window. Pickersgill followed, though not without a customary cautious glance.

Another coughing fit ensued as Finch studied the cutting and Pickersgill directed him to the section headed 'Death Notices'.

Among the poor East Anglian souls to have shuffled off this mortal coil this past week – the '*dearly beloveds*' and folks now '*resting in peace*' – was one Bertram Brandon, Pickersgill indicated, aged thirty-seven, of Endthorpe, '*perished at sea*'.

'He was a crewman on my boat.'

'I still don't understand.'

'A day boat, thirty-footer, small steamer. We used a-crew with four.'

'Look, I'm sorry for poor Mr...'

Finch examined the cutting again.

'...Brandon. But...'

'The other two, and now Bertie,' Pickersgill cut in. 'That's three of us in the last nine days. All dead.'

'*Dead?*'

'All in boating "accidents".'

Finch handed the cutting back. He set about tying his neck-wear, a golden silk cravat he'd worried was a tad too flash but was prepared to take a chance on.

'Go on...'

'Look, Dr Finch. You hear wha' happen on the Dogger Bank recently... the *incident*... those trawlers from Hull...?'

'How could I not? It's all anyone's talked about. War, war, war and more bloody war...'

Finch gestured to his *Times* lying on the settee. After bottling up the Russian fleet in Vigo, Spain, the Royal Navy was now shadowing the warships on the high seas, primed to engage if necessary. The front page was full of items about the public clamour for retribution and how London and St Petersburg were locked in a frantic diplomatic scramble.

'I was there,' said Pickersgill.

'What do you mean?'

'I mean I was *there.* My boat, the *Kittiwake.* We take har out. We're o'er the Dogger Bank that night.'

'I'm sorry to hear that. Must have been quite an experience.'

Finch wasn't sure where this was going.

'Bertie… That's *three men*, Dr Finch. *Three men.* I know for a fact two of them hant even put out to sea in that time. They didn't die in "accidents", believe you me. They were…'

He fumbled for the right words.

'You mean they were *killed*?' asked Finch, suddenly pausing mid-knot.

'Murdered.'

Finch's tone turned serious.

'If there's something sinister afoot, Mr Pickersgill, then take it to the authorities. Go to the police.'

'If only it were that simple.'

Pickersgill folded the cutting and inserted it back in the Bible. He put the good book back inside his jacket.

'And Bertie Brandon didn't just *die…*'

The vowel was round, like 'doy'.

'…He be decapper-tatered.'

'*Decapitated?*'

The man nodded.

Finch winced. 'Propeller blade?'

'No, Dr Finch! Although funnily enough… not so funny, as it happen… that's what they say… the police. But I see his body. That wa'nt a clean cut made by no blade. It was ragged… everythin' stretched, elongated, ripped… the wound, the tendons. Like his head a-been torn… *wrenched* orf.'

There was a furious rapping on the knocker. Pickersgill darted into the kitchen. Finch noted his jitters, pleaded for calm and answered the door slowly.

It was Maude standing there.

'What the hell is keeping you?' she scowled.

'I was just on my way.'

'Damn you, Ingo. I've been waiting three quarters of an hour.'

'You said half past eleven.'

'I said *eleven.* We changed it, remember?'

'Sorry.'

She huffed.

'We'll have to get the next train.'

Though it was inopportune to say it, she looked stunning: a green satin bolero jacket over a tapered bustle skirt, a matching pashmina wrap, long ivory gloves and tasteful tam-o'-shanter adorned with a small peacock feather.

As she made her way in, Maude caught sight of Pickersgill lurking in the rear.

'*Oh*.'

Pickersgill had clammed up, the words unable to come.

'What a *pleasure*,' she added with unconstrained sarcasm.

His coughing fit returned. He pulled the blanket in tight.

'Is he ill?' she asked Finch, not addressing the man directly.

Finch nodded. He went to the bureau, on which sat his medical bag. He rummaged through it and returned with a thermometer. He sat Pickersgill down in front of the fire. He loosened the blanket.

'Listen, be a good fellow...'

He shook the thermometer, popped it in Pickersgill's mouth and looked at his watch.

Maude touched Pickersgill's shoulder.

'He's soaking wet.'

'Look, Maude. I know this seems rude, but do you mind waiting outside? Just for a moment.'

She sulked and stamped to the front door. Finch paced about till three minutes were up. He removed the thermometer.

'Ninety-eight. Borderline. But you've got yourself a dose of *something*, Pickersgill. A heavy cold, bit of a fever. Sleeping rough, the wet and not eating properly won't have helped.'

Pickersgill pulled him close.

'I've accepted my fate, Dr Finch. They'll get me soon. Make no mistake. I just thought you, as a man who worked in intelligence, one with connections, that maybe you'd be able to—'

'Dammit Pickersgill,' Finch snapped. 'I don't know where the hell you got such a fanciful notion into your head. But I tell you, you are completely mistaken!'

Pickersgill gave a wan smile. He nodded in the direction of Maude, strutting up and down outside the window.

'Must be hard, havin' t'keep it quiet all this time. I understand.'

'I'm warning you…'

He coughed some more. Finch eased off.

'Look, for the sake of *my* health, *I* need to go,' said Finch. 'And *right now*.'

Pickersgill's eyelids were beginning to droop.

'The fire. Those wet things. You can dry them out here. There's a clothes horse…'

Pickersgill sighed.

'You're very kind.'

'Help yourself to food. And grab something from the fruit bowl. But above all, get some *sleep*. You're safe here.'

Pickersgill was already leaning back into a slumber. Finch tucked the blanket around him.

The Offenbach, which had been paying all the while, came to an end. The stylus crackled in the central groove, going round and round and round.

'But I expect you to be gone when I'm back. You hear me? Eleven o'clock latest.'

He pointed to the carriage clock on the mantelpiece.

'Yes, sir. Thank you, sir,' he mumbled. 'God bless.'

'I'm looking you in the eye here. You *promise*?'

Pickersgill strained his lids open to signal his consent.

'I promise.'

'Leave everything as it is. Put the fire out. I'll draw the curtains. No need to answer the door.'

He went to his medical bag again.

'Here… two drops of this.'

He produced a brown medicine bottle and a pipette.

'What is it?'

'Acetyl chloride combined with sodium salicylate.'

Pickersgill shrugged wearily.

'*Aspirin*,' said Finch. 'Open wide.'

Pickersgill did as he was told. Finch splashed a couple of drops onto his tongue.

Pickersgill touched his arm.

'I'm glad I found you,' he said. 'It's a weight off my mind.'

'I don't see how. You haven't really told me anything.'

'Oh but I *have*, Dr Finch.'

Finch pulled on his jacket and coat. He grabbed his Homburg from the hatstand.

'You'll find a way. You will,' said Pickersgill.

'Here,' said Finch.

He sighed, as if compelled to act against his better judgement, and slipped Pickersgill a half-crown.

'God bless you, sir.'

'Goodbye.'

Outside, Maude was standing, arms crossed.

'Some treat *this* is turning out to be.'

'I'm sorry.'

'Where is he?'

'Pickersgill?'

'Who else?'

He gestured back indoors.

'He'll be gone when we return. I promise.'

'You're a fool, Ingo.'

They set off up the road.

Chapter Six

The hansom cab clipped along Brook Street. The evening had reached that magical hour – darkness falling outside, but with those indoors having yet to draw their curtains against it.

To Finch it was like a confessional, the townhouses and *pieds-à-terre* of Mayfair revealing their interiors to the world – the gold-leafed finery and crystal chandeliers, the earnestly posed portraits. In one ground-floor dining room, servants were setting out the silverware for dinner. At another, bored masters and mistresses, dressed in their formal evening wear, prodded at overloaded plates between monstrous candelabra.

'My God, this is an exhibition in itself,' said Maude. 'And thank you…'

She twitched her brochure, titled *The Dudley Gallery*.

'It was very kind.'

Finch lit a Navy Cut. He exhaled out of the window.

'Listen… Maude?'

'Yes?'

'This morning… these past few days…'

He found it awkward to say so but forced it out.

'I'm sorry,' he said.

'For which particular bit?'

'Don't rub it in.'

She squeezed his hand and smiled.

'Stieglitz goes a long way,' she said. 'But I still think you're a fool… on several levels.'

Finch clasped his cigarette between his lips. He reached inside his jacket for his hip flask.

'Do you really have to?' she asked.

'I'm a fool… remember?'

He offered her a sip. She declined. He went ahead.

As they reached the glass portico of Claridge's Hotel, red waistcoated bellboys sprang forward in expectation, only to retreat when it was obvious their cab would go sailing past. A doorman in a top hat blew a shrill whistle and waved white-gloved hands, marshalling others.

There was a fine drizzle, not much more than a mist. Finch thought for a moment of his old comrade Major Leonard Cox, who'd met his unfortunate end in a vehicle just like this one on the streets of Cape Town.

He had corresponded with Cox's family in India in the aftermath, leading to a protracted pen friendship with Cox's spinster sister, which he had indulged out of politeness but abandoned once it became a chore. Despite his withdrawal from their communication some time ago, a letter of hers had arrived only last week – pale blue, slightly perfumed, but whiffing moreover of desperation. He hadn't bothered to open it.

'Penny for your thoughts,' said Maude.

'What?'

'You were miles away.'

'Sorry.'

'What *was* it?'

He drew on his cigarette.

'Nothing.'

'What kind of "nothing"?'

He shrugged. The silence lingered. Then he felt bad about it.

'Just… you know… South Africa… the war.'

She squeezed his hand again and kept hers there this time.

'It's okay,' she ventured, tenderly. 'I mean… If you want to talk about it. My uncle… Dad's brother… he was in Afghanistan and—'

Finch banged hard on the cab's roof.

'Right along Regent Street, please,' he commanded the driver.

He turned to Maude.

'You know, they profess to know every bloody street in London, but this fellow was about to go left, I swear.'

She huffed and snatched her hand back.

'If you can't talk about it...'

He said nothing.

'*Well?*'

Nothing.

On the street corner a newsvendor was yelling out '*Evenin' Standard* latest!' Peace talks between Britain and Russia, proclaimed the one-sheet poster, were in the balance. This seemed to be presented as *good* news.

Finch took another swig. Maude dug him in the ribs, slightly too hard to be playful. Conflict, thought Finch, in all its forms, was never far beneath the surface. He capped the flask and put it back in his jacket.

'My dearest Maude,' he said. 'There persists this notion, chiefly amongst female intimates – in my admittedly limited encounters – that "sharing feelings" or "talking about things" somehow relieves the burden. In my experience it merely exports it.'

She rolled her eyes.

'Sometimes you really are the most patronising, obnoxious...'

'I know.'

On Regent Street they proceeded south down Nash's grand Regency curve. Even on a Saturday evening it was still busy with red horse-drawn omnibuses, buggies and carts clogging the thoroughfare, cyclists gliding by. An impatient buzzing Daimler automobile tried to weave its way through. Along the pavements the pedestrians teemed, some making their way home from the afternoon's demonstration in Trafalgar Square. There were more police around than usual.

A recent city statute had allowed Saturday commercial hours to extend to seven o'clock, which accounted for the bustle. Ahead, dormant cranes towered over the excavations for the new Piccadilly Underground station and the luxury hotel being built for

Swiss hospitality magnate César Ritz. Behind them, too, through the small window, Finch could see a forest of lifting machinery over Euston. In every way, London was a city on the rise – in a constant state of reinvention.

On Regent Street, the huge plate glass windows of the clothiers and milliners and haberdashers were being pored over in wide-eyed awe by pedestrians for whom shopping in such emporia was economically unthinkable. The stores relished the fact, boasting ever more elaborate window displays, their golden lights reflecting back on the wet pavement.

One shop, a purveyor of bridal dresses, had a hugely detailed display running along its whole front. It had forgone mannequins for real live young women, dressed up in all-white and sprouting feathers in a *Swan Lake*-themed tableau. It had attracted quite a crowd. Small boys at the front were pulling faces.

As they neared the hub of Piccadilly Circus, a churning wheel of traffic pivoted clockwise around the Shaftesbury memorial and its winged cherub (mistakenly misconstrued, as Finch liked to point out, as the Greek god Eros). A handful of pro-war agitators were sitting around the steps of its base, placards lowered, reduced to the odd drunken chant and bouts of internecine bickering.

Around them, under the great new illuminated green sign advertising Perrier water, queues snaked for the grand Criterion and Piccadilly theatres. The Perrier sign, composed of thousands of light bulbs, standing on high like a great emerald beacon, was an object of fascination in itself, a brand new wonder of the commercial world, not least for the fanciful Continental notion that honest-to-goodness drinking water should be purchased in a bottle.

Finch asked the driver to turn left into Glasshouse Street. Away from Nash's symmetry, the old road pattern – evolved over centuries of chaos – resumed. He got out, tipped the driver and helped Maude down. It was chilly enough now for their breath to cloud the night air.

'Here!'

He pointed.

'Oh...' she said.

Their cab was swiftly commandeered and, with a snort and scrape of hooves, was soon trotting off.

'Don't be alarmed,' he assured. 'You'll love it.'

The Cathay restaurant was brand new, its bold red paintwork with green adornments and sculpted gold dragons a shock of Eastern flash in a dull Western backstreet. Glazed, bloated duck hung in the window; above it the establishment's name was written in a cod-Oriental script. Though early, the place was already busy, those exiting having to jostle their way through the entrants. On the pavement, a dejected woman was browbeating her husband about his failure to make a reservation.

A party emerged onto the street, including a man in a jaunty panama. His group was intercepted by a pack of pushy men with notebooks.

Squealed Maude, 'My God... is *that*...?'

The man's friends fell away to let him field questions.

'George Robey indeed,' said Finch. 'Haven't a clue what he's like as an actor, but any man who can play professional soccer while turning out for the MCC is all right by me...'

Maude tried hard not to stare as Finch steered a path. As they entered, Chinese men with wispy beards, pigtails, skull caps and elaborate silk smocks with 'frogged' braided fastenings, bowed and held open the doors into a reception area dominated by a huge gong. The aroma of spices and wok-fried produce was pungent and intoxicating.

Finch had made several trips to the original Chinatown that had grown up around the Limehouse area of the Docklands – a small district of shops and cafes springing up to service the many Orientals, in particular from Hong Kong, who had come to the country as merchant ship crews. If such food were eaten by native Chinese, Finch had supposed – largely Cantonese – it had to be authentic.

This place, by comparison, though he didn't doubt the quality of its fare, had been established by an enterprising Chinaman, an ex-Red Funnel steward, as a confection for the Occidentals of theatreland. The newly voguish dish in which it specialised, chop suey – like its New York variant, chow mein – had been created specifically for the purpose, deemed more palatable for British dilettantes.

The decor of plaster pagodas and dog-like dragons bolstered the theme. As did the kitsch paintings of waterfalls, the Great Wall and junks in Hong Kong harbour. The place was festooned with paper lanterns.

'Ingo, for a stick-in-the-mud, you occasionally surprise,' declared Maude.

An attendant took their coats and a small fawning man in black pyjamas showed them to their table, weaving through a vibrant room where waiters bustled around, artfully toting huge trays of food and where meats were flamed and sizzled theatrically right in front of the diners.

'Chopsticks?' Maude panicked, toying gingerly with the porcelain utensils paired before her upon a small rest.

'Part of the fun. You'll soon get the hang of it...'

-

After a meal that had thoroughly met with Maude's approval, washed down with a fine white burgundy, they ordered jasmine tea and engaged in small talk before pondering the journey home. The stains and scraps on the crimson linen tablecloth (more on Maude's side than his, noted Finch triumphantly) bore testament to their enjoyment.

Finch excused himself, leaving Maude to flip through the dessert menu, and made his way to the gents. The white-tiled room was empty and Finch's feet clicked on the floor as he strode to the furthest of the three urinals, stepping up onto the plinth, making a note to leave some coins in the gratuity dish by the washbasins on his way out.

As he began to relieve himself, a man entered, shoes echoing as Finch's had. Finch was facing the wrong way to get a look but felt somewhat aggrieved that when the man approached the urinals, he chose not the furthest one from Finch, as decorum would dictate, leaving the free receptacle as a no man's land, but stepped up to the one right next to him.

The man smelled of lavender. A discreet sideways glance told Finch he was dressed in a fine grey suit, with a cravat and silk kerchief in his pocket to match his refined scent. In the heart of bohemian London, and in the bold new world of the twentieth century, Finch didn't think it so outrageous that he might be about to be propositioned by a person of the same gender, but considered it a tad optimistic on the man's part that he should choose to do so in a busy restaurant of an early evening, especially when it was quite obvious that Finch was enjoying female company... Or maybe that was the challenge?

The man spoke, his business brisk and to the point.

'Dr Finch,' he said.

'Pardon me... But have we met?'

Finch appreciated neither the approach nor the fact that he was addressing him sideways-on in an unfortunate situation. He couldn't see his face.

'Dr Finch, I will say this only once,' he continued. 'But the rules governing your liberty were abundantly clear – that you owe your freedom to a certain set conditions, one of which is that you are to desist from any activity that might be deemed injurious to the proceedings of His Majesty's government.'

Finch willed himself to finish his urination and button himself up. He realised that the other man was not urinating at all.

'Who the hell are you?'

'I am here to advise *you*, Dr Ingo Finch, that you are to extricate yourself from such activities on pain of severe consequences.'

The man stepped down off the plinth.

'I don't understand,' spluttered Finch, straining his head around.

The tone was now icy.

'You understand perfectly well, Dr Finch...'

The man made to leave.

'...If you know what's good for you, you'll pay your bill and see your way out of here... *You have been warned.*'

Finch desperately finished.

'Oh, and one other thing,' said the man, strutting out, only visible from behind. '...Mr Sidney Pickersgill. He is not all he seems.'

'But who...?'

As Finch buttoned up, another man entered the bathroom, obscuring the lavender-scented man as he swung open the door, casually throwing some pennies into the dish. Finch caught a side glimpse of a pencil moustache.

'And have a good evening,' he added.

Finch rushed after him and saw him turn towards the exit but, in the crowded corridor, amid the customers and restaurant staff, he lost him. He hustled through them to the pavement and looked back and forth up and down Glasshouse Street but there was no sign.

'Can I help you, sir?' asked a waiter.

'Sorry... wrong turn.'

Finch returned to wash his hands, then went back into the main dining area, head swimming.

Now a woman appeared to be calling him.

'Finch,' he heard. '*Finch?*'

What the hell had just happened? Had they had him under observation? *All this time...?*

The voice came again, louder.

'Finch! It *is* you... *Finch!*'

He turned. Standing before him was someone he would never, in a million years, have imagined to be in his presence. And certainly not at *this* disconcerting moment. It even felt strange to say her name, but he blurted it out reflexively in a state of confusion and incredulity.

'*Annie?*'

Chapter Seven

The sun had set over the striped tented village that had spread across Victoria Park. The aroma of chestnuts and hand-spun candyfloss wafted over the site, the pipe organs and screams of pleasure mixed in a sensory cocktail.

The illuminated lights of the rides – the roundabout, the helter-skelter, the big wheel – were reflected in the lake, midway between the gentrified terraces of Hackney and the lodging houses of Bow.

Mordecai and his friends had seen the young women before, nodding polite hellos on their way to the docks. There were three of them, 'match girls' from the Bryant & May factory. Dressed in aprons and pinafores then, they looked older now, more womanly – dolled up in their weekend finest, though still with the hunched, stiff-shouldered bearing of those who toiled on a production line.

No formal arrangement had been made to meet up. Indeed, save for 'hellos', none of them had every really spoken. But the lads had guessed they'd be in Victoria Park tonight. They had swapped knowing shoves and prods when they spotted them over by the alcoved seating, formed from the discarded parapets of the old London Bridge.

They had followed the girls into the Ghost House – a ludicrous palace of dangling string, fake skeletons and forced screams, where the promised 'genies and goblins' had failed to materialise. And now the dance continued, the girls this time lagging not too discreetly behind as the lads kept their over-exaggerated balance across the shifting boards of the cakewalk.

With five young men and only three young women, no one quite knew where their affections lay – maybe the girls had friends? But one of them – small, blonde, seemingly the more shy – gave a sheepish, kindly smile to Mordecai, evidently identified as a kindred spirit.

The lads weaved on, the girls came closer. Together they jostled through the melting pot of old and young; native and foreigner; top hat and baggy cap; bonnet and mop cap; soldier and sailor.

On the helter-skelter, wide-eyed kids whizzed down the chute on hessian sacking. On the great roundabout, powered by a belching steam traction engine, riders on white chargers shrieked and waved.

A man poked a mangy bear with a staff. The animal stood upright on hind legs, groaning against its muzzle, as a small terrier yapped at it. A midget one-man band played a lively ditty on a violin, simultaneously pulling a string to operate the bass drum on his back while crashing small cymbals between his knees.

Along the path, a member of the Malthusian League lectured on the principles of population while being harangued by a drunk. A Swedenborgian, standing on a wooden crate, declared the imminent advent of a new Church to sweep away the old. Not unrelated in Mordecai's mind, a member of the Socialist International proclaimed the collapse of the capitalist order – '*Let them cease with their ridiculous wars*' – and the vision of Karl Marx. Mordecai had heard enough of this man's name back home to know that it usually spelled trouble.

A brisk woman trilled 'Votes for Women' and pressed into his hand – though he couldn't read all of it – a leaflet denouncing Prime Minister Balfour. Mordecai instinctively threw it aside. He thought for a moment of the old country, where bad-mouthing anyone in authority could be met with a bullet to the back of the head.

Behind the park's great ornate drinking fountain, the cheap vodka was passed around again. This time the girls were invited to sip. They took the bottle tentatively at first, like garden sparrows testing breadcrumbs in the palm of a gardener.

On the tram ride up from Stepney, one of the lads, Yan, who was older than the others and knew the ropes, had warned his pals to keep their voices down. Pole, Ukrainian, Czech, Baltic, *Russian* – the English could not tell the difference. Though with the bottle of vodka uncorked the moment they had got on board, the advice had been long since disregarded. As usual, Mordecai had refused a drink. Not so long ago, the others would have teased him about his abstemiousness. But they were less inclined to do so these days.

Some months back, on a Friday – payday – one of the dockyard gang, a lumbering, disapproving Muscovite called Andrei, had shoved Mordecai into the back of the warehouse – there to be held down by acolytes while he forcibly poured liquor down Mordecai's neck.

Mordecai's response had stunned everyone. As his triumphant assailant had turned, arms outstretched, eliciting the strained mirth of those who had been drawn in from the quayside, Mordecai had risen to his feet. Spluttering, soaking and with a fuzziness in his head that he was willing with all his power to go away, he had blind-sided Andrei with a flat-palmed chop to the throat. Not hard, just precise. The swing had connected his fingertips with Andrei's Adam's apple.

The man dropped instantly to his knees, pained, panicked, clutching his windpipe, gagging for air. A textbook application of an arm lock, with a thumb applied behind the ear, direct to the mastoid gland, had forced Andrei face down on the ground, weeping and begging for mercy. Andrei never returned to work. And no one had ever bothered Mordecai much since.

Most violence, or threats of violence, Mordecai knew, were theatrical, ritualistic, and he did his utmost to avoid physical confrontation. If young men were posturing, fists raised, while yelling at an opponent, it meant lines of communication were still open, the situation could still be defused. It was the silent and random violence, of which London offered much, that was the most difficult to fathom. He saw the newspaper stand – *Britain and*

Russia: War Latest – and fancied that incidents against outsiders would be on the up.

It did not take long for the braggadocio of his own gang to work its way to the surface, fuelled by the vodka. It was the kind of habitual display that young men put on for young women – a chance to demonstrate their own prowess, placing themselves in a pecking order.

Mordecai declined an invitation to 'ring the bell' – a machine, in his estimation, inevitably fixed – letting his friends scrap it out over who could (or couldn't) bring down the mallet the hardest upon the pad, one that sent a puck shooting up the groove in the post to (almost) strike the bell.

Instead he stood alone (though he sensed the presence of the blonde girl), transfixed by the giant Gavioli organ and the tin marionettes that moved robotically upon its façade.

Tuned into the lads and their displays of bravado, a barker was calling from a nearby stall.

'Ten shots for a penny! Fancy your chances, lads? Win a prize for the lady!'

Duly suckered again, they took their turns with the air rifle, popping away at the eight tin ducks rotating into view on a wooden wheel, none with much success.

It was no use. Urged on, and unable to keep backing down, Mordecai stepped up to the challenge. Left-handed, he nestled the stock between his chin and shoulder and, with his designated ten shots, between a smooth but rapid snapping of the barrel to pump the compressed air, hit not just every duck in the centre of its body but, with the next shot, casually split the thin gold cord that sent a fluffy, stuffed rabbit falling into the arms of the blonde girl.

With a flourish and against a cry of 'Now hold on!' from the stall keeper, he sent the tenth vertically into the night sky. His mates cheered. The girl smiled. She was his if he wanted.

But Mordecai did not feel comfortable. He had the sense recently that someone was watching him, someone lurking in the shadows. He had felt it at the docks, that time after Andrei. He had discerned it in the street late at night when returning to his flophouse. And though this evening, amid the merriment, he had forgotten about it temporarily, someone was most definitely observing him now… their malevolent, unseen presence right there across the way.

A shiver ran down his spine. Cold sweat trickled down his brow. To the disappointment of his friends, and to the blonde girl in particular, Mordecai excused himself and left…

Chapter Eight

'Finch... Say something... *Finch?*'

His head was in such a whirl, it took him a moment to comprehend.

'I just...'

He remained impassive while she reached up and kissed him on the cheek, her lips brushing lightly.

'You look like you've just seen a ghost.'

'Two ghosts, actually.'

The remark threw her. Her smile fell for a moment, then picked up.

'Christ Finch, it's good to see you,' she enthused, as informally Australian as ever, touching his forearm for good measure. 'What are you doing here?... I can't believe it!'

'What am I doing here? What are *you* doing here?'

He looked over her shoulder, scanning the dining room. Had the lavender man slipped back in?

'Finch... *Finch?*'

There was no sign.

'Something more interesting going on?'

'Sorry.'

The imploring dark-brown eyes staring up at him were just as he remembered, as he cherished – no real-life let-down here from the fantasy. He stepped back and regarded her in full for the first time. She had on an elegant deep-silver outfit, gunmetal almost. In her pinned-up dark-brown locks was a long purple feather. There were pearls round her neck, on her ears, in her hair.

If he had thought a thousand times about what he might say or do if he ever saw her again, he had never envisaged a situation in which she wouldn't command his full and absolute attention.

'My God. Finch? I thought that perhaps you'd be just a little happy to see me... I mean, what are the chances?'

'My apologies, Annie, it's just that...'

He felt a tear straining at his eye – joy or frustration or both, he really couldn't tell. Did the lavender man's warning have anything to do with *this* very encounter? Finch felt foolish, and suddenly very rude. He overdid the conviviality and looked Annie up and down with over-familiar approval.

'You look... I don't know how quite to say it, but you look...'

He felt stupid immediately.

'So *there* you are.'

It was Maude who was now at his side, clutching his elbow.

'Oh... *hello?*' she said, directing it at Annie.

He sensed curiosity rather than jealousy. But he was suddenly ashamed, embarrassed at Maude's presence.

'I'm sorry... introductions,' he flustered. 'Miss Maude Carter, Miss Annie Jones... formerly *Nurse* Annie Jones of the New South Wales Army Nursing Reserve...'

'We were in South Africa.'

'Quite a mouthful,' said Maude, extending her ivory glove to shake Annie's black velvet one.

'Actually, it was the New South Wales Army Nursing *Service* Reserve – a mouthful and then some!'

Maude laughed. Annie turned to Finch.

'And it's not Jones any more.'

'Oh,' he said.

'It's Pointer.'

Finch looked down. Maude registered Finch's discomfort. He thought she secretly relished it.

'So, do you live here?' Maude asked. 'I mean, in London?'

'No, no, no... That's what makes this so extraordinary,' said Annie. 'Home is in Australia again... Sydney... Edward and I...'

'*Edward?*' repeated Finch under his breath.

'…We're on a sort of belated, extended honeymoon.'

'Congratulations,' said Maude.

'He had business in Europe and the United States coming up… bit of a tour… so we thought we'd combine business with pleasure. Or should I say pleasure with business. Three months at sea. Stopped in Singapore, Madras, Alexandria… Where else…?'

It seemed to be enthusiasm rather than showing off.

'…Oh, Malta,' she gushed. 'London's the base for Europe, but we've also been to Paris, Berlin…'

'Wow!' exclaimed Maude.

'Trust me. I say that to myself every day. It's really not a life I ever envisaged. *Truly*. I have to pinch myself. I mean, a suite at the Savoy?!'

'So how long have you two known—'

'Since we were young, really. I mean it was difficult, me being away for so long, but then Edward, when I got back from South Africa—'

'No I mean *you* two.'

Maude indicated Annie and Finch. Annie wrinkled her brow. She wasn't sure of the implication.

'I suppose we were pitched together during the war over… what, a couple of years…?' she pondered. 'Isn't that right, Finch? Pretty much from 1900. The camp, then Cape Town… After that it was Kimberley for a bit. And then, well… the Transvaal…'

She seemed lost for a moment again.

'…Some unpleasant things along the way.'

'It was 1899,' corrected Finch. 'December 1899.'

How could she be so bloody casual about it?

'Yes, yes.'

'Until March 1902,' he added, punctilious.

Annie nodded. She was fudging it, he knew, gently editing her own past.

'*I* stayed on until the annexation,' he reminded her, 'but *you*… you were seconded with Major Jenkins, remember…?'

'I do remember.'

'...Went up to Bulawayo... Rhodesia... You, your friend... Nurse Sullivan?'

A stillness came over Annie. She caught his eye. He knew the look.

'Typhoid,' she whispered. Her head hung for a second.

'Oh... I'm so sorry... *Truly*...'

Maude jumped in.

'Listen, sounds like you have a lot to catch up on...'

She addressed Annie directly.

'...If you're in town, then we should arrange to get together, do this properly.'

Finch felt awkward. No matter how hard he'd wanted this scenario, *dreamed* about it... now all he desired was for it to go away.

'I suspect Miss Jones... *Mrs Pointer* will be busy...'

'Actually, you're right,' said Annie. 'We've got to be in Liverpool by Saturday. Sailing to New York. The *Carpathia*... Plus we have dinners, lunches. Edward has meetings...'

'I'm sure he does,' said Finch, trying to rein in the sarcasm.

'Then perhaps an address? For future reference,' asked Maude, gleefully rooting through the drawers of Finch's former life.

'I've got a better idea,' said Annie. 'Come and join us...'

Finch scanned the restaurant again, still uneasy.

'We've got a private room upstairs. Come and meet Edward. Have a nightcap...'

'It's okay, Annie. I really think we should be going,' said Finch.

He turned to Maude.

'I just need to settle the bill. Plus, we've got a train to catch.'

Maude contested the hint. She gave him a look that screamed it was an invitation *not* to be passed up.

'Nonsense,' said Annie. 'I *insist*. Come on, please. It will be our pleasure.'

Maude raised her eyebrows at Finch, imploring him to comply.

'Come on, Ingo. Don't be such a killjoy. Anyway, the trains run till midnight.'

He looked around the restaurant again. The lavender man was nowhere to be seen. He supposed that a quick drink would be okay.

'Yes, come on…' urged Annie.

She looked him in the eye while she said it. He felt a frisson of something in her private mockery.

'…*Ingo*.'

–

The small private room upstairs, atop a tight, winding, rickety staircase, was no more luxurious than the main restaurant. Its chief benefit seemed only in that it came with its own dedicated staff. Finch didn't quite see the point. A key component of the Cathay was its atmosphere. Up here there was none.

Finch and Maude lingered while Annie went in ahead, presumably to explain why a cosy meal for two was now about to be gatecrashed.

Edward stood upon seeing them, a look of fake sincerity playing about his lips. He was a man of medium height with receding hair – not unpleasant of features, but with the chubbiness of good living and what Finch fancied was an air of smugness to go with it. He removed his cigar, a fat Bolivar.

'Dr Finch?'

Edward shook his hand. The grip was firm but not a palm-to-palm one. More of a clasp of the fingers.

'Annie tells me that you were in South Africa together.'

She'd never talked about him?… About what they did?… He had that, *at least.*

'That's correct, Mr Pointer, sir. In the thick of it.'

Finch introduced Maude. Edward kissed the back of her hand. It seemed gauche… nouveau riche.

'Please… *Edward*,' he insisted. 'Any friend of Annie's…'

He clicked his fingers, rather too aggressively. Two extra chairs appeared and a small man in black pyjamas came over and bowed.

'Now look here, my little chap, we'd like some brandy. Courvoisier,' instructed Edward. 'That all right with everyone?'

There were nods of assent. Except from Finch.

'Actually, if you wouldn't mind, I'd prefer a drop of scotch.'

'Of course.'

'Talisker if you have it,' Finch said to the waiter, 'but any single malt will do.'

The waiter bowed.

'Understand you, old boy,' said Edward.

His Englishness seemed forced to Finch, a pointless thin veneer upon the Antipodean.

'In which case it would be rude of me not to join you.'

He called after the waiter.

'Same here. Make them doubles.'

He put the fat brown stogie back in his mouth and puffed a pungent, purple cloud. Finch took out a packet of Navy Cut and indicated that he would like to join him in a smoke. Edward produced a flint lighter and wafted the flame.

Annie noticed the programme poking out of Maude's bag.

'My God, you went to the Stieglitz exhibition…?'

'The Dudley Gallery, Park Lane. Yes…'

'I just *love* his work. He's elevated photography to an art form…'

'He absolutely has.'

'Did they show any of his colour… the autochrome…?'

-

It had not taken long for Finch to get the measure of Edward, the very same man whom Annie had once professed to despise… *to be running away from…* but was now brazenly calling 'darling', while fiddling with the oversized diamond on her left hand. Unless it was another extraordinary coincidence…

Edward's shoddy treatment of the waiters as they cleared away the leftovers, together with what Finch considered a heinous crime – boasting of his avoidance of military service so that he might capitalise on its commercial dividends via his father's shipping business – did not endear him. Though, Finch knew, the man could have been a saint made flesh and he'd still have hated him.

That the 'girls' seemed to be getting along like a house on fire – secretly giggling in some sort of sisterly conspiracy – only accentuated Finch's sense of dislocation. Though the fact that Edward seemed demonstrably uninterested in Annie's doings in South Africa, as if it were some errant chapter to be skipped over, at least gave Finch the comfort that there *was* something of Annie he still had to himself.

What nagged at Finch most, though, was the lavender-scented man. He replayed countless scenarios in his mind but failed to place him. Finch could not recall the man's presence at the inquiry at the War Office or at any of the security hearings in which Finch had become embroiled, whether in Cape Town or on return. And the fact that he had mentioned Pickersgill…

Mindful of the warning he had been issued, he was right, he told himself, to spurn Annie's extended invitation – to attend a *soirée* with the singer Michael Maybrick at the Café Royal – in favour of returning home. ('A little indulgence for the lady,' confided Edward, in candour. 'Not one for music, nor any of these damned paintings or photographs she's always dragging me off to see… A bit like yours…')

As they bid their farewells, Finch supposed he might never see Annie again. And though the thought pained him greatly, parting's sweet sorrow was lost amid the unusual circumstances of the evening and the fact that he would now have to mollify Maude.

Maude… Here was a woman – ostensibly perfect for him in every way – who had shown him nothing but affection and whose quest for adventure, for an experience beyond her lot, had once again been dashed… And by *him*… And on her birthday outing to boot.

The cab pulled up outside Finch's house just before midnight. The suspension squeaked and the body tilted as he helped Maude down. The driver pocketed his tip, twitched his whip and the horse clip-clopped off.

'You like her, don't you?' said Maude.

The gaslight on the corner hissed.

'Annie?' he dismissed.

She rolled her eyes.

'Who else?'

'Of course, we spent a lot of time together. We were in some pretty…'

He fumbled for the word.

'…*intense* situations.'

'Intense?'

It was the wrong one.

He delved into his pocket for his keys. The lights were off inside. Pickersgill would be long gone.

'It's more than that, Ingo. I saw the way you looked at her. I mean, she called you "Finch". You'd have to have been pretty familiar with a woman for her to address you like that.'

'It's not what you think, Maude. I promise.'

He found the right key.

'Look, I can't blame you if *you* don't like her,' he added. 'It would only be natural.'

The smile she gave was for herself.

'Like her, Ingo?… I think she's wonderful…'

The pause had a vaudevillian's timing.

'…Too bad about that pig of a husband.'

He laughed. She did too, but only momentarily.

'I'm serious, Ingo. She's wonderful. *Too* wonderful.'

She laid her hand on his forearm.

'I think I'll say my goodnights now, if I may.'

She turned to go.

Damn!

'Maude, *please*!'

'Sorry, Ingo. Not tonight.'

He put the key in the lock and turned around. He motioned her towards him.

'Just five minutes. Tea… we'll talk… I'll walk you home…'

He nudged the stiff oak door open with his shoulder and flipped on the electric light.

'*Shit!*'

'What?'

His alarm had her swivelling back. She joined him at the threshold and stared in. Books had been pulled off shelves, the furniture overturned, cushions slashed, picture and photograph frames smashed. Anything, any ornament or item, that had occupied a horizontal space, a shelf, a table, the mantelpiece, lay strewn across the floor. The place had been well and truly ransacked.

'Like I said, Ingo. You're a fool… On every level.'

Chapter Nine

When Finch awoke, the dagger was at its most sadistic, its blade so keen, so cruelly inserted, he half wished it would simply slide all the way into his brain and finish him off.

He found himself on the settee, still clothed, with Pickersgill's wet blanket pulled over him. He could smell the man's body odour on it, mingling now with the toxic aroma oozing from his own fetid pores. His mouth felt like it had been hibernated in by wild animals. He needed water and lots of it. He started to shake.

As Finch roused himself, gingerly, he kicked the empty whisky bottle, which rolled across the floor. He had barely time to take in the mess around him – the books, the papers, the smashed ornaments and pictures, the explosion of feather down from the ripped upholstery – when there came a loud staccato rap at the front door. Finch waited a few seconds – the curtains were drawn, he could conceivably be out – but it thundered again, harder, persistent.

Instinctively – though it pained him gravely – Finch got up and crept over in stockinged feet, still with the blanket round his shoulders, trying his best to avoid the shards of glass from the smashed picture frames. That someone should have chosen to shatter a photograph of his mother and father on their wedding day hurt him more than anything. They gazed up at him forlornly.

He reached up above the front door to the false panel, cut beneath a beam, where he kept his loaded Webley service revolver. He unwrapped it from its oily rag and flipped off the safety catch. Then he positioned himself on the hinge side of the door jamb – his right…

There was a loud pounding again. But this time it came with a voice.

'Finch? *Finch!*'

He sighed with relief and undid the lock.

'Jesus, Ingo. What the…?'

Despite his years in England, the rolling Edinburgh burr was unshakeable. It was as soothing as any balm.

'I know we lawyers aren't popular,' the man quipped, noting Finch's clumsy attempt to conceal the weapon. 'But what the *hell*…?'

'Jilkes.'

The man surveyed the damage.

'Quite some bender you went on…'

Finch gave a pained smile.

'…And look at *you* Ingo, you're a mess.'

He entered with a sense of purpose. He wafted a hand in front of his face to alert Finch to the pungency of his breath.

'Come on,' he urged, and made his way to the kitchen. The rattling of implements stirred the dagger again.

'Got any real tea or still on the South African stuff?'

Finch reached for the water jug he'd drunk from last night, still half full, and drained its contents, sloshing a fair amount of it down his shirt. He staggered back over and took to the settee. He pulled the blanket back round him and placed the gun on the floor. He could hear Jilkes at the stove. He fumbled for his Navy Cuts, lit a match and sat back.

Suddenly inspired, he reached forward again… the whisky bottle.

It was snatched away from him.

'Come on, wee pal. This stuff's caused you enough trouble.'

There was barely a drop left but Jilkes shook it ceremoniously onto the fire where it hissed on embers not quite dead. He then went to the curtains and yanked them back. Finch squinted against the light. He also opened a window. Finch pulled the blanket in tighter. There was a sharp stab in his left big toe. A shard of glass had got him.

'Smells like a Tangiers brothel in here,' Jilkes winced. 'Hearsay, of course.'

'Of course,' Finch groaned.

He picked up his foot and saw the spot of red.

Jilkes was a man of medium height, well-dressed in his Sunday best of a fine charcoal suit. He had kindly blue eyes, a healthy outdoor hue to his complexion, was in reasonably good shape – even though he toiled in an office – and was clean-shaven. He was, supposed Finch, the nearest thing he could call to a friend… not that he ever really had a *best* one.

Jilkes smacked away some feathers with his leather gloves before perching himself on the chair opposite. A lawyer and a doctor – they were, in theory, twin pillars of the local community, thought Finch… *very* much in theory.

'Ingo?'

'What?'

He held his arms wide, indicating the mess surrounding them. 'I'm not going to ask. I'll wait for you to tell.'

Jilkes reminded him to a degree of his old army doctor pal Hawley Jenkins… *Major* Jenkins… another soft-spoken Celt – Welsh rather than Scottish – a man razor-sharp in intellect and who also, seemingly, had all the decent human attributes which Finch himself was so sorely lacking.

The kettle began whistling. Jilkes left and returned a minute later with a pot of *rooibos*, two cups, some milk and a teaspoon.

He pulled two saucers out of his jacket pockets, like a conjurer. 'Just to make it decent,' he said.

Finch had pegged Reginald Jilkes as an ex-military man the first time he set eyes on him. And when he found out that he'd also served in Africa – albeit *West* Africa, when the Royal Niger Company had mounted a counter-insurgency campaign against the Aro Confederacy – he felt him to be a brother of sorts, if not quite in arms (both of them had been non-combatants, officially at least).

'Jilkes?'

'What is it, Ingo?'

Jilkes didn't talk about it much but Finch understood his legal skills had made him of great value in military circles. He knew that he'd been somewhere in the delegation that had brought an end to the slave trading that had been rampant along the Niger.

Finch picked at his foot. He teased out the thin glass sliver.

'You think there'll be war?'

Jilkes blew out a hiss. There was sarcasm in his voice.

'Any war in particular? Germans, Russians, Austrians…? I still wouldn't write off the French.'

'The Russians. This North Sea business.'

Jilkes eyed Finch's cigarettes.

'Mind if I pinch one? Agatha's with the bairns. Sunday school… While the cat's away…'

'What time is it?'

Jilkes flipped back the cuff covering his wristwatch.

'Almost noon.'

'Christ!'

'Now now,' said Jilkes sarcastically. 'The Lord's name in vain on the Sabbath?'

Finch tossed his matches to Jilkes but missed. Jilkes scooped them from the floor.

'You went too…? To *church*?' asked Finch.

'You think I dressed like this just for you? Don't flatter yourself, laddie!'

Finch almost grinned.

'Do you believe in God?'

Jilkes smiled, an ironic one.

'My, my… I wasn't expecting *that* one, Dr Finch… Questions don't come much bigger than *that*.'

Jilkes looked around the mess of the room.

'…Why, you think *He* did this?'

'I couldn't blame him.'

'If you must… I believe in *Church*, Ingo…'

He lampooned his own accent.

'…*Aye, the good auld Kirk*… I believe in Church. I believe in community. And if doffing my hat to the Big Man on a Sunday is what it takes for me to keep my affairs in order and put food on the table, then…'

He puffed cautiously in the manner of the casual smoker.

'…You know, maybe once in a while *you* should…'

'No sermons, please.'

'Sorry… And as for those Russians? I don't know…'

He coughed.

'…I mean it's a good opportunity though, I must admit… while they're engaged in the Far East. Back door's wide open. But name me a military campaign that ever went to plan… and especially one against Russia.'

Finch drew hard on his cigarette.

'There's nothing to gain from it either,' Finch said.

'Since when has *that* ever mattered? I don't know, Ingo. By the terms of international law, if there *is* such a thing, we do have every entitlement to exact our pound of flesh.'

Finch smiled to himself.

'"We"?… You said *we* have every entitlement. Not the kind of thing a lawyer—'

Jilkes laughed. He fished the strainer from his breast pocket and began pouring the tea.

'For a man with a hangover, you're still quite the pedant.'

'And the pound of flesh?'

'Legally, Britain has every right to seek recompense. Whether that be financial, territorial… Honour must be upheld in certain eyes. Maybe it *won't* come to armed conflict. I mean, what would be the objectives? Bombard St Petersburg? March on Moscow?… In *winter*?… I don't think so. That said, what the Russian navy did was a crime. Don't lose sight… Russia conducted an illegal military act against British citizens… *civilians*… in British territorial waters… And you can bet your last drop of single malt there will be old duffers in Whitehall pushing hard for punitive action.'

Finch breathed out a large cloud.

'You know what I think, Jilkes...?'

Jilkes shrugged.

'...I think Russia's a powder keg. You take a society that was in serfdom until relatively recently... It's still an autocracy... Bloody inbred Romanovs... You conscript those barely-liberated, illiterate peasants, dress them up in uniform, send them to sea for the very first time and ply them with vodka...'

The cigarette was now spent. He stubbed it out.

'...Add a drunken aristo captain who needs to manufacture an external threat to stop his own men from lynching him and so fills his crew with paranoid nonsense about an enemy lurking out there in the dark... Do *that* and it only takes the slightest thing – a strange light, a strange boat... a *fishing trawler* – to set the men blazing away at anything that moves... and with highly mechanised weapons that more than exceed the capabilities of the persons operating them.'

Finch nodded at the newspaper lying there.

'I mean, for Christ's sake, it turns out that, after attacking the fishing boats, they started shelling each other!'

Jilkes sipped his tea then put down his cup and saucer.

'Dare say you're right, Ingo. But if you do *nothing* this time, then someone will do it again. Give 'em an inch... Britain has interests all over the world. If you don't stick up for your own...'

'You were in the army, Jilkes. Look at the mess we've made of the Niger Delta. Christ, look at the carnage "*we*" wreaked in the bloody Transvaal: scorched earth, burning down farms, herding women and children into camps...'

Jilkes extinguished his cigarette.

'And so *that's* why you trashed the room?'

The joke fell flat.

They lit second cigarettes, poured more tea and, for the next quarter of an hour, Finch recounted the main points of his encounters with Pickersgill, his trip to London with Maude and, though he didn't go into full detail, the fact that he had been approached by someone last night who had warned him to keep his nose out of business that didn't concern him.

When he was done, Finch leaned back – the invitation for Jilkes to venture an opinion. Jilkes sat there, trying to process it all. When he'd done so, he craned forward…

'Then you think that your house was *not* simply burgled… robbed? *Not* just ransacked by this Pickersgill character? You're suggesting *what*?'

'I don't know.'

Jilkes pressed his fingertips together in contemplation, making a steeple of the index fingers upon his chin.

'The law of Ockham's razor, Ingo…'

'You sound like a chap I once knew.'

'…The simplest explanation…'

'…is probably the most likely one… I know. You mean that Pickersgill was simply an opportunist who took advantage?'

'It's what the law of averages would dictate.'

'Then why on earth was he name-dropped by this other fellow… this man in the gentlemen's room?'

Jilkes hummed thoughtfully.

'Maybe it was a sort of aside, a little gesture of goodwill on their part… Whoever *they* may be… You know, "*Watch your back*", that kind of thing… Or, I don't know, just a plain simple way of demonstrating just how closely they've got you monitored. "*We're watching you*"… "*We told you so*"… "*We warned you*"… Something of that order?'

'That's a lot of "what ifs",' said Finch, rubbing the back of his neck.

'Well, have you looked? What did Pickersgill take exactly?'

Finch sighed.

'That's the thing, Jilkes. I had a good root around last night. Upstairs is barely touched. He took nothing of import.'

He pointed to the revolver on the floor.

'He'd have found my Webley if he'd looked hard enough. There's money in a vase in the kitchen that's still there. All that's gone are some silver candlesticks, a trophy I won in a pub darts tournament and a carriage clock. The only thing that was of any worth was my medical bag – the drugs and the prescription pad inside – and he'd even seen where I kept it. I forgot to tuck it away. And he left it.'

'Your point?'

'I'm saying that if Pickersgill *was* a burglar, he wasn't a very good one, especially given all the trouble he'd gone to to ingratiate himself. You'd think he'd have come away with pickings a little more rich.'

'You said he seemed pretty desperate. Maybe he just grabbed what he could in a hurry. Maybe he was disturbed?'

'Possibly. But all this ripping of the cushions, the smashing of the pictures. It just seems a bit, I don't know, *theatrical*... like someone wanted to give the *impression* of a burglary... The stuff he took has no value. He'd have to shop it around... pawn it... and that's a one-way ticket to getting caught.'

Jilkes rubbed his cheek.

'How about value to *you*? Forget monetary worth.'

Finch spluttered incredulity.

'Come on, Jilkes... The emotional value of a darts trophy?!'

'I'm just trying to explore all the options.'

'My finest hour... Only three of us turned up for the tournament. The first player was so drunk he couldn't hit the board. I beat the other chap because he couldn't score properly.'

'I see.'

'And the candlesticks? They were a present from Mrs P-A. I know someone got them as a gift for *her* originally, bless her, and she quickly packaged them up for me when she realised she'd forgotten my birthday. She knew they'd still end up on our mantelpiece. Clever move actually.'

Finch laughed but Jilkes didn't this time.

'And as for the carriage clock...'

Jilkes signalled that Finch had made his point.

'Then my advice, Ingo, is get this lot tidied up...'

He waved his arm around the room.

'...Get the cushions stitched, reframe the portraits... Just let the whole thing go...'

He nodded to the floor.

'…And whatever you do, stow that bloody gun away.'

'You know,' said Finch. 'I'm surprised that you, of *all* people, didn't tell me to report it to the police. You're the one person I can always rely on to tell me to do the sensible thing.'

'Ingo. Given what you've told me… *and* given that you just answered the door with a Webley in your hand, I suspect we're operating on a level higher than the one on which the local plods operate. They're not going to trawl the land looking for Pickersgill. If that's even his real name.'

Jilkes hummed to himself in contemplation.

'What is it?'

'This lass… this Annie… Is there something you're not telling me here…? It's your eyes, Ingo. You say her name and they dart around, then look away…'

'It's nothing, Jilkes. Nothing.'

'You sure?'

'I'm sure.'

'Well you know I think you're a bloody fool, Ingo…'

'Not you too.'

'…Maude… What are you *playing* at?… You know Agatha and I adore her… the *kids* adore her… She's beautiful… She's kind… She's intelligent… She's funny… She's feisty. There couldn't be anyone more perfect for you… And you're not getting any younger.'

Jilkes put his palms up in apology. He looked at his watch again.

'I need to go soon, Ingo.'

He stooped down and started piling up books.

'But while I've got a few minutes…'

Finch put a hand out to stop him.

'No need, Jilkes. It's *my* bed. I'll lie in it. But I do appreciate your being here…'

Finch wrinkled his brow.

'…Which begs a question, Jilkes. Why *are* you here?'

Jilkes stood. He smoothed down his trousers and put on his gloves.

'You know, I thought you might ask me that...' he sighed. 'You mean, how I didn't just suspect that you somehow might have been burgled and I thought I'd better wander on over to investigate...?'

He cleared his throat.

'...It's just... And I don't know quite how to say it...'

'Out with it.'

'...but I don't think I can represent you any more, Ingo... not in a legal capacity.'

Finch slumped back.

'Christ, when it rains it really does bloody pour... *Meaning?*'

'Meaning that as your legal counsel, the one who brokered your "arrangement" with the War Office, I'm running a high risk.'

Finch slammed his cup down.

'Jilkes, for Christ's sake. You were given absolute assurances *and* from the highest authority – a document signed by Joseph Bloody Chamberlain – that as my legal counsel your position is inviolable and that all dealings between us are bound by legal privilege... You have a complete guarantee of security.'

To Finch, Jilkes looked genuinely pained now.

'I'm sorry, Ingo. Truly I am. But I have a wife... kids...'

Finch groaned in resignation.

'Someone got to you, didn't they?'

Jilkes averted his eyes. Finch understood. He backed down.

'I'm sorry,' said Finch.

'Look, I can find someone else for you. Someone good.'

Finch exhaled loudly. He pulled his blanket tightly round him again. He rubbed his foot. Jilkes made his way out. He turned before exiting.

'Be mindful of your obligations, Ingo... and for God's sake, *be careful...*'

Chapter Ten

After Jilkes had left, Finch bathed, dressed, scavenged some remnants from the kitchen and procrastinated over the business of tidying up the mess. A torrent of thoughts streamed through his head. Though, while soaking in the tub, one thing dominated – *Annie*.

With all that had happened, the encounter with her in the Chinese restaurant had since assumed an almost dreamlike quality. It beggared belief that a chance meeting with someone he hadn't stopped thinking about for the last two years, and whom he'd genuinely never expected to see again, should now be just *one* item in a bizarre series of events.

That said, the very real business of having his home ransacked seemed of lesser injury than the fact that Annie – and despite it being none of his business – should have sought love with the very man, Edward, she professed to have enlisted for South African service to escape… And *he*, Finch, had been forced to bear witnesses to this unedifying spectacle.

What he would do, he didn't quite know. Last night seemed like unfinished business. The goodbye had seemed so tame, not a terminal adieu. But she had also stated quite clearly that, within days, she was sailing for the United States and there was no further opportunity for meeting up.

Amid the thoughts whirling in his head – about Pickersgill, Maude, Jilkes, the lavender man – Finch did resolve to do one thing. And it was not a decision to be taken lightly – he would ignore Jilkes' advice.

If his house *had* been robbed by an opportunist, whether Pickersgill or somebody else, then it was Finch's duty to report the matter to the police. There lurked some sense of civic duty. He toyed with the irony in Jilkes' words when it had come to the Empire:

> *'But if you do nothing this time, then someone will do it again. Give 'em an inch…'*

He thought back, too, over his – and Annie's – previous experience when dealing with the dark arts of state intelligence. And, on that basis, he wanted everything on record. The last thing he needed was to be arrested further down the line, be put in the dock and have some supercilious wig turn to a jury and announce, smugly:

> *'And yet, Dr Finch, despite your claims, you chose not to report this so-called "robbery"…'*

Jilkes, Jilkes, Jilkes…

He felt no sense of betrayal on his friend's part for terminating their professional relationship. Indeed, he would have done the same in Jilkes' position, he was sure. But there lingered disappointment. He owed, in part, his liberty, perhaps his *life*, to the brilliance of Jilkes. He had acted as Finch's counsel on a particularly bleak day in Whitehall when the storm was gathering. But now his friends and allies were evaporating fast.

After an initial and pained assault on the disorder of his living room – sweeping up the debris, but leaving the books in piles to be shelved later – Finch gathered his hat and coat to set out for the police station. Then it was just a matter of counting down the hours till Sunday evening pub opening.

Wait… He still had some claret stashed somewhere. Didn't he? He'd hidden it for emergency use. And once he remembered where… He would search for it on his return.

Things were clearly running ahead of him, for as he opened the door, he found a police constable marching towards him down his front garden path.

'Dr Finch!' he bellowed.

The officer was middle-aged, sported a beard and would have been an impressive physical specimen were it not for the portly midriff straining at his belt, or his helmet seeming a little too small for his head.

'Morning, Percy,' replied Finch, with a strong note of curiosity.

'Ceased bein' mornin' about two hours ago, sir.'

Finch went into his usual routine of professional feigned jollity.

'One loses track of time at the weekend. How are you?'

'Oh, mustn't grumble. You know how it is.'

'And Mary?'

'Better these last few days, sir. Thank you, sir. Said she was goin' to knit you some socks. You know, as a thank you.'

Finch waved a dismissive hand.

'Don't mention it. Just make sure she gets plenty of rest.'

'Easier said'n done.'

Finch suddenly realised that PC Percy Woodruff's wife – a sufferer of a recurring, debilitating viral condition – might be the reason for this inadvertent encounter.

'Goodness… Is everything okay?'

'No, no. Nothin' like that, sir. It's somethin' else.'

PC Woodruff jabbed a discreet thumb over his shoulder.

Following through the small picket gate was another officer… the three stripes of a sergeant.

'Good day. *Dr Finch?*' the man asked – a statement more than a question. He barked it in the brusque manner of someone wishing to demonstrate authority.

The sergeant had a clipped moustache, was well-built and reminded Finch of just about every NCO he'd encountered during his time with the army. He was shorter than Finch, barely minimum height for a copper. He had the demeanour to compensate.

'Mind if we come in, sir?' Again, not really a question.

Finch shrugged and opened the door.

'We have a few things we'd like to ask.'

PC Woodruff rolled his eyes at Finch apologetically.

'Funnily enough, I was just coming over to see *you*,' said Finch. 'Something I needed to report.'

'Is that so?' said the sergeant. 'Well, well, well...'

Finch didn't like the tone.

The men removed their helmets and each took an armchair, rearranging the large wooden truncheons to allow them to sit. Finch offered tea. Woodruff accepted but then changed his mind once it was clear the sergeant was declining. Finch bundled the blanket away and took the settee.

'Been having a clear-out, have we?' the sergeant asked, noting the piles of books and the picture frames now stacked against the skirting board.

'Not quite,' said Finch. 'In fact, it's the reason I was coming over to the police station. You see, I've been robbed... burgled... Not quite sure what the legal distinction is.'

The sergeant motioned to Woodruff and the constable flipped a brass button on his tunic breast pocket. He pulled out a small photograph. He went to hand it directly to Finch but the sergeant coughed. Woodruff passed it to the sergeant, who then handed it to Finch.

The photograph was a tattered, creased, black and white portrait – almost sepia from exposure – of a man and his wife posed before a wooden rowing boat on a shingle beach. The man was standing, the grim-faced woman, presumably his wife, sitting. She was done up in a fairly stiff-looking dark dress, buttoned up to the throat. He had been posed awkwardly with one hand tucked into his waistcoat, the other behind his back.

'You know this man?' asked the sergeant.

The picture was a few years old, but there was no mistaking its subject.

'I do,' said Finch. 'His name is Pickersgill... Sidney Pickersgill. At least that's what he told me.'

'Turn it over, sir.'

On the reverse was written, in a loopy pen stroke: *Sidney and Edna Pickersgill, Cley-next-the-Sea, 1892.*

He handed the photo back.

'What do you mean, sir... that you *know* him?' the sergeant asked.

'I mean I've *met* him... two... *three* times, actually, over the past few days. I don't want to point the finger of blame without evidence, but there's a strong possibility he was the one who robbed me. You know, Ockham's razor.'

'Ockham's what, sir?' asked Woodruff.

'Sorry... I mean the simplest explanation... You know, law of averages.'

There was no response. Finch took out a cigarette. He didn't bother offering the packet.

'Robbed you when?' asked the sergeant.

'Some point yesterday. Between noon and midnight, if you're looking for the window of opportunity. I mean that's when it seems my house was turned over, some stuff stolen. Again, I'm not saying it was necessarily *him*...'

He pointed at the photo.

'...Pickersgill... But it happened around the time he was here.'

'*Here?*'

Finch lit up and took a puff.

'Yes. He was in a bit of a pickle, you see, living rough. He'd sought me out. He was a little paranoid about something...'

Finch circled his finger at his temple to indicate mental health concerns and to remind them of his own professional status.

'...He showed up here again yesterday... Saturday morning. About eleven-ish. He was penniless, soaking wet, cold, hungry and was also coming down with something. It was not a situation I could tolerate as a physician... or a Christian...'

He hoped the playing of the God card would appeal to this congregation... and on a *Sunday*.

'...I gave him some medicine, a bite to eat, let him dry out his clothes and laid him down on the sofa. Poor chap was in quite a state. Thing is, I had plans... was going out... off into London. Told him he could stay for a bit but should see himself out.'

'That's very trusting of you.'

Finch handed the photo back.

'Too right. I came back that night to find the house ransacked and some items missing, as I've said. Again, I'm not accusing Pickersgill specifically, but it happened on his watch, if you know what I mean?'

The sergeant gestured to Woodruff. He took out a notepad and read from it.

'Two candlesticks, a carriage clock and a trophy… It had your name engraved on it, sir…'

He gave Finch a wink.

'…Never 'ad you pegged as a darts man, sir.'

'No end to my talents, Percy… But *yes*, those are the items that are missing.'

'We found 'em in an 'essian sack, Dr Finch…'

'Swift work, gentlemen. Thank you.'

'…on Sidney Pickersgill's person.'

Finch sighed. Jilkes had been right.

'Only thing in 'is pockets, other than the photograph, was a silver 'alf-crown.'

Finch, you are a mug.

'Then you've got him?' asked Finch. 'Down at the station?'

'In a manner of speaking,' said the sergeant.

The policemen exchanged a glance.

'We mean 'e's dead, sir,' added Woodruff.

'*Dead?*'

'Found 'im in a ditch out on the old Roman road,' the constable explained. 'Bloke on the estate was ferretin'. Came across 'is body 'bout half past seven this mornin'. Looks like it was dumped there.'

'Dumped?'

'Was killed with a single shot to the left temple…'

'My God!'

'…from about five to ten feet.'

Finch looked around for an ashtray. He settled on the empty teacup by his feet.

'But the body's position was not one of a man felled by a bullet, if you understand, sir,' said Woodruff. 'It was of someone who'd been rolled, *dumped* down there... There are ways of tellin', sir.'

Finch nodded.

'Yes, I understand.'

Finch felt genuinely sad. Pickersgill had predicted his own imminent demise. He thought now about the man's final words to him. It was a goodbye. He'd known then and there that his time was up. But then why waste time with a pointless robbery?

He flipped ash into the cracked saucer.

'We contacted our colleagues in the Norfolk Constabulary,' said the sergeant. 'A telephone call from Norwich confirmed Pickersgill had history – a drunk, a petty thief, a conman...'

A drunk?

'Upset quite a few people, he did. Worming his way into their lives with tall tales. Invoking pity, scamming food, bits of cash...'

The sergeant looked around the room. He harrumphed.

'This "ransacking", as you've called it. Looks pretty tidy in here.'

'Well I've broken the back of it. Was quite a mess before.'

The next question put Finch on the defensive.

'Are you *sure* that's what happened, Dr Finch?'

'What on earth do you mean?'

'Exactly as I asked.'

The sergeant nodded to PC Woodruff who, on this signal, licked the stub of a pencil and began taking notes.

'Now look here, Sergeant. I'm not sure I appreciate the insinuation.'

Woodruff scribbled furiously.

'And what insinuation's that?' sneered the officer.

'I don't know... that I'm somehow being... *deceitful*.'

'And why would that be?'

Finch had had experience of police interrogations. They seemed to rely on a standard routine of turning every statement into a question. He did the same with his answer.

'And why would it *not* be?'

Woodruff looked up. His face suggested Finch's tactic might not be the most prudent, a silent imploration to desist. The sergeant upped the ante.

'Dr Finch, we have several witnesses who can place you at the Six Bells public house around twelve noon on Tuesday. Said witnesses also claim that Pickersgill entered the pub, sought you out and that the pair of you then entered into an intense conversation – some would allege a *confrontation* – which concluded with you berating Pickersgill, then storming out of the pub and slamming the door.'

Finch smiled a wry smile to himself. They had an agenda. He suspected there was little he could do now. He bent down and stubbed out his cigarette.

'Something funny, Dr Finch?' asked the sergeant.

'I'm glad you place such faith in the testimony of a bunch of drunks.'

The sergeant nodded at the empty whisky bottle which Jilkes had stood on the occasional table.

'Does that include *yourself*, sir?'

'How dare you!'

'People talk, you know.'

Finch stood.

'I'm going to have to ask you to leave.'

'Not so fast. I advise you to sit down again.'

Finch huffed, then complied.

'Did you have something against Mr Pickersgill?'

'No!'

'It's just this whole robbery thing. It seems something of an amateur cover-up…'

Now it was the sergeant spluttering an ironic laugh.

'…I mean, stealing something with your *name* on it. How *convenient*.'

'It's exactly as I told you,' bleated Finch, frustrated now that the sergeant was employing the very same logic that he himself had used earlier.

'One final thing,' said the sergeant. 'Pickersgill was killed with a .45 bullet. It had lodged in his skull. Most likely from an Enfield or a Webley revolver.'

Finch's heart sank. He knew what was coming when he saw the sergeant's eyes dip down to the area beneath the settee, right behind his ad hoc ashtray.

'What's wrapped in that rag?' he asked.

He had tucked it away but not yet returned it to its hiding place.

'You can probably guess,' said Finch.

'Do you have a licence for it?'

'It's my old service pistol. No.'

There, he knew, was their pretext.

The sergeant turned to PC Woodruff, who looked personally pained at what he would now be obliged to do.

The policemen stood; so did Finch. Woodruff produced a pair of handcuffs.

'Sorry sir…' he said.

Chapter Eleven

Finch sat on the bed in the police cell. The room smelled of carbolic and urine. The thin, worn mattress had a rough horse blanket upon it and a stripy pillow stained a nasty yellowy brown. The ensemble acted as a deterrent to any notion of lying down.

Periodic footsteps and police shop talk echoed off the bare walls of the corridor. After about an hour or so they were followed by the clanking of keys and the swinging open of the heavy metal door. Beneath a police arm, Jilkes ducked in. The door clanged shut again. A copper glanced in through the grille then slid the panel back across.

Sure that they were alone, Jilkes' voice came in a strained whisper.

'For Christ's sake, Ingo. I told you to let this bloody thing go!'

'It was they who came for *me*, Jilkes. The poor bastard's dead and they're suggesting I had something to do with it...'

He shrugged.

'...Then again I suppose I did, in a way... Hastened it, maybe.'

'Don't start saying that. You acted most charitably to Pickersgill.'

'Come on, Jilkes. Executed and dumped in a ditch just hours after I took him in? Single shot from five to ten feet? And with a bullet from a Webley revolver...?'

Jilkes nodded that he was familiar with the facts.

'They'll be taking a look at your pistol later. It shouldn't be a problem.'

'Forgive me for being cynical, Jilkes, but I'm sure they can make that bullet match it if they really want to. Ballistics is an inexact science. *You* know that.'

Jilkes exhaled. He let the pause hang for maximum impact.

'Hold on, laddie. Let's get one thing clear. The law's an ass, sure. But the law's still the law. If you lose complete faith in it, there's no point fighting your corner; no point in my even being here…'

'It's just—'

'I know what you're saying, Ingo. But you can't just storm off, take your ball and go home. You have to play the game to the rules. To the very letter. Play it *better*.'

Jilkes looked paler than he had done earlier, thought Finch. He dabbed at his forehead with a handkerchief then sat down on the bed next to him. He opened his brown leather briefcase and shuffled some papers.

'Well I guess if we've learned anything, we now know what message your friend in the gents was sending you,' he said. 'It was a warning. A good old head on a spike, stuck there to make sure you keep your nose out of this business. Whatever "this business" may be.'

'*My* head on the spike, Jilkes.'

'Not quite. They're holding you without charge on a technicality – possession of a firearm without a licence, that's all. It's a typical tactic. Bring you in while they see if they can amass enough evidence to charge you for the bigger deal…'

'You mean the *murder*?'

Finch put his head in his hands.

'Listen to me, Ingo. The ballistics – inexact science or otherwise – will only be advisory. They can't pin *anything* on you. Our local bobbies, especially that sanctimonious wee arse of a sergeant, have already broken just about every rule governing the processing of a crime scene. Even if you *did* do it…'

Finch looked startled.

'…which I'm not suggesting for one second, I'm merely talking hypothetically… we'd get it thrown out by the judge. It's inadmissible.'

Finch sighed.

'More immediately, I've corroborated everything you've told me that happened over the past few days. Ralph the bartender is happy to give a more favourable account of what happened in the Six Bells. I have the names and addresses of two others who I'm certain will sing the same tune. Here...'

He passed Finch a packet of Navy Cut and a box of matches.

'God bless you,' said Finch.

The packet was already open.

'Hope you don't mind. Thought it'd calm my nerves.'

Finch offered him another.

'Better not. Two in one day.'

Finch lit one himself. He drew deep and sighed. From a sheaf of papers Jilkes pulled out a document. He handed it over.

'Excuse the two-fingered typing... It's a signed statement from me to say I was at your house this morning, saw all the mess – I've catalogued it in detail for them – and that you'd fully intended to come and tell the police sooner... were it not for a bastard of hangover.'

'Which is actually true, Jilkes. I had a change of heart. Was on my way here. Only wish I'd done it sooner.'

Jilkes didn't react, just handed him another sheet, a list of names.

'You also have witnesses who can account for your whereabouts yesterday evening: Maude, Annie Pointer, her husband if necessary. I dropped in on Maude on the way here. Not only will she attest to the fact that she witnessed you extend your charity to the unfortunate Mr Pickersgill – and against her better judgement – but that she was also witness to the aftermath of the ransacking and robbery when you came back from London.'

Finch sighed again.

'Thank you.'

'You should thank Maude most of all, Ingo. The wee lass was prepared, if needed, to state on record that she spent the whole night with you. If that had gone to court she'd have lost her job... her honour...'

Finch stared down at the floor. It was a hell of a thing for Maude to have done. But he couldn't stop thinking of Annie.

'One last thing. I got on the phone to a colleague, a specialist in military law, worked with him in Lagos. Told me that if you raided the home of every serviceman who saw action in the colonies, you'd find over half of them had illicit hardware… stuff they brought home as a "souvenir"… And that includes an awful lot of coppers, by the way. So at the very least we can pick the police up on their inconsistency. Our ass of a law has to be applied fairly. But it also seems you chaps in the Medical Corps were a special case…'

'We were?'

'The South African War marked the first time in combat that field medics, battlefield surgeons, weren't just volunteers in mufti…'

Finch nodded.

'…The Royal Army Medical Corps had been formed specifically as a uniformed military unit. For medics in the field, carrying a sidearm was optional, a matter of conscience. Remember that?'

'I do.'

'Thing is, the whole expedition was so shambolic to begin with, especially after the defeats and retreats of the Black Week – you know, when the Boers gave us a bloody nose – that no records exist of who was issued what in the field. Whether you signed the weapon out or back in again is something no one can prove. Nor whether, after hostilities… and I want you to listen very carefully, Ingo… you paid cash to the quartermaster to purchase the gun in your own name and with the paperwork duly processed to go with it.'

Jilkes grinned.

'The retail value of a used Webley in May 1902 was about eight guineas, Ingo. I'm asking you – and you don't have to answer – do you remember handing eight guineas cash to a quartermaster in Cape Town whose name you can't recall on the promise that the paperwork would be forwarded to your home address in England…?'

Finch smiled.

'M'lud, I do believe the defence is leading the witness.'

'The burden of proof's on *them*, not us… So here, sign this…'

He handed Finch a sheet which summarised all that they had just discussed.

'You did this all in the last hour, Jilkes? I'm very impressed.'

He took Jilkes' fountain pen and added his name.

'Not as impressive as my fee, Ingo… Waived in your case… Anyway, you're free to go…'

His face was still grim, his jaw tight.

'But this is the last time. I told you, I can't represent you any more, I simply can't. I'm sorry. I truly am.'

Jilkes pointed at the cigarettes.

'Think I *will* have one of those after all.'

He took one and lit it up. They sat in silence for a moment.

'Have you eaten?' Jilkes asked.

'Some stale bread. A few hours ago now.'

'Then you're coming with me. Agatha's cooked a topside of beef. Roast potatoes, vegetables, the whole works. More than enough to go round.'

Finch began to protest about the imposition.

'Nonsense, Ingo. Always a seat at our table.'

They stood.

'Thank you, Jilkes. Sincerely. *Thank you.*'

Jilkes noticed the tremors in his Finch's outstretched right hand before he shook it.

'Best way you can thank me? Give up the bottle.'

Jilkes banged on the door and PC Woodruff opened it. Jilkes escorted Finch out.

'Sorry 'bout all that, sir,' the constable offered. 'I feel a right charlie.'

'Not your fault, Percy,' assured Finch. 'Your *sergeant* made an honest mistake.'

'Thank you, sir. No 'ard feelings?'

'None whatsoever.'

They shook hands.

'The socks. As soon as Mary's finished, I'll bring 'em over...'

-

Jilkes lived in large detached house in a newish development on the edge of the city, but the ivy that trailed artfully across the façade and the Georgian-style sash windows gave it an older feel. It was getting dark when their cab pulled up and the front door opened to reveal a house of heat and light, the aroma of a home-cooked roast dinner and the excited noise of children. It was, as Finch had described it to Maude once, in one of his more sentimental digressions, 'a house full of love'.

Agatha – petite, beaming and pretty – stood in the doorway, untying her apron.

'Hello, Ingo,' she said, greeting him with a warm embrace and a kiss on the cheek.

A seven-year-old boy and a five-year-old girl whose front teeth had recently fallen out, rushed into the hallway and thundered noisily into Finch's legs.

'Sorry, Ingo,' added Agatha. 'Since Albert and Agnes heard you were coming they've been whipping themselves into a frenzy.'

Finch squatted down and, with sleight of hand – and having checked en route that the police had returned his small change – went through his magician's routine of producing a sixpence from behind Albert's ear and then pretending to cough up another one for little Agnes. The kids shrieked with delight, then upped the volume further when Finch acceded to Agnes' request and got down on all fours so they could hop on his back and pretend he was a horse.

'Children, give poor Uncle Ingo some rest,' said their mother. 'Now run along and put that money in your piggy banks. And after supper it's straight to bed.'

They departed in a chaotic whirl.

'Don't believe they heard a word you said,' smiled Finch.

'You know how they love seeing you... how *we* love seeing you, Ingo... *and* Maude.'

'Now now, Agatha,' admonished Jilkes, as he pressed a whisky into Finch's hand.

'An amnesty,' Jilkes whispered. 'You can quit tomorrow.'

After a slap-up meal which Finch declared to be the finest roast he'd had in a considerable while – which was true – and an exquisite bottle of Jilkes' favourite Bordeaux, he sat with the kids and read them some passages from *Through the Looking-Glass, and What Alice Found There*. He impressed them with his impassioned, by-heart recitation of the *Jabberwocky* poem before they were prised away, objecting noisily to the unfair prospect of being dispatched upstairs to wash faces and brush teeth.

Agatha and her husband exchanged a look and Jilkes led Finch into the drawing room for a glass of port and a smoke. Finch wondered whether he had brought him home just to underscore how sacred his family was. He couldn't blame him.

'Jilkes, until such time as you reverse your decision, I solemnly swear that I will not call on your professional services again.'

'I'll let you off today. It was a "little bird" who tipped me off you were in trouble.'

'PC Woodruff?'

'Aye. He's a good copper. Old school. You can't police a community unless you understand that community.'

Finch's voice was tinged with sadness.

'Seriously, I don't know what I'd have done without you. Not just today. I mean *everything*.'

'It's me who should be thanking you, Ingo. I was a bit of a star for a while in the War Office. Your case got me a long way.'

They both smiled.

'But you know what, Ingo. It doesn't hurt for a man to share some of this stuff... your troubles... Not all of them, but at least *some* of them. You know you can talk to Maude...'

'Jilkes, can I ask you something?'

'Not the God question again.'

Finch laughed, then turned serious.

'Who got to you?'

'What do you mean?'

'You know what I mean. Someone approached you… told you to wind up your affairs with me.'

Jilkes sighed.

'I suppose I owe you this. But when you mentioned the scent of lavender…'

'It was *him*… in person?'

Finch could sense that Jilkes wanted him to leave it at that.

'Look, this is just so you're clear…'

He hesitated.

'Go on.'

Jilkes caught Finch's eye and stared intently for a moment.

'You cannot breathe a word. You understand?'

Finch nodded.

Jilkes pinched another of Finch's smokes and struck a match. He kept his voice down so Agatha couldn't hear.

'Friday morning. Came to my office. Had made an appointment by telephone, ostensibly to discuss some minor concern, a contractual dispute – something I was going to pass on to a junior partner. But it was a pretence. Kept it short and to the point. Just said that I should terminate my professional relationship with you with immediate effect.'

'Did he make a threat?'

'Didn't need to.'

'And then…?'

'Gone. Was in and out in five minutes… Which is why you should just stick to the narrative… as shaky as that narrative may be. Pickersgill was a petty crook… a drunk… and someone did him in as a consequence.'

'He was no drunk, Jilkes. That was horseshit. He was a religious man, a teetotaller.'

'Or so he presented himself…'

'No, Jilkes. And I don't believe he was a conman, either. That was no act.'

His volume was increasing. Jilkes motioned for him to keep it down.

'Then make yourself *believe* it was an act. It makes no difference to Pickersgill now… God rest his soul.'

He raised his glass in a silent toast. Finch did the same.

'Then why did he seek me out? Why go to such great lengths? There must be something I *know*… Something I've done in the past…'

'He was fixated on you, that's all. You treated him in the war, mended him. In his mind you were his hero. Such things are not unknown. You have some training in psychology…'

'And all this stuff about the Dogger Bank incident?'

'Half the country's speculating on crackpot conspiracy theories about what happened in the North Sea that night; every other person is sounding off about war. Hell, we did it *ourselves*. What made Pickersgill so different?'

A small human dynamo entered the room, running around the front parlour in her nightdress, giggling mischievously, pulling funny gap-tooth faces. Jilkes chivvied Agnes away playfully.

'Up to bed, you wee monkey!'

He turned back to Finch.

'Ingo, I'm away tomorrow… for a few days… I have some business in Oxford… When I return, I hope we can say that we've all moved on.'

-

On the way home, in the moonlight, Finch stooped by the side of the road to pick some woodland violets whose bloom had lingered on through autumn. He then commandeered a cab to Maude's. Her door was answered by her stern landlady who reminded him that it was after gentlemen's calling hours. He handed her the bunch, which she regarded with disdain, and asked if she could pass them on. She bade him a curt 'good night' and closed the door.

He walked the rest of the way home, if only to clear his head and exercise his knee, which had stiffened up. The wind whipped up and dead leaves swirled. The gas street lights were on. In the amber glow of the one at the far end of his road, he thought he saw, momentarily, the strange hulking presence of a man who was there one minute before slipping back into the shadows. The fleeting image was of someone huge, with broad muscular shoulders and the thickest of necks – a neck so meaty that it gave the odd impression of a near conical head set upon it, the likes of which he had never seen before.

It made Finch shiver and he hastened into his house and locked and bolted the door, cursing the fact that his beloved Webley had been confiscated.

He kept the light off, the better to peer out. But after a while, he was driven by a greater necessity to seek out the emergency bottle of claret. Finding it under the sink, he was emboldened by sufficient Dutch courage to draw the curtains, switch on the light and carry on with the business of tidying up, driven primarily by the fear of what Mrs P-A might say when she arrived back tomorrow.

As he placed the books back on the shelves, trying to remember how they had been arranged previously – classics, reference books, mysteries – he came across something. Though stashed amid the others, the volume was unmistakable: small, black, leather-bound and stained by damp round the edges. On the front was a gold-embossed crucifix. It was Pickersgill's Bible.

Had he left it for me?

In it, still, was the newspaper cutting Pickersgill had shown him only yesterday morning and Finch unfolded it – the sad death notice of poor old Bertie Brandon.

But there was something new this time… an addition. On the top of the page, above the strap carrying the newspaper's title and the date, was a word written in pencil, scrawled as if in a hurry.

'*Ursa.*'

Chapter Twelve

It was not yet light when Mordecai crossed the iron swing bridge over the lock. The road followed the line of the old marsh wall with its derelict, crumbling windmills. The earthworks skirted the western shore of the Isle of Dogs – the great teardrop of land pinched within a meandering loop of the Thames – preventing it from becoming a flood plain.

The trudge became more purposeful, the numbers swelling as they approached the gates of the Millwall Dock, the silhouettes of masts sprouting like an unkempt hedge. The men jostled hard to be at the front, marshalled by constables of the Dock Police, though they knew better than to touch the chain that extended across the entrance. There was wry amusement as the newcomers had their knuckles rapped.

The crowd had grown more fevered these past few days. Last week, a particularly sadistic foreman had chosen his gang by flinging brass washers into the air. The men who grabbed one and managed to hold on to it, scrabbling in the dirt, punching and kicking and eye-gouging the opposition, had been rewarded with labour. Those who failed had not.

The Dockers' Union had assured there would be no repeat of this stunt. The rogue foreman had been 'dealt with' by the management. But no one ever believed the word of the management. Or, for that matter, the union.

At six o'clock the gates opened and the foremen stepped through, ready for the 'call on'. They fanned out along the wall. It was palpable – the suspicion, the contempt… the desperation. It began to rain. Men twitched their caps and pulled their collars up.

It had taken Mordecai a while to divine the muddled hierarchy of the workforce. He knew the ship-loading stevedores were at the top, along with the lightermen and watermen. Below them came a raft of tradesmen whose names, in English, meant nothing to him: porters, coopers, riggers, tallymen, warehousemen, pilers, baulkers, blenders… What was clear was that, right down at the bottom, came the ordinary dockers, first the regulars, then the casuals – miserable bastards like himself, scrapping for labour on a daily basis at sixpence an hour.

Though even the casuals had their rankings – from the dependable favourites, the so-called 'royals', descending to the lowest of wretches, the filthy coalers; or the men willing to toil in the deep freezers where they wore sacking over their boots to stave off the frostbite.

The 'royals', it was said, were either friends or relatives of the foremen, or ones who had bribed them in advance. To Mordecai this made no sense. The gang system relied on emptying a ship's hold as quickly as possible to gain the 'plus money'. Good business sense surely dictated that a foreman select the fittest, most able gang, not one based on patronage? There was more logic in selection based on tossing out brass washers.

'Mordecai Plavinas.'

He raised a hand. This foreman, Mr Morris, knew him by now – knew he was strong, knew he was reliable. He was, he supposed, a royal, whether he liked it or not. The feeling of resentment around him told him he was, especially from the native-born. The others had been called on too – Viktors, Fjodors, Vlad, Nikolajs… permitted with the lucky few to pass through the chain, each group then following its master.

'Call on' complete, the constables stood to block the gates and the rejected men grumbled and walked away. Most knew which foremen were 'theirs' and had probably calculated the odds. One frustrated individual was dragged off by his mates, swearing and swinging while the constables moved forward, patting truncheons into their palms.

In through the hallowed portal of the dock gate and the chosen ones stamped their feet beneath the McDougall flour mill and its four giant granary towers.

The air was rich with the smell of grain. Timber too – bread and soil as Mordecai liked to think of it, much of it channelled via the Baltic Sea and the land he still called home. It was a pungent cocktail, fighting hard against the fetid stench of the Mudchute and the dumped silt and spoil from the harbour's dredging.

Before dawn, it was always the smell that hit you: the tar and the hemp of the rope stores; the rank animal hides; the delicate aroma of coffee and spices as you crossed the West and East India Docks. Tobacco, rum, sulphur, cork, copper ore, stale sweat…

Sound too: the shouts of the gangs; the creaking of the chains; the hollow drums rattling down the cobbles. Beyond came the cries of the mudlarks, searching at low tide for anything they could sell – cigarette butts… even dog turds to flog to the tanneries.

And then the sun would come up… It never ceased to amaze Mordecai – that forest of masts that stretched all the way out to Tilbury. The watery November light could not dim the shine of this, the 'workshop of the world', the most powerful city on earth. The scale of activity was monumental.

It was only when the hooter sounded, and the slow march back up the Westferry Road began, that the complexity of the operation was fully revealed: the shops stocked with shiny compasses and sextants; sailmakers' stores crammed with rope; grocers touting indestructible tins of meat and biscuits; clothiers with brightly coloured flannel shirts; the pubs teeming with boisterous, rum-soaked men.

There were the sailors: fair-haired Scandinavians; shivering black Africans; turbaned Lascars. There were the store hands, some with faces stained blue from indigo. There were the customs officials in their brass-buttoned jackets…

Though the modern Millwall Dock could accommodate steamers, the ship they were unloading today was a sailing vessel, a steel-hulled barque, a large four-master, Finnish, its hull full of wheat grain – though not from Scandinavia but Australia, that strange Other England on the far side of the world that seemed so rich in everything.

The fabled pneumatic elevating machine could suck the grain straight out of a ship's hold and into the granary – with its hoppers and sifters – but McDougall's would still only mill a third of it. The rest had to be sacked up – half hauled to the rail yard, the remainder to the lightermen, who would run it in barges upstream. They stood on the quayside, arms folded and smoking ('Not our job, mate'), watching with indifference while the gangs toiled.

The work was hard, back-breaking. A grain sack weighed fifty-five pounds – four stone. It was difficult to get a handhold. At the end of the day you were stooped double after carting the things, hundreds of them, back and forth, back and forth, back and forth…

Mordecai and his friends knew well enough by now to look out for each other. A gang was only as strong as its weakest member. It required the administration of private justice to a freeloader or the chivvying of a genuine struggler. One man today, in his fifties – big, strong, but with diminished stamina and lungs gurgling from a lifetime of smoking – tried hard but was clearly not up to the task. They helped him along, wheezing and panting and apologising, giving him the easiest chores.

At noon they had a break, half an hour. It was still cold but Mordecai was dripping with sweat, his undershirt soaked. As the men hung about – eating, smoking, resting – the dock manager looked out from his office, a raised wooden structure next to the grain elevator, and crooked a finger in Mordecai's direction.

Mordecai put down the hunk of bread he had stowed inside his shirt and walked across the cobbles and up the steps. He guessed what this might be about. The older man, the struggler, the one they had helped – he would vouch for him no matter what.

The office was cramped – the desk, the windowsill, the chairs piled high with papers and ledgers. The man, a sneery-looking individual with a paunch belly, half-moon spectacles and wild whiskers, informed him of some news. The foreman, Morris, had been singing his praises. McDougall's were in the process of recruitment. It had been recommended that Mordecai become a regular – work that was guaranteed, and with the possibility to start learning a trade.

Mordecai smiled.

'But unfortunately there's this…'

The manager produced a bottle of rum and stood it in what space he could find on the desk. 'Mount Gay', the label said, 'Barbados'.

'There,' he said. 'What have you got to say for yourself?'

Mordecai did not know what he meant.

'Found it in your things.'

'Things?' He did not have any 'things'.

'Don't deny it. Pilfering's a criminal offence.'

'I not understand…'

'You, son. Stealing. The job was yours had it not been for this…'

There was a knock on the door's pane. A dock constable had been summoned. The manager beckoned for him to enter.

'Too bad, Plavinas. Now get out. Sling your hook. Go quietly. You hear me?'

'But—'

'Docked your morning's pay and don't show your face here again.'

'No, sir. There is mistake! I not take drink. I not—'

The manager nodded to the constable who grabbed Mordecai by the lapel. Though Mordecai could have overpowered him easily, he knew better than to resist.

'Such a shame, Plavinas. And we thought you were a good 'un.'

'There is mistake!'

'Think yourself lucky,' snapped the constable as he ushered him out and down the steps. 'Bloody McDougall's and their do-goodery. Myself? I'd have slung you in the nick.'

His gang mates looked on, raising palms, gesturing. Morris, puffing on a clay pipe, looked confused. He hastened to the steps up to the office.

'This is wrong. There is mistake,' yelled Mordecai.

The copper yanked him away, manhandling him more roughly than was necessary. Mordecai shrugged the hand away, meant to demonstrate that he was coming quietly. But a truncheon was stabbed hard, end first, into his thigh, deadening his leg.

'All the same, you lot. Always thieving. Always causing trouble…'

Mordecai writhed on the ground, clutching his leg.

'…Fuckin' Russians.'

The pain of the accusation was greater than that in Mordecai's thigh – greater even than the news of his dismissal.

'I not Russian…' he yelled. 'I *Latvian*… LATVIAN!'

Back in his office, the dock manager opened his hand and admired the ten shining shillings the stranger had given him.

Chapter Thirteen

With all that was whirring through his head, Finch endured a restless night. A couple of times, in the wee small hours, he got up and peered out of his window, but was satisfied that no malign presence lurked.

With sleep a stranger, he rose early and busied himself with tidying the house in advance of the return of Mrs P-A, who was due back in the afternoon. He bathed, shaved and did his best to purge the smell of the police cell.

After breakfast, and at the chime of eight, he grabbed his medical bag and set off for work, his mind toying with the significance of 'Ursa'. He knew from his schoolboy Latin, and from the constellations, that it meant 'bear' – 'Ursa Major: the Great Bear'. But the bear was what… *Russia?* Maybe not the country… Perhaps it was an organisation? An acronym even…?

Had the word been scrawled on the newspaper cutting previously and it was a case of him simply not noticing it? Had Pickersgill left his Bible by accident – dropped it, maybe, perhaps when he was drying out his jacket?

Finch had barely walked for five minutes when he hatched upon an idea. Turning to swim against the tide of bowler hats drifting towards the station, he zigzagged across town, through the side streets, away from his surgery. Tucked away in a tastefully converted mews (the man had impeccable taste, Finch conceded), was the whitewashed brickwork and the hanging sign in Brunswick green for 'Jilkes and Co.'.

'Good morning,' he said, as he entered the small lobby.

'Oh hello. Good morning, Dr Finch,' replied a cheery blonde girl with tight curls, sorting through the post.

'Just wondered if I might catch Mr Jilkes before he got stuck into business?'

She paused, momentarily confused.

'Oh,' she said. 'I don't think... Not sure he's in today, sir.'

'Oh dear,' said Finch, screwing his face in mock consternation. 'You see, I have something...'

From his inside jacket pocket he pulled out the corner of an envelope.

'...which I'm meant to see him about.'

She gestured to the corridor that led to Jilkes' office. Finch replied with a raised eyebrow that asked, 'Are you sure?'

'Of course, sir. Go ahead.'

Finch walked down the passage with its pale green carpet and expensive olive and white striped wallpaper. A clerk passed him carrying a pile of ledgers and box files wedged under his chin.

'Morning, sir.'

'Morning.'

Finch knocked on the door.

'Come in.'

He entered to find Jilkes' legal secretary at her desk in a sort of anteroom. Behind her was the dormant, dark office of Jilkes – neat, tidy, businesslike and with photographs of Agatha and the kids on his desk.

'Morning, Susan.'

'Morning, Dr Finch. What a surprise. How *are* you?'

'Oh, as well as can be expected. And you?'

'Very well, sir, thank you.'

'And your mother?'

'She's a tough one. *You* know that. Feels the cold on mornings like this. Why, we were talking about you only yesterday.'

'All good, I hope?'

She laughed.

'I'm sorry but Mr Jilkes isn't in today. He's in Oxford. Back Wednesday.'

Finch uttered a fake and convincing 'damn' under his breath. He took a furtive glance at Susan's desk. Amid the work stuff and some unnecessary knick-knacks, plus a brand new telephone, there was a large black ledger with a ribbon place marker in it.

'Oh dear,' he said. 'Now you mention it, I do remember he said he might be away. That's rather unfortunate.'

He dipped his hand into his jacket again and revealed the corner of the envelope.

'Not a problem, sir. I can pass it on to him if you like.'

He gave a little anguished wince.

'Actually, don't worry. It's a *personal* matter... I'll catch him when he returns... Wednesday, you say?'

'Yes, sir, Wednesday.'

There were two seats for visitors. Finch deposited himself in one. He rubbed his knee. Genuinely it *did* hurt, but he milked the opportunity for all it was worth.

'Oh dear. Playing up again?' asked Susan.

'Afraid so. Change in the weather. Couple of minutes, it'll be fine.'

'Of course, sir.'

He made himself a little more at home. He massaged his knee overly theatrically.

'My goodness, how rude of me,' she apologised. 'Can I fetch you a cup of tea?'

He waved it away.

'Really, I wouldn't want to impose...'

'Not at all, not at all.'

She got up.

'How do you take it?'

'Milk, no sugar, thanks.'

'Be back in a minute.'

'Make it five, Susan. I really like it to stew.'

She smiled and bustled out through the door.

She hadn't closed it fully but Finch sprang to his feet, nudged it a few inches further and went to her desk. He was about to open the big black book when Susan bustled straight back into the room again.

On the right-hand side of the desk was a telephone – the new kind with the transmitter and receiver both in the handset, which was mounted in a cradle above the rotary dialler. Finch snatched it up.

'Sorry, is it all right to use the telephone…?' he improvised. 'Inform my surgery I'm going to be a few minutes late.'

'Of course, sir… I'm sorry, sir…'

She sighed and rolled her eyes self-mockingly.

'…Memory like a sieve. Did you say sugar?'

He shook his head. She bustled out again and he waited for the swish of her skirts to recede.

Finch replaced the phone and opened the book. It was, as he had guessed, a diary, the ribbon marker wedged into today's date, *Monday, November 14th 1904*. He turned it around to face him and flipped the page back to the previous Friday. It, like the other days, had a column of entries.

Friday afternoon had been reserved for a partners' meeting, it said. There was some other legal scrawl he didn't recognise. For the morning, however, there were three entries. The scrupulous Susan, not wishing to betray legal confidence, had avoided jotting any names, only initials – which he assumed to be cross-referenced with a client book somewhere. Alongside them were corresponding phone numbers:

G.C. – BAY 365
E.S. – BAR 271
M.T. – ELS 905

He reached into his jacket again and pulled out the envelope he had been using as a prop – a bill from his grocer – took a pencil from the desk and jotted them down. He could hear the bustle of Susan's skirts again. She entered with the tea to find Finch sitting back in his chair, flexing his knee back and forth.

'Super, thank you,' he said as he took the cup and saucer.

After ten minutes of idle chit-chat and protestation that he was surely keeping her from her work, together with an entreaty that she would be sure to tell Jilkes he'd called on him, he was walking back through town.

-

Finch strode through the door to his surgery to find Daphne – calmer now she was serving her notice – leafing through the new edition of *Lady's World*. It had an illustration of a woman in some ridiculously oversized hat on the cover. She didn't even try to hide it away.

'Morning, Daphne.'

'Morning, Dr Finch,' she replied, without looking up. 'You have a nine o'clock. Mrs Cummings will be here... a new patient... something about bunions.'

'Jolly good.'

Inside, he shut the door, hung up his coat and went to his desk with the old-fashioned candlestick phone, the possession of a man not yet moving in Jilkes' financial circles. He sat down, placed the envelope with the numbers written it on before him and picked up the receiver. He tapped the switch hook to establish a connection.

'Hello, operator.'

'*Good morning, sir,*' came the cheery female voice.

'I'd like to place a call... BAY 365.'

'*Very good, sir.*'

'Oh, operator... can you please tell me the name of the exchange?'

'*B... A... Y... is Bayswater... London, West Two, sir... Hold the line, please.*'

He could hear an electronic dial tone. Then, after about twenty seconds...

'*Putting you through now, sir.*'

An older woman's voice was now on the other end. It was deeper, slower.

'*Hello, may I help you?*'

'Good morning. Yes, I was just...'

Finch suddenly realised he didn't know what to say. He mumbled something in frustration.

'*I'm sorry, sir. Could you please repeat that?*'

'Yes, of course… Are you… are *you* the householder?'

Her tone suggested offence. He cursed himself for such a ridiculous opening gambit.

'*Why, no… the householder… the master doesn't answer the phone himself.*'

'Then, perhaps if…'

'*Is this Freeland business?*' she asked.

'Freeland…?'

She was cross now.

'*It either is or it isn't, sir. If you'd like me to take a message…*'

'That won't be necessary.'

'*Then good day to you.*'

She hung up.

There was a knock on the door. Daphne poked her head round.

'Mrs Cummings is here.'

'Shit!'

'Dr Finch!'

'Sorry, Daphne. My apologies. Could you tell her I'll be ready in a few minutes?'

Daphne exited.

Finch stared at the numbers. He must formulate a strategy. Cheeks burning with humiliation, he reached into his lower drawer for his bottle of Talisker. He uncorked it and took a good long glug.

It was no use, he knew, he was going to have to lie… pretend to be from Jilkes' office. No! He had a better idea. He scribbled down a few lines of dialogue, crossed them out and rewrote them.

He called the operator again. A different woman answered, but one who had the same chirpy demeanour, as if the product of some telephone operator finishing school. He wondered what her tone would be like by the end of the day.

'Could you put me through to BAR 271, please?'

'*Right away, sir.*'

He forgot to ask for the name of the exchange but it didn't matter. Nor did his script.

'*Barnet taxicabs. Elijah Swithuns at your service. Hello...*'

He hung up and crossed out the number. He dialled the operator again – another young woman similarly schooled. He asked to be put through to the next number which, she informed him, was in '*Elstree, Hertfordshire.*'

A woman answered; she sounded elderly.

'Good morning, Mrs...?'

'*Thomas,*' she replied.

'Of course, Mrs Thomas...'

He consulted his lines.

'...You know, I'm calling you on behalf of British Legal Services. We're a body set up by the Home Office to assess the performance of local solicitors, just to ensure that you have been satisfied with their performance...'

'*I see.*'

'I understand you've had some recent dealings with a company named Jilkes & Co.'

'*Why, yes, just this last week,*' she said. '*Friday...*'

'Jolly good.'

'*They were sorting out my will. My husband's long gone. I'm getting my affairs in order.*'

'Very wise, Mrs Thomas, very wise...'

There was a knock on the door. Daphne popped her head round again, saw that he was on the phone and mouthed, with a discontented expression, that his patient was still waiting.

'And were you satisfied with their service?'

'*Very.*'

'Good, good. They really are one of the best firms in the area, if not the entire country. They've been scoring full marks.'

There was a pause.

'*Who did you say you were again?*' she asked.

'Thank you for your time, Mrs Thomas,' said Finch. 'I can assure you that all information will treated in the strictest confidence. Goodbye.'

He hung up and crossed that number out too.

Enthused now, he went via the operator and tried the first number again. He lowered his voice, hoping to disguise it, and tried to ooze confidence. He imagined, in fact, that he was that pompous ass, Edward.

'Good morning,' he bellowed.

'*Good morning*,' came the first woman's voice again.

'Now look here,' he said. 'I'm calling you because of Freeland.'

She was meeker this time.

'*I'm sorry, sir, but Mr Chilcot's not here at the moment.*'

'Not in, dammit! When *will* he be in, for goodness sake?'

'*We're expecting him at eleven, sir.*'

'Well then, I shall be sending him a telegram. It is of the utmost importance.'

'*I shall see he gets it right away, Mr...?*'

'Your address,' Finch thundered. 'Remind me again... Bayswater...'

'*11 Chepstow Place. Please, sir, who shall I say...*'

He thanked her, hung up and blurted a satisfied, 'Yes!'

He looked at his watch. It was ten past nine. If he got the next train...

He breezed out through reception. A sixty-something woman with a walking stick and a foot in a bandage sat waiting, face contorted with pain.

'I'm terribly sorry, Mrs...'

'Cummings,' the woman grimaced.

'...But there's been a bit of an emergency... Have to dash...'

He turned to Daphne.

'Could you please reschedule Mrs Cummings, perhaps for tomorrow...?'

He faced the woman and winked.

'...and make her a nice cup of tea.'

She looked glum.

'There will be no charge for either appointment,' he added.

Her face lightened.

Daphne threw him a look of daggers as he pulled on his coat and hurried out of the door.

Chapter Fourteen

Two hours later, Finch was amid the white stone Regency townhouses of a west London side street. It was quiet, away from the thoroughfare of Bayswater Road, though the boom of the piles being driven for the foundations of the giant Whiteley's department store nearby caused a periodic visceral shudder.

Other than that it was the last house in the row, on the corner of a cross street, 11 Chepstow Place was exactly the same as the others. It was neat, tidy and smelled of discreet money. The only differentiator between each tall, terraced dwelling was the type of potted and topiaried shrubbery that stood beneath the neoclassical porticoes.

Finch hadn't really got a clue what to do now that he was here. Several plans swirled and none of them was convincing, so he sat in the communal gardens opposite, where glum nannies wheeled perambulators or vaguely tolerated the infants in their care. He positioned himself on a bench with a vantage point of the house, lit a cigarette and, with half an eye, reread bits of *The Times*.

There seemed no slackening of the tension between Britain and Russia. Russia and Japan, for *their* pains, were embroiled in Manchuria in the kind of trench warfare and industrialised carnage that the conflict in South Africa had begun to hint at.

Kaiser Bill's exhortations for his cousin the Tsar to thwart the 'Yellow Peril' rising in Asia seemed to Finch a cynical ploy. In a complicated arrangement, the intervention of another power in the Far East – whether Germany or even France – would force the direct military entry of Britain. Britain had obligations to Japan under yet another of the treaties that seemed to be signed willy-nilly. He thought of Jilkes. An army's most lethal weapon these days was its battalions of lawyers – pens mightier than the sword. This profusion of pacts seemed mere sub-clauses to an impending cataclysmic contract.

Depressed by the turn in international politics, he leafed on. In the United States, the election triumph of Teddy Roosevelt had been eclipsed by news that, in Ohio, the Wright brothers had made another flight, powering their aerial machine for over five minutes this time. How long before America was dragged out of its isolation and into a European war? How long before someone construed an aeroplane as another kind of weapon?

Finch studied the house. The curtains were all drawn. It seemed that nobody was home. He replayed the various scenarios he had entertained while in the train carriage and contemplated one of them – once life was evident within – of going straight up to knock on the door and bluster his way in over something or other to do with 'Freeland'.

But *what* exactly? And what would be his line of enquiry? He didn't even know what Freeland did. All he knew was that there existed the *possibility* of a link between this address, someone called Chilcot, a business or company called Freeland, a person sent to menace both him and Jilkes and the murder of Pickersgill. Perhaps he should scoot over to the post office and organise the delivery of a telegram, just as he had threatened on the phone. But what would he *say*?

He cast his mind back to South Africa again and the mess he'd got himself into there, but how he – and Annie – successfully for a while, and against all odds, had pitted their wits against the machinery of state intelligence.

Annie…

Amid the languid ambling of horses, the creaks of their carts and buggies and with the sun coming out to spread a brief blanket of warmth, Finch got lost in his thoughts. The activity of the last couple of days was catching up on him. The boom of the pile-driver had stopped. He felt his eyelids droop.

He was stirred as a red rubber ball bounced across the grass and tapped into his foot. A small boy trussed up in an uncomfortable-looking sailor suit ran over. He stared up at Finch, unsure if he should approach further.

'Hello, young fellow,' said Finch cheerily.

He picked up the ball and threw it back gently. The boy, with his young, uncoordinated hands, mistimed the catch and the ball hit him four square on the nose. He started to bawl.

'Oh, I'm so sorry,' said Finch.

He knelt down to comfort the child – 'There's a brave boy' – as a stern nanny, the caricature of a middle-aged spinster, swept in to scoop up her young charge and deliver him from evil. The other nannies regarded Finch with equal scorn and pulled their young wards in close. As if picking up a cue, other children began wailing too.

'Sorry,' repeated Finch.

The piledriving started up again.

Amid the howls and the *boom-boom-boom*, Finch nearly missed the sound of a motorcar. It purred along the road then slowed to idle at the kerb. He rushed back over to the privet hedging that screened the gardens within the iron railings. A bright blue Rover automobile was now parked, engine running, alongside the pavement right outside number 11 – a high, open-topped vehicle with a single leather bench seat. The driver appeared to be a chauffeur of some sort. He was dressed in a light-grey outfit trimmed with piping. He nodded to acknowledge some signal.

And there, descending from beneath the portico – they *had* been in – came the man Finch recognised, or at least imagined he recognised, from the gentlemen's room in the Chinese restaurant. He wore a grey suit with an astrakhan-collared coat over the top. He had a pencil moustache, a purple cravat, a Homburg hat. From his left lapel sprouted a sprig of… *yes*… lavender.

He had barely clapped eyes on him when, a step behind, followed a man whose appearance delivered a sharp, icy jolt to Finch's spine. He was a veritable man mountain, a quite extraordinary specimen of a human being. The man was *huge* – about six foot seven and probably weighing in at about twenty stone, though his body mass seemed comprised almost entirely of muscle, squeezed into a black suit and raincoat that must have been tailored specifically for his unusual proportions. For, what was even more impressive than his size and weight was his physique, his shape. His torso rose north from a trim waist to a pair of broad shoulders that would have seemed excessive on a circus strongman.

Bare-headed, the man had a close-shaved crop, the type beloved of the Prussians, skin that was swarthy, and narrow black eyes that were extremely close-set within a flattish, Eurasian face. More than that he had the thickest neck Finch had ever seen. It was like that of an oversized bull. It was as if his head were made of wax and it had melted down to pool on his shoulders; suggesting the product of some sort of genetic mutation.

Finch's cold shiver was an instinctive confirmation. He knew right away this was the man who had appeared within the glow of the street lamp last night, not yards from his own house. The man followed closely, barely a pace behind his lavender-scented colleague as they descended the six or seven steps to the pavement where they climbed on board the vehicle. It tipped on one side against the big man's weight.

The chauffeur went through some fussy ritual about putting a blanket over their knees but the fat-necked man swatted the request away. Under the creak of the lopsided suspension, the driver executed a U-turn and headed back up to the Bayswater Road.

Finch saw a taxi cab clip-clop past to deposit an older couple a few doors down, the woman proudly carrying a brand new hatbox. As the Rover drove off, Finch darted across the road and commandeered their cab, almost shunting the husband out of the way.

'Cor, someone's in a hurry,' quipped the cabbie.

Finch pointed up the road.

'Please… Follow that car.'

'I'm afraid that's just in the penny novellas, sir.'

'I'm serious. That blue motorcar about to turn left up ahead. Can you follow it?'

'Where's it going?'

'If I knew that I wouldn't be asking you to follow it.'

The cabbie sucked on his teeth.

'Not as easy as it sounds.'

'I'll double the fare.'

'Right you are, sir.'

Finch climbed in. The cabbie twitched his whip, the horse whinnied and he worked it up into a trot.

Due to a hold-up at the T-junction, they managed to get within fifty yards of the Rover as it turned left, towards the West End, along the northern edge of Hyde Park. The cabbie was no slouch and weaved aggressively through the traffic, eliciting expletives from the wagons and carts he cut up. He nearly knocked one man off his motorcycle.

The traffic slowed to a near halt, placing them at a discreet distance behind the blue car. Finch could not get over the sheer size of the man with the neck. Viewed from behind, his lavender pal and the chauffeur looked like children sitting next to him, all squashed together on the seat, the lavender man wedged in the middle.

To the right, the midday sun dappled the trees, not all having shed their leaves yet. It glinted on the Serpentine lake, which marked the division between ornate Kensington Gardens to the west and wilder Hyde Park.

Further along, they rounded Marble Arch – Nash's cod-Roman ceremonial gate to Buckingham Palace, relocated, ignominiously, to the site of the old Tyburn gallows. Curiously, and perhaps appropriately, it now had a police station housed within it.

As the traffic picked up and they crossed the north end of Park Lane, they were clearly going to be no match for a motorised vehicle that could travel at thirty miles per hour. Onto Oxford Street and the Rover was now just a bright-blue speck. The cab got jammed up in the usual London mêlée of carts and cabs and wagons and horse-drawn omnibuses.

The Westminster authorities were still refusing to allow the laying of tram tracks which, to Finch, rendered the West End curiously old-fashioned and chaotic, especially given the pedestrians who swelled on the pavements and were apt to wander out into the road without a second thought. It seemed out of step with the other cities he'd been to, even the London suburbs. The Cape Town of five years ago seemed more modern in its public transport – above ground anyway.

If not quite as chi-chi as the Bond and Regent Streets that crossed it, Oxford Street had succumbed to the march of commerce. The few residential buildings left were fighting a losing battle against the spread of shops and entertainment venues: the Princess Theatre, the John Lewis drapery shop, the department store owned by American retail magnate Harry Selfridge.

The explosion of advertising grew more and more astonishing every time Finch came here, the whole place geared up to sell you something from every conceivable angle – signs and hoardings, even on the sides of buses, imploring you to drink Guinness... Bass Ale... Ovaltine... or wash with Pears Soap.

There were posters for the latest West End shows... at the Daly's Theatre... at the Apollo... and, at the Duke of York, home of the new fairy-tale sensation, J.M. Barrie's *The Boy Who Wouldn't Grow Up*.

At Oxford Circus, a bobby with white oversleeves stood on a box and blew a whistle at the traffic, trying to impose some order. Up ahead, the blue Rover was long gone.

Finch told the cabbie to stop, paid the exorbitant fare, which was gratefully received (though with hand still extended for a tip), and decided to take the long walk back up to St Pancras and a train home.

No sooner had he done so than a flash of cobalt blue streaked across Oxford Street – as if the Rover had turned around somewhere on the north side and was now cutting back to the south. It was heading into Soho... Wardour Street, it looked like.

As fast as his stiff leg would carry him, Finch took a right onto Poland Street then a left onto Broadwick Street, weaving around the fruit and vegetable stalls and bustling crowds of Berwick Street market, the barrow boys hawking their produce at the top of their lungs.

The bustle of activity and the narrow streets had slowed the car. Finch loitered in the doorway of an ironmonger's as the Rover pootled past. It then dog-legged onto Dean Street – Finch following at a distance – where it puttered to a halt.

The two mismatched men got out and the car drove off. They crossed the road and Finch watched them enter an alleyway – the lavender man going first with his thick-necked beast of a friend very close behind.

Finch caught his breath, dabbed his brow, composed himself, pulled his collar up, turned his hat brim down and walked past on the opposite pavement. He glanced up to see the pair ascend a metal stairway, much like a fire escape, and go through a cracked and faded pale-green doorway.

Opposite the alleyway was a pub, the York Minster – a typical artsy Soho hangout, Finch assumed. Though once inside it seemed rougher, the saloon bar full of drunks, tattooed lowlifes and those for whom booze was just another medicine. There were a couple of scrawny women at the bar, tartily dressed, with decaying teeth and sporting too much make-up.

One thing the bar *did* have was a window overlooking the alleyway, so Finch ordered himself a pint of overpriced, watered-down ale and parked himself up against it, lighting up a cigarette. He waited for twenty minutes, keeping himself to himself, but the pale-green door at the top of the stairs remained closed. No entries, no exits.

He'd been in the pub long enough to know that tension was brewing, the scent of violence in the air. A surly individual asked him what his business was, to which he replied that it was to drink his pint in peace.

He lit another cigarette to calm his nerves, gave another away to someone who asked if he could bum one, but it was clear he was an object of suspicion and had outstayed his welcome. At the far end of the bar, through the fug of smoke, voices were raised, though it seemed to be an internal dispute of some sort. A burly man in a baggy cap was threatening to administer physical justice to someone or other and was having to be calmed down. A petite woman with straight, copper-coloured hair was screeching at him.

Just as the situation seemed to have been defused, it happened. The burly man swung a fist and the woman was sent sprawling across the sawdust into the middle of the room. Even in a place such as this, so obvious and public an act of violence conducted towards a female caused howls of indignation. The large man was sent packing, staggering off out into the street.

The woman was in her late twenties and wore a tattered long blue dress; the copper-coloured hair Finch had noted was actually a wig, which now sat askew upon her head. But it was her skin that was her most striking feature. She was ebony black, the kind of person you saw in parts of London, in the communities from West Africa or the Indies. It reminded Finch of his time in South Africa… of that accursed refugee camp near Paarl.

She groaned and sat up. There was a trickle of blood from the left side of her mouth. Her eyes were out of focus. Despite giving her assailant short shrift, no one seemed that bothered. No one went to help her.

Finch leaped from his seat and crouched down at her side. He helped slide her over and propped her up so that her back rested on the bar. He handed her his fresh white handkerchief and she pressed it to her mouth.

He pestered the barman for a pint glass of water and got the young woman to sip. He felt around her jaw, determined that there was nothing broken and performed a rudimentary test, asking her to focus her eyes on his index finger.

It was only then that he noticed…

'Thanks, sugar.'

…the Adam's Apple.

'Oh… that's okay… really.'

She stroked his face.

'My knight in shining armour.'

Momentarily flustered, she noticed him blush.

'Don't be shy now.'

Her voice, not too deep, but still a giveaway, betrayed an accent from the Caribbean.

'I'm not shy… It's just…'

'You mean you never met someone like li'l old Lulu before?'

He ignored the comment.

'Come on, let's get you on your feet.'

She put her arm around his shoulder and he helped her up. The rest of the pub got on with its business. At her request, he walked her over to the toilets.

'Er… which one…?'

'Now that would be telling… *Hero*,' she said and disappeared on her own through the main door to leave that question tantalisingly unanswered.

Five minutes later she came out, face cleaned up, wig pinned back in place. She had also applied some powder. She had spotted Finch back in his window seat, where he was back on lookout, and took the stool next to him.

'You mind if I have a smoke?' she asked.

Finch offered her his packet of Navy Cut. She took a couple, tucking the spare behind her ear.

'Keep them,' he said, and offered the whole box.

When he lit a match for her, she cupped her hands round his and pulled them in close. The touch of her palms and the confident, suggestive way she did it made him feel awkward.

Who knows, amid the commotion, if he'd missed any activity from the door at the top of the stairs across the road? He gazed at it again.

'Something bothering you?' she asked.

'I didn't like you getting thumped like that.'

'Not the first time… nor the last.'

'Who was he… that man?… What was it about?'

'Nuthin', honey… but that's not what's *really* bothering you. Is it?'

'What do you mean?'

'You've been here half an hour, you've spent most of it staring up at that door across the street.'

'That's *my* business.'

She shrugged and rolled her eyes.

'If you say so.'

The barman came over and plonked another pint of ale in front of Finch. He set a glass of port down in front of Lulu. Finch reached to pay for them. He feared a clip joint scam – that the woman's drink would end up costing a fortune, to be extracted from him by some burly bouncer if need be.

'No need. Present from the lady,' said the gruff barman.

Discreetly, Lulu flashed a stuffed wallet at Finch that looked like it wasn't hers.

'You gonna take a slap, might as well make it worthwhile.'

She grinned. Finch stifled a chuckle. He raised his glass.

'Thank you, Lulu. Good health.'

She clinked hers in return.

'Charmed, I'm sure.'

She… he… *she* had kind, liquid eyes.

She leaned in and whispered.

'You know I can give you a proper thank you if you like. No charge… On the house.'

Finch spluttered into his beer.

'Lulu, you know I appreciate the offer, really I do, but I think I'm just going to finish this drink and leave.'

Chapter Fifteen

Mordecai sat in front of the fire and smoked a meagre roll-up. There were barely any coals left but – what hell – the code of communal living had been broken by everyone else in the house. And, besides, he hadn't eaten properly. He was cold. He'd endured hours of back-breaking work for no money. He was exhausted. He'd been humiliated. He felt sick to his stomach.

There would be kids – street urchins – round later, selling stolen fuel. They brought it on a sledge door-to-door, coals pilfered from the railway yard. His pals would be back when the dockyard hooter sounded. Let *them* shell out some pennies then.

Mordecai looked around the filthy, spartan room which passed as a kitchen. There were wicker laths visible through the gaping holes in the lime plaster, huge and pungent damp stains colonising the walls.

At a time like this, when it was quiet, no one around, you could hear the scrabble of rats beneath the bare, grimy floorboards. By the fire was a blackened cooking pot, with its mouldy green residue of ancient broth. There were cigarette butts stubbed out everywhere.

He thought about a nap, a means to write off the rest of the day before getting up at dawn to try his luck at the East India Dock. But the prospect of the miserable upstairs room which he shared with six others – their thin, stained straw mattresses pushed together and covering the entire floor – did not appeal, even in their absence.

The slop bucket, he knew, would not have been emptied. Even if he did it himself, tipping it into the alleyway out the back, he would still lie amid the lingering stench of other men's urine and excrement with the wind howling cold through the broken window. Last winter, in the thick of it, they would shiver under moth-eaten horse blankets carpeted with snow.

The house on Sidney Street had become a magnet for disaffected Livonians – Latvians and Estonians. The area of Stepney, too, was a safe haven for Jews like himself, who could go about their business without fear – especially the fear of an oppressive Russian overlord. You could not put a price on freedom. Staying in Riga had not been an option.

But *this*…?

There was a knock at the door. Mordecai had no watch but guessed it to be about two o'clock. At this time of day it could be anybody: – the kids with the coal sledge; a costermonger with his handcart; a socialist pamphleteer; a do-gooder from the Salvation Army; someone just casing the house prior to a burglary, not that there was anything to steal. Occasionally, of an evening, there would be a desperate hollow-eyed woman – sometimes with a child in tow – offering her undernourished body for rent.

Once a month came the neighbourhood 'committee' with their demand for a fee to offer 'protection', something that was paid without question. Mordecai did not know who these protectors were. He did not know who his landlord was. Nobody did. The house was a sub-let upon a sub-let upon a sub-let. Mordecai just worked, paid what he owed, kept his nose clean.

He opened the door to a narrow crack and peered out. It had started raining again. Women were frantically hauling in the lines of washing which had been strung across the street. Standing before him was a thin man in a black suit, his slicked dark hair crowned by a bowler hat, hunched under an umbrella.

'Mr Plavinas?'

'Yes.'

The man half turned.

'If you'd just come this way, sir.'

Mordecai resented the arrogance.

'Who are you?'

The man turned back.

'Please, sir. If you'll come with me.'

'I go nowhere.'

The man pulled a pained expression, as if it were Mordecai who was being unreasonable and that the prospect of a stand-off was simply tiresome.

'Please, Mr Plavinas. Let's not make this any more difficult than it needs to be.'

Mordecai did not budge.

'Look… Mr Plavinas… *sir*…'

He tried a different tack.

'…I… *we*… hear you're now out of a job.'

'How you know?'

'Please, sir, time is pressing. There's someone who wants to meet you.'

'Meet me?'

'Yes… So, *please*…'

He beckoned for him to follow.

'I go nowhere.'

'Believe me, it will be worth your while. *Very* worth your while. I can say no more than that. Take it or leave it.'

Mordecai stepped out into the street. He saw, at the top end, a motorcar. It had already been surrounded by curious children. Even a horse cart had slowed down to allow the rag-and-bone man to take a peek.

'Please…' implored the man with the umbrella.

Mordecai shrugged. What was there to lose? He buttoned up his collarless shirt, pulled on his coarse wool jacket and his baker boy cap.

The green car, which sat like a shimmering emerald between the grim slum terraces, was unlike anything he had seen – no mere functional automobile but one of absolute luxury, a long-wheelbase limousine. As he neared it, he saw the gold-plated metalwork and lamps, the white-walled tyres and the completely enclosed rear passenger section. There were shades pulled down in the windows. Out the front, in the open cockpit, a uniformed, goggled chauffeur sat under the canopy, minding his own business.

The man led Mordecai behind the car. Unusually, instead of doors at the side, over the running board, entry to the main cabin – the tonneau – was via a door mounted in the rear, centrally, above the bumper.

The small crowd parted and Mordecai was beckoned on.

'Please…'

The man opened the door and extended his palm, bidding him to enter. Mordecai had second thoughts. He had heard of things… of West End toffs travelling east for 'a bit of arse'…

'No.'

The man rolled his eyes, as if Mordecai were a petulant child.

'Please.'

A boy yelled out, 'Go on, mister… go for a spin!'

And with that, Mordecai stepped up and in, and the man closed the door behind him.

It was dark in the car's cabin, just the yellow glow of dimmed electric lighting. It smelled of expensive leather and cologne. Whoever was in there, in the gloom, he sensed, was taking wry amusement at his disorientation. Eventually they spoke.

'Good afternoon, Mr Plavinas,' came a deep, resonant, plummy voice.

Mordecai was sitting opposite him, on the edge of the seat and on edge in his demeanour.

'Do you like my car?'

Mordecai shrugged an 'I suppose so'.

'A Darracq. French. I had it shipped over from Paris.'

The automobile was already moving, Mordecai realised, its engine smooth, its suspension so gentle that you barely noticed.

'Who are you?' asked Mordecai. 'What do you want?'

The car glided into a higher gear, picking up speed. The man turned a dimmer switch and the lighting increased a fraction. He was about sixty years old, well fed and had on an expensive chocolate-brown silk suit; his silver hair was brushed back behind his ears and he had bright-blue twinkling eyes. Around his shoulders was draped a fur coat.

'The essence of conversation, Mr Plavinas… may I call you Mordecai…?'

Mordecai shrugged again.

'…especially in a tense, maybe even *confrontational* situation, is never to betray that the circumstances are beyond your control. Not to reveal your hand, as you might put it. You must at least create the *illusion* of having the other fellow in your pocket. Your question here… *two* questions… indicate a man who is confused… afraid.'

'I not afraid.'

'My goodness, your English,' he mocked. 'It's "I *am not* afraid," or the contraction "*I'm not* afraid" if you really must.'

Mordecai's anger was rising.

'What you want?' he growled.

The man casually fiddled with the signet ring on his little finger.

'And there you go again…'

Mordecai balled his fists, but the man gave no hint of feeling threatened. He exuded nonchalance. There was something wriggling. Mordecai hadn't noticed, but within the fur of the coat, nestling on the man's lap, was a small dog, a bony thing with sleek brown fur, pricked triangular ears and oversized saucer eyes.

'Please, let us not have this turn vulgar.'

Next to the man, on the seat, was something covered in a tartan blanket. He pulled it back to reveal a large wicker hamper. He unfastened the buckled strap and opened it. It was packed with breads, meats, cheeses, pâté and garnishings. There were some lavish sandwiches already made up. The inside of the lid was stamped with the word 'Harrods'.

'I'm assuming you are hungry… Please, dig in, help yourself…'

The rumbling in Mordecai's belly dictated his response. He grabbed a steak sandwich, the fine meat and its accompanying salad and ripe tomato slices packed within floury white bread, and tore into it like a savage. The man, pointedly, offered a linen serviette. He pulled out a sliver of luncheon meat and fed it lovingly to his lapdog. There was a half-bottle of champagne in an ice bucket… Moët et Chandon. He uncorked it and untethered two crystal glasses fastened inside the hamper lid.

'Oh, I forgot… you don't.'

He offered Mordecai a bottle of Perrier water instead and popped its lid with an opener. Mordecai swigged from it. The man poured a glass of champagne for himself.

'Hope you don't mind,' he said, though Mordecai was too engrossed in his eating.

'Well here's to *you*, Mordecai,' he added. 'Glad to have you on board. And in answer to your question – *two* questions… *One*: who I am is of no great relevance, not at the moment. And… *Two*: what do I want? I want you to do something for me.'

Mordecai's face fell. He thought again – 'the gent'… 'the bit of arse…'

The man read his expression.

'My goodness, you really are such a base creature,' he scoffed. 'No, no, no, nothing like that at all. But you *must* come with me. In fact you already are.'

'What time I… What time *will* I be back?'

'My dear fellow, *never*,' he said. 'You can never come back to this place ever, ever again.'

Chapter Sixteen

Finch opted against public transport and wound his way out of Soho. He cut through the alleyway by the Pillars of Hercules pub, traversed Charing Cross Road with its antique bookshops, got a bit lost around Seven Dials, till he emerged amid the cobbles, hustle and bustle of the Covent Garden market. He proceeded along Long Acre and turned south down Bow Street, past the grand rebuilt Royal Opera House. He clipped the edge of the crescent of the Aldwych, coming out opposite the red-tiled Strand Underground station of the Piccadilly Railway.

He crossed the Strand itself – once upon a time the north shore of the Thames, he was fond of dropping into conversation – and passed through the street façade into the courtyard bordered by the neoclassical grandeur of Somerset House with its magnificent arches and elegant stonework.

Before entering, he strolled around to the terrace, took a moment and looked out across the Thames. The river was the city's… the country's… indeed the *Empire*'s… lifeblood and he liked to remind himself of it. Even here, upriver, there were barges ploughing back and forth, steam ferries crossing here and there, pilot launches bobbing in between. A creaking vessel rolled past, laden with sacks of grain.

He had never ceased to admire the sheer scale of activity that was occurring just a few gentle curves away downstream, the other side of Tower Bridge – the hundreds of ships arriving daily to disgorge their wares transported from around the world and the army of men engaged in unloading it all.

It started to rain. He pulled his collar up. As a child, he had been transfixed by a painting by the artist Canaletto which he had gazed at while clutching his father's hand in some gallery or other. In a near photorealistic manner, the artist had captured the view from this very spot, rendering London and the river in honeyed Venetian hues, like some jewel of the Enlightenment. Even the boatmen were standing, sculling as if they were on gondolas.

Today, in contrast, the scene was far less romantic. Scaffolding and a temporary boardwalk covered the crumbling Waterloo Bridge.

What would the Iron Duke have thought?

The grey clouds now gathering and the pall of smog made him question whether things really *were* that beautiful in the past, or if the Italian painter was just thinking wistfully about home.

Inside Somerset House's great lobby, with its black and white tiled floor, Finch was directed to the General Registry of Births, Marriages and Deaths, whose public reading room occupied a large hall on the first floor with its row upon row of wooden cabinets and file drawers.

After filling in some forms, the acquisition of a 'day card' and a by-rote, unenthusiastic orientation speech on the part a bored and halitotic clerk, Finch set about his business. It was something he had hit upon while sitting in the Soho pub – he would try and gain some background information on the various players in this unfolding drama.

He started out by looking for the public file on a certain 'Mr Chilcot'. Though without a Christian name or names – Jilkes' secretary had listed him merely as G.C. – it was a wild stab in the dark. There were several drawers alone containing information on thousands of people named either Chilcot or Chilcott. Christ, he didn't even know the spelling.

The drawers were long thin troughs full of handwritten index cards, separated by dividers and full of coded letters and reference numbers. He had made a few notes on how to decipher the coding with the pencil and rough sheet of paper he had been provided with ('*No outside material in the reading room!*'). But he was going nowhere fast. He had an address: 11 Chepstow Place, London W2, but found no way of cross-referencing it.

He looked around the room. Seated on the periphery, at the reading tables, were people – mostly men, but a few women – making discreet notes about some nugget of information they had just unearthed. Tax collectors, solicitors, private detectives, bailiffs, wronged spouses...? He suspected there was either professional interest or private desperation behind most of the investigations, the gold all panned in perfect silence. There were others like him, less adept novices sighing in exasperation over the drawers.

The bored clerk reluctantly indulged him with a further tutorial but it was no use. The Bayswater address seemed absent from the Land Registry altogether. The information from the 1901 census was still incomplete, or hadn't yet all been transferred by hand to the files, recounted the clerk with an acidic *schadenfreude* ('*Sir did appreciate there were forty-two million people resident in Great Britain and Ireland?*').

Finch, irked, pulled rank, flashed his medical credentials and spun the clerk a line about needing to track down information as a matter of urgency... no... *life or death*. Browbeaten, the snippy man agreed to make a telephone call on Finch's behalf to Companies House. But, again, after an endless interlude, it yielded nothing. There were several small 'Freelands' – a garage in Portsmouth, a lettings agency in Wolverhampton, a joinery in Cardiff, but there was no company or society listed that fitted the bill.

On a whim, Finch tried something else. He went back to the files and worked his way through the trays marked 'P' till he came to the name 'Pickersgill'. Despite it being an unusual name, there were far more Pickersgills listed than he had anticipated. Most were in Yorkshire but there was a pocket in Norfolk.

Finch took the information over to the county records, put his new-found skills to use and, after a few minutes – and some under-his-breath swearing – managed to locate the index card for *Pickersgill, Sidney John, b. February 22nd 1854* (still officially alive and kicking) who resided, as a tenant, at an address in

Endthorpe, Norfolk. He had a wife, Edna, but no children listed. His profession was recorded, intriguingly, as 'servant of the parish' rather than 'fisherman' or 'seaman', but then the man could have changed jobs. As of 1901 there was no evident criminal record (despite the police suggestion). Yes… it *had* to be him.

There was a room off the hall, at the far end, marked 'Military Records'. Finch went in and searched on. He took his details on Pickersgill and looked in the various files for the Norfolk Regiment. Again, he wondered why a fisherman had enlisted in the army over the navy. But the South African War was a land campaign and volunteers and reservists had been deployed on that basis.

The Norfolk Regiment had a long history. There was some information given on its founding – at the request of James II, it turned out, to put down the Monmouth Rebellion of 1685. As a foot regiment it had served in various guises over the years: at the Battle of the Boyne, in the War of Spanish Succession, the American Revolutionary War… Back then, regiments were designated by number rather than county. From the nineteenth century, it gained a permanent base in East Anglia and had served in the Peninsular War, the Crimea, Afghanistan, the Boer War. Though it was only since 1881, when the regiment was established in its modern identity, that thorough records existed.

Finch spent an hour going through files, but to no avail. He then found a different way into the system and cross-referenced the name (he was getting quite good at this, he fancied). He was, nonetheless, heading up another blind alley, his eyes watering over the endless rows of cards and their fussy, minute copperplate type. He checked his Zeiss wristwatch and was about to give up completely when, lo and behold, he found it. He felt his heart race and a little thrill after all his efforts. *But*…

He looked again, double-checked. It couldn't be… *could* it?

All roads led him to the same place… to the same conclusion. Sidney John Pickersgill had served in the South African War all right, of that there was no doubt, and had been pretty much in all the places he had claimed. But he had not been an infantryman at all, let alone in the Norfolks. He had attained the rank of corporal in the *Military Foot Police.*

Confused, Finch closed the drawers and left. The prissy clerk called out, asking if he'd found what he was looking for. He did so with the tone of one hoping for failure.

Finch knew he shouldn't have done what he did next but he was so close, he was driven to it. A couple of hundred yards away, along the Strand, stood the Savoy Hotel. As he was in the neighbourhood… it would not be unreasonable… *Would* it? Five minutes later he had turned off into Savoy Court, the curious, anomalous stub of a road, the only one in Britain where traffic drove on the right.

The hotel had been bought and done up a few years back by theatre impresario Richard D'Oyly Carte – his Savoy Theatre stood on the corner – and founded on the profits of his Gilbert and Sullivan productions. It was regarded as one of the world's most luxurious. Finch had visited it before – it was the first time he had ever ridden in an elevator, a 'lift', he remembered – though he never fancied he would ever be well heeled enough to stay here himself… or know anyone who did.

Finch walked beneath the gilded canopy that overhung the entrance. Two top-hatted doormen snapped alert and ushered him in. The place was exquisite: fine marble stonework and mahogany panelling with gold leaf inlays, beautifully upholstered furniture. There were potted palms and ferns sprouting from golden tubs. In the corner of the tea room, where cake stands were piled high, amid the waft of tea and coffee, a string quartet was playing Brahms. The ambient music, the genteel hubbub, the added aroma of food, perfume and cigars, even the temperature, immediately spelled comfort of the highest order.

A valet of some sort asked Finch if he was resident or visiting and steered him towards reception. Beyond, he could see into the American Bar, furnished in the new modernist *arts décoratifs* style. It was famous for its cocktails, its female bartender one of the hotel's most celebrated employees, whose gin and vermouth concoction, the suggestive 'Hanky-Panky', was perennially name-dropped in the society pages. Finch wondered whether he should try one for himself.

He enquired at the front desk – per etiquette, he decided – after Mr and Mrs Edward Pointer, even though the words felt awkward, distasteful in his mouth.

'Certainly, sir,' replied the obsequious receptionist and telephoned up to their room. 'Whom may I say is calling?'

Though after a minute of ringing, it was obvious that the Pointers were out.

Finch sauntered through the lobby and out of the riverside exit. He entered the Victoria Embankment Gardens, with the obelisk of Cleopatra's Needle beyond, and walked to sit near the bronze statue of Robert Burns – perched on a tree stump, quill in hand. Finch smoked, craved a drink and wondered what the hell he was doing. Couples in their *haute couture* and Parisian finery promenaded down winding paths through the trimmed shrubbery. Even though the weather was dull, some women carried frilled parasols.

Finch reflected on his whimsical adventure and wondered whether Jilkes' advice hadn't been the best – get your head down, keep your nose clean. He looked at his watch again and was contemplating his route back to St Pancras – the better to beat the rush hour – when he suddenly realised she'd strolled right past him, and on her *own*. She was in a maroon dress and jacket and wore a beret with her hair tucked up.

'*Annie?*'

She startled and wheeled round. Finch sprang to his feet.

'What on earth…?' she spluttered.

'Sorry,' said Finch.

'My goodness, you're quite the one for surprises.'

His words flowed out in a torrent.

'I had some business nearby. It would have been rude not to… I just left a message for you at the front desk… Had no idea… Didn't expect to catch you here… on your own.'

'Edward's in Glasgow. Business,' she said, dropping his name at the first opportunity, he noted. 'There for a couple of days. I like to take a turn along the river, through these gardens, in the afternoon. This little patch of green. It's a well-kept secret.'

She came and brushed her lips lightly on his cheek, just like the other night. She wore a pair of pearl earrings, minimal make-up and her hair smelled of juniper berries.

'My… Finch. So here we are… *Again!*' she added, seemingly genuine. 'And how's Maude? It was lovely to meet her. She's delightful. You're a very lucky chap.'

He didn't know why, but the comment made his heart sink.

'Something wrong?' she asked.

'Nothing.'

She sighed.

'Come on, Finch, I know you better than that.'

The endearment didn't help either. It reminded him of how they *used* to be.

'It's nothing.'

'Finch, you're doing it again.'

'Doing what?'

She was irked. The rising inflection of her accent was amplified by her temper. He remembered that. He remembered, too, the rebellious, uppity streak from the first time they had met – she and her pals, fellow nurses, all rather boisterous, spirited.

'The other night,' she prickled. 'Christ, what are the odds we'd run into each other like that?… And then you… you…'

'I *what*?'

'…I don't know, Finch. You act like you'd rather be anywhere else *but*—'

'That's not true.'

'…Couldn't wait to tear yourself away.'

He flustered.

'It's a little more complicated than that.'

She shrugged a truce and indicated that they should continue walking. He extended his arm and she took it. Just the feel of her touch, even through several layers of clothing, sent a charge, some primeval shock through him.

They strolled for a moment in silence, westwards, the great Palace of Westminster looming up ahead.

'*O sweet, to stray and pensive ponder a heartfelt sang,*' he said.

'What?'

'Robbie Burns…'

He pointed.

'…There, the inscription.'

'Oh… What do you think it means?'

He thought he did, but it suddenly felt wrong.

'I'm not sure… I mean…'

He shrugged.

'…I don't know…'

He felt foolish.

'…How's your stay, so far?' he asked, ridiculously formally, as if he were now supposed to address her differently, and hated it the moment he said it.

'London? I mean, it's great, there's so much to do. So much life… culture. But, I don't know. I mean, the weather… I guess you get used to it.'

'The cold?'

'The cold's fine. A chilly day and blue sky is all right by me if you're wrapped up well enough. It's just… I don't know… days like today… everything's so *grey*.'

'Grey?'

'It's like the greyness, the damp, seeps into your soul, colours your mood. It explains a lot… I mean about you… not you specifically… I mean, the English…'

'Steady on!'

'No, no, no, don't get me wrong. That's not a negative. I mean it's how you carry yourself, like you're always wearing several layers, speaking with your mouths half closed, everything internalised, no external stimuli. Australians, we're cut from the exact same cloth, and yet…'

'Psychology? Nurse Jones, I think you missed your calling.'

She failed to laugh.

'I haven't been Nurse Jones in a long time, Finch.'

'I'm sorry.'

'I'm happy, Finch. You want to do something? Be *pleased* for me.'

He said nothing.

'And you?... Maude?' she continued. 'You didn't do so badly. She's beautiful, clever, funny... She's adorable, Finch.'

He was uncomfortable and she sensed it. She changed the subject and went on for a few minutes about the glories of the Savoy Hotel. Mark Twain was staying there presently, didn't he know? – Mr Samuel Langhorne Clemens himself. She told him some story, with considerable glee, about the actress Sarah Bernhardt who had also been a guest recently and was rumoured to sleep in a coffin which she took with her everywhere she went.

'I think Miss Bernhardt has a very good publicist,' said Finch.

This time she did laugh.

A young married couple strolled past, the man in a striped blazer and boater, humming a tune which made his wife giggle.

Emboldened by the thaw in relations, Finch tried to make amends for his awkwardness by diplomatically enquiring after Edward, feigning enthusiasm as to his very evident success in evidently every field.

The fact that he had just secured some kind of lucrative contract with the Admiralty – the reason he was currently in the Glasgow shipyards – and had further shipbuilding deals about to be brokered in Brooklyn and New Jersey, did not enhance Finch's mood. It was why they were embarking from Liverpool in a few days' time, she explained.

The finality of it all forced him to his point.

'Annie, can I ask you something?'

They had stopped for some reason. She turned and faced him. He wanted to stare at her with impunity, to get lost in her deep-brown liquid eyes, but felt awkward and kept looking away.

'South Africa... the trouble we got ourselves into... Do you ever...?'

She looked embarrassed. Even though no one was listening, she strained to keep her voice down.

'How can I *not* think of it, Finch? We were bloody lucky.'

'It's just that—'

'*What*, Finch?'

He led her to a bench, her favourite she said, and, on a promise of secrecy, he told her everything that had happened: Pickersgill, Jilkes, the newspaper cutting, the lavender man, his fat-necked friend, Chilcot, Bayswater, Soho, Lulu, Somerset House, *everything*...

Annie was a good listener. She always had been, like the very first time he had unburdened himself upon her, on the run through the vineyards of Stellenbosch. She didn't judge. He thought again of the scores of deathbed confessions she must have been party to during the war, dying Tommies reaching out to clutch her hand. After he had finished going through the details, she sat in silence contemplating it all.

'Well Ursa's Latin for bear,' she said matter-of-factly, in the manner of someone nonchalantly tossing off an answer to a too-easy crossword puzzle. 'You know *that*, right?'

'I'm not that stupid. And given Pickersgill's mention of the Dogger Bank incident, I'm guessing the bear here has something to do with Russia... the country itself, a society, an organisation...?'

A woman walked past with a mournful-looking dachshund. Finch wondered if it too didn't fit into Annie's weather theory.

Annie now looked concerned, sad.

'Finch. Your friend... Jilkes. He's right, you know. We owe our liberty to staying out of trouble. What happened in South Africa... I never want to go through anything like that ever again... as long as I live. You know what, now that you've said it, I don't like the fact that you've told me all *this*. Now I feel implicated.'

Finch turned apologetic, soothing.

'Sorry, it's just that you, Annie... you're the only person I know who would understand. And you being here... I don't know, it's just what... again... *fate*?'

She stood. Her tone turned brisk.

'Finch, I don't know how to say this any other way but let me spell it out. I am a married woman – a *happily married woman*.'

He could feel himself regretting the words as they left his lips.

'Annie... South Africa... After you left for Rhodesia... All those letters...'

'Goodbye, Finch,' she snapped and stamped off.

Finch cursed himself. He went to go after her but her curt 'Leave me alone' and a rejective shrug as he touched her arm was just about the most painful thing another human being had ever done to him. He couldn't see, but he thought she might be crying.

The heads of the promenaders were turning. They'd been causing a scene. There would be Savoy guests among them. He let her go. But it would not be the end of it, he swore. Somehow, he would see her in the next few days... or write to her... *anything*... He would apologise and make it right. He'd been an arse.

-

When Finch got home to St Albans, Mrs P-A had returned and he felt obliged to sit with her, drink tea and explain the robbery (missing out the part about his own arrest and the fact that the burglar had also been murdered – he didn't want to cause her unnecessary alarm). He listened to her enthusiastic tales of her trip to Bournemouth. He refused... but then gave into her insistence that she cook him some dinner (bangers and mash but constructed with some unique South American flourish), then waited for her to retire for the predicted early night.

Once he was on his own, Finch dug out his set of Ordnance Survey maps – a fortuitous Christmas gift from a few years back – and which he used for the odd bit of country walking. He found the one for Norfolk. As he studied it, following the line of the coast with his finger, he noticed, on the occasional table, an envelope with a card inside. He knew it must have been delivered by hand to Mrs P-A earlier but that she had had the decency to let him discover it for himself – although it must have agonised her not to foist it upon him when he walked through the door and sit there studying him while he read it.

The lovingly curved hand which had inscribed '*Ingo*' on the front told him it was from Maude. Inside was a picture postcard, a cross-hatched etching of the ruin – Old Gorhambury – they had sat at just the other day on their bicycle ride. She must have spent a lot of time on the words on the back, and doubtless been through several drafts before committing it to card with little margin for error and little space to fit it all in.

Indeed, what she wrote was quite beautiful in its composition – a baring of the soul, a confirmation of the fact that she cared very deeply for him, with an accompanying, gentle plea that she could forgive him if he would only just explain what had been going on of late (she'd evidently run into Daphne). But, in order for absolution, in order to share herself with him, to *love* him, she stated, she needed to *understand* him.

Finch thought about what he might need for his trip and began throwing a few things together. He would slip out at first light.

Chapter Seventeen

Mordecai could just see through the gaps at the bottom of the blinds. By the looks of it, the car was proceeding along the Commercial Road. Yes, they were rounding the Limehouse Basin and going over the Cut. The smell alone told him that they were passing Billingsgate fish market, heading east. Indeed, they soon crossed over the hump of the bridge on the River Lea. Sliding down in his seat he could see, beyond, the huge Victoria and Albert Docks with their miles of quays, an excavation so massive it dwarfed the berths on the Isle of Dogs.

After their initial exchange, the man said little, other than asking him whether he'd had enough to eat. When Mordecai *did* try to speak, the man raised a palm to indicate he should desist. Mordecai began to view him with contempt – this self-important man with his stupid little dog.

Soon after Billingsgate, the air was charged with another pungent aroma, that of natural gas mixed with the unmistakeable sulphurous tang of human excrement. The man raised a white silk handkerchief to his mouth. They were near Beckton, Mordecai knew, with its gasworks and sewage treatment plant, built on the outskirts of the city before it rolled into the Essex marshland the other side of Barking Creek. There was one last dingy settlement, the village of Creekmouth, built for the workers of the guano works, which yielded another toxic aroma altogether.

The car turned off the main road and began to wind down side tracks. Eventually it stopped, the rear door opened and the man who'd knocked on Mordecai's door, evidently a sort of manservant or valet, extended a hand for the man with the fur coat to alight, still clutching his minuscule canine.

Mordecai followed. He could see him fully now. He had a rounded belly, the mark of good living. His coat was made from sable, a fur Mordecai recognised. It would have cost an absolute fortune. The gold cufflinks alone would probably keep Mordecai in food and rent for six months.

'Where are we going?'

'You'll see,' said the valet.

Once more, he lofted his umbrella against the fine drizzle – though over his master this time – and led them across a disused yard towards a derelict warehouse. There was no one around. Not a soul.

Again, the bright, shiny, expensive car seemed wildly out of place, this time in an industrial wasteland. It was open and windswept, the breeze whipping in from where the Thames opened out on its course to the North Sea.

There were mangled stretches of chain-link fence around the perimeter. Weeds and nettles and thistles poked up through the cracks in the concrete and patches of gravel, the dents and unevenness pitting it with mucky puddles.

Behind them, upriver, loomed Beckton's cylindrical gas holders, hundreds of feet high, the giant containers at varying levels of capacity within their ornate steel skeletons.

Their feet crunched across the ground. Mordecai wasn't forced to follow. He knew he could walk away if he wanted to. And if anyone tried to stop him he could outfight, outrun them easily. He went nonetheless.

The warehouse had holes and missing panels in its corrugated-iron roof with the fine rain cascading down. There were wooden planks absent from the walls and patches of light came in. There was the constant drip of water from a pipe somewhere. Mordecai could see from the equipment – crates, tanks, hosepipes, shreds of netting – that it had once been a plant for processing fish, part of the near-dead Barking trade.

They stopped. Ahead, in the dark, someone was advancing towards them with big shuffling footsteps. When he emerged into the light, Mordecai was taken aback. The man standing before him was not only the most peculiar, but also the most *shocking* specimen of a human being he had ever seen. He was *huge*, a man mountain, but powerful-looking, his upper body completely disproportionate to his legs. And his neck… it was as thick… *wider* than his head…

The man had something in his hand. It was a rifle, British army issue, a Lee–Enfield, Mordecai knew. Mordecai was not a man who gave in easily to fear but he felt a pang of it when the enormous, grotesque man began a slow, deliberate lumber in his direction. His dead, black, close-set eyes were fixed upon him.

He stopped and held out the rifle across his two huge palms – a gesture. Mordecai took it. The man pointed back outside, across the yard. To what exactly, Mordecai did not know. The man did it again. About a hundred yards away was a low wall, about three or four feet high. There appeared to be objects set up upon it – bottles. They were standing in a row, equidistant, probably with water in to weight them against the wind.

The man pointed again. Mordecai deduced that it was an invitation to shoot at them. Mordecai shrugged and turned for a second opinion. The valet nodded his assent.

Mordecai had never fired a Lee–Enfield but had used a Swedish version of a German Mauser and, on examination, the principle was the same. He pulled back the bolt. The box magazine was empty. They had had the good sense not to hand him a loaded weapon right away.

The big man reached in his pocket and tossed Mordecai the bullet clip. Mordecai rammed it into the breech and expelled the charger. It pinged out onto the floor. He was left-handed and tucked the stock under his chin. He wound the webbing of the strap around his right hand and tugged the weapon in tight against his left shoulder.

He was not sure of the gun's sighting. From an unsteady standing position, it would be difficult to calibrate. He turned deliberately to his left, just a few degrees – so they knew what he was doing. On the ground, some five yards to the left of the wall, was a brick. He closed his right eye and took his time. Slowly, smoothly, he squeezed the trigger.

The bang echoed thunderously around the warehouse. He had forgotten how loud it could get. Out in the yard, a splash kicked up in the puddle just a few inches to the right of the brick.

Mordecai trusted his aim implicitly. Gently, he moved the slide on the rifle's back sight. He pulled the bolt and ejected the cartridge, which clinked onto the concrete. He took aim again, this time at the end bottle. With the remaining four shots, he shattered bottles unfailingly and sequentially, left to right.

The large man tossed him another clip. With the next five shots he proceeded along the line. He did not miss. They exploded in distant green clouds. Mordecai lowered the rifle.

The valet nodded. There was no need to carry on.

'Do you love your country, Mr Plavinas?'

'What?'

'Do you love your country?'

To Mordecai it was an absurd thing to ask.

'My country? I *have* no country,' he spat. 'Latvia, she has been stolen.'

The valet showed no reaction.

'You were a soldier. You fought bravely for Mother Russia. A sharpshooter in Peking. The Boxer Rebellion.'

How the hell did they know?

'What the fuck Russia doing in China?' Mordecai snarled, suddenly thrown. 'I have nothing against Chinese. I had no choice. And now?… We are Jews. We are treated like dirt. We leave. To come here. To England.'

The rich man in his fur coat began laughing. It was as if Mordecai's outburst was just a twee show, a diversion, the tantrum of a child, something to be humoured. Mordecai felt his blood rising. It must have been obvious. The large man stepped forward in warning.

Eventually, the rich man stopped his splutters, dabbed his eyes with his handkerchief and petted his dog.

'What if I offered you a chance to correct that?' he asked.

'What do you mean?'

The valet nodded and the large man retreated into the shadows at the rear of the warehouse. Mordecai heard a door open. A minute or so later, he was aware of some whimpering, like that of a scared animal.

Slowly hulking into the light came the large man again. But this time he had someone with him. He was dragging them. As they neared, Mordecai could see the person was dressed in ragged trousers and a ripped, collarless shirt. He was filthy dirty. He had bare, bloody feet. He was shackled at the ankles. His hands had been bound behind him. And, over his head, was a sack. The captive was staggering, limping.

As they came closer Mordecai could see the bruises, the blood, the sweat. Around the man's groin was a large stain of urine. Mordecai recognised the pathetic words that were being mumbled from within the hessian cloth. It was Russian.

'*Pozhalyusta. Net...*' Please. No.

Mordecai recoiled. Whatever this man had done, this treatment was sadistic. The outcome did not look good. Another thought froze him. What if they turned on *him*...?

The big man yanked the hood off. The captive winced, blinking into the light. His face had been beaten severely. It was bruised, swollen. One eye, within a bulge of dark flesh that looked like the skin of a rotten, black banana, was just a slit. His nose was obviously broken. And he had no teeth, just stubs of them. Blood dripped from his mouth.

The rich man spoke.

'What if I told you this man was Russian secret police... *Okhrana?*'

Mordecai did not know how he was supposed to react. Of course he should therefore hate him. It was a given. But here? Like *this*...?

'We found him on the run here, posing as a Pole,' added the valet.

Mordecai shrugged, feigning nonchalance.

'You have heard of *Jaunā Strāva*, the "New Current"...?' the rich man said.

Did they know *he was in the liberation movement?*

'No... I never heard...'

His inquisitor sighed an exaggerated exhalation of disappointment. He shook his head.

'Come come, Mr Plavinas. You can do better than that.'

Mordecai shrugged again.

'Then what if I told you, this man, the *Okhrana*... He was in Brigade 52?'

The fat-necked man, in one clean movement, ripped off the victim's left sleeve. He turned him round to face them. Mordecai saw the blue-black tattoo marking on the forearm: the double-headed eagle, the insignia of the Russian Secret Service; the Cyrillic script, '*Охрáна*'.

The rich man laughed.

'The fool is even proud of it.'

The wretch began to whimper again.

'The torture and execution of New Current members and other so-called dissidents...? The rounding-up of Jews to be sent to Siberia...? You do not need reminding of the exploits of the *Okhrana* – in particular, Brigade 52 of the *Okhrana*. This fellow is so satisfied with his work, mere roubles are not enough. He's wearing his allegiance as a badge of honour.'

Challenge them, Mordecai. You have to...

'How do I know that you are telling me the truth?'

The rich man snapped, the first crack in the veneer – a loud guttural bark.

'Part of your new remit is not to question that which you are told!'

The shouting upset his dog. It yelped. He cooed, soothing it apologetically, as if comforting a baby.

The distraction gave the Russian captive his opportunity. He shuffled across the warehouse as quickly as he could in a bid to escape, the chain around his ankles clanking along the way. But it was an agonising, pitiful spectacle. Pathetic.

The big man strode not towards the man, but to the far wall. There were some implements hanging there, one of them a rusty gaff – a curved, sharp hook attached to a wooden handle, a device for hauling in a large fish.

He marched back over, swung and casually plunged it into the escaping captive's shoulder. The man shrieked in agony and collapsed, falling face first, his arms having been lashed together behind him. The big man took the handle of the gaff, embedded deep, and dragged him back across the floor, leaving a fresh smear of blood, most of it now oozing from the new savage wound.

The valet nodded. The big freakish man let go of the tortured Russian and reached into his pocket. He produced another clip of bullets.

'My gift to you, Mordecai,' announced the rich man. 'Your chance to avenge your people… Or, at the very least, put this lamentable creature out of his misery.'

The poor wretch was grovelling now – agonised, whining, slobbering, begging…

'*Pozhalyusta… Pozhalyusta…*'

Mordecai stood firm.

'No.'

'*No*… Why?'

'Because I cannot kill a man in cold blood.'

The rich man sighed, disappointed again.

'In our business, Mordecai, death, in its various unpleasant guises, is a mere occupational hazard… a bruised thumb to a carpenter… a paper cut to a clerk… Dispensing death is a task you performed with distinction when in uniform.'

'That was different…'

Mordecai could not look him in the eye.

Said the man: 'Then it is something I suggest you re-familiarise yourself with.'

The valet gave a nod to the big brute. He yanked the snivelling captive up and put the Russian in a head lock underneath his left armpit. There followed the crunch of bone and cartilage as he twisted, wringing his neck like a chicken. He then elaborated with the most grotesque signature Mordecai had ever seen given to a casual act of violence. With a flourish, while the man's last moans were still echoing, he wrenched the head around a full 180 degrees.

He then stooped over the silent body, now on its front, placed his boot between the man's shoulder blades for leverage and proceeded to twist, turn and pull at the head – like a troublesome cork in a wine bottle – till he had separated the spine, the ragged flesh and all but a few shreds of sinew and tendon.

Mordecai's guests did not bat an eyelid.

Blood pumped like a geyser, clear spinal fluid dripped from the jagged shards of bone. Then, with one final two-handed heave, the big man yanked the head clean off. It landed with a soft thud and rolled across the floor – the dead eyes staring, the stricken tongue lolling between the sad, broken teeth. The big man clapped his hands together casually, no more inconvenienced than a gardener brushing off the dirt after uprooting some carrots.

The rich man's dog was giving some excited little yaps, his paws pedalling in the air. He set it down. It padded straight through the lake of blood and began licking at the stump of the neck, sucking on the open wound, gnawing on the meat, wagging its stubby tail.

'From now on,' said the rich man, 'you will do exactly as we ask.'

Chapter Eighteen

Something told Finch not to travel directly. He left at dawn, caught the first train into London and walked from St Pancras to Euston past the giant, palatial neo-Gothic Midland Grand Hotel. Lest he be followed, he hoped to give the impression of intended travel northwards (he had family in the Midlands). After queuing rather obviously in the ticket office of the London and North Western Railway, he ducked out of a side exit and took a circuitous route via public transport to Liverpool Street station.

From Liverpool Street, Finch took the Great Eastern locomotive service to Norwich. While delayed at Ipswich, he used a telephone in one of the new public booths and frustrated the put-upon Daphne, who'd just arrived for work, with the news that he was unwell (he'd 'picked up something' from Mrs Ashby) and probably wouldn't be in till Thursday.

After Norwich came the East Norfolk Railway, a draughty, regular stopping service that groaned north, skirting the Broads waterlands on its way to the Victorian resort of Cromer, perched atop a steep escarpment with its pier nestling down below.

At Cromer he boarded a train on the branch line that traced the coast westwards for the remaining few miles of his journey. The countryside, up on the clifftops, was flat and exposed. Rain lashed against the carriage window, like someone throwing gravel. Beyond, to his right, the North Sea was a foreboding slate-grey with white breakers kicking up.

Unsure of what would be required of him on his mission, Finch had dressed in a worn tweed jacket with cap and knee-length corduroy knickerbockers. He wore a jumper over a checked shirt and knitted tie, thick woollen socks with walking boots, and carried his basic supplies for an overnight stay in a canvas rucksack. He lit himself the latest in a long line of cigarettes. And, when no one was looking, suckled on his hip flask.

After delays from the earlier engineering works somewhere in Suffolk and a consequent missed connection, it was mid-afternoon by the time the train pulled into Endthorpe. The rain had stopped and a patch in the clouds yielded a brief burst of sunshine. A partial band of a rainbow revealed itself against the purple-grey backdrop. The reflected sunlight glared up from the wet pavement.

Amid the engine's hiss and a great belch of smoke, Finch exited the small station by the level crossing – the gates of which the signalman was opening by hand to let the traffic through – and wandered down the pleasant high street with its attractive flint-fronted buildings and new clock tower built over the public water pump. A smattering of locals mooched in and out of the shops: the greengrocer, a large ironmonger's store, the tobacconist…

It was clearly very quiet outside of holiday season. Finch walked past the evidence of busier seasonal times as he neared the seafront: the shuttered ice-cream parlour, a closed summer tea room and various boarded-up amusements. Soon he found himself leaning on the marine wall, head cleared by the cold sweet sting of sea air.

The clouds rolled back over again and he felt the temperature drop. He watched their great dark shadows move across the water and thought for a moment of the wild weather swings on the South African veld. Herring and black-headed gulls, the latter now in their winter plumage, just a black dot on the side of a white head, squawked and whirled.

The beach had a steep bank of large grey pebbles with tidal shelves worn into it. A hundred-yard stretch of flat, compact sand lay beyond it to the water, the beach subdivided by a line of defensive wooden breakwaters that jutted straight out. But the grim, dark sea was fast coming in, its speed exaggerated by the flat sand.

For a seaside resort, unusually, the sun was behind the town, over the land, the shore facing due north, nothing between it and the Arctic. Out there, studding the grey water, small single-masted crab boats bobbed between the coloured cork floats that marked the location of their pots.

To Finch's left, along the crumbling clifftop, above the promenade, were several impressive large modern hotels. They owed their living to the holiday trade that had sprung up with the advent of the railway, turning remote fishing villages such as this one into seaside resorts.

To the right, beneath the gulls hovering on the breeze, was what he had come to find – the fishermen's slope. A number of crab boats had been hauled up it or alongside it on the pebbles. There were stacked wicker pots and mounds of round cork floats all around; the sharp tang of crab hung in the air. There were wooden tubs with the creatures in, piled on top of each other, trying in vain to crawl up and out, unable to gain any purchase on the slippery smooth sides.

There was a handful of fishermen, some at work sewing up nets and patching up the weave in their pots, others tending to ropes, sails and oars, some just leaning back, smoking. To a man they were weather-beaten, dressed in oilskins and woollens, seemingly unbothered by the wind and cold. Several had thick beards.

Finch watched for a while. There seemed an intrinsic nobility to these men – hard men... men of the sea... of nature. Their labours were punctuated by the odd burst of playful, indecipherable banter. Finch felt conspicuously soft, pink, childish... *urban.*

To the side of the slope, the doors were open on a newly built shed. As if in testament to the perils of the fishermen's trade, there sat a brand new lifeboat with its white-glossed hull and ropes for hand-holds looped around the dark-blue band below the gunwale.

Finch jumped down over a wall, overtaxed his knee, and hobbled along. The slope was slick with seawater and seaweed slime and his cautious footing, along with his dress, singled him out immediately as an interloper.

He approached a man in his twenties, clean-shaven but his face a reddish-brown, woolly blond hair matted with salt, at work with a knife on a rope, the stub of a hand-rolled cigarette clenched between his lips.

On the assumption that news of the death would not have reached these parts yet, Finch bade him good day and enquired politely if he happened to know of a man named Sidney Pickersgill. He was an associate, he said, and he was looking for him. As had happened before – a constant failing, Finch admitted to himself – he wasn't prepared for every eventuality.

One thing he certainly *hadn't* bargained for was that the name Pickersgill would be met with an outright look of hostility. His follow-up enquiry, that he understood Pickersgill to have been a colleague of the late Bertram Brandon, caused the man to call over his shoulder.

'Tommy… Spud… Squinty…'

Three men abandoned what they were doing, came up the slope and stood behind their friend in a not exactly friendly manner.

'Pickersgill? Who want a-know?' asked the shortest of the men, one of his eyes on a sharp inward cast towards his nose. His accent was so thick it took a few seconds to register.

Finch didn't play the 'medical card' or give his name but alluded to his credentials as someone in a position of standing. It was a professional call, he said. He needed to find Mr Pickersgill or speak to his associates. The first man flipped his cigarette in Finch's direction. He turned his back and returned to his whittling. With a sign-off of black looks, the others wheeled about too. One of them muttered an expletive. Another nodded to someone at the top of the slope.

Looming over them was a seafront pub. It was doing a brisk trade for the time of day. Finch went back up, entered it, took off his cap and ordered a pint. The place was warm and cosy. It had low beams, a fire and a lively atmosphere, full of loud and booming conversation. He stood at the bar and made some chit-chat with the barmaid, letting it be clear he'd just arrived in town, was an innocent abroad, and was there to tidy up some business affairs.

The young woman was friendly, clearly proud of her town, and told him of a few things locally he might like to do. She made a joke about the miserable weather. Ice duly broken, Finch felt safe enough to drop Pickersgill's name again. The smile fell swiftly from her lips and she moved on to another customer.

Finch was shaking. It was absurd, he told himself. He'd been in the heat of battle, been shot at on several occasions, seen death and destruction on an unimaginable scale. He'd been tortured. He'd faced summary execution. He'd even killed a man with his own bare hands (technically speaking, his hobnail boots).

But *this*...? Suddenly he was afraid of asking a few not-unreasonable questions of some locals. Maybe it was the delayed reaction – that after all that had happened in South Africa, he was once again ensnared in something much, much bigger than he'd bargained for and with the potential for bleak prospects the further he got in. He sipped the ale and let it hit the sweet spot behind the eyes, willing 'the bliss'. It wouldn't come.

By the fireplace, in a partly partitioned section down a couple of flagstone steps, was a group of fishermen. They were talking, laughing loudly. One of them – an older, large man, with a thick grey beard, a round belly and a fisherman's cap – held court, heartily regaling his pals with some loud, bawdy story in between puffs on a clay pipe. Whether he *was* or not... he gave the impression of being the one in charge.

Finch bided his time, went over to the fire, ostensibly to warm himself, and, half-drunk pint and cigarette in hand, gradually ingratiated himself into the man's audience, nodding and smiling along. When a pause presented itself and a round of drinks was ordered, Finch, as politely as he could, went into his routine about being a stranger in town. When one of the men enquired as to his business and he announced that he was seeking 'a Mr Sidney Pickersgill', the request met with the same grim silence.

As if to underscore the point, the four fishermen from the slope had appeared through the door and were nodding to their colleagues, glowering in Finch's direction. He had walked straight into the lion's den… One of the men whispered in the ear of someone drinking at a nearby table. He and his friends – evidently not part of their gang – got up and left immediately, their ales unfinished.

'This here gen'leman want a-know 'boot Pickersgill,' announced the man with the belly to his mates. 'Say he a friend o'his.'

One of the others – a well-built man with bushy black eyebrows – pushed Finch hard with both hands on his shoulders.

'What you want a-know 'boot Pickersgill, eh?'

'Please, I was just—'

Finch flew straight into the man with the belly, who shoved him straight back into somebody else.

'Bloody Bible basher, do-gooder,' he heard someone mutter.

The barmaid suddenly appeared, at which point they stopped.

'You forgot your change,' she said, looking directly at Finch, and pressed some coins into his hand. Her look to the others was a plea to call off the bullying.

'He's now-a-gorn, see?' she said.

She took Finch by the arm and steered him up out of the bear pit and towards the door.

'Thank you,' he whispered.

'*He'll* help,' she breathed and patted his hand.

The fisherman with the blond hair, the first one he'd spoken to, stood blocking the exit. She scowled at him.

'*Eddie?*'

He glared at her but relented and stepped aside. Finch had safe passage out of there.

Outside, he hurried along the prom and ducked into the cubby hole of a public shelter. He hadn't forgotten his change at all.

Wrapped around the few pennies that had been pressed into his hand was a scrap of paper. On it the barmaid had written a name: 'Nathan Cole' and the address of a cottage in Blakeney.

Finch checked his watch. The daylight was not only receding, but the leaden clouds were ominous. The wind had picked up and the tide was almost high. He felt a visceral boom as a wave hit the sea wall and sent a great explosion of water into the air. Spray smacked him, salty, cold and wet.

For a moment he was back in that accursed sea cave at Cape Point, on the Cape of Good Hope, where he and Annie had nearly met their end. There followed another boom. He needed to get out of there.

He headed up an incline, under the arch that led down to the seafront and went between the huge hotels on the esplanade and the well-kept borders that lined the road and roundabout, all being dug over for the winter. Back at the train station he got a cab and asked the driver where he might lodge for the night on the road to Blakeney. The cabbie knew of somewhere en route, a bed and breakfast.

Half an hour later, as the horse ambled away from having deposited him, Finch found himself standing in the hallway of a smart, detached flint house set back off a bend in the coast road by a small, pretty church, which had been built into the ruins of an old priory.

The house had a guestbook on a table, various mounted pictures of wild birds, a bookcase containing well-thumbed volumes on seemingly every conceivable matter ornithological, and a rather forlorn-looking stuffed curlew in a case mounted on the wall. The fireplace in the sitting room was pumping out some very welcome heat.

A jolly grey-haired woman shut her excitable cocker spaniel in the kitchen, ushered Finch in and showed him upstairs to a cosy, if chintzy, room while simultaneously firing off information about mealtimes, local amenities and the coastal bus service. It was out of season, she said, and he was the only guest there tonight.

They'd thought about closing for next winter. It was a lot of work. Though they did have some folks in last week.

'Are you with them?' she asked.

'Who?'

'The Freeland people?'

Finch tried not to betray any reaction.

'Freeland? No. Who are Freeland?'

'I don't know rightly know, sir. Some marine company, something to do with the fishing, I think. Up from London.'

She informed Finch she had a copper bed warmer if required and asked if he'd like a full cooked breakfast – bacon, sausages, mushrooms, black pudding, fried tomatoes, and how did he like his eggs? She wondered if she might make him a sandwich and a cup of tea if he wanted to avail himself of the lounge and the fireplace for a spot of reading. He said he'd be down shortly and she left him to it.

A short while later, Finch was back in the hallway, fountain pen in hand, poised over the guestbook. With the landlady in the kitchen attending to the assembly of his sandwich, he flipped through it, though there was no entry for any guest beyond early October, as if the page containing anything else since had been removed. Yes, there were the remnants of a tear along the page gutter. There was certainly no clue as to whom the 'Freeland' guests might have been.

As close – or as far – as he might be to uncovering what might be going on, Finch felt a very real sense of danger still. He decided to leave a clue, lest anything should happen to him.

The woman emerged, valiantly bearing a tray overladen with a pot of tea and a huge doorstep of bread and cheese.

'Here you are...' she said.

She looked over his forearm at his freshly inscribed signature.

'...Mr Cox.'

Said Finch: 'Please, call me Leonard.'

Chapter Nineteen

Nathan Cole lived in a remote cottage on Blakeney Point. From the village itself, with its flint cottages lining the slope of the only real road, which led down to the small harbour, Finch began the long walk out on the coastal path. It sat atop one of the dykes that the Dutch engineers had constructed along this stretch of the coast in the seventeenth century, reclaiming miles of farmland from the sea but rendering the original small ports stranded and silted-up miles inland. Turning back to face the old coastline, he felt like he was already way out offshore.

The Point was a hook of land that curled round the salt marshes of the estuary of the narrow River Glaven, which meandered out across the mudflats. The ambient tinkling of the rigging of the sailing craft retreated as he proceeded. On the wind now, in staccato blasts, you could hear the barking of the grey seals – and get a whiff of them, too – from the colony on the far shore. The winter breeding season was upon them.

It was a cold and blustery morning but mercifully dry, the sea air invigorating. Finch found Cole's cottage easily enough. A good mile away from anything else, it was a remote, rundown shack – a brick foundation that had been embellished and patched with wood – smoke wafting from the rickety chimney, buffeted about by the onshore breeze.

A young woman in a long grey dress and white apron, her hair in a loose bun, was pinning out tattered washing on a line in a nominal garden of coarse grass fringed with yellow gorse and a fence made from driftwood. There was a toddler at her feet waddling around, merrily banging on stones with a stick.

Finch bade good morning, but his voice was lost on the wind. He tried again, louder, and the woman turned round with a start. The presence of a stranger who'd walked all the way out here caused inevitable suspicion. She stopped her pegging, pulled a shawl around her shoulders and picked up the little one – all mischievous grin and ruddy cheeks – who smiled at Finch and offered him his stick.

When Finch asked if he might speak to a Mr Nathan Cole, the woman pointed twenty yards away, seaward. On a shelf of the shingle beach, amid patchy clumps of samphire, was a man hunched over, paintbrush in hand, attending to a ten-foot skiff with a single short mast at its bow.

Finch crunched across the stones.

'Mr Cole?'

The man looked up from the boat and studied him with inquisitive hazel eyes. He was in his thirties, had tousled dark-brown hair and tanned skin.

'Who want a-know?'

Finch was beginning to think this was the standard Norfolk greeting. The man set down his brush and stood up. It was only then that Finch saw – he was missing his left arm. It had gone from just below the elbow. His frayed canvas shirtsleeve had been rolled up accordingly.

Cole wiped his right hand on a rag. He was lean and fit-looking, his extant forearm strong and sinewy.

Finch, judiciously, didn't offer up his name.

'I've come from down near London,' he said. 'I'm an associate of Mr Sidney Pickersgill.'

Cole took his time. He chewed the word over. He uttered it with cynicism.

'*Associate?*'

'I mean I had some dealings with him.'

One-handed, while bracing a jar of varnish in his left armpit, he screwed the lid back on.

'How I know tha' be true?'

'I saw him just the other day, Mr Cole. Saturday. He was at my house.'

He set the jar down.

'Then how come you don't give me a name…?' he said. 'Man with nothin' a-hide han't got no business withholdin' his name. Normal passage o'introduction, 's the first thing you sayin'.'

He was right, knew Finch.

'The barmaid at the Coronet said I should speak to you.'

There was a faint flicker of a smile.

'Ole Betsy?'

'I'm afraid she withheld *her* name.'

He muttered something under his breath.

'She's a good girl, Betsy, but she gotta be watchin' harself. Some rum 'uns in there.'

'Rum 'uns?'

'Folk none too particular. Sure you meet some already – the big 'un, Fat Pete… Spud, Squinty, Tommy… Shitty Eddie…'

'Why do they call him Shitty Eddie?'

'Why you *think*?'

'The barmaid… Betsy… She got me out of a spot of bother. You say you know her?'

He held on to the pause again.

'She's my sister.'

Finch dug into his pocket. He pulled out the scrap of paper and showed him her handwritten scrawl.

'Tha's har,' he confirmed.

Cole continued to take his time.

'She vouchin' for you, suppose *you* think I owe you a hearin'?'

Finch was in no mood for games.

'Before we begin *anything*, Mr Cole. I need to know how well you knew Mr Pickersgill.'

'Sid? Pretty well. *Why?*'

Finch chose his words carefully.

'I'm afraid I have some bad news… Sidney Pickersgill… He's dead.'

'Oh.'

Cole turned and gazed out to sea for a moment. Finch left him with his thoughts.

After a minute or two, he proffered his packet of Navy Cut. Cole took one.

'Thank you.'

Finch got out his lighter and sparked it up for him. Cole gestured for them to sit. The shingle was dry.

'How?' he asked. 'How'd he die?'

'Shot.'

He exhaled.

'Jesus… Do anybody *else* know?'

Finch got out his hip flask. He offered it and Cole took a sip, cigarette gripped between his fingers while he did so. He gave a nod of approval at the Talisker and raised the flask slightly in toast.

'You're the first I've told up here,' said Finch. 'I was assuming word hadn't reached these parts yet.'

'Generally the last to know on everythin',' he conceded. 'Someone say th'other day ole Napoleon be done for.'

He gave a sardonic smirk.

'And when I say "shot", Mr Cole… Whoever it was that did it tried to frame Pickersgill as a petty crook, a desperate drunk.'

'Sid don't drink.'

The Norfolk dialect, Finch realised, had no past tense, everything in the present; at least poor old Pickersgill would live on. Awash with glottal stops and yod-drops, the stress on random syllables and the rising inflection at the end of each sentence gave the broad accent a musicality – no burred 'r's like the West Country but a big round sound full of sea air and country flurries. His ear was beginning to adjust.

Cole stared out to sea again. He took another swig of the whisky.

'To Sid Pickersgill…' he said, wistfully.

Finch nodded.

'…So, ole boy. Get you in the end, they do…'

Finch let it hang for moment.

'What do you mean by that?' he asked.

Cole turned to face Finch.

''xactly what it sound like. After the others? Only one way it going to finish up.'

His tone became more conciliatory.

'Listen, I don't want no trouble...'

He nodded back to his house.

'...I've a wife, a kid. I tell Sid, I warn him not'a pur-*soo* things. He dint ought a-done that – come after you, I mean. I told him, boy, just leave 'im be.'

He dragged on the cigarette. Finch extended his hand.

'You're right, Mr Cole, I do owe you an introduction. My apologies. My name's Finch... Dr Ingo Finch.'

Cole parked the cigarette in his mouth and shook. His one hand had the power of two.

'I know,' he said.

Cole's wife appeared. She crunched across the shingle with two enamel mugs of tea.

'Milk,' she said to Finch. 'Takin' a guess at no sugar.'

'Thank you, Mavis,' said Cole.

Finch took both mugs and drilled them an inch into the shingle to secure them.

'Perfect,' he said. 'Much obliged.'

She smiled and returned to the house.

'Wife keep a pot goin' near constant,' Cole added.

Finch took a sip.

'What do you mean?' he asked. 'That you *knew* it was me?'

'I mean puttin' two and two t'gether. See you a-comin' up here. I know Sid set orf a-try find you. He think you can help him... That you're... you know... *connected*... That you might have a way a-stop this thing. Fearin' for his life.'

'I just don't get why a fisherman from Norfolk would go to such lengths...'

'*Fisherman...?*'

Cole gave a small, incredulous chuckle.

'...Hold you hard, boy.'

'What?'

'Sid wa'nt no fisherman... Sid run a mission boat.'

'A mission boat?'

Cole explained how the mission boats – small steamers – put out to supply the box fleets sitting out there on the North Sea, stuck out over the Dogger Bank for weeks at a time. While the company cutters took care of the catch and ferried out everyday supplies, shuttling back and forth with food and suchlike, the mission boats supplied spare clothes, reading material, tobacco. Many of them, like Pickersgill's boat, the *Kittiwake*, came under the patronage of the Church, run as charitable operations...

Servant of the parish.

...They did most of their work, not with the local crabbers, he said, but with the trawlers out from Hull and Grimsby up beyond the Wash.

'Crew with him myself awhile,' he added, 'but just wa'nt worth it, money-wise.'

Finch recapped how Pickersgill had come to him; about his state of agitation; his presence at the Dogger Bank incident; and how he was on the verge of revealing something he believed to be of great importance. He skipped over reference to any of his own interaction with military intelligence.

'He said he'd been wounded, shot in the wrist,' said Finch.

'Tha's right. Army medic fix Sid up better'n me.'

He waggled his stump.

'...Cop me a good 'un at the Zand River... the Transvaal...'

'You were in South Africa, too?'

'Uh-huh.'

'Sorry.'

'For *this*? Don't be...'

He waggled it again.

'...I be dead otherwise. That's the way I look at't. That's the way I *have* t'look at't.'

'I mean, just sorry… South Africa, the whole bloody mess.'

'T'ent *your* fault, Dr Finch. Despite my arm, I still get orf light. Join up with the Norfolks. By the time they ship me out, Pretoria's aboot a-fall. Just a few skirmishes. Nothin' at all… then some ole Boojer, he creep up the railway line, do our blockhouse with some 'splosives. Catch me with a round when we're all a-scarper. Dum-dum bullet. Smash right through the bone.'

'Again, I'm sorry. Battlefield surgeons. Trust me. They don't take such decisions lightly.'

Cole shrugged it off as if it were no big deal.

'Be havin' a tough time, Ole Sid…'

He gazed out to sea again, lost for a moment.

'…Was older'n me, above ten yar n'more. Not an active service type. Enlistin' like a lot o'locals. Hoped for the Norfolks but, 'cause o'his age, end up in the Military Foot Police…'

He bummed another cigarette.

'Queer thing, he see a lotta mischief. More than me. After the big show's over, he's stuck clearin' up the stink. The guerrilla war. Women, children, old 'uns. Burn down their farms. Herd 'em into camps…'

His jawline tensed.

'…I tell you, Dr Finch. What he tell *me*? If I'd a-know it then…'

'It was a mess, Mr Cole. A scandal. I saw it myself.'

'Sid say that plain *wrong* – him torchin' farms by his own hand, destroyin' their livelihood. Folks just like us. Say the military police's just scapegoats, there t'do the dirty work o'thems higher up…'

Cole's sadness swelled. He explained how Pickersgill's wife, Edna, had died while he was in South Africa. Cancer, they thought, but no one knew for sure. It happened quickly. The man had no children. No other family.

'He always sayin' that God's way a-punish him for what he do down there. I mean he always a Christian man, a church-gooer. But his life ever since, this last two yar? That be all aboot *atonement*. Turned into a devout good-booker…'

He pointed at Finch's flask.

'...Never touch another drop.'

Finch swigged.

'But how... How did he know *me*?' asked Finch. 'Where do I fit in? What made him seek *me* out?'

'Because if you're who you *say* you are, Dr Ingo Finch... *Cap'n* Ingo Finch of the Royal Army Medical Corps... as *was*... then you one o'his victims.'

'*What?*'

'Tha's right, boy. Tell me a rum ole tale, Sid do – 'boot how they arrest you in Stellenbosch, take you down a-Cape Town and work you o'er all night long... Good ole thumpin', he reckon.'

Jesus... *Pickersgill?*

'He never felt right aboot that either.'

He *was one of the little bastards?*

Finch felt light-headed. The shock must have been evident to Cole.

'Y'all-right?'

'I'm fine, really,' said Finch.

He sipped the tea this time.

Christ. He'd been trying for so hard and for so long to block it from memory, that black night in Stellenbosch. And now he was in the perverse position of trying to recall it all.

For a moment he was back there, naked, in a darkened, stinking room, curled double against the pain of the beating, the drug they had pumped into him, and the sheer desperation – though he could not single out the individual faces of his tormentors... The captain in charge, yes, but certainly not the underlings.

Nathan Cole was either oblivious to the full extent of what had happened to Finch, or simply didn't care. Finch hoped it was the former.

'This stuff in the North Sea,' Cole went on. 'Men dyin' since – Bertie, the others. It's been hard on us locals.'

'*What* stuff in the North Sea?'

'...But then the money...' he continued.

'*What* money?'

Cole threw him a look as if to suggest Finch's mental impairment.

'From *Freeland*, o'course. Everyone suddenly very rich and no one complainin'. This kind o'thing never happen a-folk like us...'

'The North Sea, you say... *What* happened out there?!'

Their talk was interrupted by the sound of a car – unmistakeable in the silence. The rasp of the engine rose on the breeze. They turned to see a black, open-topped Ford advancing along the coastal path. There were four men inside and the shapes of police helmets.

'Shit!' blurted out Cole.

Finch went to duck into the boat.

'No point in *tha'*,' said Cole, almost mockingly. 'Will have had eyes on us. Binoculars.'

He was probably right.

'And anyway, we got nothin' t'hide, *right*?'

They got to their feet.

'If you say so.'

'You're a man up in the country, 'quirin after ole Sid Pickersgill. All legal.'

'Right.'

The car came to a halt about fifty yards away. They heard the ratchet of the handbrake. Then four men got out, one in plain clothes and three uniformed policemen. They strode towards them.

'Don't worry, I know 'em,' said Cole. 'Just play 'ar cool. Follow my lead.'

The plain-clothes man led his men over. He wore a long mackintosh that flapped in the breeze and a wide-brimmed fedora.

'Fancy 'imself does *this* boy,' Cole asided.

He threw Finch a reassuring wink.

As the man crunched across the shingle, the uniformed bobbies trailed in his wake.

'Morning, Nathan,' he called out.

'H'ar y'all *right*, Chief?' replied Cole. 'You care for a cup o'tea?'

The man oozed condescension.

'Another time, Nathan. Afraid it's official business.'

'How can I help you?'

The man turned to Finch.

'Superintendent Dryden, Norfolk Constabulary,' he announced.

'Good morning,' said Finch.

But the man did not return the pleasantry. There was certainly no handshake. He was in his fifties, had a piercing grey-eyed stare and carried himself with the air of someone who did not beat about the bush.

'Word's come in there's a stranger in town, snooping around, asking questions…'

'I'd hardly call it snooping,' Finch retorted.

Dryden raised his palm, indicating that Finch should keep his mouth shut.

'Others'll be the judge of that.'

Finch kept his counsel.

'Word's *also* come in that Sidney Pickersgill is deceased. You hear that, Nathan?'

'Sid's *dead*? Dear Lord,' Cole faked.

'That's right… *murdered*!'

'Murdered?'

Finch wasn't quite sure where Cole was going with the charade.

'Shot dead,' explained Dryden. 'And *this* 'un…'

He pointed at Finch.

'…has been accused of it.'

'Now hang on a minute,' protested Finch. 'There was no such charge. I was questioned and released. And *I* was the one he was supposed to have burgled.'

'Burgled?' tutted a copper. 'Sid Pickersgill?'

A constable came up and thrust his hand into Finch's inside jacket pocket. He tugged out his wallet and threw it to the superintendent, who caught it and flipped it open, pulling out his medical card in the process.

'That *right*?' growled Cole.

Said Dryden to Finch: 'Why don't *you* tell him…'

He read the card, then nodded to his men that Finch's identity was confirmed. He spat the words out.

'…*Dr Ingo Finch*… Or is that another of your aliases…? Yes, that's right, we stopped off at your lodgings along the way.'

Finch turned to Cole.

'What he says… It's horseshit.'

He was caught unawares by Dryden's hard, open-palmed slap across his left cheek.

Stunned, he felt his heart pound, his ear ring. Beyond the stinging pain, he felt the adrenalin pump, the cold sweat begin to trickle down his temples.

'How dare you!'

Cole, meanwhile, continued to play his part a little too convincingly.

'That why you out here… *harassin'* me… harassin' my Mavis?' Cole snarled, with full theatrical gusto.

He lunged at Finch. Two policemen jumped in to restrain him. The third copper, the one who'd removed Finch's wallet, moved behind Finch and… *Click!*

…snapped on a pair of handcuffs. He patted Finch down and pulled out his whisky flask. He handed it to Dryden, who opened it and took a sniff.

'Well… we also got a telephone call this morning…' he declared – smug, satisfied.

He threw the hip flask to Cole, who caught it.

He turned to Finch.

'…Seems our friends in Hertfordshire haven't quite finished with you, Finch… And I tell you what, boy, neither have *we*.'

Chapter Twenty

Finch was bundled into the back of the Ford and squeezed between two policemen, his rucksack abandoned. With his hands cuffed behind his back he had to be helped up onto the running board. Constricted in his movement, the rough handling nearly forced a shoulder out of joint and he winced at the pain. But he knew better than to protest.

Superintendent Dryden was a man who clearly liked the sound of his own voice… a classic authority bully. He relished his ongoing criticism of the copper behind the wheel, who seemed a perfectly competent driver to Finch, but who had, within a few hundred yards, lost so much confidence he began to make unforced errors – crunching gears, over-revving the engine.

Beyond the pain and humiliation of the slap, Finch was fuming – firstly because of the sense of injustice at being arrested again for the same alleged crime (although he had still yet to be formally charged with anything) and with the sinister hint of some small-town retribution thrown into the bargain.

Secondly, there was Nathan Cole. To hell with playing it cool.

Granted, Finch hadn't admitted to Cole that he himself had been momentarily *accused* of Pickersgill's murder – just that he had been taken into the police station for some questioning, which was pretty much the truth. But the man had plain sold him out. He had *trusted* him, for God's sake. And now Cole knew far too much.

'Over here,' barked the superintendent.

In the distance, the white sails of a windmill gently turned on a solid flint tower. Before the path straightened out onto the last leg ahead to the shore road, the driver pulled the Ford off to the left, down a slope. Without his hands to brace him, Finch lurched forward and banged his forehead on the metal back of the seat in front, right on its top edge, where it met the leather. It was a bad knock and he could feel the sting of an open wound on his hairline. The blood began to trickle. It ran down and collected in his eye socket, forcing him to blink it out of the way.

No one helped him. The three policemen seemed locked in some silent lawman's equivalent of the Endthorpe fishermen's *omertà* – as if some unpleasant task lay ahead.

Unlike the main path, up on the bank, this track was at sea level, directly on the flood plain. The grass and the last remnants of token field division soon gave way to salt marsh, the car splashing through the puddles across the winding course, the wheels slithering around. A pair of binoculars swung back and forth on a seat hook – just as Cole had predicted.

'Stop,' growled Dryden.

The driver hit the brakes and the car skidded. The path was not navigable much beyond this point. There was no one around.

The two policemen in the rear dragged Finch out and down from the vehicle.

Dryden clicked his fingers.

'My waders.'

One of the policemen pulled down the flap of the car's boot. He came over with a pair of long green rubber fishing boots. Dryden twisted sideways on his seat, untied his leather brogues and handed them to one of his men. Fastidiously, he tucked his trouser legs into his socks, then wrestled the thigh-high boots over them. He jumped down with a satisfied squelch.

'You can turn the car around there,' said Dryden to the driver.

There was a patch of compacted shingle to the side. The copper behind the wheel manoeuvred the vehicle.

'Okay, this way.'

Then he led them, stamping across the mud.

They were well away from the village, not a house visible, not a soul in sight. A lone heron stood on one leg, conserving its body heat. Beyond, some black and white oystercatchers dipped their bright red bills in the silt. The temperature had dropped again. With the wind chill it felt bitterly cold.

Finch was giddy, his head in splitting spasms of pain from the bash in the car. He could see the drops of blood on his shirt front. His shoulder hurt still and, right on cue, his good old knee decided to join the party. No matter how he tried, his walk was an unsteady, shivering, shamble. His state of distress elicited no sympathy from the two policemen. One of them, a man with the demeanour of a bulldog chewing a wasp, gave him an unhelpful shove every few paces.

Around them, Finch saw that the mudflats were criss-crossed with creeks and tidal flows. The tide had turned from low water and was now ebbing back in. There were some large concrete blocks ahead, remnants of an ambitious but long-abandoned sea defence.

Said Dryden: 'Right, that'll do. Bring him over here.'

Finch was led up and manhandled against one of the blocks. It was a cube-like structure, each side about six feet square, its surfaces a composite of concrete and shingle. It had tilted forward in the mud, the upper side facing out to sea, sloping at a forty-five degree angle, the underside covered with seaweed and barnacles. On each corner of the block's surface was a corroded metal ring.

Finch was pushed hard against the seaward face. He yelped at the discomfort and whacked his head again. He was half lying down, given its slope. One of the policemen flipped him round and undid the cuff on Finch's left wrist. He handed the keys to Dryden who slipped them into his breast pocket.

'Constable…' he instructed.

On Dryden's nod, one of the coppers yanked up Finch's right arm. Finch struggled, but with two policemen holding him down he was no match. Dryden re-cuffed him to the uppermost rusty red ring on the block.

'What the hell… *You have no right to do this!*' Finch yelped.

'You can go now,' said Dryden to his men.

'Right you are, sir,' said the one with the bulldog face and they stamped back over to the car which the driver had turned. They got in and it drove off, gently splashing through the puddles again and straining its way up the slope. Soon you could hear it no more.

'Well, well, well, Dr Finch... *Captain* Finch,' said Dryden coldly, sarcastic.

'What?!'

'Poking around, sticking your nose where it's not wanted.'

Despite his anger, Finch tried to employ reason.

'Look... I don't know what the hell you think you're playing at... or what you heard... I have been completely exonerated from any suggestion of foul play with regard to Pickersgill. I have a lawyer... It is all on record...'

'Shut your mouth, Finch!' he snapped. 'Truth is I don't rightly care who did in old Sid Pickersgill. Can't blame *you* if you did. Things were going nicely round here till he started yowin'. Three good men died because of him whining his mouth off. If he'd have just kept quiet – Bertie Brandon, the others, they'd still be alive.'

'What the hell are you on about?'

He ignored him.

'And you, Finch... Dr Finch... *Captain* Finch...'

In one deft, swift move, defying anticipation, clearly practised in a hundred interrogations, Dryden spun and punched him hard in the stomach. Unable to double over, Finch coughed and choked and jerked his knees upwards, yanking his handcuffed wrist hard against the metal ring. He grabbed on with his left hand to lessen the strain on the right, though it left his midriff vulnerable.

'Oh yeah, I've been reading up about *you*,' Dryden went on. 'You come up here with your smart mouth, thinking we're all a bunch of dim-witted yokels, asking questions. But I tell you something...' He spat the word out... '*Doctor*... I've got friends. Friends in high places. To hell with "classified".'

Knowing Finch's physical predicament, he deliberately took his time. He wound his arm back at his own leisure and...

BAM!

…casually punched Finch again. This time he caught him hard in the solar plexus, sending his diaphragm into spasm. Finch strained hard, trying to raise his knees for protection while gulping, groaning in vain for air, making a guttural, animal noise.

'That one was for my boy.'

Finch voice came weak, confused.

'Your… your *boy*?'

'That's right. My boy. My *only* boy… South Africa. Lost him… Spion Kop.'

Finch mouthed an 'I'm sorry.'

'Don't need *your* pity.'

Dryden looked wistful for a moment, incongruously emotional.

'We left some fine men down there, dying in that murderous stink hole at the bottom of the world. Brave men doing their duty for queen and country, king and country. And then there's the likes of *you*, running around, thinking they know better, trying to discredit our own intelligence services, pissing all over our armed forces, our lads. Oh yeah, your file's quite a read, Dr Finch.'

'That's not true! I've never done one thing in my life to compromise national security. Quite the opposite.'

'I'd have more respect for you if you'd suited up with a bandolier and a slouch hat. At least the Boers fought with honour… And now you're at it *again*!'

Finch coughed… and then the coughing, the spluttering wouldn't stop. He had trouble breathing, trouble getting the words out.

'I don't know what you've read, what you've heard,' he wheezed, 'but that's not even one half of the story. Anything I've been involved in… been *rumoured* to have been involved in… was to secure the defence of the realm. I'm a loyal servant of king and country… as much as the next man.'

'Oh yeah?… And so that's how you show it, is it?… Pitching up here to defend a miserable turncoat? Sidney Pickersgill was a snivelling little weasel. He's likely ruined everything for us… and a good few ex-servicemen among them. Unless…'

The fist came hard, blind-siding him again. It caught Finch on the left side of the jaw. The knuckles glanced off expertly. The pain shot up the side of his face and down the nerves in his neck. His ear rang again.

'…Unless we shut you up.'

Finch spat and coughed, retching on his words, protesting.

'I don't what the hell you're talking about… I'm a physician… Pickersgill was ill, a man in a mental state… by the terms of the Hippocratic oath, I was obliged…'

A long viscous drool of blood trailed from a fat split upper lip.

'…And then he was killed…'

'I'm sorry, I can't hear you,' Dryden mocked.

'…*murdered*,' he spluttered. 'He'd asked me for help. I owed it to him to come here to try and find out what happened. No one else seems to be lifting a finger.'

Dryden laughed to himself. It was derisive.

'You think I *care*, Finch? The government "cared" so much about the death of my boy, the death of *all* our boys, it went and sold out the peace in South Africa to the very enemy it had been fighting, gave the Boers… the Afrikaners a seat at the top table. A cosy little "Union", the foe now running the show. Was all a waste of time. Those boys… *my* boy… died in vain.'

He waved his hand, shaking out the impact of the last punch. He rubbed his knuckles.

'Only thing that bothers me is this… What do you know about Ursa?'

'Ursa… I… I…?'

The fist came again. Harder. Finch felt a molar loosen. And he'd bitten a chunk off the side of his tongue. He spat out clotted dribbles of blood and saliva. He tried to raise his head but his neck had been jarred. The peripheral vision in his left eye was now just a blur.

'Ursa,' yelled Dryden. 'What do you know about Ursa?!'

He struck him again, this time with his left, connecting with the right side of the bridge of his nose. A searing jolt shot up into Finch's brain. His eyes watered instantly.

'Nothing…'

Finch's voice was pained and weak now.

'…I… know… noth— nothing.'

Dryden turned.

'See that out there…?'

He waved his arm.

'…the North Sea…'

Finch had slumped, his whole body weight now dangling on the right wrist chained on high.

'…It's where us folk up here make a living. Where my father made a living. Where people round here have made a living for centuries. The cold North Sea's claimed the lives of many a good man… bad ones too.'

Finch looked to his right. The water in the creek had eddies forming in it. Whirlpools were swirling in the fast, incoming current.

'Please…' winced Finch, his mind flitting in and out of consciousness.

Dryden turned back again.

'In order to contain this situation… like I said, I need you, Dr Finch, to tell me everything you know… everything you know about Ursa…'

Finch blinked up through the blood still clogging in his eyes. His mouth and gums were so swollen, he could barely form the words.

He thought of Maude; he thought of Jilkes and his picture-perfect family. He thought of his mother, father, his sister. He thought of the little girl Emily in South Africa. She would be what now, twelve? He thought of her panicked mute mother, of the brave African man who had helped them. He thought of his old friend Hawley Jenkins. He thought of Inspector Brookman, of Ans Du Plessis. He thought of George Robey.

He thought of the big green illuminated Perrier sign at Piccadilly Circus. He thought of chicken chow mein. He thought of Mrs P-A. He thought of a stuffed curlew in a glass case… But mostly he thought of Annie.

The man was shaking him.

'Finch. Goddammit…!'

Finch blinked up into the dispassionate grey eyes. He could feel cold water around his ankles.

'Don't you black out on me, you shit!'

'I know… I know nothing.'

The fist connected again.

-

When Finch came to, he was pained, dazed. How long had it been? It took him a moment to orientate himself. Now his legs were cold, numb. The water was way over his knees.

'Freeland…' he whispered.

He looked to his right again. The creek was no longer there. It had been completely submerged.

'*What?* Speak up, man.'

Dryden sloshed over in his waders, grabbed Finch's hair and yanked his head back. The pain in his neck was a searing fire. He didn't know how much more he could take.

'Freeland… I heard something… about Freeland,' he offered.

Dryden let his head drop.

'Not good enough, I'm afraid.'

He smacked his hands together and looked out to sea as casually as a beach fisherman who'd cast a good line.

'See how far the tide is out, Dr Finch? It's deceptive… Over flat ground like this, out here, now it's turned, it comes in fast.'

Finch tried to focus. He could see white breakers. The salt marsh beyond was now a sheet of water.

He willed his mind to be sharp – to appreciate the gravity of the situation. It was true, he knew. Yesterday's high water had come around four o'clock. It was about one o'clock now but they were a good half a mile out from the old original shoreline...

'Don't suppose I have to instruct you on the intimacies of drowning, being a medical man and all. Water goes into the lungs, choking, spluttering... that we all know. But it's the blind panic that gets you, the foreknowledge... that as the water level rises you're forced to raise your head as high as you can to try and outpace it.'

'Please, you must understand—'

'Funny thing, breathing. Do it from the second we're out of the womb. Instinctive. Twenty-three thousand breaths a day. Eight and a half million a year. Never even give it a thought. But we're a frail species. We can survive three days without water, three weeks without food. But air...? Just three minutes and your number's up... That burning in your chest as you gulp for oxygen... for dear life itself... Only there isn't any.'

'I tell you... please... I don't know anything about Ursa. I saw the name written down, that's all... Is it "bear"?... Something to do with Russia?'

Dryden took his time. Ominously, Finch felt the first cold swirl as a low wave passed, the white foam head running along its peak from one side to the other.

'Reckon you got a good hour's thinking time afore you start gulping and spluttering. Will be a right pretty picture. Shame I won't be here to see it. Wife packed the "thigh-highs" not the "chests".'

'Please!'

'You know I once knew an old boy, a fisherman, who'd just about drowned, till they fished him out and managed to pump the water out of him. Said the worst thing of all, while going under, trapped in his boat, not far off the beach... was that he could *see* people... ordinary folks on the shore going about their everyday business, oblivious to the fact that he was about to meet his maker.'

'Listen... I'm telling you... I know nothing about Ursa!'

'And therein lies my dilemma, Finch. Whether you do or don't. It's immaterial now. You're a threat. The best thing for everyone concerned is that you just disappear.'

He turned to face Finch again.

'One for the road...'

He balled his right fist and swung it back. Finch closed his eyes.

BANG!

Dryden hung there for a moment, a strange quizzical look on his face. Then he staggered forward.

BANG!

He took one... two... three steps and slumped right on top of Finch, his face pressed right into his, the grey eyes gone, unfocused. A terminal rasp of breath rattled on Finch's cheek, expelled from a man who'd just been shot... Dead.

Chapter Twenty-One

Finch used every last ounce of energy to kick Dryden's body off him. With lifeless limbs lolling, the man rolled over and splashed face down in the water. Finch strained his neck and blinked through the blurring and the blood. Ahead to the left, behind the mound of a mudflat, he thought he saw the tip of a short mast.

He willed himself to focus, but he could now hear it too – a person advancing towards him, sloshing through the water…

Nathan Cole.

He had a rifle slung over his shoulder.

Cole reached the concrete block and gave Dryden's capsized body a prod. The superintendent's feet dragged in the mud, holding him in place.

'Believe me, I want a-do that fr'a long time.'

He turned to Finch and examined his face. He hissed out a sigh, pulled out a blue and white spotted kerchief from his pocket, dipped it in the water and handed it up, indicating for him to press it to his left cheek.

'Here.'

'Thank you…'

'Give you a right beltin'.'

'No… I mean…'

Finch nodded at the body.

'…*Thank you.*'

Cole shrugged, as if dispatching Dryden were no more a courtesy than holding the door open for someone.

'Don't thank me… thank ole Sid,' he replied. 'You were good to him. Help him in his hour o'need. Least I can do's show my gra'itude.'

'But I thought…'

He chuckled to himself.

'*Wha'* you think? I lead you on a merry dance with my little show for the boys in blue back there… Gettin' all roiled up…? Believe me, I know more'n anyone, there's only one way ole Dryden's mind work.'

Finch eyed Cole's rifle, slung about him with a webbing strap. A Lee–Enfield. He'd seen enough of those to last him a lifetime.

'What you might call a souvenir,' Cole quipped. 'Arms for an arm.'

Finch thought for a second of Jilkes – what he'd said about ex-servicemen keeping hold of their weapons.

Cole switched his attention to Finch's handcuffed wrist.

'Don't make life bloody easy, do 'e?…'

He poked at the body again.

'…Never did. Ole bastard…'

He rolled Dryden over.

'…Creeks and channels all over these parts. Know 'em like the back o'my hand… my *right* hand. Tha's how I sneak up orn ya.'

Dryden's face was blank, the eyes dull. For someone who had exerted such power over him not five minutes ago, to Finch he now seemed so pathetic. There was a ragged exit wound… *two* exit wounds… on his left chest, right over the heart. Cole, even with one hand, was clearly a very good shot.

'The *key*,' said Finch. 'He put it in his jacket. The breast pocket.'

Cole dug his hand in.

'Wha' I call self-preservation,' he recounted, as he felt around. 'But one thing, sure as eggs is eggs. Regardless o'what happen a-you. After Sid, I'm next…'

'*The breast pocket*,' repeated Finch, with more urgency.

'Hold you hard.'

Cole patted around. Finch did not like the look on his face. After the breast pocket, he tried the others, then, with greater desperation, every fold in the material, front and back, from every conceivable angle.

He looked Finch in the eye.

'Bad news.'

'What?'

'T'ent there.'

'Try again.'

He did so but to no avail.

'Maybe in the mud…?'

As adept as he was with one arm, the rising tide and the encumbrance of a rifle slung around him made it tricky for Cole. He lay his gun down on the block next to Finch, threw his jacket on top, then ducked under the water. He came up for air.

'Impossible to see.'

He plunged again. Finch got a glimpse of his white hand feeling around. He came up, shook his head, then scaled the block. With its bottom half wet and the seaweed now a billowing slippery carpet, it was not easy to get sure footing. Once up, Cole pushed and pulled at the rusty ring, then the handcuffs. They cut deep into Finch's wrist.

Finch felt the cold shock in his groin as the first low breaker hit him full on.

'Here…' Cole said and beckoned for Finch to pass up the rifle. But he had not reckoned on the extent of Finch's incapacity. His grip on it was unsure.

Splash!

It slipped into the water.

'Shit!' yelled Cole.

He slid down on his backside, jumped back in and fished it out. He was standing waist-deep.

'Well that's buggered the next part o' the plan,' he said.

'What?'

Cole tilted the rifle. Water poured out of the barrel.

'I was goin' a-shoot through the chain on the handcuffs.'

The pain in Finch's wrist was increasing. The wetter the block got, the more he slipped down. The more he swung on the handcuff, the more it cut into the skin, the more it acted like a tourniquet. He was too weak to keep shifting position. He grabbed the rusty ring with his left hand also, trying to relieve the pressure.

Cole wedged the rifle's stock under his left armpit and pulled back the bolt; the chamber was water-logged too.

'Nope,' he muttered.

He shuttled the bolt and tried firing a one-handed round into the air. The pin just went *click*. He ejected the cartridge and put it in his jacket laying there on the block. He tried another to no avail.

'S'all I had, the five in the magazine. Two o'them I used on Dryden.'

He climbed up again and tried the remaining bullet, firing with the thin chain of the handcuffs pressed right across the barrel.

'This work, you'll get a burn on your wrist, a right good-un,' he said.

Finch didn't even brace himself. He knew what was coming. Again, all they got was *click-click-click* as Cole repeated the exercise for good measure.

With all three cartridges set aside in his jacket, he slid down and rifled through the floating Dryden's pockets once more. There was nothing else in them of any significance – a wallet, some coins – they could use to free Finch. Cole bobbed underwater again and felt around on the seabed.

But… *nothing*.

He climbed up again. He pulled at the corroded metal ring for all he was worth. He even shoved the gun barrel in to it to try and use it as a lever. All he did was bend the barrel. Finch pulled the chain taught for him while he smashed away at it with the rifle butt, and then repeated it on the big rusty metal ring of the block. After five minutes of hammering it was clear it was a futile exercise.

The water was above Finch's waist now. Small waves were beginning to break around them more frequently. It was so cold Finch was shivering uncontrollably. Cole lay his jacket over him.

'Be a while t'get help. Even if I sail back home 'gainst the tide, not sure I've anythin' there. And then I've got a-get back.'

Attached to his belt was a sheathed hunting knife. He removed it for Finch to see. It had a curved steel blade, about eight inches long.

'You'll never saw through solid metal with that,' said Finch.

'That's not wha' I meant.'

He registered the look of shock on Finch's face.

'It's oiled, sharp...'

'Wait! No!'

'I can skin'n gut a rabbit in under a minute. I know how t'get in between the bone.'

'WAIT!'

'Wha' else you suggest for Chrissakes?'

Finch fell silent. And then...

'A cartridge.'

'What?'

'A cartridge... From the rifle...!'

'Hold on.'

Cole stopped him.

'*What?*'

'He's floatin' orf.'

Dryden had started to drift. Cole jumped down yet again. With his legs near numb with cold, Finch could feel Cole tugging at his own ankle.

'What are you *doing*?'

'Tuckin' the toe o'your boot into his belt... There, he's tethered good n' proper.'

The weight of the body put even more strain on Finch's wrist.

'You were sayin'?' asked Cole.

'A cartridge,' winced Finch. 'In my inside pocket, there's a cigarette lighter. We use some dry clothing. You can rip up my shirt. Whatever you need. We wedge some material under the ring, then place a cartridge under the chain link on the handcuffs. We set the material alight. Build a fire. It will heat the metal bullet casing. When the brass is red hot, it'll ignite the powder in the cartridge… the cordite. The bullet will be expelled from the casing. It's how a bullet works.'

'You sure?'

'You got any better ideas?'

A hundred yards or so away, Cole's skiff had risen on the tide. It was near fully visible from behind what was left of the mudbank, which had been reduced to a small islet.

The water was creeping over Finch's stomach, halfway up the exposed side of the block. Cole got the lighter out of Finch's pocket just in time. Doing the best he could with his one arm and with Finch shackled, he partially wrestled off Finch's jacket, then pretty much ripped the shirt straight off his back.

He screwed the dry cloth into a ball for a fire, just as Finch described, packing in the material under the handcuff links, and squashed in Finch's knitted tie for good measure. He wedged the bullet in vertically, nestling its nose into a link, pointing upwards.

'No, the other way,' said Finch.

'Wha'?'

Finch was so exhausted, he could barely get the words out.

'Bullet's held in place by a crimp in the metal casing… In a gun, the cartridge is held fast… so the bullet is released… Here… with it being insecure…'

'For Chrissakes… *What?!*'

'…It's the other way round… Law of physics… It's the bullet that's solid, heavy. The metal of the cartridge is hollow, light… So it's the *bullet* which will expel the *cartridge*…'

'Will it work?'

Finch gave him a look.

Cole splashed Finch's jacket sleeve and pulled it up as a protective barrier over his wrist. He ripped some more of Finch's shirt, wet it and bound it round his hand.

'Here goes...'

The dry material for the fire did not light at first. But, sheltering the flame from the wind, it took.

'Now you'd better stand clear,' ordered Finch.

Cole hooded his own jacket over Finch's head, then turned his back, ducking out of the way, and hoped for the best. After a couple of minutes, Cole looked up.

'S'not workin'.'

'Needs to generate some serious heat. Needs to get red hot.'

''ll take forever. The lighter... There naphtha in it?' ventured Cole. 'That'd add to the flame. I could open it...'

Finch yelled straight over him.

'Another cartridge... Split it open... The butt of the rifle... Use the powder within... the cordite... Extract it...'

'Tha's an explosive, Doctor... Raw 'splosive... Not stable...'

'I don't know what else to do. The only thing I can think of...'

The water was up to his chest. A low roll came in and, for the first time, washed over his face. Finch spluttered the water away.

Cole took the first of the two spare cartridges, climbed up and wedged it in a crack in the block's uppermost edge, with the bullet head poking out. Swinging with one arm, he brought the rifle butt down hard. The bullet and its casing just pinged off into the sea.

'Shit.'

'Try again!' urged Finch.

'No... I mean the fire's gorn out.'

The water was up to Finch's shoulders.

'Don't worry, it's dry up top for now... still two foot clear... we can relight it... *Just do it!*'

Cole repeated the exercise with the second.

This time he whacked so hard he simply forced the bullet into the crack.

He sighed and reached to his belt again.

'Sorry, Dr Finch. Reckon it's the knife.'

'NO... TRY AGAIN...!'

'Really. S'not that bad, once you get used to it.'

A breaker swamped right over Finch's face again.

'JESUS FUCKING CHRIST, COLE…' he choked. 'GET BACK THERE RIGHT NOW AND BREAK THE HEAD OFF THAT FUCKING BULLET!!!'

The concrete block was now just an angular ridge poking three feet above the water. Cole fiddled for what seemed like forever, teasing the bullet out of the crack with his knife. He then braced himself, took a sure swing from well behind his head and, with a manic, one-handed thump, brought the rifle butt down on the cartridge.

'YES!'

He stooped, prised off the loose bullet-head then gently eased out the metal casing, being sure to keep it upright. Finch gestured for Cole to pass it to him and to light a new fire. There was a strip of dry shirt up by the ring still.

While Finch struggled to keep his head above the water, he raised his left hand in the air, keeping the cartridge clear. Cole complied and set to work on the material with the lighter, starting a new fire. This time, using his hands to shield it, he got a flame first time, right under the chain of the handcuffs.

'Okay, she's alight.'

The fire burned with the original cartridge still wedged in place.

'Right… Again…' panted Finch. 'Take cover.'

Cole ducked into the water and placed himself on the leeward side of the block, pulling himself in tight. Flames licked at the chain.

'Okay, here goes,' said Finch.

He mouthed '*One… Two…*' and on the '*Three*' reached up with the bullet casing to tip the gunpowder directly onto the flame.

BANG!!!

With a huge jolt to go with it, Finch felt a searing burn on his wrist in the gap between the wet material protecting his arm and hand.

Cole lifted his head.

'You beauty!' he yelled. 'IT WORKED!'

Finch was choking, having to hold his breath between waves.

The chain had only partially shattered. But Cole climbed up again and swung the rifle butt down hard on it. With brute force he bent the remainder of the link open.

'There!'

Cole pulled Finch clear and down into the water. Pushing the floating Dryden before them, they paddled through the icy water against the growing force of the incoming tide.

Towards the mudbank it grew more shallow, but the current was strong, like hands grabbing at their shins. They were sinking in up to their knees. Finch had no energy. Cole struggled to help him. White breakers began to crash with force. They had to turn their backs with each one.

The mudbank island had been reduced to just a pimple. They squelched onto it on their bellies, dragging Dryden behind them.

'Here, lemme get you on board,' said Cole.

He sloshed into the water again and pulled the boat over, straining on its anchor line. Once alongside, Finch rolled over the gunwale, taking a good portion of seawater with him, and lay prone. Cole tied Dryden to the stern of the skiff, fastening him securely round his chest. He then threw his dud rifle on board and hauled himself over.

He weighed anchor, then pushed off with an oar and unfurled the triangular sail. He wound the halyard round his left vestigial elbow and, with his right hand, grabbled the tiller, pointing her into the wind. He kicked an empty corn beef tin in Finch's direction and urged him to bail out. Finch propped himself up and did the best he could. They tacked against the onshore bluster.

'First thing we need t'do is dis-*poos* o'*him*,' Cole said, nodding at Dryden, trailing behind them. They could use the anchor, he explained… and there were some fishing weights they could also use to send him to the bottom.

'Won't it be obvious? I mean, if he washes up ashore?… I mean what *happened* to him?'

'Trust me,' said Cole. 'Tides 'n' currents round here, the rough stones 'n' rocks, he come ashore ten mile away – over to the west beyond Wells… Hunstanton. Yip, they put two and two t'gether. Know it's him just aboot. But he be mashed to a pulp. Won' even know the ole boy's been shot. If no one see us… and I don't think they do, we be blocked from view… we're fine… *Here*…'

He got Finch to sit up. He was battered, broken, had just the shreds of a shirt under his jacket and was caked head to toe in mud.

'…'Fraid you got work t'do, boy…'

Cole tethered the billowing sail to a cleat on the port side. He placed Finch's hand on the tiller.

'…Hold'ar hard this direction. See that red lobster float yonder. See it…?'

'Yes.'

'…Aim for har.'

Finch nodded.

Cole made better work of the bailing and got rid of all but a puddle. When done, he reeled Dryden's body in to the stern. The man's waders had come off, pulled away by the weight of the water in them.

'Shame. They're good 'uns… Hodgsons.'

Cole began shoving the lead fishing weights into the dead man's pockets.

'Just in case the anchor line break.'

He stopped suddenly when he got to the breast pocket.

'Look!' he exclaimed.

'What?'

He pulled out the key for the handcuffs. He dangled it gleefully from his finger.

'Must a-been tucked right in deep.'

Finch was beyond being able to formulate a response.

Cole took over on the tiller again. Going against the tide and tacking against the wind was tricky in an overladen boat and with a one-armed man at the helm. But Cole's skill was impressive.

Finch really didn't have any sense of time, but they must have got nearly a mile out when Cole reached over again and tied his anchor to the line round Dryden.

'Can they trace it… the anchor?' asked Finch.

Cole's look suggested that Finch was an idiot.

'Right, here goes.'

The boat rolled almost to the water line as Cole leaned over, undid the rope and heaved clear. Dryden hung there for a moment, just the hump of his back visible till the anchor took hold, and then went straight under. The few bubbles didn't linger.

'Crab food,' said Cole.

'Thank you again,' said Finch.

'Like I say…'

They drifted beyond the spot and Finch thought about the unknown world down below… the secrets that lay hidden in the fathoms. Back to landward, Blakeney Point was just a smudge.

'So what happens now?' Finch asked.

Cole blew out a sigh.

'First light I get my wife and child out o'here… Mavis… my Isaac… We got friends all over. Head up north most likely. Well away from Norfolk.'

Beyond the tidal breakers, the sea was rolling rather than rough. Finch was so cold it didn't seem to matter any more. Cole reached inside his own jacket and retrieved Finch's whisky flask, the one that Dryden had thrown to him.

'Here…'

Finch took a grateful swig.

'I reckon you're a man o' 'spensive taste, Dr Finch,' Cole smiled.

Finch just about managed to reciprocate.

They sat there for a moment. There was not another boat in sight. They both knew it but neither said it – they had been lucky.

'Tell me, Mr Cole.'

'You can call me Nathan by now.'

'Then tell me, Nathan... please... What the hell's going on...? You have to be into something pretty deep to shoot dead the local chief of police?'

'He was aboot a-kill you, Dr Finch.'

'For which I'll be forever grateful... But you said something else. You said he "had it coming".'

Finch passed the flask back. Cole signalled for Finch to take the tiller again while he changed the tack, tethering the sail to starboard this time. Tucked under the bow was his rucksack, Finch noticed. Cole had retrieved it from the shingle.

''xactly as I say. Man was no good. 'specially since...'

'Since what?'

Cole reached under a shelf at the boat's prow. He pulled out a small rubber bag.

'There she is...'

It contained a wax pouch of tobacco and cigarette papers.

'...My life preserver.'

With one hand he crafted two roll-up cigarettes and passed one to Finch.

'Thank you.'

Finch handed him his lighter... the lighter that had saved him. That and a half-remembered lecture by some anonymous instructor at Aldershot who'd given a group of RAMC officers a crash course in basic weapons training prior to shipping out for the Cape and had painstakingly – to a bored-beyond-belief classroom – described in forensic detail the properties of a bullet.

'That's it, hold 'ar steady. You doin' a good job, Dr Finch.'

Cole puffed on his cigarette and gazed out to sea.

'Well I s'pose I do owe you some sort of explanation,' he mused. 'I mean... after all you been through...'

Chapter Twenty-Two

While Finch held the tiller, Cole smoked and finished the story he had been meaning to tell… before the police had shown up. Four weeks ago, he began, Pickersgill's mission boat, the *Kittiwake*, a thirty-footer, had been chartered by some out-of-towners up from London, supposedly for scientific purposes – 'this Freeland Corporation,' he said.

'Dryden made the introductions. Did it discreet. According to instruction, Sid and his crew were to take 'ar out o'er the Dogger Bank. These so-called scientists, they were goin' to monitor some of the fishing stocks. "Oceanographers" they call themselves.

'There were two o' them, these academics, an Englishman and a yeller 'un, some sort of Oriental… I don't know. Had some gear with them, electronic, which was carried on board in a packing crate.'

It was all done in secret, added Cole; no one else knew about the trip or saw them boarding. It was prearranged that they were to be over the Dogger Bank at a specific time – 8 p.m. on October 21st.

'Trafalgar Day, as it happens,' Cole added. ''Ole Nelson, he born round these parts, y'know – Burnham Thorpe.'

Finch nodded.

'Sid ask me t'crew that night,' he explained, 'but I'm already commit to a crab boat that weekend… Shame, it pay better for once. But ole Sid, he know right away that the academic, the English one… reckon he military… armed forces. *You* know wha's like, Doctor, can spot 'em a mile orf…'

It was true.

'...An' the gear they carryin'? Well Bertie Brandon he reco'nise it right away... A wireless radio set... big coil transmitter an' a battery pack. He's in South Africa too, see. Royal Engineers. Be relayin' signals from the army scouts outside o'Mafeking. An' the Oriental? Everyone call him a Chinaman. But Bertie, he reckon the li'l fucker Japanese. You pardon my French.'

Finch waved away the apology.

'Just like we seein' in the pictures... the *noos*-papers – you know, all skinny, round spectacles... an' dressin' like *us* now, like some London toff – suit, cravat...'

'That's a stereotype, Nathan.'

'Call it wha' you want, Dr Finch. Make no difference...'

He paused to redo his sail.

'Anyway,' he continued, 'tha' night, eight o'clock, just as I 'stablish, they get to within a mile range o'the Hull fleet. Well guess what they do?'

'Pickersgill's crew?'

'No, these other two...'

He said it with contempt.

'...these "oceanographers"...'

'I don't know,' Finch shrugged.

'Send up a kite... Big thing, silk and bamboo, with a wire attached back down to the boat. For "meteorological purposes", or so they claim. As if a seaman hant got the gumption to work out the weather for his self. But really, it's an aerial as you call it. And then they start transmittin' is what. You know, a Morse tapper, the Jap doin' all the tippy-tappy.'

Asked Finch: 'You mean, what, *radio telegraphy*?'

Ahead, out to sea, hung a thick grey curtain of rain. It would be moving inshore, Finch knew. They were in its path.

'If you say so, Doctor,' said Cole. 'Keep at it awhile, they do. Dint take too much to figure later that they tryin'a 'tract the attention o'those ole Russian warships. Just a con trick. You know, Japanese chatter in the North Sea bein' picked up soon enough on a battleship wireless receiver...?'

Cole was watching the horizon, too. Finch deduced he didn't like what he saw.

'…Them Russians, they soon hear the chatter, then when they see those Hull trawlers, they put two'n two together, make five. They think they really *are* Japanese gunboats an' start firin'. You know, just like the Russkies in the *noos*-papers's sayin' all along. Tha's wha' Sid think anyway.'

'Christ!'

'Tha's right. 'xactly what I say.'

Finch was stunned, momentarily speechless.

'Nathan. If this is true… If it can be *proven* to be true, then this is *devastating*… The issue is exactly as serious as Pickersgill was trying to claim… Something of national… *international* significance. Whoever did this could be about to start a war. At the very least they've got several good men killed, and I include Pickersgill and his friends among their number.'

'No doubt aboot that, Dr Finch. But who? Who *you* think do such a thing?'

He hauled a lanyard and instructed Finch to push hard on the tiller, swinging her about. The boom veered right across and they had to duck. They were heading back to shore.

'Therein lies the problem, Nathan. God knows I've had my own brush with them in the past… the secret service, military intelligence… Thing is, they all move in mysterious ways… and every country's got their own versions. Usually they work against each other, sometimes they act in consort, operating on a level that most governments can't. But there are plenty of reasons for wanting to start a war between Britain and Russia, *that's* for sure. There are plenty of people willing it right here in our own parliament. But can you imagine if, say… I don't know, *Germany* was behind this thing… whether it be state-sponsored, or a freelance, rogue operation…? I mean, a war between Britain and Russia would suit them down to the ground.'

'I'm thinkin' along those lines myself, Doctor.'

With the wind behind it and its load lightened, the boat picked up speed.

'So what happened?' said Finch. 'Pickersgill gets back from sea, and *then* what?'

'Well, back ashore, these "scientists" disappear into the night along with their gear. Dryden starts taking care of Pickersgill's crew on Freeland's behalf. You know, gin'em a few extra quid on the absolute guarantee they keep their traps shut. Thing is none of 'em actually *sees* what's goin' on over the Dogger Bank that night…'

The boat was zipping along now, skimming over the swell.

'Hold on… Pickersgill… I got the impression he was *witness* to events – the Russian warships, the trawlers? Saw it all?'

Cole rolled Finch a new cigarette. He lit it for him.

'No… not at all… You makin' an *assumption*, Doctor…'

Finch thought for a moment of the venerable detective he knew in Cape Town, Harry Brookman, who'd chastised him repeatedly for his impulsive conclusion-jumping.

'…Just said that he was *there*, tha's all. Course, Crabby Stamshaw, Buster Compton, they never look'a *noos*-paper in their lives. But Sid, he soon read aboot what's goin' on out there at sea that night. Say he think he hear rumbles, big guns, see flashes in the fog after they leave the area. Round midnight or so. Anyway, he start t'smell sumpin' fishy. Now *he* put two an' two together. So he resolve t'do, in his mind, what he think is the right thing…'

'You mean go to the police?'

''xactly… Get to the bottom of it… But o'course the police *is* Superintendent Dryden. He shut Sid up. He tell him he's a "fantasist", he call 'im… He got a screw loose.'

'So Sid takes it elsewhere?'

'Again, 'xactly right… Ole Sid, he do sumpin' bold. He call a meetin' o' the Fishermen's Collective, the local crab boys. Goin' t'get 'em all come down the Oddfellows Hall. He even invite a local *noos*-paper man. Get it all on record. Plans t'tell 'em all 'boot what happen that night – the radio, the Japanese, the Russians…'

The boat was going too fast for her own good. Cole took in some sail, slowing her.

'Now in my defence, Doctor, ole Sid, he already tell me 'boot it all. Swear me to secrecy. I tell 'im t'keep his mouth shut. T'ent nothin' he can do t'bring those Hull boys back. An' nothin' he can achieve by takin' on the likes of Dryden and those higher up.'

'I hate to say it, but you were right… I mean about Pickersgill…'

He nodded his appreciation.

'An' then the inevitable. Dryden, he get wind o'the meetin' tha's goin' a-happen two day hence. He get to Fat Pete and the Fishermen's Collective first. Tell 'em all in advance that Sid, he men'lly defective, him just sore aboot some petty local charterin' matter and that by raisin' it in public like he intend, it mean ole tax man's goin' a-come in', pook his nose around in their business, stop all the back-hand trade they do – fish they sell black market to the big hotels and the like. Get 'em all in trouble. Get 'em all in debt.'

'And so, what, Pickersgill's an outcast as a consequence, a black sheep?'

With the tiller tucked under his arm, Finch tried crafting a roll-up himself. He packed the tobacco in way too loosely and half of it fell out when he went to light it.

'Worse'n that. Dryden gets this Freeland lot back in to pay *them* all, the Fishermen's Collective, a handsome slice… on the sly, o'course… cash. Recompense, if you like, for all the "inconvenience" that Sid, this one l'il ole boy's caused. They dint mean t'open no can o'worms, they say. They just humble "Oceanographers"…'

He spat the word out again.

'…Dint mean to cause a stir. Want a-say sorry an' all that. Apologise. And o'course Sid's meetin' gets cancelled.'

Cole made Finch a fresh, tight roll-up. The wind was starting to buffet from different directions, the water getting choppier. Finch steadied himself as he lit it up.

'But Christ,' said Cole, nodding Finch his reassurance. 'I mean these boys, they get paid *huge*. Tens o'pounds. An' the promise there's plen'y more where that come from, if they can all sit tight. More Freeland business in future…

'I must stress, *none* of the Endthorpe fishermen knows aboot the Japanese feller and all that stuff, by the way. *Still* don't. Word never get out aboot that. They all think Sid just some busybody, some God-botherin' do-gooder out a-spoil their big payday – their mistrust pretty much confirmed when ole Sid go orf on the run.'

'But what about the deaths… Sid… his crew…?'

Cole shrugged.

'Accidents… Enough said… It *happens*… Everyday hazard… And Sid… When they find out he die too… Well he'll just turn out to be a rum 'un after all…'

'What about the dead men's families? Didn't they think it odd… a mighty coincidence?'

The first rain hit. But the big squall was still behind them. It seemed just a prelude. They hunched themselves against it, Cole playing the sail the whole time.

'That for me's the saddest thing, Dr Finch. Ole Crabby… Buster… Neither one of them's "thinkers", as you might say. Bertie Brandon too for that matter – their brains made o' dynamite it still wouldn't blow their hats off. Yet Sid, once he start yarpin' to them 'boot this stuff with the Russian navy, he put ideas in their heads. An o'course, none too bright as they are, *they* go straight to Superintendent Dryden…'

He gave a look that suggested to Finch he knew what happened next.

'…What you might say a case o'people cutting their losses. The Fishermen's Collective, they're all wise enough to be discreet 'boot the money they come into. Right careful. No trouble. But ole Bertie Brandon, the little bit he'd already copped for the keepie-quiet, and some more they give the *Kittiwake* boys besides, he's fool enough to start blowin' it all on the drink. Drawin' attention… enough to convince Dryden's lot that them off the *Kittiwake*'s a liability, a dead loss. Literally. Hence, four men now gorn. Though I tell you, boy… The first three… Their widows… This Freeland? Pays 'em handsome. I mean *handsome.* More money they ever 'arn a lifetime. Enough to make 'em *believe* their husbands died in accidents at sea…'

He gave a sardonic smile.

'…Can't blame 'em. We're poor people. Fishin's no money. This sort o'thing never happen t'people like us. An' Dryden, he got the town in his pocket. Never been more clear. You cross him, you finished. You tattle, he know aboot it… Though not any more.'

Cole was scanning the sea now, watching the movement of the water.

'And so, what, the *Kittiwake*'s crew were killed – three men, then Sid?' said Finch. 'Me too, nearly… Just so everyone can sit on their fat piles of hush money?'

Cole blew out his cheeks.

'Tha's one way t'put it. Maybe. But *me*? These fishermen… the others? I reckon they just *scared*. Know they take money they don't deserve and feelin' guilty 'boot it. A-feared a-bein' rumbled. And are just naturally suspicious o'anyone who arrive in town askin' the wrong sort o'questions…'

He mused on it.

'…Conspiracy o'silence, Doctor? More like conspiracy o'*fear.* Way I look at it – Buster, Crabby, Bertie… Sid. They're *warnings* to 'em… Crows nailed to a fence… Christ knows they'll shit their britches when they find out ole Dryden's been done for too!'

He hauled the lanyard, pulling the sail in closer still as they got within distance of the breakers. Cole was right, noted Finch, the current had already taken them well to the west, just empty shingle beach ahead, beginning to merge into more flats of sand and mud.

'An' tha's why I'm gettin' out a-here, Doctor. I'm a marked man. Guilt by association… with Sid… an' now with *you*. Word'll be out *we* crossed paths… Oh… an' I never take a penny, by the way.'

Finch had no idea what he was supposed to be steering towards; it was a struggle to keep the tiller under control.

'Just run with the current,' instructed Cole. 'Let the boat do the work.'

'So what about Ursa?' asked Finch. 'What *does* it mean?'

He sensed that he had perhaps asked a question too far.

'Don't rightly know,' said Cole, eyes on the water still. 'Tha's a word Sid heard on his boat. Like a code word.'

They were three hundred yards off shore. There were still the breakers to contend with.

'But then, get this – me and Sid. End o'October. After the rumpus with the Fisherman's Collective. One night, when we know he not around, we go over to Dryden's house. He live on a back road out in the pine trees. Ole Sid, o'course, he get his Christian cold feet; don't wan' a-break in – a sin and all that – so I make him stand lookout instead...

'But I get in there, Doctor. Smash a pane an' unlock the back door. Do some snoopin' around. Ole Dryden, he got this back room he use as an office. There some stuff in there I see... some handwritten notes. But nothin' as you might say, *'crimin-atin'*... Then again, he's not going to be printin' up dossiers o'his misdeeds, is he?'

'*What* exactly? What did you see?'

They were no longer running ahead of the storm. The grey sheet was closing in.

'...I don't know. I can't make it all out. An' o'course I can't rouse suspicions by takin' sumpin' obvious. But I do manage to grab *this*...'

He reached into the rubber bag under the seat at the bow, the one he'd kept his tobacco in. He pulled out a ripped page from a notebook.

'Tha's in Dryden's own hand. Only thing I could find with any reference.'

He passed it to Finch. It had on it, inscribed in pencil, the words: *Ursa, November 4th 1904*.

'What happened on the 4th of November?' asked Finch.

'I don't know...'cept tha's the day Crabby Stamshaw died.'

'And he was the first of Pickersgill's crew... to be killed?'

'Yup.'

'So you think it's an order? An *execution* order?'

Cole shrugged.

'Seems a dramatic way a-puttin' it. But maybe.'

And then the real rain hit, *hard* – a ferocious lashing.

'The families...' Finch asked. 'Crabby... Bertie... the other one...'

The boat wobbled.

'Buster...'

'Can I speak to them?'

They were having to shout now to be heard.

'Are you out yer head, Doctor? You a marked man. We both are. How the hell you think you gorn do that anyway?'

'I don't know... You're right.'

Finch yelled it out in short sharp bursts, over a wind that was now starting to howl, about his investigation of a company called Freeland operating from an address in Bayswater, west London, and of the two men he had followed – one of them, the 'lavender man' who had warned him to stay away from matters which didn't concern him; and the other, the oversized, strong-looking freakish man, and how he had seen him loitering outside his house the other night.

Cole stopped hauling on his lanyard. Behind the water dripping off it, his face was suddenly stony.

'You see this man, Doctor, the big 'un, you in real trouble. We all are. I'm *serious.* Ole Sid heard... *I* heard, that he once pulled a tongue clean out o'someone's head...'

'Pickersgill said that Bertie Brandon had been decapitated.'

'Tha's right.'

The way Cole said it carried a weight of implication.

'So, you go on the run with your family... what happens after that?'

Cole flipped his cigarette into the air. The boat started to pitch and roll. Finch clung on tight.

'Have to ride 'ar out,' bellowed Cole and hauled in the sail completely. It was hard work; he collapsed back on the deck, sitting right next to Finch.

'You mind I have another swig?'

Finch passed the flask to him.

'Well, I reckon I discharge my duty so far,' Cole hollered. 'Sid tell me you might show up...'

He gave the flask back.

'...He say you do, it probably mean he's dead. In which case I'm to tell you everythin' I know. Which I just have.'

'You were a good friend to him, Nathan.'

'*What?*'

Finch yelled it again.

'*You were a good friend to him, Nathan!*'

'But as for what happen next, as you ask?' replied Cole. 'I think I just have a change o'plan...'

Finch scrunched his brow. Water streamed off it.

'How do you mean?'

'That body o' ole Dryden. It wash up sooner or later, or the torso will, just like I say. Always do. No matter what you do – weight it, tie it, a body has an uncanny way a-declarin' itself... 'specially a murdered one. An' I can tell you now, they'll want a-pin it on someone. So that's *one* problem. And two...'

'Two?'

'...There's not only someone know I do it, but he now also know everythin' *I* do about this Freeland, this Ursa business... Everythin' to do with Sid Pickersgill... And a bit too much more besides...'

'What do you mean?'

'I got a wife, Dr Finch, I got a child... They on *your* tail? They only one step from me. And if this big feller...'

They were two hundred yards from the beach, running parallel to shore.

'Way I see it there's a very simple solution to *my* problems. Tie everythin' up neat and tidy in a nice l'il bow – keep my secret safe, my family safe and also hands the authorities the murderer they be lookin' for.'

Cole rose and lunged for his rifle.

'Sorry…'

And, with a sharp horizontal swing, he caught Finch square on the left temple. Cole looped the rifle over Finch's shoulder as he tumbled backwards into the water.

Chapter Twenty-Three

'See… there…?' he was told. 'Take a good look.'

It was four storeys high and painted a soft grey with white sills and frames around the rectangular, multi-paned windows that the British seemed so fond of.

There seemed a presence, an arrogance to the building – those pillars either side of the door, like an image of a Greek temple he had once seen in a school book. Though its most arresting feature was what was hanging over that entrance – a large, horizontally banded tricolour in white, blue and red. Beneath it was mounted the emblem of a black double-headed eagle.

'Mr Plavinas?'

Mordecai stared at the flag.

The horrors that have been inflicted in its name.

'Mr Plavinas?!'

'Yes?'

'Are you ready?'

It was the valet doing the talking again. His name was Weathers, Mordecai had learned, an appropriate one, he thought, for one who spent most of his time toting an umbrella.

'The suit. How does it fit?' asked the man's master.

The suit?

The rich man stood there, his fur coat round his shoulders, his ridiculous little dog in his arms, nestled on his belly. He stared intently at Mordecai. He made him distinctly uncomfortable.

'The suit… Is good,' he said.

'It *is* good,' he was corrected.

They had had him measured up in a street called Savile Row, a far cry from the Jewish tailors who had patched together denim in the lumberyards on the Daugava River – old men who sat and gossiped and kvetched in their dim, cramped workshops about the ongoing Russification of Livonia and shrugged at the creeping curtailment of their liberties.

My, how much better things were under the Germans, they would say – the good old enlightened Germans, friends of the Jew.

Savile Row hosted the finest tailors in London… in the *world*, the rich man had declared, and put the suit on his account. He had stood and watched while Mordecai stripped – the men with the tape measures fussing over him, prodding and poking and toying with his inseam.

The colour of it was a light brown… 'beige' he was told. It was not dissimilar to the one sported by the rich man, his evident new patron. Mordecai could not believe that such material had been spun from the cocoons of worms fed on mulberry leaves. It seemed like a proposition from a fairy tale. The cloth was as fine and sleek as his old clothes were coarse and rough.

'Be a dear boy. Turn around for me,' said the man.

Mordecai complied, reluctantly.

The new plaything.

'My, you do look splendid. We'll make a gentleman out of you yet.'

The gentleman… A bit of arse.

Then, lumbering up behind them came the huge, freakish, thick-necked brute, the one whose handiwork in the old warehouse created an image that had proven impossible to shake.

Mordecai wondered again whether he shouldn't just run.

The Brute… I could outpace him easily… surely?

But he knew it wasn't that simple. Human bondage took many forms. There were no chains. But there were other ways of holding a man captive. And he had seen what the Brute was capable of. The Brute didn't speak, just flicked his head in a 'let's go' kind of way. There was no light in his black, close-set eyes. He didn't even seem human.

Was he human?

The rich man set down his pathetic little dog. He attached a lead to its jewel-encrusted collar. Weathers, the manservant, led the way. They must have been an unusual sight, this unholy caravan, thought Mordecai: the fawning valet; the big-bellied rich man in his fur coat, his cane and his silly little pet; and then the monster, the Brute, the freak of nature.

They turned left onto Lyall Street and followed the line of yet more elegant townhouses. There were cars and horse-drawn taxis going back and forth, delivery men in their carts and wagons. There were members of household staff huddled, furtively puffing on the crafty cigarettes that were no doubt banned within. A scullery maid scrubbed at steps with a bucket of soapy water and a wire brush. She looked up, then quickly looked down again, averting her eyes.

There was no smell here in this part of town. The streets were clean. Even the gutters were clean. There was so much obvious wealth, Mordecai found it hard to be believe they were in the same city – the city of slums and hovels and near-slave labour down at the docks.

'Now, I require your complete attention, Mordecai,' said the rich man. 'You hear me?'

'Yes.'

'I want you to memorise this route… this route from the embassy – every street, every path, every cut-through. I want you to know every shopfront, every crossing point…'

They ambled on, reduced to the speed of the pathetic little dog, which got tired after a hundred yards and started whining, forcing the rich man – 'Daddy' – to pick it up again. He kissed it and petted it.

They soon arrived at a square, as the British liked to call them – actually an oblong – which extended along the main east–west road, a set of gardens with grand houses lining either side.

The traffic here was much busier, rushing round the corner at one end in an endless stream – carts and wagons and several motorcars. A horse-drawn omnibus, the number 11, came to a halt and Mordecai watched passengers get on and off. A man on a bicycle nearly fell off at the sight of the Brute.

A bored newspaper boy on the corner sat behind a box with its hand-drawn headline: *Daily Mail – Russia's 'Mad Dog Squadron': Exclusive*. An elderly man in a top hat, with a finely dressed woman on his arm, tutted about how such a vulgar publication should have been allowed in these parts.

What would the newspapers be saying in St Petersburg?

The rich man put his hand up, the signal to stop.

'Eaton Square, Mordecai… the most expensive real estate in London… which probably makes it, by default, the most expensive real estate in the world.'

Mordecai had no reason to doubt it.

The townhouses set back behind the gardens were serviced by their own perimeter access road. They were, without question, magnificent. A rare burst of afternoon sun was reflecting off the white and cream. The porticoes, the columns… 'Doric.'

Was that how you said it?

Belgravia spelled money. But here? This square? This was an impossibly elevated level of affluence.

The square was lined with ornate gas lamps, black with gold trimmings; the gardens, too, were contained within black iron railings detailed with filigree. Behind the hedges, nannies wheeled perambulators and mothers held the hands of small, shining children.

'Here,' the man beckoned, bringing Mordecai to his side. 'I want you to study the traffic, to see which way it moves, how it flows. Traffic is like a stream of water coursing down a riverbed, Mordecai. You have to see how it strikes the banks, how it seeks out the deepest channel; note where it moves quickly, where the shallows lie…'

Mordecai didn't know why he said it, but the words flowed like the river the man had just been describing.

'And if I don't?'

The slap came hard, stinging, right across his face. It had been administered by the man himself. Mordecai was shocked less by the smarting in his cheek than the fact that it had been done so boldly and brazenly, right there in public.

'Might I remind you, Mordecai,' said the man, in the manner of one admonishing a mischievous child. 'That you have already borne witness to what can happen to our enemies...'

Mordecai straightened his tie – a reflex. He was already living the part.

'...And, if one can be indelicate for a moment, might I also point out that you still have family in Latvia – a mother and a sister in Riga, a sister with *children*...?'

Mordecai felt his blood rise, the pounding in his chest, heard a rushing sound in his ears.

'What you try to say!?'

The man put his hand up to stay him.

'At the moment they are being looked out for, perfectly safe. "Protected", if one might employ such crude terminology...'

Mordecai thought of the men in Stepney who would knock on his door.

'But your cooperation is most essential to the pursuance of this arrangement. Fail us, Mordecai, and I'm afraid we will not be able to prevent their lives from becoming *extremely* uncomfortable.'

The rage rose further. There was a thumping in his head.

'HOW DARE...!'

He was gripped so artfully and powerfully round his throat that he could make no sound. With a single, oversized hand, the Brute lifted him effortlessly and discreetly so that he was not only fighting for breath but also struggling to stay upright on his tiptoes. The Brute walked him a few steps to a recess in the railings, surrounded by bushes, and with a park bench in it.

I cannot breathe. My eyes, I cannot see.

There was a burning in his arteries. The more he sucked at air, willing it to fill his lungs, the less it came. As if for some comedic punctuation, his bowler hat fell off and rolled along the pavement.

After a minute of spluttering and gagging, the rich man gave the signal for the Brute to desist. Mordecai staggered, flopping against the bench, gulping in great lungfuls for all he was worth.

The man went back to petting his stupid dog, pulling out from a waxed bag some titbit, a sliver of meat. He raised his cane and pointed. It was as if what had just passed were all entirely reasonable.

'As for the circumstances, Mordecai, it is a case of perfect timing. Look around you…'

Look around me?

Mordecai did so, panting all the while, rubbing his throat, though he didn't know what he was supposed to see. The man beckoned for him to stand again.

'…London plane trees. A marvellous case of biological engineering, a hybrid, you know – part Oriental, part American sycamore. A hardy species, most suitable for urban use – highly wind resistant and, while we're at it, intriguingly asexual…'

He gave a little cough and dabbed his handkerchief to his mouth.

'…Though problematic, I must confess, for asthmatics – the fine hairs of the young leaves can get into the air. But the London plane tree, dear Mordecai, is, to our immense fortune, just the same as every other tree of its kind… It is deciduous…'

Deciduous?

'…It sheds its leaves in winter. Not two months ago this square would have been basking under sunshine dappled by a lush green canopy. But now…?'

A gardener was raking dead, wet leaves into piles.

'…As you can see, Mordecai, the upper windows of the building have a clear view right across the thoroughfare. And on this side, the north, there will be no sun in your eyes. The bare branches also provide enough of a screen to confuse those at ground level suddenly looking upwards. That and the glorious architectural triumph of Eaton Square – handiwork of Mr Thomas Cubitt – a sublime achievement in disorientation… Each house is *identical*.'

'What you want from me?'

'Aged twelve you enlisted in the Imperial Russian infantry,' said the man. 'You were a soldier for seven years.'

Mordecai spat the word out. '*Enlisted*... I not join, I kidnapped. A *khapper*... a "grabber" from the *Kahal*. The boys, they take us, send us away.'

'After basic training near St Petersburg you served in the regional reserve where you distinguished yourself as a marksman... a sharpshooter,' the man went on. 'As such you were attached to the 12th Siberian Rifle Regiment, which in July 1900 docked at Port Arthur as part of the Eight-Nation Army, on its way to relieve Peking. You were credited with twenty-four kills. *Clean* kills.'

'How you know?'

'Six months later, you unilaterally... How shall I say..."left" the service...'

How did they know?

'...Which also makes you, Mr Mordecai Plavinas, a deserter, liable to be executed should your whereabouts be notified to the authorities. Not that we should ever do such a thing. You are, after all, whether you know it or not, on our side.'

A khapper... He had been 'grabbed' again.

The rich man nodded to his valet. Weathers reached inside his jacket and handed Mordecai an envelope bound with a thick rubber band.

'Your down payment,' said Weathers.

Mordecai untucked the flap. It contained white sheets of paper, the size of a letter, promising '*to pay the bearer on demand*'.

The rich man relished Mordecai's confusion. He chuckled to himself.

'...But of course. How quaint...'

Do not mock me!

'...You've never seen such things before. Five-pound notes... "White fivers" in common parlance...'

Ten of them?

'Fifty… *fifty pounds*?!'

Mordecai felt weak in his legs. He sat on the bench.

'Half up front, the rest on completion,' said Weathers.

The valet brushed off the bowler and passed it back to Mordecai.

'You're a valuable member of our organisation, Mordecai,' declared the rich man. 'Take good care of it.'

He set his little dog down again. Weathers went to lead the way.

'Learn the terrain, Mordecai,' said the master. 'Follow the road down to Westminster and back. And pay special attention to this square, the routes in and out of it. Familiarise yourself. Make yourself at home.'

He turned to go.

Said Weathers: 'We will be in touch very soon.'

Chapter Twenty-Four

Annie sat on the bed and cracked the spine on the new book she had purchased on one of her wanderings down Charing Cross Road. She wondered whether Henry James' *The Golden Bowl* – raved about by the critics – was a novel she felt she *ought* to be reading rather than one she might genuinely enjoy. The prospect of a story about an outsider caught in a web of wealth, class and strained romance in the capital of the British Empire was subject matter, she suspected, she should perhaps steer clear of.

The telephone rang. The device, like everything in the penthouse suite, was not just something of function but also form. More than that, it was an object of beauty, all ivory and gold – genuine ivory, she figured, on the hand receiver anyway. She wondered what a poor elephant had done to deserve such an inglorious memorial.

She had a sudden, grimly ironic thought about the name of the new process of long-distance dialling, allowing callers to circumvent the operator, that was now possible in some parts – a 'trunk call'.

The hotel operator announced that it was Edward on the line. He was in Glasgow (still). Something to do with the Clyde shipyards. He would be there for another day or two, longer than he thought. He would have to travel to Liverpool directly to catch the boat. She should make her own way. He would meet her there on Saturday. Was that okay?

She had little choice, she knew. She had little say, either, in the fact that his secretary was with him again… or that said young woman, a surprise fellow traveller on their voyage – a belated honeymoon tour, of all things – would now be accompanying them to the United States.

As she hung up the phone, there was a knock at the door. Annie let the bellboy in. He was attired in a braided drummer-boy tunic and hat and brandishing clothing trailing from a wooden hangar, held beneath a paper covering.

'Suit… for Mr Pointer.'

'Thank you.'

'D'you want me to hang it in the wardrobe, Miss?'

'Hook on the door's fine.'

He attended to it.

'Right clever this dry cleaning, ain't it, Miss?' he chirruped.

Her thoughts were elsewhere.

'*Miss?*'

'I suppose so… yes,' she said, fumbling in her purse for some change. 'Tell you the truth, I'm not even sure how they do it.'

'Chemicals or something, Miss. Not right sure myself.'

She pressed some pennies into his hand.

'Thank you, Miss. Anything else I can do? The tray? Shall I take it away?'

He nodded at the pot, the cup and jug of milk on the tray on the dressing table and the remnants of toast, butter and preserves.

'No, that's fine.'

'Very good, Miss,' he said and left.

The penthouse suite contained everything Annie had imagined and more. It had burgundy velvet curtains, a Persian carpet, Queen Anne furniture, the biggest bed she had ever slept in, as well as the deepest bath she had ever sunk into. There was no food, no luxury, no delight, that was not a telephone call away, twenty-four hours a day.

There was a bedroom, a bathroom, a drawing room for entertaining. There were top-lit oil paintings on the wall – French and Impressionistic. Originals too. If not of the masters, then of those whose work was of passable quality.

Annie went to the French doors onto the terrace and looked out across the Thames with its endless stream of barges and tugs and river transports, the panorama bisected by Cleopatra's Needle – Hungerford Railway Bridge to the right, the dilapidated Waterloo Bridge to the left, covered in ugly scaffolding. There were the Pleasure Gardens on the South Bank opposite. Were they worthy of being a destination on another of her epic strolls? She hadn't yet explored the other side of the river, around by the grand Waterloo station.

She wolfed the last of the toast, polished off the contents of the coffee pot, laced up her boots and pulled on a hacking jacket and sensible cloche hat. (Why, oh why, in this country, did she *always* have to wear a hat?)

On exiting the lift in the lobby, she crossed the marbled floor, heading for the rear exit to the Embankment. The place was busy, people standing around with luggage, waiting to check out. She sought solitude. She had her Henry James in her bag. She would walk for a while, then sit somewhere and read. She had also sneaked in a packet of cigarettes – Player's Navy Cut, a secret habit – and trusted that she could enjoy her own company, unchaperoned.

As she headed for the revolving door, she heard her name being called. It was the lanky, fawning concierge. Probably a confirmation of some other errand that had been run on Edward's behalf.

'Sorry, Miss, but there's a gentleman waiting for you,' he said, throwing her somewhat. 'Says it's important. He's been here a while.'

He led her to a recessed area off the busy lobby, set back behind potted palms, where a man sat in an armchair drinking tea, his raincoat slung over the armrest, Homburg on top. He rose as he saw her. He was middle-aged, smallish, was wiry in his physique and sported an anonymous grey pinstripe suit. He was bald on top, with dark but greying hair around the sides. He had a full moustache and wore round, wire-framed spectacles around brown beady eyes. To Annie he looked like an insurance salesman.

'Mrs Pointer?' he ventured.

'Yes.'

He nodded thanks to the concierge, who departed.

'Sorry to ambush you like this, ma'am. My name is Coates.'

He gave her an apologetic look and raised an index finger, as if to suggest that he'd forgotten a detail of the ritual. He fumbled in his jacket and produced a leather wallet. He flipped it open to show a Metropolitan Police badge and identity card.

Annie, from her previous scrapes, knew enough to at least convey the pretence of studying it. Though in this case it got her attention.

'*Scotland Yard?*' she emphasised.

'That's right, ma'am.'

'Oh.'

Thoughts rushed through her head.

'Edward… Is it *Edward*?!' she panicked.

'Your husband, ma'am? No.'

He gestured.

'Please… sit.'

She took the edge of the chaise longue opposite, between them a coffee table. Despite the busyness at the front desk, the civility of a five-star hotel continued – the hushed chatter of the guests, the silent business of the staff, porters artfully wheeling trolleys of suitcases.

'Can I get you anything?' the man asked.

'I'd rather you just told me what this is about,' she urged. 'Detective… Is it *Detective*?'

'Detective will do, ma'am. I'm afraid at Special Branch we're not permitted to divulge rank.'

'Special Branch?'

'New unit, ma'am. Let's just say our business concerns matters of national security.'

She began fussing with her bag, rearranging its contents nervously and unnecessarily. Coates watched as she removed her book and set it on the coffee table, followed by her gloves, her cigarettes.

He picked up the Henry James and flicked through it.

'Hear it's all the rage, this one.'

She took it back.

'Some other time, perhaps.'

Coates rolled his eyes and reached into his inside jacket pocket again.

'Mrs Pointer, I don't know whether this is an indelicate subject...'

'Indelicate?'

It was a photograph, about six inches by four. He handed it to her.

'...but I wonder if you happen to know *this* man?'

She did, instantly. Despite the sepia tinge and the blurred reproduction, it was a posed portrait of a man in the uniform of a captain in the Royal Army Medical Corps. It had been taken pre-embarkation for South Africa, 1899, in some army studio, a standard shot, one arm resting on a pillar, pith helmet in the crook of the other, some kind of painted backdrop of trees and a triumphal arch in the background – an absurd suggestion of Greek or Roman glory. She once had a copy of it back home... till, on engagement to Edward, it had mysteriously 'disappeared'.

'Yes... Dr Ingo Finch,' she said.

He tucked the photograph away.

'Look... Mrs Pointer... I don't like to ask, but have you *seen* him of late... Dr Finch? I know that you were former associates and—'

'Please, Detective, I'm not sure what you're getting at.'

'It's just that we looked up his file... his military file... *your* file. When I say associates... Yes, you served together in South Africa but there's... I mean, you were...' he fumbled, '...you know...'

'We were *what*?'

If there was going to be an exhumation of her former private life, she was going to make damn sure she was indignant about it. She shoved her possessions back in her bag again, with purpose.

'...It's just that there's a gap in the records – for *both* of you – a period marked "classified".'

It was something of a relief to Annie that he had gone off on a different tack.

'I'm afraid I'm not at liberty to—'

He raised his palms in apology.

'No, Mrs Pointer, *no*. I wouldn't dream of it. Classified is classified. I'm an ex-military man myself. Royal Navy. Seven Years in Way-High.'

'Way-High?'

'Wei-Hei-Wei… Port Edward as we call it. The China Station. Was attached to Royal Naval Intelligence… Signals… It's why I'm here alone. Normally I'd have a constable with me. You know, working as a pair.'

She nodded that she appreciated his discretion.

'It's just that, if you *have* seen him – Dr Finch – and I know you're not long in the country… I *do* need to know.'

He pulled out a notepad and pencil and shrugged a 'do-you-mind?' She nodded that it was okay.

'It's no secret, Detective. I saw him… *we* saw him, my husband and I, on Saturday evening. He was with his lady friend, a young woman called Maude… quite charming… I didn't catch her last name… oh hang on, yes… Cutler… *Carter*… a schoolmistress…'

His pencil was blunt.

'Sorry, ma'am,' he said, as he took out a penknife and whittled it to a point.

He tried again.

'There, that's better. Saturday night, you say…? A Miss Maude Carter…?'

'Yes… We ran into each other at a Chinese restaurant in Soho… the Cathay…'

He pulled an approving face.

'Very nice, ma'am. Hear it's a right feast. The missus has been pestering me to take her. Loved the grub when I was out there, the Far East. Miss it rotten. Have always been trying to explain it to her.'

Sincere as he might seem, Annie didn't feel like getting side-tracked into pleasantries, though she knew – the small talk, the penknife, the police badge – it was more than likely a tactic, a means of lulling her into a false sense of security.

'It was a purely chance encounter,' she went on. 'Dr Finch had no idea I… *we*… my husband and I, were even in London. We hadn't seen each other since the war, you understand. We went our separate ways in early 1902. Two and a half years ago.'

'Your husband can corroborate all this?'

She knew from his reaction that her face thundered disapproval.

'Is my word not good enough?'

'No… no… Nothing like that. Forgive me, ma'am. I mean the lady friend…'

He referred to his notes.

'…Miss Carter, too. Just so we can cross-reference details, times… Build a comprehensive picture.'

She started to get concerned again.

'Why, what's *happened*?'

He stopped his note-taking.

'I'll come to that in a moment, ma'am, if I may… I need to be clear on movements, times. This was the only occasion you saw him, you say?'

'No.'

'Please, go on…'

She huffed.

'Very well… Monday.'

'Monday?'

'Yes. I met him again.'

'Where?'

'Here, right outside…'

She pointed across the lobby, towards the river exit.

'…on the Embankment… the gardens.'

'You were with your husband again?'

'No.'

'Oh.'

The word hung awkwardly while she waited for to him to catch up with his pencil-work.

'It was just after lunch. Half past one… two o'clock-ish. He'd been in the neighbourhood… Again, a chance encounter… Well not *completely* chance… I mean he had come into the hotel first… asked reception call up to the room. When he found out I wasn't in… that *we* weren't in… he went and sat in the gardens for a smoke. I just happened to be walking past.'

'I see…'

He jotted some more, breathing heavily in concentration while he did so. Whatever had been said seemed to carry significance.

'Were you aware that he'd been at Somerset House?'

She decided to play ignorant. It was plausible for a non-native not to know.

'I'm not entirely sure what Somerset House is. A library?'

'The Public Records Office.'

She thought he'd bought it.

'What did he say… What did he talk about… Dr Finch… The first occasion?'

'Saturday…? It was just polite stuff really. I mean, he'd never met Edward before, and we'd never met Maude… Miss Carter. It was all fairly superficial. To tell you the truth we were probably a bit shell-shocked by the encounter. I mean, what are the odds? Edward and I, we asked them on to a show afterwards… the Café Royal… but they declined. Had to get back.'

Coates scrawled on.

'And on the Monday? What did he talk about *then*?'

She paused for a moment. She had been told things by Finch in the strictest confidence and did not wish to betray it. She thought, given that he had already been questioned by the police, it was safe to rehash information that was probably already in their domain.

'Well… there was that awful business with Mr Pickersgill. I had no idea on the Saturday that Dr Finch had taken in a man who was clearly ill and in a desperate situation. It must have been weighing on his mind. I'm supposing that's the reason he left early. But then, yes, on Monday, he *did* tell me about it. He was quite shaken. He said he had acted in the interest of a poor fellow who had turned up on his doorstep and was not only suffering from possible influenza from sleeping rough, but appeared to be afflicted by paranoid delusions…'

'Delusions?'

'Yes, fearing for his own safety… So he took him in under his own roof, just temporarily, only to discover that, when he returned on Saturday night, the man had not just robbed him of some of his possessions, but had then wound up dead… *murdered.*'

In the lounge, the string quartet started up. Vivaldi's *The Four Seasons* – 'Spring'. It sounded a bit thin with just four instruments, thought Annie.

'Did Dr Finch tell you that he himself had been brought in for questioning the day before in *connection* with the murder?'

'Actually he *did*, yes. He was very disturbed by the accusation. He thought it frankly ridiculous that anyone should think he might somehow be culpable. But he also said he'd been swiftly exonerated. He did add that he *was* culpable in the sense that he blamed himself indirectly for Pickersgill's death. He should have kept him out of harm's way.'

'Meaning?'

Had she said too much?

'I don't know, referred him somewhere or something, some medical establishment, I suppose?… The police maybe…?'

'And why didn't he?'

'I really don't know. But he did say that the next morning, after the man's disappearance, he *was* on his way to the police station to report it all.'

The detective wrote some more and collected his thoughts.

'Somerset House… the Public Records Office… It's a national archive, ma'am… personal details, census returns… Do you think it likely that Dr Finch had been in there to seek information… look something up… perhaps with regard to tracking someone down?'

'Goodness… I don't know… I really couldn't say.'

'The clerk there has furnished us with information as to the type of thing Dr Finch was researching.'

'Like what?'

'I'm not at liberty to say, ma'am. But I can tell you Dr Finch was a man with specific intent.'

'*Intent?*'

The detective let out a sigh. He leaned back. She could tell he was searching for the right words.

'I don't know quite how to say this, Mrs Pointer, but you are a very lucky woman.'

'Lucky? How so?'

'This Dr Finch... the one you talk about in such an affectionate...'

He checked himself.

'...*considerate* manner... He is a very dangerous man.'

She laughed.

'Finch? Come on!'

He leaned forward.

'The police in Hertfordshire now have every reason to believe he *did* kill Sidney Pickersgill, ma'am... He was shot with Finch's own gun, to begin with... The body had been moved and dumped, with a very poor attempt to disguise Pickersgill as a thief.'

'That's just ridiculous!'

'On Tuesday morning, two days ago, Dr Finch then went absent from his work. After laying a false trail, he took a train to Endthorpe on the Norfolk coast, home, as it happens, to the late Sidney Pickersgill. We also have good reason to believe that Pickersgill was aware of Dr Finch's past – something that happened in South Africa. Maybe he was using it against him. Blackmail, possibly. We don't know yet...

'What we *do* know is that a man fitting Finch's description made himself unwelcome there, angered some of the locals. Yesterday morning, Wednesday, on confirming his identity, the Norfolk Constabulary rearrested him in connection with the murder of Sidney Pickersgill. He was placed in the custody of the local police superintendent. Neither of them have been seen since.'

Annie sat in stony silence.

'Now here's the thing, suspicions were aroused when some footwear of this arresting officer… a pair of wading boots… items of clothing he was last seen wearing, in the company of Finch… were found washed up on the shore at Blakeney, the place where the arrest was made.'

'That doesn't mean—'

'This morning, the body of said police superintendent pitched up on the shingle beach just to the west of there. It had been knocked about by a rough sea and was pretty bloated, but there was enough physical evidence to suggest that the man had been shot… Twice, as a matter of fact.'

'Shot?'

'Most likely with a .303 calibre weapon… a rifle… the bullets had passed right through.'

'I still don't see—'

'Mrs Pointer… Does Dr Finch have a problem… with alcohol… drinking… in your estimation?'

'I mean, he likes a drop, who doesn't?'

'Is he a man, in your experience, prone to rages… blackouts even…? Is he capable of things, perhaps even *violent* things, beyond that suggested by his everyday persona?'

She was starting to question it herself.

'I really couldn't say. As I told you, I hadn't seen him in a long time.'

'Dr Finch was seen to have an altercation with Mr Pickersgill in his local pub a few days before he died.'

She shrugged. There really was no opinion she could form.

He exhaled a whistle.

'Like I say, you were lucky.'

'And what, I'm still in danger…? Not in danger…? *What?*'

The first movement, the *Allegro*, had finished. The quartet took a polite round of applause.

'I would say *not*, Mrs Pointer, for this very reason… We also found some of Dr Finch's clothing – the clobber he was last seen in – washed up further still along the Norfolk coast, near Wells… his rucksack too, along with a Lee–Enfield rifle – a *.303* calibre Lee–Enfield rifle – standard army issue, just like his pistol… There's no body as of yet, but it's only a matter of time.'

'Are… are you saying…?'

'They were last seen alone on the beach… Finch… the superintendent. We've no concrete evidence, but… putting two and two together…'

Annie felt a swirl, a sudden rush, as if she were instantly detached from her surroundings.

'You mean…?'

'Most likely he killed again…'

'No, I… I… mean *Finch*.'

The musicians eased into the slow *Largo*.

'Yes ma'am, almost certainly… *Dead*…'

–

Looking back, Annie didn't remember the next bit – saying goodbye to the detective, or her leaving the hotel. She found herself by the Covent Garden Market in a daze, lost in an early morning crowd, stumbling into people, then drifting over to the Charing Cross Road, retracing the steps she'd taken only yesterday – some subliminal means of repeating the past, she told herself later, as if to prevent the future from occurring again.

She got lost in thoughts of South Africa – of Finch, of his stubbornness, his kindness and, in the last few days, his sadness. And she thought of how, in her darkest hour, when they were on the run, facing the cruellest of ends, he had saved her… saved her life.

That Finch might be dead was, in itself, perhaps not unsurprising. She had considered more than once that she, and especially *he*, might be on borrowed time – not that it had lessened the blow. But the stuff about his rages, his violence…? She supposed that the detective would be travelling up to St Albans right now to impart the very same news to a heartbroken Maude.

There was one hope. As Detective Coates had flipped his notebook shut, tucked it away, she had asked a question. Some instinct had compelled it.

'We just have to have the police in Norfolk ask a few more questions,' he said. 'At the bed and breakfast where he stayed and suchlike.'

'If Finch were on the run… or on some kind of secret, murderous mission,' she replied, 'what on earth was he doing checking into a guest house?'

The detective had stood, pulling on his raincoat.

'He used an assumed name, ma'am.'

'What was it?'

He had wrinkled his brow at her wanting to know. He got his notebook out again and thumbed through the pages.

'Cox… Leonard Cox.'

Finch would not have used Cox's name lightly. It was for outside consumption. Or rather the consumption of those in the know.

She needed an ally. Someone to help her.

The detective had laid his credentials out. She had no reason *not* to confide in him. He had seemed sincere. But there was a party line, she felt, an official narrative, and he was subscribed to it. She had to find someone to trust – to get to the bottom of it all. Wasn't there a lawyer? Someone Finch had mentioned in his letters?

And then there was Edward… She thought of Finch again and of their visit to Lady Verity back in Stellenbosch – the bird in the gilded cage, desperately sad and unable to confide in her own unfaithful spouse. *Yes*, she had loved Edward once. But she had gone to South Africa to escape all that… and had humiliated him in the process.

Her brother… the gambling debts, the impending jail sentence… Edward's money and influence. It seemed like a worthwhile trade. One she could learn to live with.

Annie returned across the Strand, went down to the Thames and sat in the Embankment Gardens again. She looked up at Robbie Burns.

O sweet, to stray and pensive ponder a heartfelt sang.

She got out her cigarettes, lit one, and felt the tears trickle down her cheeks.

Finch, Finch, Finch…

She had been there for what seemed an eternity, while people, heedless of her sorrow, promenaded up and down without a care in the world.

This bench, this very bench, where not three days ago…

There was a rustle in the bushes behind, a pained groan. It came from beneath a thick screen of leylandii.

Annie rose and turned. Amid the roots, tucked in deep, was a man, lying in the soil. He was filthy dirty, had no shirt on beneath his jacket and was caked in dried mud and black, encrusted blood.

He said something. It was barely discernible. But then he repeated it.

'*Annie.*'

She knew right away.

'Jesus Christ… *Finch?!*'

Part Two

Chapter Twenty-Five

He was swirling, swirling, swirling in the blackness, as if in a dream where you were once flying but now suddenly plunging to earth. Finch tumbled over and over and over, reaching out, waiting for something to break his fall. And then he realised… the primeval force within him compelling him to seek it…

Air… He needed AIR!

He had no idea which way was up, which way was down. He knew, if he kept still, he would begin to rise. But the pain screamed in his lungs. The panic shot like electricity through his limbs, imbuing them with an unnatural energy and strength.

His foot clipped the bottom and then he understood. With an almighty, instinctive push, he thrust himself up, pleading, pleading, to break the surface. His burning lungs were ready to burst. And then, with an eruption of relief, his head was above the water, mouth sucking in the oxygen for all he was worth – sucking in life itself amid the howling wind and sea.

A breaker crashed over him and he ducked under. When he came up again he could see Cole's mast, heading west. He was consumed with an overriding desire to physically climb out of the water and strike him dead.

But the hands were pulling him under, the undertow tugging. He knew to shrug off what clothing he could, to shed the encumbrance. Another absurdity… the dead weight, the rifle slung around his neck. He pulled it off and thrashed his arms, flailing off his jacket as he went below the water again.

A wave caught him and flung him further in. There was a searing pain in his head – not just his jaw, his forehead, but on the side. Cole's low blow. Though it had not landed squarely, it had glanced. Stunning him, not knocking him out.

Finch went through the motions of swimming. The saltwater stung his wrist and scoured his forehead. It was impossible, amid the raging foam, to effect any kind of stroke. But as soon as he hit the shore shelf, the sea became shallow. The swim became a frantic deep wade, and then a wide-legged stagger through the surf. Without the buoyancy of water came the sharp stabbing pain in his ribs.

Finch couldn't see Cole any more. He must have passed round the bend. The beach here was sand, not shingle. Amid the storm and the blackening sky, he stumbled up the shore, every step sending darts into his midriff. He flung himself into the dunes and curled up in a leeward hollow. He didn't think he would be able to get up ever again.

It was only when out of the water and in the air that the delayed shock of the cold became apparent. He was in his corduroy knickerbockers and woollen socks. He still had his boots on. But his upper half was clad only in an undershirt. He was freezing, shivering. There was no option. He would have to move. *He had to keep moving.*

In the distance there were lights – a village. He concentrated, like a Saturday night drunk, on the very art of walking – slowly, deliberately, placing one foot in front of the other. Using tree trunks for support, he dragged himself into the pine woods which lined the beach and which screened him from the worst of the wind and rain. The scent, combined with the sea air, was potent.

He trod on, with difficulty, through the sand and loam, stopping to rest. Over the hump of a dune and the slats of a wooden walkway, he came to the coast road. The grim weather had put paid to any traffic. The tops of the trees swayed violently. His shivering was almost uncontrollable. To his left he saw house lights and billowing, spilling smoke. And, beyond it, a hundred yards away, there was a pub.

He limped on, driven by desperation. Past the house, he hugged a wall for cover, trying not to scream out in pain. Leaning in the pub's side passage was an old black pushbike. From inside came the sound of chatter, bursts of laughter. He could see through the window – men gathered in the saloon. The smell of ale was like an elixir. And then, in the doorway, *coat hooks... coats...*

He targeted one, a waxed jacket with a quilted lining, the kind a gamekeeper might wear. There was a tweed flat cap hanging on the peg above it. He summoned every strength, stiffened every sinew and casually opened the door. He lifted them from their hooks and walked straight back out. No one noticed.

He took the bike, wheeled it clumsily and climbed on. The saddle was too low, the bar brakes ineffectual, but it made no difference. And then someone came running out.

'Oi, YOU!'

Buffeted by the wind he swerved round them – a fist swung but missed – and kept just ahead as they raced after him before giving up.

He hadn't realised, but he was now laughing, delirious. He was hurtling along the coastal road, heading, he assumed, towards the east.

The clouds scudded along on the wind and there was a deep patch of navy blue, a magnificent splash of silver across it. He saw Orion and his belt. There were other lights – up ahead, the headlamps of a car coming towards him. He pulled off the road into the darkness of the verge. It droned past.

In the distance he heard the toot of a train. The railway sprung like a stream from its source somewhere around here. It trickled slightly inland before curving east, following the coast along to Cromer, from where the main line bent south to Norwich.

Finch cycled on and dog-legged inland. There were places he passed whose names seemed straight out of the pages of fiction: Stiffkey, Cockthorpe, Letheringsett. Fuelled by adrenalin, he just kept going. Within half an hour he was nearing the small market town of Holt. He could see the train in the distance pulling away, the lights from the carriages a streak of yellow in the night. He remembered the trains ran in each direction hourly.

The storm was easing, the rain letting up. There was road traffic now, more people the nearer he got. He rode on in. There were shops and pubs, a bank. He ditched his bike in an alleyway and walked.

That he was soaking wet was not a problem, given that he could simply have been drenched in the downpour. But his face? He caught sight of himself in a window and felt momentarily sick. He certainly didn't want to come within sight of an inquisitive policeman. He pulled his cap down and his collar up. There was no way to disguise it.

He limped around the edge of the town, his long-standing troublesome knee having announced its presence, too. He found a place in the bushes a hundred yards upstream of what was little more than a sleeper station, a raised wooden platform either side of the track. There were two or three passengers huddled there.

Finch bided his time. Sure enough, to the hour after he heard the first whistle, came another. The smoke billowed as the shape of the train emerged from the western darkness, gradually slowing down. As it came within sight, he could see in the gloom three passenger carriages and – yes – a goods wagon, coupled to them in front of the guard's van at the rear.

With a great visceral hiss, the train slowed. It was still travelling too fast to climb on board and too risky – too dangerous in the dark. With a squeak and a shudder, it came to a halt. To his advantage, the last two wagons fell short of the stunted platform. The guard alighted and walked up, boots crunching on the gravel. Finch went around the rear to the blind side of the train. Against the shards of pain plunging deep into his ribs and the fire in his wrist, he pulled the lever to slide back the door.

It won't budge.

He heard the conductor's whistle. The steam hissed. The guard was crunching back down the gravel. He tried again with all his might. It opened a crack. He pushed himself up on the wheel's pivot, praying that it wouldn't yet turn. He just managed to wriggle in.

The smell was overpowering. Though empty, it was clear there had been pigs in there – most probably on their way to slaughter. Pigs were clever. They knew what lay in store. Their anxiety had coloured the air and stained the floor. But, at one end, were piles of unused straw. Finch buried himself in deep. He heard the guard tut at the unsecured door and slide it back shut.

Finch's face ached like hell. He was a mess. He felt scared and nauseous. For the first time he could discern the great egg of a bump above his left ear. Though it was his forehead that hurt the most. Of all that had happened to him, it seemed perverse that his worst injury had come from bumping his head in the car.

He wondered whether the police *knew* that he was 'dead' yet or just suspected it. They would no doubt already be concerned for Dryden. He suspected that Cole might have stage-managed the dumping of *his* body, too, yanking off the anchor with a quick-release knot, a highwayman's hitch – ensuring that the corpse would wash up before too long. Maybe he had since spun the police a yarn – witnessing a 'struggle'. Finch hugged himself tight and drifted off into a strange, dream-laden, hallucinatory sleep.

He awoke with a shudder as the train nudged the buffers. But he was not at Cromer, he was at… *Norwich.* The goods wagon must have been recoupled and steered on. He had slept right through it.

It was late at night, after eleven, and still no one seemed to care much about the sad, empty abattoir wagon. After the few passengers had been discharged from the passenger carriages, the wagon was shunted into a darkened siding.

Dressed in his gamekeeper's jacket and cap, Finch figured he could bluff his way out of any situation – beaten-up face or otherwise. He thought that, with his medical knowledge, he might blind any interrogator with science. He concocted in his head a story about how he was an agricultural inspector, there to check on the hygiene of animal transportation. (And if anyone asked, he'd been kicked by a horse.)

So thoroughly did he rehearse his lines in his head that it was a disappointment when the station began shutting down and he was able to climb out – albeit with difficulty – limping up the track to a side platform, and then on to the covered station concourse. It was pretty much empty. There were people sweeping the floor.

The cafeteria was closing but there were tables outside with unfinished meals left here and there, attracting the attention of the pigeons. Finch saw something that looked like a sandwich – a slice of French baguette filled with a kind of ham. He calmly took it, shoved it in his pocket and retreated to a bench to eat it.

He noted the time of the first train to Liverpool Street station, 5.15 a.m., and the fare – two shillings and sixpence. There were a few spare pennies in the pocket of the jacket – the unwitting fist-swinging benefactor to whom he'd be forever grateful. He noticed some more copper coins lying on the floor under the cafeteria tables which he discreetly gathered up.

He remembered something he had once heard about industrious tramps, and how rich pickings were to be found in left-luggage lockers. There was a row of them against the station wall on the far side.

They had a coin-operated system. You inserted a penny, turned a handle and took your key out to lock it – the same penny being returned when the key was inserted to reopen it. He was sure that of the two hundred-odd lockers, there must have been at least a *few* hurried travellers who had left their expelled coins behind. He was right. He found seven pence among them, which left him with another shilling to find.

He went into the men's toilets, a large tiled chamber with a high ceiling. There was a line of toilet cubicles, fully enclosed, with the doors and their glass panels above extending all the way from floor to ceiling. None displayed an engaged sign.

He inserted one of his pennies into the door lock of one of them ('speculate to accumulate,' he heard a voice in his head say). Once inside, he stood on the wooden toilet seat – wincing as he did so – and lifted off the heavy iron black cistern lid. He tried to use it to smash off the box inside the lock that contained the money – the 'spent pennies' – but it was too unwieldy.

Instead Finch pulled the chain, flushed the toilet, stood on the seat, reached over and jammed the ball cock to prevent the cistern refilling. He prised off a section of the flush pipe, giving the copper tubing a twist along the way and, using the sharp metal edge as a chisel, slowly and surely managed to dig the lock out of the door, releasing the coins. He could now afford his train fare with three pence to spare.

The man was pulling down the shutters in the ticket office but Finch caught him just in time and bought a single to London for the next day – in effect, less than six hours' time.

'H'ar y'all right, sir?' asked the man, taken aback by the blood and bruising on his face.

Finch explained that he'd been in an automobile earlier which had skidded down a slope – the reason he was travelling now by train. In doing so it had caused him to bump his forehead. One of the passengers, a man sitting in the front, had fared far worse than he had (which was the truth). Judging by Finch's accent that he was no barroom brawler, the man took pity and, touching his nose conspiratorially, gave him a ticket for first class instead.

'Just between me and you, sir. Make sure you look after y'self.'

Finch half slept on a bench and thought of the time he and Annie, when they were on the run, had camped out amid the sea of bodies at Cape Town railway station.

At some point the adrenalin would wear off, he knew. At some point the injuries would catch up with him, and probably very soon. He also knew – death of Dryden or not – he was a marked man and so, instead, he roused himself, forwent the bench and tucked himself away in the shadows with a good vantage point. He opted for rest over sleep.

He was dreadfully thirsty but the toilets and their washbasins had closed and the public drinking fountain wasn't working. He thought about venturing into the city but he was in too much discomfort.

It seemed to take forever but, before first light, the new day's station activity began. He had enough money for a cup of tea from a stall and then, at five, he headed painfully, unsteadily for his train.

The odd person had stared at him and he knew that his injuries would draw attention. On a near-empty train, the luxury of first class was redundant, but he appreciated the ticket clerk's kindness, and it probably made him less conspicuous should anyone be looking out for a man on the run. When the inspector came, he pulled his cap down low and – affecting the manner of a man half asleep – handed his ticket over for clipping without looking up.

Two hours later he was at Liverpool Street station, amid the sanctuary of the rush-hour crowds, armed with the only plan that made sense. He had just enough change for the fare to the West End and, after waiting for the rush to subside, rode the number 11 omnibus back via St Paul's and Fleet Street to the Strand. With his body about to give up, he began a painful hobble down Savoy Street, alongside Waterloo Bridge, to the Thames and the Embankment Gardens.

His eye was now swollen and black. He thought he might have broken his nose. He had a near-dislocated right wrist with severe abrasions and a burn; not to mention the agony of his ribs, that stinging deep cut on his forehead and the accursed lump that Cole had given him.

He knew where to find Annie but couldn't risk going into the hotel, so instead he staggered and stumbled round to collapse at the back of her favourite park bench.

Chapter Twenty-Six

With the help of a hotel porter, paid handsomely for his assistance, Annie managed to get Finch to the tradesmen's entrance of the Savoy. Finch was filthy and he smelled, though the porter knew better than to complain.

Loitering out of sight till the coast was clear, they bundled Finch into the service elevator. The porter, a young man from India, who looked upon the mission as something humanitarian rather anything clandestine, assured her that they hadn't been seen.

At the penthouse they got out, thankful there was no chambermaid lurking in the private corridor. With Finch's arms around their shoulders, the porter helped Annie walk Finch to her room, where they propped him on a Queen Anne chair which she had the foresight to cover with a blanket first.

She gave the young man a huge five shillings as a tip, thanking him for his absolute discretion. She knew Mr D'Oyly Carte personally, she said (she didn't). She asked him – 'Pandit', he said his name was – if he could arrange, privately, some room-service food to be delivered along with access to a first-aid kit of some sort. As a seemingly exciting diversion from the quotidian, not to mention a lucrative one, the porter snapped to the task.

Annie hung a 'do not disturb' sign on the door and went to run a bath. Then she helped Finch out of his clothes, stripping him down to his underwear. He had a badly bruised midriff, with – she determined on a cursory examination – a possible cracked rib or ribs. His face was cut, bruised and swollen, particularly on the left side, with a black eye to go with it. There was an impressive lump on the top left-hand side of his skull.

Running along his forehead, just below the hairline, source of much of the encrusted blood, was a nasty, deep cut – about three inches long – that gaped open and was liable to infection. Finch's right wrist was cut and bruised and appeared to have a flash burn on the underside – the kind she had seen on the battlefield, a common injury for those discharging firearms.

She wrapped the blanket around him, as much to preserve the chair as for warmth, went to the drinks cabinet and poured him a large brandy. Finch cupped the bowl glass in his left hand and took a long sip.

'Thank you,' he mumbled.

She then lit him one of her cigarettes and placed an ashtray stand next to him. He nodded his gratitude again.

When the bath was ready, run to a good temperature, she helped him stand and led him into the bathroom. Leaning on the edge of the tub and assuring her that he could get in unaided, she left him to it, urging him not to get hot water in the head wound or on the burn on his wrist.

She knocked periodically on the door to check that he was all right. But, half an hour later, Finch emerged, cleaned up, looking vaguely human, dressed in a pair of fresh gold silk pyjamas, white cotton slippers and a maroon and blue striped bathrobe with the hotel's name embroidered in gold thread on the pocket.

'Hope this is okay?'

It was, she said.

Pandit the porter had come and gone again in the meanwhile. He had rustled up some scrambled eggs on toast and a pot of tea left over from breakfast – nothing too challenging for an injured man (some story about a man he knew once in his village back home who'd had internal bleeding and eaten the wrong kind of food and it had killed him).

The medical kit was rudimentary, the kind of thing they kept on the side in the hotel kitchen, but he hoped it would help. It had plenty of wound dressings. Again, Annie had expressed her appreciation.

Finch took his seat at the room service trolley, on which the flap had been raised, locked in place, to act as an ad hoc table. Annie removed the stainless steel plate cover (Edward would have accepted nothing less than silver and made a song and dance about it). Finch ate cautiously at first but then began tucking in.

'Thank you, Annie,' he said again.

'Listen,' she replied. 'I'm glad to help, but this is not a good situation… you being here… for any number of reasons… You understand me?'

He nodded a yes.

While he ate, she told him of her visit earlier from Detective Coates of Scotland Yard. Then, when he'd finished, she helped him to sit on the edge of the bed. She had some gauze, ointment and bandages ready. After helping him off with his pyjama top, she bound his ribs, then applied a dressing to his wrist.

'Haven't done this in a while,' she said. 'Getting out of practice.'

He'd put on a bit of weight since South Africa she thought. There was a softness to him. She stood over him and studied his forehead, gently turning it back and forth in the light from the window.

'It's going to need stitching.'

There were no such items in the first-aid pack so she went to a drawer and came back with a hotel sewing kit, the kind used for replacing buttons. She threaded a needle with black cotton, then upturned a bottle of iodine onto some gauze and dabbed gently at the gash, which was swollen and sore and an angry red around the edges.

Finch winced but then composed himself. She took a match, lit it under the needle to sterilise it, then commenced with her needlework.

'Good boy,' she said mockingly.

For the first time he smiled.

When she'd snipped off the final thread, Annie helped Finch up onto the bed and propped him upright with pillows. She poured him some tea and, over the next half an hour, let him tell her all that had happened in Norfolk: events in Endthorpe, at the guest house, the trip out to see Nathan Cole at Blakeney and the agony of his encounter with Dryden. It was followed by his rescue, then, finally, the strange duplicitous reversal by Cole – a man who had committed his 'murder'.

'The weird thing was, Annie, I was so angered by it,' he growled. 'Not just the blow, but by the sheer gall of what he'd just done… I wasn't driven by any motive to stay alive… to survive… it was complete, blind rage. I wanted to climb back on board and kill him. It was adrenalin, pure adrenalin that saved me…'

She lit him another cigarette and one for herself too.

'He was clever,' he went on. 'He was watching the current, the tide, and knew just when to do his dirty work.'

'Jesus, Finch. You were lucky.'

He finished up detailing his train-hopping back down to London.

She tried to sound reasonable, to sound comforting, given all that he'd gone through, but she knew her tone sounded hostile to him.

'And you chose not to go to the police, not to your lawyer friend, not to Maude… but instead you came *here*?'

'It was the only thing I could think of. All I could afford. My gratitude again, Annie. I'll not hang around. As soon as—'

'Edward's still away,' she said. 'In fact, he won't be coming back here at all. Going directly to Liverpool from Scotland. I'm meeting him up there on Saturday. But like I say, Finch you… *we*… have to be discreet.'

She poured him some more tea.

'Finch?'

'What?'

'I'll be honest with you… something Coates said. The stuff about the drinking, the personality changes, violent mood swings… He had me convinced for a moment. And then, what you just said, about *rage*…'

He tried to laugh it off but it was a weak effort.

'Please, Finch, you have to tell me. Is there something here you should worry about… something *I* should worry about?'

'No, Annie, I promise.'

She went to the French doors and looked out over the Thames again. The river traffic was ploughing up and down as ever.

'So, do you have a plan?… What's next?'

'I don't know,' he said. 'I need to sleep on it… *literally*.'

'Fair enough. You must be exhausted.'

While he shifted position, she pulled back the counterpane and the quilt. She rearranged the pillows.

'The only plan I had till now,' he sighed, 'the only thing that kept me going… was getting back to *you*.'

The silence was awkward. His words sounded to her like the lyric to some cheesy music hall ballad.

'Here,' she said, businesslike.

She helped him off with his dressing gown and he climbed right in. In a matronly fashion, she realised, perhaps even a maternal fashion, she tucked him in.

'Just an hour or two. You understand?'

But he was already asleep…

–

'Finch… *Finch?*'

He stirred. Rare sun was streaming in through the window.

'*Finch?*'

He was groggy.

'What time is it?'

'Ten past eleven.'

'How long…?'

She could tell by his face that he was in considerable discomfort. He probably had a thumper of a headache. He was putting on a brave show.

'Couple of hours, a little more… *Here*.'

She had ordered some more tea. His own Zeiss wristwatch lay on the bedside table. He reached for it and nodded approval that, for all its tribulations, the time was correct. He strapped it on.

He also noticed, in the corner, that she'd bundled up his old clothes.

'Is that a hint?'

She hoped her face conveyed the necessary gravity.

'Finch, I've been thinking. It's like I said the very first time… in South Africa. You need to go the police. We can find someone sympathetic, I'm sure and—'

'Annie, I'm the apparent killer of a policeman!'

'No, Finch. You've been wronged. You're innocent and you know it. Someone tried to murder *you* for Christ's sake. This Nathan Cole, they can arrest him.'

'*No*, Annie, the local coppers in Norfolk are up to their necks in this thing. It'd be Cole's word against mine about what happened. And I know who they'd believe.'

'What about this solicitor friend… this lawyer…?'

'Jilkes? I'm afraid not. They got to him too, remember? Plus he's got a wife, kids. And I made a promise.'

'What kind of promise?'

'That I'd keep him out of it.'

She shrugged.

'The bigger picture, Finch… Ursa… If it's as you say… What happened in the North Sea, this is *deadly* serious… of national importance.'

'*Exactly*, Annie. Which is exactly why I need to get to the bottom of it, find a trusted person…'

'The detective… Coates… *Yes*, I know, he was singing from the official hymn sheet. But he seemed reasonable… I'm sure if—'

'NO!'

'Jesus, Finch, there's no need to be so bloody rude.'

She saw the guilt flash across his face.

'Look, Annie. If I go to the authorities, I *have* to have everything cast iron. Everything *has* to be proven. Otherwise, to them, it's just supposition and fairy stories. I'll come over to them just like Pickersgill did to Maude and myself. Like some ranting lunatic.'

Annie sipped her tea.

'That's the first time you've mentioned her, Finch.'

He cast his eyes down.

'Finch?'

'I don't want to talk about it.'

'Why not?'

He shrugged.

'Maude, come on, she's lovely… What's not to like?'

'Please, I—'

'Damn you, Finch! You were forthright enough with your opinions about *me*.'

She felt the rush of blood.

'Are you *trying* to pick a fight?' he snapped. 'It sounds like it.'

Damn you, Finch.

She huffed and slammed her cup down on its saucer.

'You can't just *do* this, Finch… come crawling back here. I'm happy to help… *really*, I am… but I'm *embarrassed* that you're my first port of call.'

'Why?… Because we signed papers…? Official Secrets…? Jesus, Annie. Lord knows I wanted to steer clear of this thing altogether. But it came to *us* Annie, not us to *it*…'

She swung her arms in exasperation.

'Because I'm *married*, for Christ's sake.'

She had got him.

'*Happily* married?' he retorted.

'To hell with you, Finch. Get out of here. This is your mess… *again!*… *You* sort it out!'

Finch tried to get up. It was hard work. She took pity, came over and helped. He sat on the edge of the bed. He could probably smell on her breath that she'd had a brandy herself. Could he see that she'd been crying? She looked away.

'Here…'

She unhooked Edward's dry-cleaned suit from the back of the door.

'…You're about the same size. Help yourself to a shirt, tie, whatever you need…'

She pointed at the wardrobe, the dresser…

'You sure?'

She nodded.

'Thank you.'

'Your shoe size?'

'Ten.'

She rooted in the bottom of the wardrobe. She handed him a pair of brown brogues.

'May pinch a bit but they'll have to do… And you'll need a hat to cover the bandage.'

She went off into the sitting room to allow Finch to get dressed. On her own, she sat and smoked another cigarette. Five minutes later Finch entered. He was not completely sure on his feet but markedly better than before.

She found it difficult to speak. There was her husband's suit – royal blue with a navy-blue pinstripe – only the man inside it *wasn't* her husband. She wondered for a moment if…

'This any good?' he said.

'I'm sorry?'

'*This…*'

He casually scooped the Henry James from the coffee table and thumbed through it. She had forgone the dust jacket for its reddish-brown linen binding and had turned down the corner on page seventeen.

'Oh… I don't know, I haven't really had a chance to get into it yet.'

On the marbled endpaper, at the top right, she had written her initials in ink. She knew he would have seen it: 'A.J.' – 'Annie Jones' – not 'A.P.'

The clothes fit well. He looked good in them. She couldn't deny it.

'How are you feeling?'

'Like I've been kicked by a mule.'

He looked down, shuffled a bit.

'Look, Annie… about earlier… this whole thing. I'm sorry for landing you in it.'

'The police, if they come back – I won't lie,' she said. 'I can stall them, that's all…'

He nodded his understanding.

'It's not *just* that, Annie… It's…'

'What?'

'Seeing you the other night… I still can't… I don't know…'

'Finch?'

She stood up and came over. She faced him.

'I didn't tell you everything,' she said.

'What do you mean?'

'Remember… my brother?'

He said it jokingly.

'What's he done this time?'

She touched his arm.

'It was worse than that, Finch… He was in *serious* trouble… gambling… debts… sucked up into the crime that goes with it. He was looking at prison, a long stretch… and then… Edward…'

'I'm sorry. I don't follow.'

She got cold feet.

'It doesn't matter.'

He looked into her eyes. She gazed up and saw someone deeply unhappy. She knew, in her heart, it was probably what he saw in her too.

'Annie…?'

He took her hands.

'I'm going to go… and I'm going to get to the bottom of this.'

She felt the warmth… the touch of his skin…

'Oh… sorry… hate to ask…'

'What?'

'You know…'

He pulled a mock wince.

'...Money.'

She rolled her eyes and fetched her purse. She stuffed into his hands every note and coin she had.

'I owe you,' he said.

'Where will you go?'

'The lavender man... Chilcot... There are still questions...'

She kissed him lightly on the cheek.

'Be careful, Finch.'

And he was gone...

-

Annie sat in her penthouse living room, head in hands, stomach churning at her feelings for Finch, her fear for Finch... and for the awful sense that she had just kicked him out in his hour of need. His sad bundle of filthy clothes sat there like a memorial. She knew that he, too, would probably have redone their farewell if given a second chance.

There was a knock at the door and she sighed with relief. He was back.

Right compose yourself, girl.

They would sit down. They would rethink his strategy... how he... how *they* could alert the authorities... and then she would tell him everything... *everything*.

Carpe diem.

Her heart beat fast as she skipped to the door and threw it open.

Standing there was the strangest-looking man she had ever seen. He was tall... massive... powerful... with the broadest shoulders and thickest neck...

Chapter Twenty-Seven

Mordecai watched the blue Rover pull away. He stood on the pavement outside the gate to Battersea Park, going over in his head the verbal instructions that Weathers the valet had just imparted. There were people going about their business: morning strollers entering and exiting; carts, wagons, buses and motorcars jostling in the queue to go over the narrow Chelsea Bridge.

The rich man, who'd stayed behind, had told Mordecai to forgo his suit today. Instead he was clad in the outfit of a tradesman, or rather what his benefactors *supposed* was the uniform of a tradesman: a tight-fitted woollen work suit and cap, boots and with a red neckerchief over a thick twill shirt. (Brown again, thought Mordecai. The rich man liked him in brown.) He wondered why, for complete authenticity, they hadn't just made him wear his old rough work clothes.

In his hand was a trusty, deceptively voluminous Gladstone bag, tastefully worn and distressed. He checked it again. It contained various tools, though non-specific to a particular trade, more that of a handyman: a couple of hammers, a bag of nails, screwdrivers of differing types, a hacksaw, some chisels, a set of spanners, a sink plunger.

He crossed the suspension bridge, where frustrated motorists beeped horns at the congestion, their exhortations failing to make the blindest bit of difference. Ahead stood the ornate tower of the Bazalgette pumping station. The denizens of west London, Mordecai observed, preferred their sewage dealt with discreetly... *beautifully*, in contrast to the brazen shit factories of the east.

To the right of Chelsea Bridge, downriver, was the railway bridge taking the trains in and out of Victoria station. Through clouds of steam, the passenger services of the London, Chatham and Dover Railway hissed, creaked and trundled back and forth. Amid them a line of shiny blue and cream Pullman cars rolled south. With dark wood, festooned drapes and crystal lamps, their luxury was obvious. They were towed by a gleaming powerful engine, resplendent in full company livery. Mordecai had heard about this train – it went down to Dover then, the other side of the Channel, continued on through Paris, Munich, Vienna, Budapest, Bucharest, all the way to Constantinople.

There was something incongruous about this little parcel of gentility – the swells in their gowns and furs and fine suits – being dispatched against the backdrop of the Pimlico tenements, the swirling murk of the Thames below and the pervading aroma of the Battersea Dogs Home.

Once on the north side, Mordecai crossed over the swing bridge on the Grosvenor Canal and wound his way onto Buckingham Palace Road.

Everywhere, folks were lugging suitcases and carpet bags on and off buses, in and out of cabs – or with paid staff do it on their behalf. The locality exuded the excitement and tension that came with impending journeys and, in Victoria's case, the added thrill of trips to the Continent. The air was rent with whistles and hoots and public announcements from the grand station behind the houses.

Mordecai cut north onto Elizabeth Street with its twee patisseries and cafes and jewellers. He was back in the rarefied air of Belgravia again, an area whose street patterns he now knew like the back of his hand.

Elizabeth Street cut across Eaton Square, and soon Mordecai was traversing the open space – past the grand townhouse terraces on the south side, then the gardens themselves and the busy main road that ran west to east along the square's length.

He thought, with anger and humiliation, of the slap that had been delivered to his face, and then the near-choking administered by the Brute. His rising anger was tempered by the money and the envelope he still carried on his person, tucked in an inner, deep pocket of his jacket. But then there was his family in Riga. The fear of what might... He was in a daze of confusion again. He willed himself to snap out of it. Maybe, just maybe, there was a way to get revenge? Silently, anonymously. *Later*... the dish served cold. He would do his job, complete this task and bide his time.

As before in the square, traffic flowed fast and heavy round the western end till it began to slow – Elizabeth Street, which turned into Lyall Street on the north side, acting as a tidal barrier.

The flow of water, just as the rich man had said.

On the corner, the *Daily Mail* was still banging the drum for war, ridiculing the latest Russian excuses for its actions at sea, relishing the failure in diplomacy. Mordecai strolled on nonchalantly past a policeman walking his beat.

The British bobby with his strange, domed helmet.

Behind Eaton Square's grand houses ran a 'mews', the stable yards, tucked away behind the servants' quarters. Though when Mordecai turned left, through the arch into the narrow cobbled alley that backed the houses on the north side, it was clear that here, in the moneyed part of town, the householders were eschewing horse-drawn transport for the motorcar.

Save for a couple of outhouses, which still exuded equine snorts or the tang of straw and manure, the stables had largely been converted for automobiles. Some of the doors had been reconfigured.

The mews alleyway was otherwise quiet, except for one garage, where the double doors were wide open to reveal a mechanic's feet stuck out from beneath a gleaming new silver luxury car – a Rolls-Royce – the man cursing as he banged at some nut or valve unwilling to budge.

The blue wooden garage door to number 95, halfway along the left-hand side, had a recessed door built within it. It had been left unlocked as he had been told. He looked back and forth and turned the knob. The garage was empty, dusty and carried the smell of disuse. He went through into the side passage and up the steps to the back entrance to the house. The aroma of roast beef wafted from somewhere along the way. He could hear the clink and clatter from nearby kitchens.

Mordecai knocked on the door in the prescribed fashion – a memorised pattern of long and short raps. It seemed to take forever, but he heard footsteps coming down the stairs, then echoing along the hallway. He heard bolts being released and the lock being turned.

The woman was dressed in the simple plain grey dress of a housekeeper – another 'costume' he wondered? It was done up to the throat, her hair tied back. She said nothing, just stared at him grimly.

He recited the words he had been told to say.

'I am here...' he raised his bag, 'to "fix the problem".'

'And who sent you?'

Her voice had a trace of Russian.

'Ursa,' he replied.

She stared for moment, weighing him up, then opened the door fully for him to enter. It was clear that the house was empty. She locked the door behind him.

'You must exit from this door only, the rear,' she said. 'You understand?'

'Yes.'

She demonstrated how the door locks worked – two deadbolts, turned by lever, and a conventional latch operated by key.

'Here...'

She pressed it into his hand and made him open and relock it three times. She asked him to repeat the exercise from the exterior. He was to be sure to take the key with him when he left, she said. This part was crucial. There was a clinical iciness about her insistence.

'Yes. I understand.'

The house smelled fusty, not lived in for some time. They moved into the hallway, past the stairs that led down to the kitchen. The hall had a chandelier that had been covered with sheeting and a large mirror on the wall with a sculpted gold leaf surround. A grandfather clock ticked away, its big old pendulum swinging slowly back and forth.

The house had been furnished expensively – it was not dissimilar to the one that the rich man had put him up in. The open door to the dining room showed a long table and chairs covered with white sheets also. There were bare patches on the walls where paintings had been removed. Before the front door, the mat was covered in unopened post.

They ascended three more flights of stairs past a drawing room, a study, a music room with a shrouded grand piano, and bedrooms. The tall Georgian windows on the street side, though partially shuttered, still threw generous light. They afforded views straight across the square.

At the top, within the roof, above a tight, switchback staircase, they arrived at an attic room. It gave the impression of a games room of sorts – an unofficial one, like a hideaway, a den for children. It had a dartboard on the wall with a pitted cork surround and the odd dent in the plaster from where a dart had gone astray. There was a vacant doll's house and various sealed cardboard boxes.

Pushed up against the interior wall was a half-size billiard table, two shortened cues leaning in the corner, balls nestling in the cotton mesh of the pockets. The shelves along the end were empty. A portion of the carpet had been rolled up to allow access to the unvarnished floorboards, some of which had been taken up and piled to the side. The planks of wood were spotted with white paint from when the room had been decorated.

Was this where it was kept?

The woman indicated the two small sash windows overlooking the square. He set down his bag, went to the right-hand one and tried it. It was impossible to open as it was. It had been warped solid into its frame, its runners stuck and since painted solid. He pushed and pulled at it several times, trying to ease it, but to no avail.

'*Here*,' she said, pointing at the other one. She opened it easily, the bottom half sliding up on its counterbalanced cord, just like it should.

Mordecai had already made his choice from street level.

'No.' he said. 'No good.'

She did not like being countermanded.

'There will be no excuses. There will no failure,' she snapped.

He continued with the stuck window frame, trying to unjam it. He was *that* sure, he didn't need to double-check.

'Do you hear me?!'

He carried on.

'*Do you hear me?!*'

He had no time for such histrionics.

'The money. When do I get the rest of the money?'

'You will get the balance, the rest, upon completion as promised,' she barked. 'But your insolence will not serve you well.'

'But I—'

'Silence. You will be paid in full when you have fulfilled your duty.'

He shrugged.

She pointed to the billiards table.

Not under the floorboards after all.

'You are to leave nothing behind. Not a trace.'

He nodded. She left the room.

He knelt by the table and examined its underside. He opened his bag and got out a flat-head screwdriver. The long package, wrapped in brown paper, had been secured in a brass cradle, screwed into place at eight points.

He released the holder and slid the heavy object out. He placed it on the green baize. He carefully untied the paper, done up with twine, and removed the waxed layer within.

He relished the smell of oil and the newly lacquered wood. It had been broken in, tested and sighted. The telescopic scope was attached along the top of the extra-long barrel – a customised Mauser rifle, model 1895.

The Russian version he had used in China seemed immediately an inferior copy. Even Mauser's licensed Serbian and Turkish models, of which he had experience, though identical in many aspects, lacked the overall precision and detail in the workmanship.

He carefully packed away the parcel paper, the metal cradle and the screws, tucking them in his bag, leaving no evidence. He laid the rifle back down carefully and reached around under the table again. He slid out a clip of five 7-millimetre silver-tipped hunting cartridges.

Chapter Twenty-Eight

Finch felt awkward – humiliated even – dressed in Edward's suit. The worst part about it was that it fitted so well. Only the tight shoes gave him gyp. He wanted to get out of the damned outfit as soon as he possibly could. He suspected that might not be for some time.

As he strode out of the lift, he skirted the lobby, heading towards the rear exit, the one that led out to the Embankment Gardens. He sidestepped people without drawing attention, being sure to pull his Homburg – *Edward's* Homburg – down over his forehead, doing his best to obscure the bandage.

He was almost there when a voice called out from behind.

'Good morning, Mr Pointer.'

Finch carried on walking. The voice rang out again.

The bellboy… the one who had delivered the same suit earlier, suddenly caught sight of a man who clearly *wasn't* Mr Pointer. He thought it odd that another man should be wearing the same item of clothing, a pretty unique garment – royal blue with a navy-blue pinstripe – and tapped the concierge on the arm. The concierge glanced at the copy of the photograph that the detective had had left him earlier.

He abandoned his business at the front desk.

'Excuse me… *sir*?'

Without turning, Finch picked up the pace. He was immediately aware of his physical limitations. His ribs hurt with every footfall. The concierge lifted the telephone while nodding to the bellboy, who alerted a burly-looking man in a suit loitering behind a rubber plant.

Finch threw a look back and saw the man dart out. He performed an ungainly jig down the steps, causing considerable pain in his abdomen, and plunged into the revolving door, which he immediately jammed by not taking into account the elderly woman with her mournful dachshund entering from the other direction. The woman was now stuck in the revolving door but with her dog marooned outside. It was the lead she was still clutching which had caused the obstruction.

The burly hotel man banged on the glass.

'Sir, I need a word with you… *sir*!'

The woman with the dog was so wrapped up in the plight of her pet that she hadn't taken in what was happening.

'Madam,' yelled Finch, tapping on the glass divider. 'Your lead, it's jamming the door. You need to let go…'

He pointed at the obstruction.

'But my dog…'

'I'll pass him back in.'

'She… It's a *she*.'

'Then I'll pass *her* back in!'

The burly man was banging on the glass again.

'Sir, wait there, please!'

Finch saw him signal to someone else. They had surely sent someone round to catch him on the pavement.

'Please, madam…'

'But what if she…?'

'Just do it!'

With the woman panicked into letting go, Finch pushed the door, and, in one move, shoved the dog back in and spun the whole revolving apparatus so that the woman was thrust into the burly man, blocking his path.

Finch turned right. He would head for the crowds around Charing Cross station. But he saw a broad-shouldered man at the far corner coming towards him. He was similarly attired, in a dark suit. On turning in the other direction, a heavy in a suit appeared there too.

There was a knot of people. A man held an unfurled umbrella aloft in one hand and a sign saying 'British Museum' in the other. A collection of fur coats, expensive perfume, silk suits and cigars gathered around him for their morning tour. A private sightseeing omnibus stood at the kerb.

Around them, porters wheeled trolleys of luggage. Finch eased his way through, exacting a 'Now look here!' from a man with an upturned moustache and a monocle.

The hotel men were closing in.

'Quick!' came another voice.

A hand reached out and pulled him off the pavement into the tradesman's entrance, then shoved him into a broom cupboard and shut the door. Finch waited in the dark for what seemed an eternity. Eventually the door cracked open. The light hurt his eyes.

It was the Indian porter, Pandit, standing there.

'They're gone. But leave now,' he urged. 'They may be back.'

'Thank you,' said Finch.

He stuffed some of Annie's money into his hand. Too much, probably, but worth it.

Having checked up and down the pavement, Finch staggered off...

–

Half an hour later, after winding his way across the Strand and up through the backstreets round Covent Garden and Cambridge Circus, Finch found himself, once again, in the York Minster pub in Soho. He bought himself a much-needed pint of ale, a whisky chaser and a packet of Navy Cut from behind the bar.

'Someone's been in the wars,' said the barman, nodding at the bandage.

He caught his reflection in the engraved mirror behind the shelves of spirits.

With his hat having eased back, the bandage was barely disguised and now a touch bloody. Finch said nothing, took his drink, and placed himself on the same stool by the window, looking out at the alleyway across Dean Street and the tatty green door at the top of the iron staircase.

The pub was full of the usual lowlifes. But he didn't care. He was now one of them. He lit himself a cigarette, sipped his beer, willed the 'bliss'… and this time it came.

Over half an hour and two more drinks he waited, watching a door that never opened. He pondered all that had happened since he was last in here… of what might happen next… and, again, of Annie.

Annie…

'Hey, Hero.'

While he was lost in his thoughts, Lulu had sidled up to him.

'Oh, hello,' he said.

She wore a green dress this time, her auburn wig replaced with a blond one with abundant Bo-Peep ringlets. For a black man… black *woman*… it seemed an unusual choice.

'You like my hair?'

'It's most becoming.'

'Sugar, you're a terrible liar,' said Lulu, and gave him her most devastating grin. It was hard for Finch not to smile back.

She eyed the bandage round the crown of his head, the one on his right wrist and the swollen mess of his face.

'Something tells me you're in trouble.'

'You could say that.'

She laughed politely and touched his arm.

'Buy me a drink, you can tell me all about it.'

'I'll buy you a drink, Lulu,' he sighed. 'But as for *this*…'

He pointed to his head.

'…I'd rather not.'

He nodded to the barman to fetch Lulu whatever she wanted.

'Actually there *is* something,' he pointed out. 'That good old door up there. You know what goes on behind it?'

She shook her head.

'I don't… and neither does anyone else…'

She leaned in close.

'…I was looking out for you, see,' she whispered. 'Figured I'd ask around. There's the occasional person going in and out… but beyond *that*…?'

She shrugged and helped herself to a cigarette. The barman came over and deposited a port and lemon.

'You behave yourself, Lulu,' he warned. 'You understand?'

'What? L'il ole me?' she said and batted, exaggeratedly, her false eyelashes.

Now it was Finch's turn to whisper.

'Lulu, this may sound like a strange question…'

He thought about how to phrase it.

'…But if I wanted to hire… some *muscle*…'

She gave a knowing grin.

'So that's the way you like it, huh? You really *are* full of surprises… Hero.'

'No… I mean, if I wanted a strongman or two, someone to help…'

He picked over his words again.

'…*extract* some information.'

'You mean, work somebody over?'

'In a fashion.'

Lulu looked serious for once.

'Go on.'

'I mean… in here, for example…'

He looked around the room.

'Can I… you know… make the necessary connections?'

Lulu frowned, sipped her drink, sucked hard on her cigarette and exhaled.

'You know, as my mama used to say, "Be careful what you wish for."'

'It's just…'

She let out a disapproving sigh.

'Sugar? You in trouble, that's one thing. You hurtin', that's another. But *this*…?'

She waved her arm around the room.

'…This ain't your world.'

Finch laughed to himself.

'What's so funny?'

'Believe me, Lulu. I inhabit a circle of hell well below this one.'

No sooner had he said it than there, walking down Dean Street with a casual, carefree stride, came a man in a grey suit, a cravat, an astrakhan-collared coat and a Homburg. He had a pencil moustache and a sprig of lavender in his buttonhole. He turned into the alley, skipped up the steps, took out some keys and let himself in. The green door closed behind him.

Lulu had seen it too.

'Actually, I have a better idea,' said Finch, discreetly flashing her the pound notes Annie had given him. 'I need some rope… and a gun.'

Chapter Twenty-Nine

Finch walked across the street and into the alley. Despite his intended soft footfall on the metal staircase, his shoes – *Edward's* shoes – clanged all the way up it, the structure wobbling with each step.

There being no element of surprise to his advent, his right hand moved to the Colt snub-nose revolver in his side jacket pocket, the one with the serial number filed off. His left hand patted the twelve-foot length of thin rope – a washing line by any other name – that had also been rustled up the minute cash had been flashed.

Finch stood outside the door and its worn, chipped, pale-green paint. He paused for a moment then gave a short hard rap.

'Come in.'

The voice was cheerful, welcoming. Finch tried the knob. The door was unlocked. Gun drawn, he pushed it open with an extended forearm and leaned back against the wall, taking cover, letting it swing far enough to afford him a view inside.

But there was no trick, no ambush… Sitting behind a desk, poring over some notes, was the lavender man. He hadn't even looked up.

Colt raised, Finch threw a glance back over his shoulder, stepped in and closed the door. Caught mid-flow, without lifting his head, the man raised a palm in apology, finished scrawling, then, with a touch of self-satisfaction, set down his fountain pen. His tone carried the air of someone greeting a new customer.

'Now what can I do for…?'

His smile fell immediately.

'…You?… What are *you* doing here?' he spluttered.

It was the first time Finch had been able to get a proper look at him. He seemed less refined under close scrutiny – the black hair suspiciously dyed, the pencil moustache and eyebrows possibly touched up with mascara.

'Put your hands up!' Finch yelled.

The man's palms shot north and quivered. Finch turned the key in the lock.

The office was cheap and smelled of damp beyond the man's buttonhole posy – possibly the reason he wore it – and was cluttered with papers and files, some of them stacked or just scattered on the cheap linoleum. The grubby lone window, with its wire-meshed opaque glass, was flecked with pigeon muck. Overhead swung a bare light bulb.

Finch moved behind the man. He raised his gun, as if to clout him about the head, and the man flinched and gave a little whimper. He ordered him to stay sitting and lower his hands again, keeping them at his side. Finch kept himself at arm's length, prepared for any false move.

The man saw Finch pull the cord out. He had already fastened the rope into a loop with a slipknot, working it like a lasso.

'Listen, there's no need—'

'Shut it!' Finch barked as he looped it over the man's shoulders and yanked it taut, using his foot against the armrest for leverage.

The man winced.

'Please,' he panicked. 'What are you going to—?'

Finch went for the fake pistol-whip again and the man cowered.

'I said, "Shut up!"'

Finch wound the cord round him several times, tying it off with a reef knot. The man's arms and torso were now bound tightly to the back of the chair. Finch moved round to the front of the desk again. He waggled the gun, showing he meant business.

'Okay, Chilcot,' he said. 'Start talking!'

The second he had uttered it, he was reminded again of his failure to think things through. The man's face was a picture – a mix of incredulity, humour and what seemed like… *pity*.

'*Chilcot?*… I'm not Chilcot,' he scoffed.

Finch's head hurt, his face hurt, his ribs hurt.

'For Christ's sake,' he said. 'I'm in no mood for games.'

The man sighed, as if it were all just an honest mix-up.

'I'm *not*. I swear.'

The expression of doe-eyed innocence suddenly seemed compelling.

'Then if *you're* not Chilcot…?'

'There,' said the man, nodding towards the front of his desk.

The brass nameplate had been obscured by papers. Finch brushed them off. It was a cheap item screwed to a wooden block, the kind of knick-knack they'd knock up in any local ironmonger's.

'*Vax… Clive Vax?*' read off Finch.

'Private investigator,' said the man, cheerily. 'How can I be of service?'

Finch tossed the nameplate down. It landed with a thud. He pawed at some letters in the overflowing in-tray. 'Mr C. Vax' or 'C. Vax Esq.' appeared on all of them.

'My God, I'm so pleased to see you…' the man added.

His weasel response to Finch's invasion had now shifted to one of smarm.

'…Seriously. We thought you were dead!'

'*We?*'

'I mean I… *I* thought you were dead.'

Finch was thrown and he couldn't deny it.

'What a relief… I can't begin to tell you…' the man continued, his high-pitched voice betraying working-class London beneath the studied elocution of the aspirational professional.

'You're bluffing!' snapped Finch, waggling his gun again.

'Bluffing? Not in the slightest. I'm on *your* side,' the man trilled, relishing the confusion. 'Always have been. Just wish you'd taken my advice.'

'Your advice?'

'The men's room… the Cathay… You know, to stay away… keep out of this whole thing… It was done for your benefit, believe me.'

'What do you mean?'

'Given your history… your inquisitive nature… you were bound to be heading for trouble. Pretty much borne out, too, if I may be so bold. Plus, I hate to remind you, you *had* signed papers with the War Office, made a promise to king and country. A case of keeping you on the straight and narrow, as one might put it.'

Finch tilted back his hat. He felt the blood on the bandage.

'Why the hell should I believe *anything* you say?'

The man shrugged as best he could under his restraints. He nodded at Finch's gun.

'Colt? Those things are two a penny in Soho. A handy piece, no question about it. I hope you didn't get fleeced.'

Finch thrust the gun closer to his face.

'You can cut the lip, mister. I'm warning you!'

Finch cocked back the hammer.

'Look, don't shoot the messenger,' the man bleated. 'I was just doing what I was told.'

'By whom?' barked Finch.

'Sorry, can't say… That's the one thing I *can't* help you with… Just be assured you're being looked out for… I promise!'

The gun was now just six inches from the man's left eye. He strained his head away, sweat beading on his forehead, a rivulet of black dye heading south.

'Please,' he gibbered. 'Don't shoot!'

Finch kept him squirming for a second then lowered his weapon. He watched the man's tension subside once again. He didn't know why he did it – catharsis as much as anything else – but this time, catching him unawares, he swung the pistol, connecting the stock and trigger guard hard with the man's left cheek. It was pretty effective, he had to admit. It made a nasty *clunk*. The man groaned and snivelled. His head slumped.

There was a wicker chair opposite. It was covered with papers. Finch swept them off and took a seat. He lit himself a Navy Cut. He trod the match out on the floor then exhaled a lungful of smoke for maximum theatrical impact. He took a good look at his quarry. Blood dripped from the cut on the man's cheek. Slowly, he lifted his eyes.

'My goodness, you look a bit, how shall I say it… discombobulated,' groaned the man, somewhat groggy, but still seeking a tactical advantage, employing mateyness now. 'Say, you want a drink? I keep a bottle of Scotch in the filing cabinet over there. You know, "for medicinal purposes"…'

For a brief, flickering moment, Finch thought about it.

'…That's right… could use one myself…'

He could feel the man worming his way in. He was a sly operator.

'…Good stuff, Dr Finch… single malt… twenty years old… Your poison, right?'

Finch willed himself to get a grip.

'What do you mean,' Finch growled, 'that I'm "being looked out for"?'

'I mean that you *are*, Dr Finch. People have got your back.'

'It doesn't feel like it.'

'I know… Best laid plans of mice and men and all that…'

Robert Burns. Again.

The man gave a faint smile.

'…Christ… you don't have to tell me about *that*.'

Finch stopped short of an apology for hitting him, but he lit a second cigarette from the embers of the first. He leaned over and placed it between the man's lips. He dragged on it. Finch took it away.

'Thank you.'

Finch continued to keep his gun trained on him.

'Answer me this, Vax… if that's who you really are…'

'It *is*.'

'…Care to explain what were you doing at the house in Bayswater?… I mean, I saw you coming out of it, down the front steps… with my own eyes. And that freak? The man mountain you were with…?'

Vax's eyes conveyed comradeship now… patronage even.

'You did well, Dr Finch. You've been amassing the pieces of the puzzle, just not assembling them in the right order. Yes, that's Chilcot's house, as you correctly deduced… Or the house *used* by him at any rate.'

'Who is he?'

'You know, you really need to get this rope off.'

He wriggled.

'*Who is he?*'

'We don't really know… not yet. Will be an alias, of course. Wields some kind of political clout, that's for sure. Has contacts in the Foreign Office, pretty high up… the dark arts… you know how it is?'

If this was bait, thought Finch, he wasn't taking it. He said nothing.

'And Freeland? Who are they?'

'Seriously, this is very uncomfortable. I wish—'

'*Freeland!*'

'That's how I came to be involved in this thing. A client of mine—'

'A client?'

'…Can't say… confidential… but yes, a client had some suspicions about the company, wanted something checked out. Comparatively minor matter, considering where this whole thing has led us. Freeland is a legitimate marine scientific company… with some wealthy benefactors, too… academic patronage and everything… Oxford… But there seemed some shady business going on… this thing in East Anglia…'

He nodded for another puff on the cigarette. Finch obliged.

'…And as for our friend… that fat-necked beast? You really shouldn't mess with him… He's done some things… *believe* me…'

'Who is he?'

'Is this one of those games where you're just pumping me for information to confirm something you already know? You know, like a courtroom lawyer?'

'*Who is he?*'

'Name's Smert...'

He pronounced it *Schmert.*

'...was some kind of hit-man... an assassin, served in the Tsar's Imperial Guard...'

'The Tsar?'

'Your friend Pickersgill was right, there are Russian hands all over this... Comes from some one-horse town on the Volga... part Tatar... A killing machine, strength like you wouldn't believe... A sadist, I mean a clinically diagnosed one... the more unpleasant the death, the greater the pleasure... Mute, you know... I say the Tsar, but that was a while ago. Is now what you might call a "private contractor"...'

He gave an ironic chuckle.

'...though I doubt he's big on paperwork.'

Finch stood. He thrust his gun again.

'Hang on. It's pretty convenient you suddenly distancing yourself from these people, burning all your bridges. You looked pretty cosy with them all a few days ago. You... this Smert...'

'*Schmert*... you pronounce it *Schmert.*'

'...You hopped in a car with him and came right here.'

Vax breathed out a sigh, conciliatory.

'You're absolutely right,' he said, nodding as sincerely as he could. 'Absolutely right. Hadn't realised you were following. In which case, if I were in your shoes, *I'd* be pretty suspicious of me too. I concede that point entirely. But what if I told you he... Smert... was marching me down those steps at close quarters with a gun in his pocket, right in the small of my back, and then, when we got out of the car, he marched me up these steps here the same way?... You saw him. He was right up close behind me.'

'Why would he be doing that?'

'They'd held me captive there for a while. He was then bringing me back here to search the office on the strength of something I'd said… Ended up ransacking it… just like your house… Fellow's not noted for his patience.'

'How do you know about that?'

'What, Smert and his temper?'

'About my house?'

'Come on, Dr Finch, give me *some* credit… But yes, that's what he dragged me back here for. Looking for something on behalf of his master…'

His eyes darted around the room.

'…You think it's normally this messy. Please, Dr Finch, you can't run an investigative operation if your files aren't in order. That's what I've been doing, putting everything back in place. Just took out a small ad. Have a girl starting next week.'

Finch looked around. He hadn't noticed, but now Vax had said it, he saw that the curtain pole had been pulled off the wall. It was resting vertically in the corner, the material furled around it. The metal filing cabinets, too, had dents above the locks where the drawers could possibly have been jemmied open. A ransacking would also explain the piles of papers everywhere. But it was not entirely convincing – about as convincing as the turning over of his own place.

'What was he looking for?'

'Who?'

'Smert… *Schmert?*'

'Information.'

'What information?'

'On something called Ursa…'

Finch blew out a sigh. He hadn't realised it, but he'd begun pacing up and down.

'And so here we are yet again,' he quipped sarcastically. 'The mystery inside the riddle inside the bloody enigma.'

'Why, do *you* know something?' asked Vax.

Finch smiled and shook his head in mock disbelief.

'Nice try, Vax… I mean, really, that was a very nice try. You almost had me…'

'But I—'

'Come on, man, I wasn't born yesterday.'

'It's the truth!'

'Truth is, Vax, that if you'd angered these people, got in their way, why didn't Smert…'

He repeated it, pronouncing it again in an exaggerated fashion.

'…*Schmert*, just bump you off, something he seems very adept at?'

'Because I've got something *on* them… on Chilcot… something that will be passed into influential hands if anything should happen to me… Call it my *insurance* policy… Come on, Doctor, you know how to play *that* game.'

Finch didn't like the insinuation.

'Well I've got an idea, Vax. How about this?' said Finch. 'How about if I frogmarch you straight over to Chepstow Place right now? Have it out with this Chilcot character? Thrash it out in the open. Get to the bottom of it all.'

Vax squirmed beneath his bindings.

'No, Finch… No, no, *no*!'

Finch taunted him with his gun. He waved it just inches from Vax's nose this time. More hair dye had run.

'Seems like a good idea to me, Vax… Conscious or unconscious, makes no difference how I get you there.'

Finch swung back his gun again, the butt of the pistol aimed straight for Vax's nose. Vax flinched.

'Please, no… that would be madness!'

'Would it? I thought there were guardian angels watching over me? What have I got to lose? Or is it because Vax, or whoever the *hell* you are… YOU'RE NOT BLOODY TELLING ME EVERYTHING?!'

Finch was so tired, so battered, he again didn't know where the move had come from. It certainly wasn't premeditated. But this time he shoved the gun barrel right into Vax's open mouth. The man's eyes grew so wide, he thought they'd pop out of his head. He moaned and groaned and choked.

'You've got five seconds. Five...'

He could feel the bleat and whine of protest.

'Four...'

It transformed, according to Finch's ears, into what sounded, curiously, like the sound of a mewling guinea pig.

'Three...'

There were tears in Vax's eyes.

'Two...'

Finch cocked the hammer.

'One...'

'Okay, okay...!' he felt him mumble, his tongue caught round the barrel.

Finch pulled the gun out. The sight rasped on the man's front teeth.

Vax panted, simultaneously sucking hard for air and spitting out the taste of metal.

'I'll be straight with you...' he wheezed, 'but I do so for two reasons.'

'I'm listening.'

There was a water jug on the filing cabinet. Finch filled a glass and put it to the man's lips, sloshing half of it down his shirt front. He gulped and spluttered and panted some more.

'The most pressing reason, Dr Finch, is that you shouldn't be here. *Neither* of us should. Not together, not like *this*...'

'And two?'

He huffed and puffed for more air.

'Two is that I genuinely believe you *don't* know what Ursa is. You just proved it.'

'I thought you didn't know either.'

'Sorry, just part of the act,' he said. 'Though my name *is* Vax.'

'So then, Vax... talk...'

'It's not that simple.'

'Yes it is.'

'It's not. What I know... about my client... the one who commissioned me and, more importantly, about Ursa... you need to see it to truly understand. It's complex. Plus, I've a feeling this isn't going to turn out well for me… not *now*. In which case, I've just added *you* to our insurance policy… I mean, carrying things on in the event I don't make it.'

'*Our* insurance.'

'You'll soon understand.'

Vax nodded to the desk drawer.

'There.'

'What?'

'In there… my keys… take them…'

'Why should I do that?'

'I live just up towards Euston, a basement flat off Fitzroy Square, 29B. A fifteen-minute walk, ten if we go fast…'

'*We?*'

'You untie me. You take me there. I show you. You can keep your gun pressed in my back the whole way. In your custody.'

Finch laughed.

'I'll give you credit, Vax. You can talk your way out of anything. How about I leave you tied up here and go there myself?'

He slid open the drawer. There was a bunch of keys attached to a rabbit's foot.

'No, no, no, no… You can't leave me here. Not like this. If Smert were to come by—'

'I thought you had something on them?'

'Not if they think we're in cahoots.'

'We're not in cahoots, Vax…'

He swigged straight from the water jug himself.

'…in which case, yep, I think I'll leave you right here.'

There was genuine panic in the way Vax said it.

'YOU CAN'T!'

'Believe me, Vax, I *can*. So tell me… Your flat… What was it we were supposed to be looking for?'

'No, Dr Finch, YOU CAN'T DO THIS TO ME!'

'Oh yeah…?'

He scooped Vax's keys into his pocket.

'...But I'll make a deal with you, Vax. Tell me what it is I'm supposed to find and I'll take a look. If your story's genuine, I'll come right back, we'll be brothers in arms... bosom pals... whatever you say...'

'How do I know I can trust you, Dr Finch?'

Finch spluttered incredulity.

'You? Trust *me*?'

'Yes, Doctor. The issue here isn't whether you trust *me* now, but whether I trust *you*.'

'You don't... You have to go with your instinct. But given what I've been through already, I'd say I'm a pretty safe bet...'

He pulled out his silk handkerchief – Edward's silk handkerchief, navy blue with white polka dots – from his breast pocket.

'...But if you're lying to me, Vax, then maybe, just *maybe*, I'll make a telephone call to Chilcot's house... I've got his number... I'll tell him you've just sung like a canary... and that you're sitting here trussed up like a turkey... Pardon the similes.'

He nodded to the candlestick telephone on the desk.

'You wouldn't?!'

'Try me.'

'Under my bed,' he flustered, 'there's a loose floorboard... has a bent nail poking up... It's where I've hidden it... Didn't trust it in the office... You see what's in there, replace everything exactly as you found it... *exactly* as you found it, not a hair out of place... you'll see I'm genuine...'

He stared Finch directly in the eye.

'...And if you want to talk about trust? Goddammit, I've just placed my life in your hands.'

Finch yanked the handkerchief taut...

'Please,' protested Vax. 'There's no need...'

...and pulled it hard into his mouth, tying the gag at the back. He took the door key, ready to lock Vax in as he left.

'If you've played your cards right, Vax, I'll be back in half an hour.'

Chapter Thirty

Fitzroy Square was less than a mile away from Vax's shabby office. Finch headed north, cutting across busy Oxford Street and up Charlotte Street, past the Hundred Marks pub, the Sass art school, the Scala Theatre and the bijou eateries.

When he had followed the blue Rover car previously, it had diverted this way. If Smert had been forcing Vax at the point of a gun on a search of his properties – going to Vax's home first – then such a detour made sense. Though they would have had barely any time there. Perhaps they had changed their mind? Perhaps Vax had persuaded Smert that what he was seeking lay in the Soho office? Maybe they were deterred for some other reason?

Who knew with Vax? He was still an unknown quantity. He had hinted at knowledge of Finch's former brush with military intelligence, which suggested he knew far more about events than he was letting on. Finch pondered that if he had simply heeded the warning Vax had given him at the Cathay restaurant, as Vax had reminded him, he might be going about his everyday business untrammelled.

Then again, looking at it from another point of view, Vax was in a desperate situation a few minutes ago and – slippery as an eel – had managed to wriggle his way out of his predicament, possibly telling Finch any old story to serve his purpose. Finch kept his hand on the Colt revolver in his pocket.

There was one thing that stung Finch and gave him pause – that parting shot, Vax's urgent insistence that he had placed his life in Finch's hands. There was something that suggested the slipping of a mask – his reference to it being part of an 'act', the brief flicker of an expression and a voice slightly changed.

Finch felt bad – less about clobbering Vax with his gun than for the brutal way he had then shoved the barrel into his mouth. It was a cruel and unnecessary flourish – sadistic. He thought of Sun Tzu: '*To know your enemy, you must become your enemy.*'

He was disturbed by the capacity for violence that lurked deep within him. He had unleashed it once before – back in South Africa, a case of kill or be killed. He was not sure any more whether he truly liked himself. A psychiatrist would have a field day.

A news stand, covered by a striped awning, had an array of newspapers and magazines on its racks, with all the usual bold-type headlines agitating for war against Russia. The *Morning Post*, however, carried an insider's hint of an 'international summit', suggestive, if not of immediate peace, then of a possible alternative way of achieving a diplomatic resolution. Finch yearned to get up to speed on current affairs – his travails of the past few days meant he was now lagging way behind.

Fitzroy Square was a large open space, set between fine Georgian buildings made from Portland stone, not far from Regents Park, hemmed in on its north and east sides by the busy Euston and Tottenham Court Roads. It had a cluster of plane trees and a circular garden in the centre. In a burst of afternoon sunshine, some children thundered past, chasing a hoop. A few adults strolled back and forth; some walked dogs, but it was fairly quiet. It had a cheap hotel for railway travellers and some boarding houses. Judging by the casual style of the people thereabouts, it fancied itself as bohemian.

Number 29 was on the western side of the square, its basement – 29B – down some dank, mildewed steps upon which water dripped. Finch kept his distance as he walked past several times, looking about him the whole while. The door appeared to be covered by a metal concertina grille, the kind that shopkeepers pulled across their storefronts.

Satisfied that the coast was clear, he descended. The dripping water from an overflow pipe had started to form into a stalactite. Or was it stalagmite? He could never remember. There was rubbish – bits of newspaper and food wrappings – that had been blown (or thrown) down into the basement well, and the dustbin itself was overflowing. He thought he heard the scuttling of rats.

Finch went through the keys attached to the sad and sinister rabbit's foot, though when he identified the correct one for the grille, he realised that it had already been forced open, just pulled back to rest in place – again the familiar work of a crowbar or some tool used to prise the lock, backed by considerable strength.

When he slid the grille back out of the way, he saw that the lower left of the nine frosted glass panes that constituted the upper half of the front door had been smashed in. It was the one right over the door handle. And the door was now unlocked.

Finch drew his gun, flipped off the safety catch and gently prodded the door open with his foot. There was enough light coming through the window for him to see inside and, with a couple of darting movements of his head, he managed to get a look around the door frame. Cautiously he entered, primed for any movement.

The main room was a sitting room but there were two doors at the rear. The door to the left looked to lead to an interior passage to elsewhere in the building. It had a white towel hanging on the back of it and a big key on a nail in the wall. Finch supposed it was the way to the bathroom or WC, probably a kitchen too, meaning the door led to up to a hallway and communal facilities. He tried it. It was locked.

The other door, hanging ajar, was surely to Vax's bedroom. Finch approached slowly, nudged it open, led with his gun and looked in. The room was barely big enough for its single bed. There was no one in there.

The main living space was cluttered, much as Vax's office was, and smelled inevitably of lavender. On the window sill was an earthenware vase with a small bush in it. A table had the remnants of a meal: a plate of bacon and eggs and a half-drunk cup of tea. They were sitting on a wooden tray, which fitted with Finch's hunch about shared facilities and carting things back and forth.

There was a small coal fireplace, a threadbare settee, a tatty rug, a bookcase and a writing desk. Vax, the detective – if that's what he was – was evidently fond of crime writer Fergus Hume. On the table was a programme from a recent Association football match, *Woolwich Arsenal versus Aston Villa.*

The desk contained various letters and bills – one from a grocer, another from a tailor – that were all addressed to Clive Vax, or Clive V. Vax if one was to be precise – the V standing for Victor as was written on one letter, a rather depressing bank statement that suggested Vax was down on his uppers.

One missive, addressed to Vax specifically as a 'Private Investigator', from a Mrs Babcock of Twickenham, thanked him for his good work in tracking down her missing (grown-up) daughter, but wondered when he might return the gold bracelet that had been used in identifying said mother to said child.

The compact bedroom had a small wardrobe at the foot of the bed. The cramped confines prevented it from opening fully – not that the door functioned properly anyway, wedged closed with a folded piece of brown card. The bed was unmade, the pillows greasy – probably from all the hair dye.

There was a gas lamp and Finch lit it. He set it on the bare floorboards next to the bed and peered under. There was a stack of periodicals – magazines. On pulling them out he saw they were of a certain kind: several editions of a publication called *Gentlemen's Monthly*. *GM*, as it styled itself, fancied itself as a publication of lifestyle, with various articles about sporting goods and motorcars, though its chief fascination, according to the well-thumbed pages, was the middle section devoted to photographs of coyly smiling women either in their undergarments or… in interesting arrangement… no undergarments at all.

Finch put his head on the ground and looked along the line of the dust-laden floor. At the far side, against the wall, he saw a crooked nail poking up. He manoeuvred the bed out of the way within the cramped confines, leaned over and yanked the section of floorboard up – a two-foot length, custom-built as a hideaway.

It was hard to see and he brought the lamp over… There was nothing in there.

Angered and alarmed by the possibility that Vax had either duped him, or someone had beaten him to the stashed information first, he leaned over again, thrust his arm in up to the elbow, poked about and – this time – felt something rectangular and hard wedged in at the back. He pulled it out. It was wrapped in brown paper and tied tightly with twine – too thick for him to snap – and with a knot impossible to unpick.

He took it to Vax's desk, set down his gun and found a letter opener with a serrated edge on one side of the blade designed for just such a purpose. As the string pinged open and he peeled back the paper, he hit a cold wall of shock, the kind that made his head swim and pulsated behind his eyes. It was a book…

…Henry James' *The Golden Bowl.*

It had reddish-brown linen binding and the corner of page seventeen turned down. It had 'A.J.' inscribed on the endpaper. He felt nauseous, light-headed and sensed the chill of cold sweat between his shoulder blades. *Annie!* Dear, sweet Annie. She had wanted nothing to do with this. And *now*…?

He knew he must get out of there, and get out of there fast. He checked his watch. He had already been gone twenty-five minutes and he speculated whether, in his absence, the person who had planted this, clearly to taunt him, to signal to him, might already have done for Vax – a man he'd left alone, a sitting duck.

Unless *Vax*…?

You bastard. Did you just set me up?

He shoved the book in his jacket pocket. Instinct told him to head straight for the Savoy. They would have got to Annie… *taken* Annie… only in the last couple of hours. But he knew his presence there would result in immediate arrest, with his plea for urgency lost amid everything else. Whoever had done this was banking on his impulsive response – his Achilles heel.

No… I must get back to Soho.

Something told Finch this was *not* Vax's doing, that Vax would be able to help him. But if he *had* got something to do with…

what?… Annie's *abduction*…? then Finch still had him right where he wanted him and he would make his previous interrogation methods look like child's play.

The room grew dark. It was as if black clouds had suddenly rolled across. But it was not the weather. He heard the heavy footfalls and saw the beast – Smert – at the top of the stairwell. It was not just Annie. Now they had *him* too.

Chapter Thirty-One

Finch's hand went to the Colt revolver. He had that at least. But then he saw there was an alternative course of action. As Smert, with his ungainly gait, shambled down the steps, he grabbed the key from the wall and opened the interior door. Once on the other side of it he went to lock it, then opted not to – encouraging Smert to follow him.

He listened to make sure that Smert had entered, then crept up the steps to the hallway, with its faded black linoleum and the smell of impermanence. Sure enough, off it was a communal WC and bathroom. A woman stood in a man's dressing gown, cigarette between her lips, towel over her shoulder, sorting through her post at a table by the front door. He breezed past her and made a discreet exit.

Finch began a brisk walk, heading south out of the square, hanging back on the corner of Charlotte Street, waiting to observe Smert emerge and gauge which way he might go, but the man-mountain was evidently wise to Finch's game and had burst straight from the basement, already striding in his direction, locked on like a cheetah stalking a gazelle.

Finch began a painful jog back down towards Soho. But going south was pointless. He was merely leading Smert to a known destination. Instead he ducked left and doubled back up Tottenham Court Road, past Euston Road Underground station.

Smert had gone. Or *had* he?

No... The man had anticipated his move and had attempted to cut him off along Warren Street. He was now a mere twenty yards behind, close enough for Finch to feel the pounding of his shoes.

Finch increased his speed, his heart thumping wildly. But he was not in sufficient physical shape to keep up a sustained run, he knew. Ahead the pavement was crowded – people waiting to cross busy Tottenham Court Road, among them an ice cream cart being manoeuvred into position by a short Italian man in a pristine white tunic. Finch plunged amid the throng. The jostling gave him a moment of cover.

It was a risky move. But with a sudden gap in the traffic and a surge of the waiting pedestrians, Finch feinted to go one way, then, screened by the cart and the wooden board sign above it, darted into an alley. It was a short narrow cul-de-sac, a filthy stub of a thoroughfare, a geographical accident that seemed to serve no purpose.

He froze absolutely still as the huge figure stopped, mere feet ahead, his back to him, blocking the entrance… and the light. For a moment, Finch could examine him, like an exhibit in a zoo – though without the safety of bars – his ridiculous fat neck twisting, eyes scanning back and forth along the street, aware that Finch must have made an evasive manoeuvre. He had looked everywhere but behind him. Finch held his breath.

The alley stank of rotting rubbish and urine. And something else. There came a low growl… an aggressive canine warning.

Finch turned.

A mangy mongrel, some kind of feral alley stray, its black fur patchy, filthy dirty, had emerged from the shadows. It was baring its fangs. Finch had stumbled onto its territory.

Finch put his finger to his lips – a futile gesture, he realised. The dog looked half Alsatian, part pointy-eared savage… and entirely without reason.

He whispered a plaintive, '*Shhhhhh*,' but the dog's growl grew more guttural, more menacing and lowered in tone. Saliva stringed from its jowls, its hackles were raised. It took a tentative step towards Finch – eyes wide, the whites fully visible.

'*Shhhhhhhhh*. Good boy!'

The dog did not respond. It moved closer… snarling louder.

Finch touched the Colt in his pocket. If he *had* to...

The bark, with an accompanied snap of teeth, resounded like a thunderclap.

Smert spun.

Finch lunged... and so did the dog.

Smert's oversized arm swung, the huge boulder of a fist arcing towards Finch's face, but with less precision than it might. The black streak of fur threw him.

As Finch ducked under it, the dog's jaws clamped down on the big man's leg, allowing Finch to tumble onto the pavement. He turned to see Smert pick the dog off, like some irritating insect, and fling it hard back into the alley where it hit the wall, yelped, slid down and whimpered. It limped off.

Finch seized his moment. With heads turning and a stranger's hand reaching to help him up, he bolted, as best he could, up to the east–west Euston Road, running straight across the traffic, weaving in and out of the oncoming vehicles, eliciting shouts and curses and the beep of a horn.

Smert's heft encumbered him and Finch kept his lead... *just*. An eastbound omnibus had pulled away from a bus stop, the twin horses already carrying it at a sufficient lick. Finch launched himself towards the rear platform, staggered, lost his grip on the pole, but thrust his other hand up to gain sufficient purchase. He pulled himself on board.

The human monster ploughed on, parting the traffic like Moses and the Red Sea. He was on the pavement now, then jumping off it again, waving down oncoming vehicles. He was clipped by the wheel of a cart – hard, it looked – but it seemed to cause him no bother. He glanced at his wound with mere curiosity, then renewed his chase with purpose.

A taxi cab pulled over and Smert climbed up. The cab driver whipped his horse and it began gaining on the bus.

The conductor appeared, a grumpy little man with a pitted nose.

'All right, mister,' he snapped at Finch. 'You're only supposed to get on at the designated stops.'

'Sorry.'

Heads turned.

'How much to St Pancras?' asked Finch, feigning cool.

'Tuppence ha'penny.'

Finch fumbled for change. The conductor wound the ticket machine that hung on his leather harness. Though no sooner had he cranked it than the bus slowed and Finch, using the cover of a coal wagon, had jumped off again.

'*Oi...!*'

The conductor rolled his eyes and got back to his business.

Finch stepped back into a pub doorway and watched the bus carry on. Smert in his cab went sailing past, still on its tail.

Another bus slowed and Finch stepped aboard. This time he went straight upstairs, the open upper deck affording a good vantage point, and found a seat near the front. St Pancras was not far. The neo-Gothic splendour of the Midland Grand Hotel loomed up ahead. Any sign of Smert and he would stay put, only getting off when safe.

He looked around. There was a mother and child, a little girl in a pinafore dress, who seemed thoroughly excited at the prospect of being allowed to 'go upstairs'. There were two men reading newspapers – one the *Daily Express*, the other the *Daily Mirror*, the gamut of opinion duly encompassed, though with war still being championed at either end of the political spectrum. An older couple sat together, the small silent husband penned in by a larger wife who was running through a breathless list of household chores for her spouse to complete once back home.

Finch absorbed the normality and, for a moment, in the late autumn sun, relaxed.

The bus stopped. The horses snorted, their hooves scraping while people got on and off, the conductor yelling, 'Fares please.' And then Finch felt it – a huge weight that made the bus tilt. He heard the creak of the stairs as the lumbering presence ascended. And there on the top floor, at the rear, blocking his exit, stood Smert.

The little girl gasped. Her mother admonished her for staring. Slowly Smert moved up the aisle. The close-set black eyes – the dead black eyes – fixed on Finch's.

Finch's pulse pounded in his ears. His mouth was dry. His hands were trembling. Yes, he had a gun. But to start a shoot-out in public…? The little girl… Her mother…

Possessed with a sudden urge to feign nonchalance, he took out a cigarette, concentrated hard and struck a match. He inhaled as the huge Smert, slowly, unsteadied by the motion of the vehicle, edged towards him.

Finch looked at the little girl and thought, for a moment, of Emily, the brave child who had been rescued in the Karoo desert during his South African adventure. He smiled at her, got a faint grin in return… then winked… as he threw himself over the side.

There was a gasp from the pavement at this sight of a man flinging himself overboard, clinging to the rail that ran atop the upper deck, then swinging his leg to gain a foothold in the open vent window of the deck below, attempting to climb down.

It turned to a shriek as a monumental man leaned over to swipe at him, grabbing him by the collar, suspending him in mid-air, swinging Finch helplessly, legs flailing, like a man on the gallows. Finch clutched at his throat, strained for breath and felt the blood pinch off as Smert, with a single giant arm, began raising him up.

Panicked, the horses picked up speed. The driver wrestled the reins and tried to regain control. One of them kept bucking. It was setting off the other, straining against its harness. There were screams now on board.

A lamp-post… fast approaching… Finch writhed, contorted, threw his arms round it and hugged it for dear life, locking each palm onto the other forearm. He felt his grip slacken and himself being wrenched away… and then a rip as his collar tore off, a bemused Smert left clutching a remnant of Edward's no doubt expensive shirt.

Finch wrapped his legs round the lamp-post too. For a moment he was marooned, alone above the crowd like a steeple-jack.

There were hands reaching up, people helping him down.

'Are you all right, mister?'

He was, he told them, panting hard, brushing off his clothing.

Ahead, thankfully – and for the sake of the little girl – he could see the bus had been brought back under control. Though behind him, in the distance, he also glimpsed a police helmet bustling along in his direction.

There were enough people milling around the Euston arch for him to lose himself. He pulled his jacket collar up and buttoned it across, covering the ripped shirt. With his hand on the gun in his pocket all the while, he walked on, hurrying up the curved ramp into the entrance to the Midland Grand.

A porter approached, asking if he was checking in, though Finch saw the man's face change when he noticed the bandage round his head. He had long lost his hat. Amid all that had happened, Finch had forgotten. He stuck out like a sore thumb.

Finch knew that Smert would follow him to St Pancras station. Sure enough, when Finch went through the hotel's cavernous vaulted lobby, past the restaurant and round to the side entrance to the Midland Railway platforms, he could see him lurking there.

Finch ducked back into the gentlemen's toilets and, looking in the mirror, unwound the bandage. It was sopping with blood, which had soaked right through. No wonder the porter looked shocked. The stitches had held, though. Annie had done a good job.

He kept on the small strip of gauze that covered them – far more discreet – and walked back to the exit. Smert was still out there, scanning the crowds amid all the smoke as passengers went back and forth to the trains, getting double takes from some of them.

Finch casually walked past the heaving, clattering restaurant and nonchalantly – he was getting rather good at this – helped himself to a long gabardine raincoat hanging on the coat stand. Following the fashion of the dearly departed Superintendent Bastard Dryden, late of the Norfolk Constabulary, he also pinched someone's fedora.

There was a departure board inside the hotel and Finch watched for the trains to Bedford – the St Albans line – knowing that Smert would probably expect him to be catching the next one. He thought of Annie, praying that no harm had come to her, and swore, if it *had*, he would kill whoever had done it, even if he had to swing for it.

An announcement for the Bedford train echoed around the station concourse and a whistle blew. He had no ticket but strolled out, mingling with the crowd, hiding in plain sight in his new guise, straight past Smert, who looked right over his head.

Finch waited till the last moment, as the green flag was waved and the final whistle blew, before jogging up the platform to the furthest carriage and turning just enough to give Smert a view of him. It worked. Smert came striding in his direction.

Finch nodded a polite hello to the three elderly ladies in his carriage and then shocked them all by sliding down the window on the door opposite, opening the handle from the outside and climbing straight into the carriage of an adjacent stationery train, in which he surprised the travellers there, too, with another 'good day', before exiting onto the opposite platform.

The Bedford train hissed, the engine strained and the squeaking carriages started pulling away. Smert had been too late. Through the windows of the train on his side of the platform, Finch saw him standing in exasperation, framed amid a cloud of steam, watching it trundle north.

A pair of constables appeared on the concourse. Finch made his way, sharpish, to the Underground station. He glanced back. Smert had gone. Inside, he caught the Piccadilly railway to Leicester Square, from where he hurried back up to Soho and Dean Street. The adrenalin and the shock had masked the pain, but his ribs sent sharp stabs through his chest. His knee, as ever, ached like hell.

He studied the alleyway, knowing that Smert would most likely turn up there again, and probably very soon. Coast clear, he clanged up the steps and, to his relief, found that the door was locked, meaning that Vax was still trussed up inside. He checked his watch. He had been gone an hour and ten minutes.

Finch inserted the brass door key and turned it. Gun raised, he kicked it open and entered. And his world went black as someone coshed him from behind…

Chapter Thirty-Two

Finch rose slowly from the blackness. For a moment, he feared he was underwater again and willed himself to swim to the surface. He was panicking, his heart working overtime, like the rapid pounding of a pneumatic drill. His arms and legs thrashed in vain, the movement commanded by his brain not yielding any response from his useless limbs. He could hear a voice but not identify it – just a distant *wah-wah* of indecipherable sound. He called out to it, whoever it was, as if in waking from a nightmare. Then his own cries became real, loud…

'It's okay, it's okay… *Shhhhhhhh*,' soothed the voice.

He could see now – just a blur, but with a dark shape moving within.

'Don't worry. *Shhhhhhhh*.'

It was a female voice. Slowly his eyes pulled focus. She had his head cradled in her lap, gently stroking his forehead. The light hit her hair and spread a halo around her curls.

'It's all right, sugar. You're okay now.'

'*Lulu?*'

She dabbed a cold wet handkerchief at his brow.

'Where… where am I…?'

He blinked into the light. He was in Vax's office, lying on the floor. His head… Christ, his head… He didn't know how much more his poor skull could take.

'Saw you rush up the steps. Saw someone else run down them and you not come out. Figured something wasn't right.'

She helped him sit up.

'Thank you,' said Finch.

'Didn't recognise you at first...'

She nodded at his raincoat.

'...but there's just somethin' about you, Hero.'

She said it playfully.

'Told you it'd end in tears,' she added.

Finch had been too eager in his movements. He wobbled, giddy. An arm buckled.

'Take it easy,' urged Lulu. 'There's no rush. Slowly...'

'Actually there *is* a rush...' he groaned. 'Someone's life is at stake.'

'All in good time.'

He forced himself to get sharp... to focus. He propped himself up again.

'The man who left, what did he look...?'

'Don't go worrying yourself.'

'*What did he look like?*'

'Jesus, Hero. An' I thought you was a gentleman!'

She pulled a spectacularly theatrical pout.

'I'm sorry, Lulu... Things are a little fraught.'

'If you must know... Thin, narrow moustache, flower in his buttonhole.'

She lit one of his cigarettes and put it in his mouth. He grunted his acknowledgment.

'Right, you need to help me up,' he said.

'Are you sure?'

He dragged hard on his cigarette and put his arm around Lulu's neck. Her strength was impressive, he thought, for a woman, until he remembered. Despite a momentary sway of his legs, she helped ease him into the chair – the same worn, wicker-backed one he had sat in, casually interrogating Vax less than two hours before.

'Lulu,' he winced, the pain throbbing in jagged bursts through his temples.

'Yes?'

He spoke through gritted teeth.

'The man... which way did he go?'

She pointed up towards Oxford Street.

'That way… But don't ask me if that's north, south, east or west, 'cause honey, I ain't got a clue.'

He thought he might faint. He struggled to concentrate.

'I need to get out of here.'

The sensation caught him unawares. He bent forward and threw up on the lino – the egg and toast from earlier now swimming in alcohol.

'Hey, these are new shoes,' screeched Lulu, swinging her red velvet pumps out of the way.

'Sorry… but listen… I really do need…'

'Don't think that's such a good idea.'

'Please, just fetch me some water.'

He pointed to the glass jug. She passed it to him. He gulped it down.

'Come on. Let's go,' he urged.

He made to get up and placed his palms on his thighs.

'You're not going anywhere, sugar.'

She pressed into Finch's hand a sheet of paper, a handbill. Under the header 'Metropolitan Police' and the notice 'Caution' was a grainy picture of himself. It was a close crop of his face from his army portrait. Underneath ran his name and the legend, in bold type: 'DANGEROUS.'

'Have been passed out all around Soho.'

He screwed it up into a ball and threw it across the room.

'Makes no difference. We need to move… *fast*.'

'*We* need to move?'

'Lulu… I need you… I need your help…'

She raised a quizzical eyebrow.

'…Please?'

He pointed at his purloined fedora, which had gone flying across the floor. It had narrowly avoided the pebble-dashing. Lulu handed it to him and he pulled it on, yanking the brim down as far as he could.

'Lulu… How'd you like to go on a date?'

'With you?'

'With me.'

'Where to?'

'The Savoy.'

'How could a girl refuse?'

He smiled as best he could.

'No time to waste.'

'Whatever you say, Hero.'

Lulu helped take his weight and, slowly, they made it to the door. Once Finch was accustomed to being on his feet, it became slightly easier.

'Now for the tricky part,' said Lulu.

It took them a few minutes, but gingerly, slowly, they clanged down the rickety iron staircase. They loitered in the alley till a free cab trotted past.

'No offence, Lulu. But I think *I* stand a better chance...'

Finch stepped out and waved his arm. The cab sailed right on by.

A minute later, another one appeared, casually clip-clopping along.

'*Here...*' said Lulu.

This time, *she* sauntered out. The cab stopped. She turned to Finch.

'Don't flatter yourself.'

Lulu helped Finch up onto the running board and, on Finch's promise of a huge tip for getting them to the Strand as quickly as possible, they were on their way. They ducked low in the cab's awning.

Lulu pointed. There was a police handbill lying on the floor, a footprint across it.

In under ten minutes, the ecstatic cabbie – who in the absence of any convenient change had pocketed a five-shilling note – had deposited them a hundred yards short of the Savoy, on the north side of the Strand, right outside the Adelphi Theatre which, with its recessed foyer entrance, afforded them a view across to the hotel.

'So what now?' asked Lulu.

Behind her hung a bright illustrated poster for the musical comedy *The Earl and the Girl* – it featured a buffoon dressed in ermine, smoking a cigar, with a young couple staring tenderly at each other in the background.

'Lulu, I'm a marked man. I have to keep out of sight. If you can only do one thing for me, and for which I'll be eternally grateful, I need to find out what's happened to the woman in the Savoy's penthouse suite. Her life may be in danger.'

'And the police ain't an option...'

'Lulu, the handbill. I'll be arrested on the spot. I'll spend hours explaining myself. They'll talk me round in riddles. Everything will grind to a halt. There's other things I'm supposed to have done. *Bad* things...'

'Honey, ain't *you* a bunch of surprises?'

'...I don't know if this woman... my friend... has that much time. The first thing I need to know is if she's there or not. If she's in her room reading a magazine, sipping tea, then I'm a fool, I've been sold a pup. But at least she's safe.'

'And if she's *not*?'

'Then, as I fear, she's been taken... kidnapped... and by some pretty unpleasant people...'

He saw the doubt on her face.

'Hero... much as I'd like to help, my kind ain't the Savoy type, if you know what I'm saying.'

'Round the back. The Embankment Gardens. There's a tradesmen's entrance and a service lift. There's a porter there, young fellow – Indian, name of Pandit. You got that?'

'Pandit, yes.'

'Tell him that I've sent you... Dr Ingo Finch... the friend of Mrs Annie Pointer he helped earlier... Tell him that, on very good authority, you have every reason to believe Mrs Pointer has been abducted and is in serious danger. And that *I'm* hiding out across the street waiting on news.'

'A married woman, Hero. You're playing with fire.'

'*Annie Pointer.* You got that?'

'Uh-huh.'

'Tell Pandit to use his initiative. Get him to check the room. If she's *not* there, then alert the authorities immediately, hotel security, whatever he needs to do. There was a Scotland Yard detective sniffing round. Get Pandit to tell the truth about everything that's happened.'

'What if the abductors are holding her in her own suite?'

'I doubt it, Lulu. But if so, it will be dealt with. Just tell Pandit that I sent you. I repeat… I have very good reason to believe that Annie Pointer is in serious danger.'

'This Pandit… what if he's not there?'

'Then you're going to have to go up to the penthouse suite yourself. You're a resourceful lady, Lulu. I have faith in you.'

'Faith *and* a lady?' she mocked.

'Lulu…?'

He grabbed her hand.

'…Seriously. Thank you.'

She looked him in the eye.

'This woman, Annie. You got it bad, ain't you?'

'That's a question for another day.'

She smiled.

'I'll be as quick as I can.'

He watched Lulu scuttle off to the Waterloo Bridge end of the street, over to the left, making her way down Savoy Street, round to the Embankment Gardens. He lit himself a cigarette and waited.

He heard a cough and turned round. There stood a small, bald, thin man in a raincoat, with a full moustache and round wire-framed glasses. He had stepped out of the doors to the foyer. He had obviously been in there for a while. They hadn't noticed.

'Dr Finch…?'

Finch knew instinctively, even in that very second, that events had overtaken him. The man cleared his throat.

'…You are hereby placed under arrest for the murder of Sidney Pickersgill, for the murder of Superintendent Dryden of the

Norfolk Constabulary and the abduction of Mrs Annie Pointer, temporary resident of the Savoy Hotel. Anything you have to say will be—'

'It's okay, Detective,' said Finch.

'Coates, Scotland Yard,' he replied.

He raised a finger, as if he'd forgotten something, and pulled out a battered wallet from an inside pocket. It contained a shiny Metropolitan Police badge and his embossed credentials. He acted calmly, unthreatened, in control. Finch knew he must have backup.

Sure enough, as he tucked the badge away again, two uniforms appeared. Finch didn't resist and offered his wrists. The cuffs were clamped, causing him to wince as they were snapped over his right one.

One of the coppers patted him down. He removed the Colt revolver from his jacket pocket, and from the other...

The constable passed the book to Coates – *The Golden Bowl* by Henry James.

'*Hmmmm*,' he hummed and flipped it open.

Finch watched him peruse the initials inked into the top corner of the blank endpaper.

'A.J. – Annie Jones, as was, I believe. Isn't that right, Dr Finch?'

'Detective Coates, I want you to listen to me and listen well.'

Coates issued an ironic smile and blew out a tired sigh.

'I don't wish to appear rude,' he said, 'but dictating terms is not really something within your powers.'

'Look, we can discuss the murders... the *alleged* murders in due course,' Finch protested. 'Right now, it is of fundamental importance that we focus our full attention on the hunt for Mrs Annie Pointer. I was in her presence less than three hours ago. I have plenty of information...'

Up ahead, he saw Lulu exit from the front of the hotel and stamp off westwards up towards Charing Cross, Bo-Peep curls bobbing. She moved with the angry demeanour of someone who'd just been ejected from an establishment deemed to be above her station.

She was followed shortly by Pandit, the kindly porter. He stood on the pavement, looked back and forth, then over in Finch's direction. Discreetly, or so he thought, he gently shook his head.

Coates nodded to one of his coppers, who headed straight over.

'In which case, Dr Finch,' said Coates, 'it'd really help *us* if you can tell us what you've done with her...'

Chapter Thirty-Three

Annie sensed a blur of white. She strained her eyes towards the French doors. The light was moving. The harder she tried to pin it down, the more it seemed to dance, wheeling around, trailing a phosphorescent streak behind it. She thought of J.M. Barrie and his magical fairies.

But the noise was wrong. There were no barges or steam horns from the river, no trains rattling in and out of Charing Cross. From the other side of the room, the far window, there came no clatter and bump of traffic grinding along the Strand.

Annie lingered somewhere between waking and sleep, her consciousness like a thick, viscous syrup slowly easing its way through the neck of an upturned bottle.

Faintly she heard a mewling… a whimpering… a sound of distress. For a moment she was back there in South Africa again… the sea cave at Cape Point… completely at the mercy of her would-be executioners. And with Finch…

Finch… Finch…?

She felt cold, like she did back then, her nerves shredded.

Blood… There was redness now… Red… Who was hurt?

'*Finch!*'

This time she called his name out loud. The sound of her own voice startled her. The blur widened, receded, widened, receded. Eventually it filled her eyelids. She fluttered them. The daylight began to sting. She was lying on her back, her head turned slightly to the window off to her right.

And the redness… It was the room… There was crimson flock wallpaper with floral swirls. There was a marble fireplace, velvet ruched curtains tied back with gold braided cord. She stared straight up. From an elaborate ceiling rose, a crystal chandelier hung.

There was a plump maroon cushion behind her head. Brushed velvet… tassels. A divan. Someone had raised her feet. And there was a taste – something chemical… pharmaceutical. Her tongue felt like dry cloth.

Drugged… I've been drugged.

'Here…'

It was a man's voice. A voice she did not know.

Something was being proffered and she reached out instinctively. Water. The glass was finely cut, the light glinting on it, a tumbler. It had ice cubes bobbing in it. The man put the palm of his hand between her shoulders and eased her forward. He inserted another cushion behind her, sitting her up.

She took a long sip. It felt better but still the taste lingered.

There was that sound again. The whimpering. *Was* there someone else in here? Were they *hurt*?

'Mrs Pointer…?'

A man's voice. Slowly, she turned her head.

'Mrs Pointer… You'll be okay. Chloroform… it does that. Twenty minutes, you'll be as right as rain.'

He was crouching down to her level. His features were starting to register, emerging from an amorphous flesh oval. He had hair that was a browny-black but which seemed altogether wrong, unsuited… unnatural. He had a thin, pencil moustache. Moreover there was a smell… *lavender.*

'You!… What are *you*—?!'

'Please, Mrs Pointer.'

She thought she heard the whimpering again.

'*Get away from me, you bastard!*'

She swung her right leg, intending to kick him in the face, but her altered state rendered it a lethargic, uncoordinated action. She missed, rather hopelessly. And then she realised, too… she was in stockinged feet; they'd taken her boots.

There came a mocking chuckle in the background. There *was* someone else.

She strained her neck but couldn't see. He stepped into view. It was difficult at first, shifting her focus. It strained her eyes. He was in his sixties, had grey hair, was dressed in a brown suit with a coat of sable fur draped around his shoulders. He had the rounded belly of good living. There was a gold signet ring on his little finger.

Then she saw… the whimpering, it had been coming from a dog… or rather a pathetic excuse for a dog. The man was cradling it in his arms.

'Allow me to introduce myself,' he said, his voice round, rich, plummy. 'My name is Chilcot…'

Finch…! It's him…!

'…Or, to be precise, before the family's insistent Anglicisation… *Chikolov*.'

Finch, I must be in his house.

The man called Chilcot stroked and soothed the dog, a light-brown, short-haired thing with big round eyes; a quite unpleasant looking creature, she thought – more rodent than canine. A chihuahua, the new fashion accessory. The Aztecs used to breed them for soup, someone had once told her… It was Finch… Finch who had said so.

Finch?

'Where am I?'

'Please, if there is one thing this residence prides itself on… that *I* pride myself on… it is hospitality, Mrs Pointer. I can assure you that you will be well looked after here, and are most safe. We will do all we can to make you comfortable.'

Annie knew she should play it calm, keep her cards close to her chest, but in the swimming soup of her mind, the lack of certainty was overwhelming.

'What do you want from me?'

The man shook his head in disappointment.

'Want?' he asked, with an air of false incredulity. 'Why, *nothing*.'

On the mantelpiece, beneath a huge mirror, was a black marble bust in the Graeco-Roman style – a head swathed in laurel leaves. On the far wall was a grand portrait in oils framed in ornate gold-leaf plaster. It was of the same person, a foppish-looking man, this time in a ceremonial breastplate, armoured sleeves and with a pale-blue sash across his shoulder – a young fellow with sad, watery eyes, and an even sadder moustache. The painting looked Dutch… Flemish…

It was the turn of the lavender man again. He was squatting down, still on his haunches. She saw now he had a fresh cut on his left cheek.

'We do offer our most profuse apologies, Mrs Pointer,' he added. 'We didn't mean for you to be inconvenienced…'

Inconvenienced?

'…But we had to be absolutely sure we had removed you from harm's way.'

Harm's way?

'There is important business to attend to. It is for your own safety.'

She had only one thought.

'Finch? Have you hurt Finch?'

'My dear Mrs Pointer…' smirked Chilcot, barely able to stifle another chuckle.

Don't mock me, you bastard.

'…I do find it peculiar yet fascinating that you should place this man's well-being above that of your own husband.'

'Why? Edward?… What have you *done*…?'

He tutted disapprovingly.

'My dear Mrs Pointer. What kind of people do you think we are? As I understand it, *Mr* Pointer has just enjoyed a rather long lunch in a discreet restaurant off Buchanan Street, Glasgow… albeit in the company of someone you'd perhaps rather not wish to know of.'

'How dare you!'

He raised a palm, commanding silence.

'Though I *dare* say he will be hurrying to London when informed by the police about your sudden absence.'

'My absence?'

'Your *temporary* absence,' chipped in the lavender man.

'…And Dr Ingo Finch,' said Chilcot. 'Since you ask…'

He shook his head, as if giving up on an errant child.

'…the only way to describe it is to say that he's been making a bit of a fool of himself, poking around in affairs that are really none of his concern.'

The chihuahua gave a little yap.

'There, there, baby,' Chilcot cooed and pulled out, from the pocket of his fur coat, a small wax bag. It appeared to contain slivers of fresh meat. The dog squeaked and yelped, licking its lips in excitement. He fed his ghastly pet a morsel and it gnawed on it eagerly.

'We suspected that his more cavalier tendencies would come to the fore when we learned that you would be setting foot in England.'

Added the lavender man: 'It's why we tried to steer him away from this whole business and, in particular, from *you*.'

She felt an ice-cold shock of fear, sick to her stomach. Her breathing rasped, her throat suddenly constricted – not for what had been said but for what her eyes were now registering.

Chilcot, the dog, the piece of meat. It was a human finger…

Chapter Thirty-Four

Finch sat in the interrogation room at Scotland Yard – not in Scotland Yard at all any more, the Metropolitan Police's headquarters having relocated just a short hop away to the Victoria Embankment and the red and white brick Gothic building of 'New' Scotland Yard.

He wondered about the propensity of an address to become synonymous with its business – Downing Street, Whitehall, Fleet Street, Wall Street... He had forced himself into such mental diversions to stave off the all-consuming worry that had paralysed his insides... *Annie.*

En route, in another rattling Ford, all protestations about her abduction had fallen on deaf ears. Indeed, they had met with a resounding silence... *indifference.* And, part of the interrogation 'game', he imagined, it also accounted for the fact that nothing much had been said since they had arrived here either.

The room was windowless and airless, the walls a faded pale green – the kind of shade, he knew, from his knowledge of human psychology, that was supposed to engender a feeling of impermanence, of discomfort, of not wanting to linger.

He sat at a worn table with two empty chairs opposite. Above him on a frayed flex, a lone light bulb buzzed. There was, on the far wall, a large mirror – from previous experience, two-way, he knew. It had grubby curtains either side, a giveaway.

His head hurt, his wrist hurt, his knee hurt. But it was nothing compared with the pain of carrying the weight of Annie's plight.

Annie, where are you?

There was a rattle and clang at the door as it was unlocked – an unnecessary precaution, he thought, given that he was already handcuffed to a long chain attached to an iron ring in the floor.

Shackled again by the police.

Detective Coates entered, followed by a mousy-looking constable, a young, skinny chap with curly red hair, probably half Finch's own age. They scraped back chairs on the other side of the table and sat down, Coates directly opposite him. The pair seemed eminently unthreatening, but the process of police interrogation was theatre, he knew – appearances, the atmosphere, it was all part of the performance.

Coates didn't look up. He spent a minute or two flipping through a cardboard folder stuffed with documents. Again, Finch supposed, per an unwritten script – any detective worth his salt, certainly on the trail of such a purportedly dangerous felon as himself, would surely know his stuff already.

Eventually Coates' eyes flicked up. He conveyed the air of a bank clerk and had affected the mannerisms of a mid-level bumbler.

That little routine about forgetting to show his badge.

But, Finch knew, you didn't rise to his rank in Scotland Yard, and certainly not within the mysterious Special Branch, by being a lightweight – not after the clear-out following the Ripper fiasco. Behind the glasses, the brown beady eyes were clear and sharp.

'Just who *are* you, Dr Finch?' he began.

Who am I?

The cryptic opener told Finch there was no rush on their part. They suspected no one of Annie's abduction but himself.

'I am, Detective, as I keep telling you, a man seriously… *very* seriously concerned for the welfare of Mrs Annie Pointer…'

The constable started taking notes.

'…As I said before, I can identify the persons I believe to be behind her abduction. What's more, I have an idea where she may be being held: 11 Chepstow Place, Bayswater, W2… Possibly by a man named Chilcot, in conjunction with another individual who passes himself off as a private investigator called Clive Vax. Vax has an office in Dean Street, Soho, and keeps a basement flat at 29B Fitzroy Square, W1, which may yield further evidence… I've told you this already… Whatever was done was most likely conducted in the company of their hired muscle, an oversized thug named Smert…'

They said nothing.

'…My guess is that they're holding her as a deterrent.'

'A *deterrent*?' blurted Coates.

'Against *me*… I've been investigating something… stumbled upon something of great importance… *national* importance… something they're involved in. They must feel I've got too close. Either that or they just want me out of the picture because of something *she*… Annie… Mrs Pointer… now knows, too.'

The detective and the constable exchanged a glance.

'And really, what might *that* be, Dr Finch?'

There was a hint of sarcasm.

'Look… I'm not sure…'

'Not sure of what?'

'It's an issue of trust.'

'You are in Scotland Yard, Dr Finch, the epicentre of British law enforcement. If there is something you wish to share…'

'In my experience the police have not exactly been my friends, either now or in the past. Your chums in Norfolk just tried to kill me.'

'That's a matter of opinion, Dr Finch.'

'It is my opinion they're as bent as a nine-bob note.'

'Is that so?'

'Yep, right up there with the Military Foot Police.'

'The Military Foot Police?'

'It's all right, Detective, you don't have to play the innocent. The whole world and his mother seem to have read my file. And you, being Special Branch—'

'Your file is a restricted matter for the military authorities, Dr Finch.'

'Your pal Superintendent Dryden didn't seem to think so.'

'True, we are aware of some previous "incident" in South Africa,' said Coates. 'But the details, officially, remain classified.'

'Look – then, as now, there's a high-level game going on. And once again I've been sucked into it, entirely unwittingly.'

'And what game might that be?'

'Nothing personal, Detective, but at this point I'm not prepared to comment. I'd prefer to speak to someone from the War Office.'

Detective Coates shrugged and returned to his folder. He flipped through what appeared to be a collection of statements and something that looked like a hand-drawn timeline.

'According to our records you went missing from St Albans on Monday the 14th of November.'

'For God's sake, man, are you not listening? Every second counts!'

'The preceding Tuesday, the 8th of November, you had an altercation with a Mr Sidney Pickersgill in the Six Bells public house, St Albans.'

'JESUS CHRIST! A WOMAN'S LIFE IS AT STAKE!'

Finch stood up, straining at his chain. The constable rose, ready to intervene, but the detective remained sitting. He casually removed his spectacles, rubbed his eyes, then looped them back over his ears – like a jaded, career-worn teacher, waiting till his classroom had calmed down.

'Dr Finch, I am a reasonable man,' he said. 'I'll have no truck with outbursts of temper or raised voices. This interview – whether you like it or not – will proceed all the way to its conclusion and in a civilised fashion. We can do it peacefully and methodically, or we can call a halt until you have regained your composure…'

Finch sat down and hissed out a sigh. He would have to play it their way.

'Please, Detective,' he urged, straining to keep his voice down. 'The reason I am so exercised is for the very reason I have been insisting all along. Annie… Mrs Pointer… It's not *me* who's taken her… I *swear*… Just hear me out on this…'

'Dr Finch. Do you really think we have been doing *nothing* while you have been sitting in here?'

'No, I didn't mean to suggest—'

'Whether you choose to believe it or not, we actually paid full attention to the information you gave us in the car on the way over…'

'Thank you!'

'…and it remains the reason why we are so – to put it politely – *sceptical* about everything you have told us.'

'Sceptical?'

Coates looked down and shuffled his notes.

'…I'm afraid we can find no such person called Chilcot, or for that matter a private investigator named Clive Vax. As for their properties – the office at the top of the stairs opposite the York Minster pub is vacant; it has had no tenant for six months and is currently home to some rather worn office furniture and nothing else—'

'But—'

'Likewise, the basement flat in Fitzroy Square… 29B. It's the registered *pied-à-terre* of a gentleman named Ingram, an importer of sugar cane who is currently away on business tending to his holdings in Trinidad… And as for 11 Chepstow Place…'

'Did you go there?'

The detective gave a faint smile and a shrug of the shoulders.

'It was an interesting suggestion, Dr Finch. Quite the riddle.'

'What on earth do you *mean*?'

'I think you know.'

He returned to his folder.

'As I was saying… Mr Sidney Pickersgill…'

Finch sighed with exasperation and put his head in his hands.

'Jesus Christ, man, am I forever to be surrounded by imbeciles?!'

'…was a known associate of yours from the South African War. We believe him to have had access to this classified information we just mentioned – possibly incriminating information about certain aspects of your involvement in the war, possibly for use as blackmail against you – and Mrs Pointer, too, for that matter.'

Finch just shook his head.

'On Saturday, the…'

He flipped back and forth trying to find the date.

'The 12th,' interjected the constable.

'…he was taken into your home. On the basis of a petty theft – a *staged* petty theft, according to our colleagues in Hertfordshire – and of a matching firearm found in your possession, we have good reason to believe that you were party to his—'

'Representation. I want a legal representation… I *demand* legal representation.'

The detective sat back. He let the pause hang.

'That's strange, sir. A minute ago you were stressing the urgency of the situation. Now time has become suddenly elastic. You wish to set back proceedings for an hour or two while we find you a brief?'

'Forgive me, but if you can't locate a four-storey townhouse in the middle of London, I don't have much faith in your ability to pursue the rest of this investigation.'

Coates nodded to the constable, who shut his notebook. The detective closed his folder. They both stood, as if to leave.

'Very well, Dr Finch. Anyone in mind?'

They had him, he knew.

'Okay, Detective, you win…'

There was no option but to let the detective unburden himself.

'…Of *course* I wish to carry on.'

He slumped back and folded his arms as best he could, given his restraints. The men sat back down.

'Like I say, the alleged robbery was most probably staged… orchestrated, by your own hand,' Coates continued, now switching his tense to the present, as if talking Finch through a crime scene, 'but the purported burglar, your alleged blackmailer, Mr Pickersgill, ends up dead, most likely killed with a bullet from your army-issue Webley revolver… On Sunday the…'

'Thirteenth,' offered the constable.

'...you are arrested and taken into local police custody, are released on a technicality, though still a person of interest, but, the very next morning, Monday the...'

'Fourteenth.'

'Thank you, Constable, I think I could manage that one... you respond by absconding from your work and heading into London where you not only have a public spat in a public park with Mrs Pointer but, according to a reader's ticket issued in your name at Somerset House, and according to the clerk who inducted you, you research the background and address of Mr Sidney Pickersgill, leading you, next day, Tuesday the...'

The constable went to help again but Coates raised his hand.

'...15th... to head, via a decoy route, to his home town of Endthorpe, Norfolk, with the intention, we believe, of finding out with whom else he may have shared this privileged information.'

Finch blew out an exaggerated sigh of boredom.

'On arrival, you harass members of the local fishing community at their place of work and in the Coronet pub, from which you are duly ejected. You then ask probing questions of a landlady at a local bed and breakfast... What's more, you are now using an alias...'

'Leonard Cox,' went the constable.

'...to throw people off the scent... You then, yesterday, the 16th, further antagonise Pickersgill's colleague, Nathan Cole, a disabled serviceman, another veteran of South Africa, whom you believe to have knowledge of your affairs also. And when the local police superintendent...'

'Dryden,' the constable chipped in.

'...is called in... a man, I might add, who had, in the process of his investigation, as you suggest, uncovered some details of your past, you then choose to silence him... *fatally*... shooting him twice with a service-issue Lee–Enfield rifle, apparently stolen from Mr Cole.'

Finch could take it no more.

'I'm sorry, Detective, but this is pure and utter bollocks.'

Coates raised an eyebrow.

'I mean,' added Finch, 'you're daresay going to throw in the bit about the same Lee–Enfield rifle being found on the beach with "Ingo Finch, assassin" self-carved into the butt.'

Coates did his glasses-on, glasses-off thing again.

'There's no need for sarcasm, Dr Finch.'

'Really?'

'But yes, the weapon in question *was* found too, washed up the next morning on the mud flats, along with, nearby, your jacket and rucksack.'

He returned to his notes.

'We're still not sure whether you were clumsy and had fallen in the water in your struggle with Dryden – you have plenty of wounds to suggest as much…'

He gestured at the gash on Finch's forehead and the cuts on his wrists.

'…to go with the flash burn on your right hand, most likely from discharging said weapon, and which had not been present during your police interview on Sunday…'

He nodded at it, too.

'…or had even been so ambitious… so *sophisticated* as to fake your own death in order to continue your apparent mission to liquidate all interested parties.'

'Well bravo for my ingenuity,' snipped Finch.

'You then appear at the Savoy Hotel this morning, having been witnessed going up to the penthouse via a service lift, duping a young porter…'

'Mr Pandit Mirza,' said the constable.

'He is entirely blameless,' interjected Finch. 'Please do not punish him.'

'…and are later seen vacating the premises, avoiding the Savoy's house security guards, and wearing Mrs Pointer's husband's clothes.'

'All true,' said Finch, 'but with a perfectly logical explanation.'

'The next thing we know is that Mrs Pointer is gone, an alarm has been raised – by your Mr Mirza as it turns out – who then destroys his own credit by tipping you off that the police are on to you…'

'I told you, he is blameless. He was, quite innocently, doing as was asked of him.'

'And so that brings us up to where we are now, Dr Finch – with you apprehended, not a hundred yards from the Savoy, in what we suspect are further stolen garments, with Mrs Pointer's book, a novel, in your pocket and in possession of Colt sidearm with the serial number filed off, a weapon which you acquired on the black market at the York Minster pub in Soho along with twelve feet of rope… as yet unaccounted for… the purposes of which, we suspect, were for the securing of Mrs Annie Pointer as part of said abduction.'

Finch sighed.

'Cole,' he said.

'What?'

'There's a great big hole in this compelling yarn of yours. *Nathan Cole.*'

Coates attended to his spectacles again. He took them off, breathed on them, got out a white cotton handkerchief and gave them a thorough polish.

'Mr Nathan Cole?'

'Damn right, Mr Nathan Bloody Cole – pull the bastard in and get him to tell you what *really* happened in Norfolk. But, for Christ's sake, in the *meantime*…!'

Coates slowly, deliberately hooked his glasses back on.

'Dr Finch… This morning, Nathan Cole's body was found on the marshes at Blakeney…'

He looked Finch directly in the eye. A chilling stare. The bumbling clerk had gone.

'So, I'm going to ask you again – Mrs Annie Pointer… What have you done with her?'

Chapter Thirty-Five

After hearing the back door close, Mordecai waited a few minutes and then went downstairs. He wanted to be sure – not only that the woman had definitely left, but that all was as it should be. He checked every room of the house. He looked under every table, every bed, behind every door, every curtain, in every cupboard, every wardrobe.

The house had not been lived in for a while. Dust and cobwebs were accumulating, there were piles of mouse droppings. He grew angry at the casual waste of space when there were overcrowded, squalid slums not five miles to the east. The inequality seemed criminal.

He descended to the kitchen in the basement. The pots and pans had been neatly stacked away. There were two exterior doors the woman had failed to inform him about, though both were securely bolted, as was the front door and all the ground floor windows.

In the hallway, the grandfather clock ticked away. The house had been tended frequently enough for someone to come in and wind it… and, for that matter, to tidy up the post, some of which had been stashed on a table by the front door.

The clock had chimed on the half-hour – half past two. He checked it against the smart silver Hunter pocket watch that the rich man had given him, one with 'Hay of Shrewsbury' stamped on the reverse.

Satisfied that he was alone and secure, Mordecai unlocked the back door in the way he had been instructed – the two deadbolts, the conventional latch – testing, checking and rechecking, to make sure that he could do so instinctively and effortlessly.

Knowledge of geography, especially of the escape route, was a crucial part of his trade. He had learned the layout of the streets and the surrounding area; now he was familiarising himself with the house and the immediate environment.

Mordecai went back out, down through the garage. Cautiously he peered into the mews alleyway. It was empty as before, only this time with the doors now pulled across the garage that housed the Rolls-Royce. There was no more banging and bashing; the mechanic had ceased his swearing.

Mordecai did not think the man had seen him and thanked God for that. If he had, he would be a witness, and would have to be eliminated. As for people looking into the alley from upper-floor windows, someone who may have observed him casually? – he could not tell. But he had kept close to the wall, restricting the sightline. He did not think he could be identified.

In the garage, he lifted the heavy, circular cast-iron drain cover with 'Willenhall' stamped on it, scraping it to one side. He dropped a small stone down and waited for the splash. It was good ten-foot drop. The water, he had been assured, was deep enough.

He re-entered the house, relocked the front door and went back up the stairs to the attic. At fifty feet up, he had a good view across the gardens and, crucially, across the road. But this is where the woman had been wrong... Yes, the left-hand window opened easily enough and afforded an unobstructed view. He could see each carriageway clearly and the traffic moving back and forth. The pedestrians, too.

But it was the right-hand one he preferred and had selected long before he had even entered the building. To the uninitiated, this made no sense. Unlike the left window, the right's view was partially obscured by a plane tree... one of the rich man's beloved plane trees. But that was the point. It gave him cover. He could take his shot right between the branches.

It was a good choice – the fact that there was no sun in his eyes and, superficially at least, that the houses *did* all seem the same. And the man had been right about human psychology. When reacting to a gunshot, people *did* automatically look up. But it would be difficult to identify a particular window, especially one screened by the remnants of autumn foliage. That the sash window did not slide open was not a problem.

He thought for a moment of his time in Peking, when the Boxer rebels and Qing government soldiers, in their brutal reaction against colonialism, had besieged the Legation Quarter, massacring any foreigner they could get their hands on… And how, one day, with a screaming mob battering at the gates, he and a colleague, spaced strategically apart, had picked off the ringleaders at will, from over a thousand yards. They had fired not just from a high vantage point across a canal, but right through the open windows of another building in between, sowing confusion amid the mob and a panic that something supernatural was afoot.

The intervention of the Eight-Nation Army – of which Russia, Britain, France and America were part – was in the name of humanitarian relief, he was told, there to thwart the wanton barbarism of the Asian horde. It was those same 'civilised' Europeans who had then tortured the defeated rebels with a bestial cruelty, executing them in gleeful public rituals. The streets, quite literally, had run with blood.

Mordecai took a chisel and hammer. Gently he tapped out the corner of the bottom left pane. Using his jacket wrapped around his hand, he managed to ease the rest of the glass inwards.

He felt a light breeze on his face – southerly. He studied the movement of the trees – just a gentle sway – and watched the motion of the pedestrians. Were they stooping? Was there anything significant about the wind that made them move differently? A swirl perhaps? It appeared not. Nor was there rain.

Carefully he gathered up the shards of glass. There was a piece of newspaper next to the piled floorboards – something about the Olympic Games in St Louis. He wrapped the shards in it and put them in his bag.

As part of his equipment he had been offered the use of a tripod but had declined. It was an affectation… unnecessary. No sniper he knew ever used one. Other than the rifle and the ammunition, the only piece of gear he needed was a screwdriver, he said.

He dragged the billiards table to the centre of the room, the balls in the pockets clacking. Against the wall, wooden dining chairs had been stacked. He selected one and placed it on the table, about six feet back from the window, well away from view. Atop the table, the seat was a good height, up to his chest. He folded his jacket to form a cushion, knowing, too, that the envelope with his money in was safe within, then rested the rifle upon it. With a bit of rearranging he found the perfect downward angle – as secure a gun platform as there could ever be – allowing him to fire from his preferred standing position.

He looked through the scope and, for sighting purposes, pulled focus on a bright-red pillar box. By zooming in he could even read the collection times. The telescopic sight worked in conjunction with the fore sight on the barrel's nose. He took the screwdriver and made a minor adjustment, turning it less than a quarter turn in the slot on the screw head.

He heard the chimes – a long jangling refrain echoing from down below that signalled three o'clock. He checked it against his watch. He was now officially in position, ready. He would remain that way for the best part of an hour.

A clip of ammunition had been provided. But a sniper did not work like that. So precious was each shot that it had become part of the ritual to revere each bullet individually. He took two and stood them up like toy soldiers, the 7-millimetre silver-tipped points like miniature mediaeval helmets.

If the first bullet didn't strike home, the sniper had virtually failed. If the second bullet missed then he absolutely *had*. He put the other three in his pocket.

Chapter Thirty-Six

The grilling of Finch was interrupted by a sudden knock on the door. Detective Coates stopped, snapped a polite 'Come in' and a constable outside swung it open.

'Jilkes!' Finch blurted.

He entered looking harried. With good reason, thought Finch. Even Jilkes' suit, normally with a razor-sharp crease on the trouser leg, looked a little crumpled.

He caught Finch's eye but Finch couldn't discern the message.

'Detective Coates?' Jilkes asked.

Coates nodded. Jilkes dumped his brown leather briefcase and stuck out his hand.

'Reginald Jilkes, solicitor.'

Coates returned the greeting without feeling.

'Mr Jilkes.'

Jilkes nodded at Finch.

'Detective, I believe I am permitted to speak to my client… *alone?*'

Coates sighed and tipped his head to his constable. They stood, gathered their paperwork and the detective flipped closed his cardboard folder. They left briskly, as if downing tools in protest.

Jilkes went to the mirror and tugged the shabby green curtains across. He took the seat opposite Finch, the one that Coates had sat in.

'Aren't you a sight for sore eyes…' said Finch.

Jilkes smiled, though it wasn't convincing. He had the bearing of a man about to take a beloved old dog for one final walk before carting him off to the vet to be put down.

'Just to let you know, I kept my promise, Jilkes. I didn't request you… didn't ask for you.'

Jilkes gave something approximating a smile again. He had brought cigarettes like before… Navy Cut. He took out two, lit them both in his mouth then passed one to Finch. They both inhaled and held the smoke deep.

'I know,' Jilkes sighed. 'And I respect that, Ingo. Truth is… it was a hard one to avoid. The police were all over St Albans, asking questions – of me, of Maude, people at your surgery, in the pub. But Christ, this is Special Branch, Ingo, not some bumbling local bobbies. These boys are only called in when it's serious.'

'But Jilkes… Agatha, the kids… What you said…?'

He didn't answer and was spared having to do by the door opening again and a constable entering with two enamel mugs of tea, which he plonked down rather pointedly, causing some of it to spill over onto the table.

'Thank you,' said Jilkes to the man's back as he marched out.

'And thank *you*,' said Finch.

He raised the mug in salutation.

'I had a rethink, Ingo. I knew *you* wouldn't nominate me as your lawyer – given our talk – so thought I'd simply invite *myself*… if that's okay. I mean, assuming you don't have legal representation already…?'

Finch shook his head and came close to a grin.

'Let's just say I'm doing this for *both* of us,' Jilkes added. 'Get this thing well and truly wrapped up.'

Jilkes opened his briefcase and rifled through his papers. He set them on the table – copies of various police reports and the statement that Finch himself had signed. He pulled his fountain pen from his jacket.

'But I have to say… Jesus, Ingo, what the hell have you been *doing*, laddie?'

'It's been a difficult few days,' Finch deadpanned.

Jilkes had got tea on one of the papers. He dabbed at the mess, then picked up the sheet to waft it dry. It looked like a copy of the arrest warrant.

'That's something of an understatement. Jesus... It wasn't enough that you were accused of murder? You then take it upon yourself to go on some crazed cross-country spying mission?'

'That's a rather sensational way of—'

'Not only that but... *dammit*, Ingo... you use some sneaky underhand tactic to worm your way into my office. You take advantage of my staff...'

'Sorry, Jilkes.'

'If everything else here weren't so bloody serious, that could be one to end a friendship.'

'I know.'

Jilkes looked him in the eye.

'Is that how you got started? Got your leads?'

Finch nodded.

'Phone numbers, yes.'

Jilkes shook his head and rubbed the back of his neck.

'Well you've got balls, Ingo, I'll give you that, as well as ingenuity... and I'll certainly be looking into how I protect my client information in future... But as for everything else... This alleged *killing spree*?'

Finch puffed on his cigarette. He gave an ironic smile at the absurdity.

'Come on, Jilkes, it's bullshit, just like before.'

Jilkes fiddled with his fountain pen. He looked nervous, uncertain. Finch had never seen him like this in all the time he had known him.

'*Is* it, Ingo?'

Finch furrowed his brow.

'*Jilkes?...* What the hell do you *mean*?'

Jilkes didn't... *couldn't* look up. He read off from his notes.

'Your gun, the Webley – they matched it, Ingo...'

He set the paper aside and moved on to another.

Finch stubbed his cigarette out in the small tin ashtray.

'For Christ's sake, Jilkes. You yourself said it was inadmissible... agreed that ballistics is an inexact science!'

'It *is*... or *was* inadmissible. It was the question of its licensing that provided us with the technical get-out, if you remember. But now that its ownership been accepted... that it's *your* gun...'

'What are you saying?'

'I'm saying yes, ballistics, as a science, is not one hundred per cent precise, far from it. But I got another test run privately – intended to exonerate you, ironically. The police test, *my* test, they *both* point to the likelihood that, in all probability, it's the murder weapon, the gun that killed Pickersgill.'

Finch hissed his disapproval. He could sense Jilkes fumbling, reluctant to come to another point. He was fussing with his cigarette and tea.

'Spit it out, for God's sake!'

'Ingo... I mean... the drinking. Is it possible that—?'

Finch stood.

'Fuck, *no*, Jilkes!' he bellowed.

'You've never blacked out? Maybe done something you weren't even aware of? That you later regretted?'

'NO!'

'Okay, okay,' Jilkes soothed.

Finch sat back down again.

'It's just this stuff in Norfolk... the police officer, Dryden...'

'He was a bastard, Jilkes. He beat me to a pulp, chained me to a concrete block and left me to drown.'

'Ingo, there are witnesses queuing up to counter just about everything you've said with regard to every incident.'

'It was Nathan Cole who shot Dryden. He actually saved me. Was on my side, it turned out... an ally... for about five minutes. Till he then decided that *I* was a loose thread.'

'And so what, you killed him too?'

'*No*, Jilkes.'

'And here, in London, all these stories – phoney people, fictitious addresses?'

'Jilkes,' he protested. 'The lavender man... Vax... you met him yourself, for Chrissakes. He came to your office.'

And then the penny dropped. Finch sat back, sighed and folded his arms across his chest.

'They got to you again, didn't they…?'

He looked Jilkes directly in the eye.

'…You're here to put me under. The executioner… Here to deliver the *coup de grâce*.'

Finch shook his head with disdain.

'You *have* to tell them what you've done with Annie,' urged Jilkes, his tone now ringing, to Finch's ears, just plain hollow. 'Please, Ingo, tell us she's still alive.'

'Get out.'

'What?'

'I said, "Get out!"… NOW!'

'Ingo… Three murders? A kidnapping? You're looking at the gallows, man. Let me get you some medical certification. Diminished responsibility. You know, your career record, your war service… These are mitigating factors. We can at least attempt to commute it to something tolerable.'

The force with which Finch leaned across the desk and screamed hard into Jilkes' face, spit flying, made the lawyer visibly blanch.

'GET OUT!!!!'

No sooner had Jilkes scurried off than Detective Coates and the constable re-entered.

'Having a nice quiet cuppa, are we?' quipped Coates.

'It was most delightful,' fumed Finch.

'It'll take a while to find you another lawyer, one of your choosing anyway. We can put a telephone call in and get a public one over a bit quicker?'

Finch sighed again.

'That won't be necessary, Detective. But I *am* ready to talk.'

The Detective looked relieved. He and the uniform resumed their seats. The constable took out his notepad.

'It's the best way, Dr Finch. The truth always outs in the end.'

Finch, with his hands cuffed together, manipulated open the packet of cigarettes and took another one out. Coates reached across and lit it for him.

'I'll make you a deal,' said Finch.

Coates' splutter conveyed incredulity.

'Yet again, I really don't think you're in any position to negotiate.'

'Actually, I think I *am*, Detective… I'd like you to take me to Chepstow Place… Number 11… Right now.'

He blew out a cloud of smoke.

'Take me there… investigate the premises… Do that and I'll…'

'You'll what?'

'Tell you what I've done with her,' said Finch. '…with *Annie*.'

Chapter Thirty-Seven

Outside New Scotland Yard, Finch was led to a waiting black police Ford. With his hands cuffed in front of him, he was placed between Coates and the red-haired constable in the back. Up front, beside the driver, another policeman perched in the passenger seat. As the car lurched away, Finch saw a second Ford exit through the gates. It tucked in close behind. There were another four police helmets in it.

At least I'm out now. That much of the plan has worked.

Across the road to the left was the river, the big old stinking swirl of brown with its barges and boats and ferries and tugs. Up ahead, and very close, loomed the Palace of Westminster and Big Ben. They were a mere half-mile or so along from the Savoy. Finch thought of the walk through the gardens he had taken with Annie, with the same view set before them.

At Westminster Bridge, the car turned in towards Parliament Square. They chugged past Westminster Hall, with grim old Cromwell standing out the front, past the Commons, and the Lords tucked away behind it, with further uniformed officers in abundance. The chimes sounded: three o'clock. If only, thought Finch, he could convey to *this* place, the seat of government, what present concerns existed inside his head.

The traffic slowed and then ground to a halt.

'It's no good, sir,' said the driver. 'It's 'cause they've closed off all the roads either side of Buck House.'

'Need to keep a clear route to Whitehall,' explained the copper in the passenger seat.

'What's happening?' asked Finch.

The driver pulled over beside great, grubby Westminster Abbey.

Said Coates: 'This crisis everyone's banging on about… the Dogger Bank… the Russians… Seems there's been a breakthrough on the diplomatic front.'

The police driver climbed down and went over to confer with one of the policemen standing guard. His cape made him look like he sported wings.

Coates turned to Finch.

'Downing Street contacted us last night. It's been in the works for a few days but yes, there's to be a summit, a signing of a joint declaration at the Foreign Office, four o'clock. They won't say a declaration of *what* exactly, but we've been tipped a wink that the stand-off's been resolved. No doubt the foreign secretary will want to make some grand announcement – how he saved the day… rabbit out of the hat…'

'Bloody Lansdowne,' harrumphed the copper in the passenger street. 'He's just waiting for the PM to turn his back. Balfour will get a proper shafting.'

'Now now, Webb,' tutted Coates. 'We're above that.'

'Sorry, sir.'

The traffic was now cramming Parliament Square, still pouring in but not getting out. All routes out to the west and north were snarled up. Horses were whinnying, scraping their hooves, the few cars were over-revving. There was the odd beep of a horn. You could hear the moaning and groaning from atop a nearby omnibus.

A paper boy weaved in and out.

'*Standard… Standard…* Getch'yer *Standard*.'

Coates leaned over and gave him tuppence. He took a paper and folded it out on his lap. Finch saw the headline in huge, bold type: '*PEACE!*'

But there was never war.

The driver returned from his caucus.

'Foreign Office have done it again.'

'They certainly have,' quipped Finch.

'He means the traffic,' said Coates. 'Whitehall has a habit of going through us, the Met, the proper chain of command for matters of high-level policing, only for the civil servants to then start dealing with individual officers directly. End up coordinating the security themselves. Left hand never knows what the right hand's doing.'

The red-headed copper spoke. It was the first time Finch had heard him.

'The paper, sir. What's it say?'

'Just as they said, Sissons. Four o'clock, Whitehall. Russian ambassador's coming to eat some humble pie. Although they'll make it sound mutual. Allow them to save face.'

'So they'll be travelling from the embassy… down through Belgravia, along Eaton Square…' mused Webb, the copper in the passenger seat.

'Be the usual,' concurred the driver. 'Mall… Trafalgar Square…'

Coates looked around him.

'If we're going to get to Bayswater, we'll have to go another way.'

'I'll take her round the back,' said the driver.

He pulled the car over to the right to go around the square and back out the way they had come in. The bobbies on the beat waved their arms and cleared a path through the traffic. They could feel the indignation of the public.

'If we can curtail our speculation about the itinerary of our Russian friends for just a minute, might I remind everyone *our* task is to resolve a missing person situation,' urged Coates. 'Potential kidnapping, a woman's life possibly at stake.'

He looked at Finch.

'I don't know what the bloody hell you're playing at, Finch. But when we're done, you'd better start talking.'

Twenty minutes later – after a detour through Pimlico, Chelsea and round the back of Kensington Palace – they emerged onto

Bayswater Road, turning off and cutting up towards Chepstow Place. It was quiet, as before, the gardens on the left, the first row of houses on the right.

'Well, here we are,' said the driver.

Coates tapped him on the shoulder and they pulled over. The vehicle behind, which had lost them briefly, had since caught up. It followed suit.

Coates told the driver to stay put. He called for Webb and Sissons to join him. On the yell of 'Babbage', a beefy-looking constable from the other car hopped out. Finch was hauled onto the pavement. They stood looking at the row of houses.

'I give you Chepstow Place, Dr Finch,' said Coates. 'The first block.'

'And I give *you* Chilcot's house,' said Finch raising his cuffed hands to the end of the terrace.

'Number 11?' asked Coates.

Finch nodded. But something wasn't right. He could sense it.

'Look again,' the detective instructed.

Finch wasn't sure what he was getting at. And then he realised… *The house numbers!* The building bore not an eleven, but a black, hand-painted number *ten* on its Doric column.

'A quirk of the neighbourhood, Dr Finch. When the gardens behind us were added, in the 1860s, some older houses on the west side of the street were pulled down. We've checked with the council planning department. When *these* houses opposite were done up – quite extensively – the Royal Borough of Kensington reassigned the street numbers. But did so somewhat idiosyncratically…'

It was plain to see.

'One to ten,' sighed Finch. 'The block goes one to ten… *only* up to ten.'

'That's right. The numbers run sequentially, in a row. *But*, the other side, north of the crossroads, where the houses resume on *both* sides of the street…'

He pointed further up, where Chepstow Place continued.

'...they carry on from number 12 upwards, odds one side, evens the other...'

He watched the realisation dawn on Finch's face.

'You mean...'

'There *is* no number 11. If you want to get specific, there's no number 13 either. Left it out because of the bad luck. Happens sometimes.'

'But it was *here*,' protested Finch. 'This end one.'

'You mean number 10?'

'No, it was *eleven*!'

The tub of azaleas had gone. Things had been rearranged.

But it had to be!

Coates pulled out an Enfield revolver. It looked strange in his bank-clerk hand. He motioned to his men and they moved in close to hug the railings. A woman walked past pushing a pram. She didn't like the look of things and scuttled away. Across the road, amid the greenery, nannies tended to their infants, oblivious.

The detective led the way, the other three close behind, gently prodding Finch on.

'Right, just in case there's any funny business, we're to stay close in. No talking. Clear?'

They nodded, Finch included. Coates addressed him directly.

'And *you*? You'd better not be pulling a fast one.'

He turned to his men.

'Webb... Babbage... The front door...'

-

Chilcot set the dog down and it scarpered off into the corner to gnaw on its meaty treat. The fear, the shock, constricted Annie's throat. Her voice came out hoarse.

'Where am I? WHERE AM I?'

She forced herself to sit up and swung her legs to the floor.

'Where *are* you?' said Chilcot. 'My dear Mrs Pointer, we've already told you – somewhere perfectly safe.'

'I demand to know… I demand to know specifically where I am… and what you want with me!'

Chilcot and the lavender man exchanged a glance. Chilcot gave the nod, the go-ahead.

'Very well,' said the lavender man, 'if you must…'

She waited for him to explain. But there was a noise. Something downstairs? Something in the street? He stood up from his crouch – his knees clicked as he did so – and darted to the window. He turned back and threw Chilcot a look.

'He's *here*…'

-

Finch watched while the officers rang the bell. With no response, they pounded on the door with their fists. Coates looked back over the street to the second vehicle. He held up two fingers and beckoned. Two more officers ran towards them, leaving just the drivers in the cars. The detective signalled for them to go around the side of the building, presumably to climb over the wall and try the back door.

Suddenly the front door cracked open. It was an elderly lady standing there. She wore a long grey dress, her white hair tied back. Her face was heavily lined, her eyes glassy, and she carried herself with a stoop. Her long, bony hands were heavily liver-spotted and rested on a walking stick.

'Yes?'

She seemed to have just a solitary tooth in her mouth.

Coates went up the steps. He tucked his gun away.

'Excuse me, madam,' he said. 'Sorry to trouble you…'

He went through his little polite routine about showing his badge.

'We are looking for a man named Chilcot.'

The woman produced a wooden ear trumpet.

'*Chilcot*,' Coates repeated, slowly and loudly.

'Or something… a company maybe… named *Freeland*,' Finch called up, with the same unsubtle tone.

Coates turned back and gave Finch a look, suggesting he'd overstepped the mark.

'This *is* Mr Chilcot's house?' continued the detective.

The woman's face was one of utter confusion.

'This is *my* house… I've lived here all my life.'

'There were reportedly some men here. Monday morning.'

'What men?'

'Does anybody else live here, Mrs…?'

She may have been elderly but she could do indignation with the best of them.

'You've got a cheek,' she growled. 'Rogers, Mrs Clementine Rogers. Just me. Sometimes my housekeeper stays.'

'Has anybody approached you, asked to use your premises?'

'The police, you say? You should be out catching criminals.'

'Sorry to trouble you, madam…'

'My father fought at Waterloo, you know. Whole country's gone to the dogs. Why, if he were alive today, he'd—'

'Have a good day.'

The detective tipped his hat. The woman slammed the door.

'Wait, look…!' called Finch.

Coates saw it too.

There, on the column, was a fresh patch of white paint upon which, in black, someone had painted over a 'one', restoring a 'zero' rather artfully.

'This *is* the house,' Finch whispered. 'See?'

And then he got it. He'd seen no one actually *exit* the house at all, not through the door. Vax, Smert… they'd merely walked down the steps… some sort of charade.

Coates nodded. Finch detected a flicker, a shifting of sympathies.

It was such a simple trick… a simple con. The number '11' he had been staking out, had stood next door to a number 9 – the normal numerical sequence for the odd side of the street – and Finch had rightly thought nothing of it.

Annie stared at Chilcot good and hard.

'You ask where you are, then very well,' he said. 'You are in Russia.'

'*Russia?!*'

'Technically,' chipped in the lavender man. 'I mean legally this house isn't standing on British soil. It's sovereign Russian territory.'

'You are in the *Russian embassy*, Mrs Pointer,' explained Chilcot. 'Where no one – if you'll excuse the expression...'

The dog yapped, gnawing on the human digit.

'...can lay a finger on you. Not that they can try, even if they wanted to. It's effectively a sanctuary. Let's just say that your absence will focus your friends' minds, diverting attention from other matters.'

Next to the fireplace, flush with the oak panelling, was another door. She hadn't noticed it. Slowly it opened.

'No,' screamed Annie. 'NO...!'

Into the room stepped the man mountain – with his flat face and his dumb expression and the thickest neck she'd ever seen.

Chapter Thirty-Eight

Coates ushered his men back to the vehicles. As he did so he took hold of Finch's arm.

'Dr Finch?'

'Yes.'

He waited till his men were out of earshot. The man looked uncertain for once, thought Finch, as bumbling and as insecure as his appearance was meant to suggest.

'What's *really* going on here?' Coates asked.

'I was hoping you could tell me.'

The detective rubbed the back of his neck.

'I don't know… It's just that some of this…'

'What?'

In the park, children squealed as they played.

'I mean… it just doesn't add *up*… Not just this house… the address… It's… I don't know… Take your lawyer friend…'

'Jilkes?'

'Back at the Yard. He was on the scene way too… *quickly*. Believe me, I've known some briefs, they have wings on their heels, they can process a huge amount of information very swiftly, but he… Jilkes… It was almost as if he came pre-prepared, as if he'd been…'

'Set up in advance… Tipped off?'

He nodded.

'It was evident you two weren't exactly seeing eye to eye on the matter,' said Coates.

'What makes it worse, is that he is – *was* – an old friend. But I know, in his defence, he's been under a lot of pressure. *Personal* pressure. He's been leaned on. *Heavily*.'

'I see.'

'Unfortunately, what started out as him just wanting to steer me away from the Pickersgill affair has seemingly transformed into him actively conspiring to put me away behind bars.'

PC Webb leaned out of the car.

'Sir, the traffic round Westminster. Unless we go now…'

'Just a minute.'

Coates looked Finch in the eye. He kept his voice down.

'Dr Finch… I have to ask you… What do you know about something called "Ursa"?'

Finch said nothing.

'I'll say it again: Ursa,' said the detective.

'Ursa?'

'Like the Latin… *Bear*.'

Coates sensed Finch's reluctance.

'I'm going to be honest with you here, Dr Finch. I *do* know about your war record. I've read the file back to front: what happened to you in South Africa, your brush with the darker elements of military intelligence, the transcript of every hearing. Mrs Pointer too. I also know far more about what you've been up to these past few days than you probably think.'

'How…?'

'Let's just say I have friends… certain well-placed friends.'

'Oh.'

'My point, Dr Finch, is that I know that the name Ursa is something that has already cropped up on your travels – a name Pickersgill had left for you. So you can drop the pretence.'

'Like I've said before, Detective, I don't know if I can trust you… Nothing personal, but trusting people has got me into hot water.'

'I assure you that you *can* confide in me.'

Finch blew out a sigh. In the background a nanny admonished a crying child.

'No disrespect, Detective, but given that you've just spent the afternoon trying to pin a kidnapping and about fifteen murders on me, you'll forgive me if I need a little more… *persuasion*.'

'For God's sake, Finch. I wasn't born yesterday,' Coates harrumphed. 'I know you didn't abduct Mrs Pointer… *Annie*… any more than I believe you killed any of those people. Been enough years on the force to be able to tell when a man is telling the truth or not.'

Finch felt his blood rise.

'Then what the *hell*…?'

There was an urgency now.

'Finch, listen to me. Annie has been taken, yes, but my sources… if you'll forgive me for being cryptic… inform me that she is perfectly safe and in a secure location.'

'*What?*'

'That said, I'm not *really* supposed to know all this. Just between you and me. Meanwhile, it would seem, I'm to persist with this official charade of keeping you under arrest until this whole thing… Ursa… is over…'

He paused to let it sink in.

'…You repeat to the authorities what I've told you, by the way, and I'll be up on a charge, drummed out of the Met. I think as a quid pro quo, that's a pretty big one. So… *now* do you trust me?'

PC Webb leaned out of the car, anxious again. Coates raised his palm to stay him.

'Very well,' Finch began. 'Ursa. It's a code word. I don't know for *what* exactly. But it was serious enough for Pickersgill to think it worth getting himself killed over. He was obviously under extreme duress, probably just about to meet his maker, when he left it for me as a clue… No, not a clue, a *plea*.'

There was safety in offering that, Finch thought. The detective would surely know it already. He watched for his reaction. He gave nothing away.

'…The same reason, if I might be so bold, that assorted people, these past few days, have either being trying to kill *me*, or at the very least have me put away.'

They could sense the policemen in the cars growing curious as to their private conversation.

'Please, you need to keep going, Dr Finch… and quickly…'

He gave a discreet nod towards his men.

'I'm not sure who *I* trust either. And you're not really *telling* me anything here.'

'I'm sorry, Detective, it's just…'

'Okay, Dr Finch. What if I tell you this?… What if I tell you that, last week, there was a secret briefing… Certain heads of department at Scotland Yard… Various Whitehall types… high-ups from the War Office… Foreign Office… a grand powwow of the "Secret Service" for want of a better word…'

'How do you know all this?'

He gave an ironic smile.

'I'm a detective. I make it my business to know.'

'I see.'

'Anyway, together they've been running counter-intelligence, feeding it to Special Branch, much of it for use against the usual suspects – Fenians, anarchists and the like. Have foiled a few bombings and things over the years, as I'm sure you know – the Walsall Plot of '92… the attempt on the Kaiser at Queen Victoria's funeral…'

'I'm aware of them, yes. The last I read, the chap who thwarted those plots, your Special Branch boss, had been hanging around with Harry Houdini.'

'Mr Melville. He does admire a bit of lock-picking, yes. A party trick…'

Finch could now sense Coates' hesitancy.

'…But anyway, this counter-intelligence discussed at the meeting the other day, I wasn't *supposed* to know about it. Way above my level. But I got fed some information… you know, from my source… That word, Ursa, it was cropping up again… No mystery in the use of a code word in itself, the Secret Service love using them. They have code words, these days, for making a cup of tea. But it was the *way* this code word was used.'

'How so?'

'It was there on the orders for your detention – Hertfordshire… Norfolk… and now in London. It's like Ursa, whatever it is, is a third-party operation, something that includes provision for *your* removal from the equation as part of the bargain… All part of some preordained plan. Some big plot that's going on.'

'Are you saying that the Secret Service are *in* on the plot?'

'No… I'm not… But they are *aware* of it, whatever it may be, and are quite possibly helping to *manipulate* it, if you get my drift.'

Finch looked up at the sky. The blue was now fighting a rearguard against ominous grey.

'With what I'm about to tell you, Detective Coates, I could be signing my own death warrant.'

'Likewise, Finch. I assure you, very much likewise.'

'Okay then… Russia… the Dogger Bank incident… the night of October 21st… It was a set-up. The Russian navy was provoked into firing on the Hull fishing trawlers. Someone was out there at sea transmitting false radio chatter… masquerading as Japanese… The Russian sailors, daresay inexperienced and ill-educated, got trigger-happy… started blasting away, just as someone hoped they would.'

'Who?… Who was behind the transmission?'

'Therein lies the question… anarchists… Germans… Irish Republicans… pissed-off Afrikaners… who knows…? *Anyone* who wants to make mischief by pitting Britain and Russia against each other… *Any* interested party with something to gain from such a situation… Maybe even the Japanese themselves – war on two fronts and all that. We have a treaty with them *too* now.'

'Don't think they need much help at the moment. Looks like they can handle themselves.'

Webb leaned out of the car again, frowning.

'Be right there, Constable,' assured Coates.

He looked at Finch.

'And so, what… Pickersgill? Out there in his mission boat? He's witness to all this?'

'It was *his* mission boat they used.'

'I see. And, what, he came to you for help…?'

Finch nodded.

'…Having some inkling that you'd been mixed up with military intelligence?'

'In a roundabout way. He was a military policemen, I found out. Had taken part in my torture in Cape Town. Was a religious man and felt guilty, apparently. I suppose it was reasonable enough for him to assume that I didn't swim in conventional channels. Wanted someone in whom he could entrust his Big Secret… and who would *act* upon it.'

'But you *couldn't* be his saviour… not officially… because you… and Annie – Mrs Pointer – had signed some agreement… your liberty conditional on some official pledge to keep away from matters of state? Something you'd signed in the aftermath of the South African business?'

'Can't fault you on your powers of deduction, Detective Coates.'

The man smiled.

'Although it's all moot now, of course,' Coates went on. 'I mean, if there's a declaration… an accord… about to be signed between Britain and Russia, kiss and make up, then this whole crisis has been averted.'

'Wait!'

'What?'

'The treaty… the agreement… If the wheels were already in motion this morning, why are the powers that be still invoking Ursa? Still detaining *me*? It can only mean that Ursa—'

'It's still happening… still ongoing…!'

Coates ushered Finch towards the car.

'Right, we need to get you back to the station as soon as possible. I need to speak to my superiors.'

Finch raised his cuffed wrists. Coates shook his head.

'You mean I'm still under *arrest*?'

'Well here's the thing… officially, *yes*…'

'That's no good, Detective. If I'm innocent, I expect to be treated as such.'

'I'm afraid I can't do that… for the moment. You have to play along.'

He gently nudged Finch into the vehicle.

Unseen, Finch worked his right wrist hard against the cuffs. He had endured enough pain these last few days. A little bit more didn't seem to matter.

–

Chilcot came over. His little dog yapped and growled and ran around with the remnants of the human finger in its mouth, leaving blood spots on the carpet.

He extended his hand, an offer to help Annie up. She had little choice but to take it. Her head felt much clearer. On her feet she was weak but not unstable.

'We will have some food sent up shortly,' he said. 'That will help restore you.'

He led her to the window and the lavender man standing there.

'There,' he said.

They were about three floors up. In the courtyard below them, within gates and iron railings, a motor limousine was being wheeled out. Its red bodywork and chrome plating were polished to a mirrored shine. It had a plush red leather interior to match. A uniformed chauffeur loitered nearby, smoking a cigarette. Over the front wheel arches, on little masts, were mounted horizontal tricolours in white, blue and red.

The whole scene seemed bizarre, thought Annie. There she was, somewhere in west London and yet, technically, she was beyond the sovereign jurisdiction of the nation. There were houses opposite, people passing by on the pavement not thirty yards away. They might as well be on a different planet.

'You… going after Finch. Detaining me here. Is *that* what Ursa is all about?'

'You could say that,' said the lavender man. 'Part of it, anyway.'

'And what, November 4th, that was the day you began your little elimination spree, killing the Norfolk fishermen and then anyone else who was party to your misdemeanours in the North Sea?'

Chilcot began laughing. It was a big fruity laugh that she found both insulting and demeaning. He shook his head in mock exasperation at her apparent misreading of the situation.

'Look there, Mrs Pointer…'

He waved his hand up towards the portrait on the wall – of the young man posed in a breastplate, with sad eyes, standing before a river and a line of trees.

'…You know who that is?'

She shrugged.

'*Pyotr Velikiy…* Peter the Great. Founding father of the modern Russian state. Conqueror of the Swedes, pacifier of the Turks. Six foot eight inches tall. A giant of a man by the standards of his own time, as indeed of today. A colossus in every respect. The man who dragged Russia kicking and screaming into the modern world…'

She feigned nonchalance.

'So?'

'You know, aside from his geographical consolidation of what we now call the Russian Empire, dear Peter performed two pieces of magic.'

'He was quite the entertainer.'

'The first one is that that he hoodwinked the Russian people into believing they were somehow "European". He sealed it by marrying its royals into Europe's great houses and introducing the notion that Russians were signed-up members of the Western Enlightenment, when, till then, Russia had been what it always was: a hybrid, a land that straddled East and West, Europe and Asia, a patchwork quilt of peoples – of Orthodox Christians, Jews, of Slavs and Samoyeds, of Tatars and Cossacks, Mohammedans and Mongols.'

He turned back to her.

'You think he bound them together with familial love for the mother country, Mrs Pointer, a shared belief in a united destiny?'

'I'm suspecting not.'

'Quite right. His enlightened ideals only went so far. He bound them together by bloody autocratic rule, a modus operandi of the Tsars that has endured for four hundred years, since the days of Ivan the Terrible, and one that can no longer, in good conscience, be tolerated. Obfuscation and lies on the part of the Russian government cannot mask an unpalatable and inevitable truth about our homeland – that Tsarist Russia, Imperial Russia, is *finished*.'

The dog began growling, a pathetic little rasp, as it dropped the finger and began play-fighting with it, batting it around with its paws.

'And *two*?' said Annie.

'Two?'

'You said old Peter performed two tricks… Our magician.'

'Really, Mrs Pointer, there is no need for such sarcasm. But, yes, Number Two. Peter's other great act of modernisation was the refashioning of *time itself*. When he was a young man, wandering around Europe, filling his head with fancy ideas, it struck him as ludicrous that Russia should still operate according to an ancient biblical diktat which considered the world to be a mere 5,000 years old, a system of calibration so antiquated that even the Catholics had abandoned it. It seemed utterly bizarre to Peter that while the rest of Europe was in the year 1700, on the cusp of industrialisation, Russia was stuck in the past… in every sense…'

'And so, he changed it?'

'Precisely… He brought Russia into the present day. And from then on she would no longer celebrate her New Year on September 1st, either, but January 1st like everybody else. Only, despite revising the years, as a sop to the Church, he kept to the old Orthodox calendar – the Julian rather than the Gregorian one which most of Europe had since adopted. Yes, Russia is still out of step with the Western world, but now, thankfully, by only thirteen days. We may be here today in grey old London on the 17th of November but on the Russian calendar it is still…'

'November the 4th!'

'You will not have heard the news yet, Mrs Pointer…' said the lavender man.

He reached to a nearby table where lay a copy of the *Standard*. He handed it to her. She saw the huge bold-type headline, '*PEACE!*'

But there was never war.

'…The Russian ambassador is shortly to have an audience with the British prime minister and foreign secretary as a way of sealing our friendship. They will sign a document which will see off any further talk of war between our nations. Or in your Australian case, our Empires.'

'*Our* nations? Which one is *your* nation?'

He gave a thin smile.

'The accord will be formally consecrated next week, presented to Parliament, followed by an international peace commission in Paris – officially an impartial inquiry, but in reality a partisan tribunal at which Russia will concede full culpability for her actions under the terms of the Hague Convention, along with the agreed payment of reparations.

'St Petersburg has done an exceptional job in selling this arrangement to the British government. An act of supreme diplomacy. There is nothing more that Russia wants than to join Britain and France in an alliance against Germany – to convert the *Entente Cordiale* into a *Triple Entente* – and will grovel accordingly, prostrating herself like the third-rate power she is, in this case by acknowledging the stated incompetence of her very own navy, a national humiliation.'

Chilcot took over: 'What many in Russia wish for, however, is not that which the ruling elite desires. Russia is a crumbling, failed state with a decadent inbred royal family – related to your own, I might add, Germany's too – that till only recently held its entire population in servitude… *serfs*.

'Russia is already engaged in a foolhardy war in the Far East with Japan. It is teetering on the brink of collapse. To which end there are some of us, of a more forward-thinking disposition, who see the bigger picture, take the longer view. We do not see war between Britain and Russia as a disaster at all. Indeed, a two-fronted war against the dominant power in each hemisphere – Japan in the East, Great Britain in the West – would actually be quite desirable, insomuch as it would give that final push, hasten the inevitable… total civil collapse. It suits *our* purpose so much better…'

'*Your* purpose?'

'…Then *we*… certain interested parties… can start from scratch and build a society fit for the twentieth century, turning our back on this stupid system of empires and alliances that will ultimately drag us, and *you*, to Armageddon. Regrettably, our plan in the North Sea failed. And unfortunately, in covering our tracks, we had to take some extreme measures. But our cause, bringing Britain and Russia into war against each other, is not yet lost…'

Down below, the chauffeur slid onto the front seat. Someone cranked the handle and, with some puffs of black smoke, the car coughed into life. Waistcoated embassy valets appeared and opened the car doors. Staff went to swing back the iron double gates to the street. A man stepped out of the building's entrance, surrounded by apparent well-wishers – a morose-looking grey-haired man in a black suit, with a full moustache, some medal ribbons on his chest and a white, blue and red sash across his shoulder. He was helped on board the car and an associate climbed in with him.

'Behold, our ambassador – poor oblivious fool; dim decadent aristocrat – off to supplicate before the British Crown,' proclaimed Chilcot.

'Fortunately,' said the lavender man, 'he will never make it.'

'*Ursa?* Is *that* what Ursa is all about?'

'As you might put it,' scoffed Chilcot. 'What better way to reignite hostilities between our two countries than by having our dear ambassador assassinated on the streets of your Empire's capital? No matter who actually pulls the trigger – we have British militant workers' groups just queuing up to take credit. Britain, thus far, has been too pragmatic to declare war on Russia. But

Russian pride can only be pushed so far. This time it will be St Petersburg spoiling for war. You think I am acting in a clandestine fashion? There isn't a single member of this embassy's staff who isn't a loyal Bolshevik. I've seen to that.'

'You arrogant bastard… You arrogant *bourgeois* bastard.'

He uttered another of his smug chuckles. His chihuahua scampered over. He picked the dog up. The chewed finger lay on the floor at his feet, left like some little tribute.

'There is hardly anyone more *bourgeois* than yourself, Mrs Pointer. The good news for you is that your husband is a valuable player in this exercise, helping fuel the arms race that will hasten the chaos, and with it our cause. As a hostage you hold great value. We can even smuggle you away under the cloak of diplomatic immunity. His anger, his determination, will be something we can use to our advantage. Another reason we wanted that irritant Finch out of the way.'

Annie swung a fist at Chilcot. With his hands cradling the dog and unable to react, she connected hard with his nose and dark red trickled from his left nostril. The dog began snarling at her and he put it down again. Seemingly taken aback by the sheer audacity of Annie's blow, he pushed her hard on both shoulders. She fell to the floor. The dog yapped at her.

He turned to the lavender man.

'Come,' he said.

They left the room. She could hear the key turn in the lock.

Chapter Thirty-Nine

In his attic room on Eaton Square, Mordecai rechecked his scope and tested the manoeuvrability of his weapon, pulling the stock tightly into his shoulder. Shooting at a moving target required him to not just lock onto it, but follow its line of motion. He would have to anticipate its speed, its path, the crosswind and everything else that could have impact upon the flight of a bullet, perhaps firing slightly ahead if the conditions dictated.

An omnibus clopped past in an easterly direction, the same way as his intended target. On the open upper deck, at the front, sat a gentleman in a bowler hat. Mordecai pulled focus, going in and out until he could see him, clear as day, right there in front of him, rapt in something of a daydream, staring into space.

Mordecai got the man in his crosshairs, the lines intersecting right over his temple. He followed him for ten, twenty yards. He pulled the trigger, squeezing it oh-so-slowly until the firing pin went *click* in the empty chamber. Life, thought Mordecai… *knew* Mordecai… was suspended by the most slender of threads.

Passing the other way was an empty horse and cart, clipping along at a fair rate, maybe twenty miles an hour, having, he assumed, just delivered its wares. Mordecai homed in. The driver and his boy sat up front, the former twitching a long whip, evidently complaining about something, the boy with a surreptitious finger up his nostril. The cart was travelling about the same speed as an automobile in such traffic. He repeated the process, this time using the man's baggy woollen cap as his target. Again… *click*!

Policemen had begun moving into the square. Pretty soon, within minutes, the last of the traffic had passed and the road was empty, blocked off. A trickle of pedestrians increased along each of the pavements, building into a steady stream. Children were being pushed to the front. They were in uniform, seconded hastily (no doubt on the promise of financial reward on the part of the embassy) from local schools.

Under the looming grey clouds, there was a sudden flowering of paper Union Jacks and Russian tricolours, waved with juvenile fervour. They were being handed out in pairs by young women proceeding down the lines... From the Russian Embassy too, Mordecai was sure, and probably with handfuls of sweets as easy bribes. Mother Russia was doing her utmost to foster goodwill, milking this occasion for all it was worth.

There had been some debate before about whether the square would be closed to normal traffic. The intelligence seemed to keep changing hourly. And now Mordecai resented the fact that not only would he have to perform his task before an audience of children, but that they would be right in harm's way should he miss.

Should he miss...

He heard the grandfather clock strike a single chime. Half past three. It would not be long. He saw policemen moving in. He looked at the two bullets he had stood to attention. He was now primed and ready. He took one, kissed it, shuttled the bolt and locked it into place in the breech.

Mordecai, do not even entertain the notion of failure.

It was a good sniping position. He had chosen well. Despite the tree's boughs, Mordecai could get a clear shot. His fulcrum was solid, secure and at a good height. He looked out again, ready, alert. And then he saw him, standing on the other side of the road, inert, just gazing up in his direction... *Smert.*

Is he here to check up on me?

He studied his flat, expressionless features through the scope, but it was unnerving. It was as if the freak were staring right back through the lens.

And then something else... Something he absolutely didn't need. *It had started raining...*

-

Back in the police Ford, Finch said nothing. Wedged again between Detective Coates to his left and Sissons the junior constable to his right, he discreetly chafed his right wrist against the handcuffs. It was working. He had drawn blood.

As the first spots of rain appeared on the windscreen, the car zigzagged down to the Bayswater Road, turned westwards and back into the traffic, with the driver and PC Webb up front moaning and groaning to each other. Finch looked behind. They had lost the other car already. Though most likely it would catch up.

There was enough noise for Finch to whisper to Coates.

'The clock's ticking. The agreement is being signed at four o'clock, you say?'

'That's what's been confirmed.'

'What time is it now?'

Finch's wristwatch had been removed at the police station. Coates carried a pocket watch. He flipped it out on its chain.

'Almost twenty to. Not long now.'

'Listen…' urged Finch, 'if *you* didn't want this signing to go ahead, *didn't* want peace between Britain and Russia, what would *you* do?… Your last roll of the dice?… I know what *I'd* do.'

There was a flash of realisation on Coates' face.

'You mean?'

'That's right,' said Finch. 'I'd eliminate the ambassador. And where better to take him out…?'

'Damn it, Finch…!'

He called to the driver.

'Jennings.'

'Sir?'

'Turn her around. West Carriage Drive. To Kensington. We're going to cut straight across the park.'

'But sir—'

'Just do as I say.'

While the detective was preoccupied, Finch chafed the handcuff some more. His wrist was bleeding freely.

Above them the skies were darkening fast, the clouds leaden and laden. The temperature seemed to drop several degrees. And then the heavens opened.

'Shit,' snapped Coates.

The car was open-topped. While the detective buttoned his coat, the policemen started pulling on their capes.

Shouting to be heard, Coates again berated his driver. Finch seized his moment. He turned to the young policeman next to him.

'I say, PC Sissons, is it?' he asked.

The young, ginger copper was wriggling on his waterproof. He nodded.

'See this here...'

Finch was bare-headed and exposed to the elements. He held his wrists up. Right on cue, aided by the rain, a crimson trickle turned south towards his cuff and then splashed onto his trousers.

'I'm in a spot of bother. Any chance you could take the right one off?'

Sissons didn't know what to do. His superior, Coates, was locked in a heated discussion with Jennings – someone, Finch realised now, who may have been working against him. Distracted, the detective waved a hand at Sissons to say that it was okay.

'I'll have to cuff you to the seat,' said Sissons, indicating a metal bar in front of them.

Finch nodded. Sissons reached for the keys.

The rain lashed harder still. It was now sweeping over in great icy sheets.

'Jennings, I said West Carriage Drive,' barked Coates, gripping the brim of his hat.

'But sir, our orders were to return straight to Scotland Yard.'

Added PC Webb, 'We go that way we'll run straight into the traffic around Kensington. It'll take us forever.'

Sissons took his key to Finch's right handcuff.

'Jennings, that's an order. West Carriage Drive!'

'But sir—'

'*Now!*'

'Sir?!'

It was Sissons this time.

'Not now.'

'SIR!'

Coates turned.

But Finch was already running through the park gate, through the torrents…

-

Annie tried the door. Inevitably it was locked, as was the concealed door by the fireplace. Frantically she banged on the window, but to no avail. The sashes on both the room's windows were screwed shut. The glass appeared to be double-… triple-glazed… virtually soundproof. She whacked the panes with a marble ashtray… toughened too.

There was a cabinet against one wall. Its top half was a bookcase, containing all twenty leather-bound volumes of the *Encyclopaedia Britannica.* The bottom drawers were locked.

In the corner was a writing desk, a bureau. On it, and in its drawers, she found a couple of fountain pens, a bottle of ink, pencils, thick wedges of writing paper, envelopes and assorted stationery. But there was no key.

She reached into her hair, fastened up at the back, and released two pins. She went to the concealed door, set flush within the wall, complete with wallpaper and dado rail to disguise it. As she suspected, the door contained a straightforward rim lock. Calmly, but as quickly as she could, she put one hairpin into the bottom of the keyhole and moved it to the left, taking up the tension. The second pin she inserted into the round hole at the top of the lock and scratched away at the lever within.

It would open eventually, she knew. It was a matter of patience. She remembered how her brother had shown her. Some locks would give straight away. Others, like this… you would have to keep at it, scraping away until it yielded. But the lock was narrow and the pins too thick. She went back to the desk. She rummaged around. In a shallow tray drawer there were some pencils, a sharpener, a pink rubber eraser and, in their own section, some paperclips. She took two and bent them out straight. They were made of steel wire, not easy to refashion. But they were thinner than the hairpins.

She went to the door and tried again. She couldn't get the correct purchase with the upper lock pick. It would take longer than she thought.

Knock-knock.

A rapping on the main door made her stop. She sprang back to the settee. She watched the glass doorknob turn, hastily refastened her hair and hid her new makeshift tools in her skirts.

It was a male arm that opened the door. She heard the man's voice in the corridor and a volley of Slavic orders. Into the room, duly instructed, came a maid – a plain-looking, scrawny woman in a grey dress and white apron, probably in her thirties, who carried a tray bearing a selection of sandwiches, a small copper samovar, a plate, cutlery and tea paraphernalia.

While the door remained held open slightly, she set the tray down on the coffee table.

'For you, Miss,' she said, her accent heavy.

Annie wondered whether she could physically get the better of her. Charge the door. But her captors would have thought of that. Was it worth the gamble? Probably not. She still stood a better chance of getting out of there by picking the lock.

The woman, with her stooped posture and tied-back dark hair fussed over the food and arranged the crockery. She checked over her shoulder, then looked up at Annie with dark eyes.

'I think you'll find the Russian ham most delightful.'

'I'm sure it is.'

Annie went to the window. There were others in the courtyard milling around the vehicle – members of staff, men in suits, women in finery. They were waving as the ambassador's vehicle motored out through the main gates. There was a line of Metropolitan Police vehicles waiting to escort it. The sky above was dark, foreboding.

The maid left and the door was relocked from the outside.

Annie went back to the concealed door and tried her implements again. She was making good progress but then a paperclip snapped. She tried another and it broke too.

A violent shudder hit the windows. The rain was suddenly lashing hard.

One by one the paperclips failed. Unwilling to gamble the last two, she slumped on the settee. She took the cup and poured herself some black tea from the small tap on the ornate samovar.

And then she saw…

It was what the woman had said – to try the ham. For there, amid the sandwiches, poking out, just about visible beneath the thick, seeded bread, between the pink meat and the green pickles, was the head of a black latch key.

Outside, the motorised procession was moving off, the sudden downpour playing havoc with the open-topped vehicles in which police capes were donned and ambassadorial umbrellas hoisted. The wrought-iron gates swung closed quickly as the valets dashed to get back inside. Amid its escort, the polished red limousine moved down the street.

The key fitted the lock. She pushed the door open.

Her boots… She was still in stockinged feet. She snatched them up from beside the fireplace and went through. She was at the top of a long, narrow, wooden staircase that led down to ground level. Not one that switched back, but that was a continuous flight, probably concealed within a false exterior wall. It smelled of wood, damp and dust, just like a cellar.

There was no lighting. When she closed the door again, it was dark. She relocked the door by touch and pocketed the key.

There was enough light creeping round the door frame at ground level for her to just make things out. As she inched her way down her eyes grew accustomed. She felt bizarrely and momentarily like Alice, on her adventure to Wonderland. There must have been at least fifty steps. She had descended from what she calculated was the second floor.

At the bottom, she tried the handle. It was unlocked. She opened it just a thin crack. She was at the side of the building, between the embassy and the line of small fir trees screening the building next door. There was no one around. She pushed it further. She was still within the compound but there was clear courtyard between her and a small iron-railing access gate, about ten yards away. The rain pelted hard and splashed up from the cobbles.

If it were locked, she could still climb over, she thought. A couple of elderly women hurried past, arm in arm, beneath their shared brolly. A greengrocer's wagon trundled along, laden with sodden cabbages. It was that close she could smell them.

Boots in hand, she crept along the edge of the building, stockinged feet in the puddles, the water cascading down from the overflowing guttering. There were no windows to be seen from. The only question was what lay around the corner. Would she have to run for it, or casually stroll on over? She could hear nothing. She hoped it would be the latter.

She counted down in her head – *one… two…* And, on *three*, stepped out.

And there, standing before her, blocking her path, collar turned up, hat brim wilting and with a small automatic pistol in hand, was the lavender man.

Chapter Forty

Finch ran along the wide tree-lined avenue that led towards Kensington Palace. He was already soaked to the bone, struggling for breath, his heart beating overtime on the sheer excess of adrenalin.

The rain came in proverbial stair rods, an explosive cloudburst that had the water splashing up hard on impact with the ground, creating a foot-high veil of spray. People out for an afternoon constitutional or casually walking their dogs had morphed into huddled clumps of forlorn humanity, gathered around the tree trunks, seeking vain shelter under near leafless branches. An umbrella, blown inside out, its spokes bent, canvas ripped, cartwheeled across the path.

In his days as a runner, he had been taught how one used one's arms as much as one's legs – and so he pumped his fists high, swinging his elbows back and forth, in strong, defined arcs, helping to lift his body and increase his stride. But his shoes were ill-suited – too tight, hindering. The rainwater tugged at him, slowing him.

He threw a look over his shoulder. Sissons and Webb were after him. Webb was a big man and not moving well. And Sissons seemed to be in the wrong profession altogether. But they were not far behind. Detective Coates and his obstinate driver, he guessed, would be trying to intercept him by car, cutting him off at one of the park's exits.

Finch pushed hard and, despite his physical limitations, moved fifty-plus yards ahead of the coppers. But then came the police whistle. Webb had it to his lips and was blowing furiously – bad in that it would draw attention, but good in that it would slow the policeman's advance. Though its sound was muffled by the downpour, Finch thought he heard another echo from somewhere. It was a constable's call to Mecca. The cry would resound from one bobby to the next.

'Police! Stop that man!' Webb was now yelling to no one in particular, placing too much faith in the apprehending abilities of drenched old ladies with sodden Yorkshire terriers.

Finch cut left past the Round Pond. The tight shoes were giving him cramp in his arches. And his breathing… He didn't know how long he could sustain the pace. In an ornate, glass-panelled public shelter, children clutched toy yachts, corralled by their mothers and nannies. He needed to get out of the park. Speed dropping, he veered straight for the Serpentine. His body hurt so much, more pain simply didn't matter.

There was an excited scampering. A drenched springer spaniel ran alongside him – white with liver markings – having abandoned its ball, and its owner, for an evidently more exciting game of chase. It barked joyfully. A man was calling it back. The dog persisted then returned.

The rain was so thick now, visibility was impaired. In the deluge, paved pathways had become rivers. Finch sloshed on. He couldn't see the policemen any more. Had he lost them?

But then, up ahead, on the humpback bridge over the water… A helmet.

The other whistle.

Another policeman was sprinting down towards him.

'Stop. Police!'

Finch changed direction, but *this* one was too fast. He was charging full pelt. Finch had lost momentum. He was struggling. The policemen's feet thundered as he made up ground.

Come on! Push yourself!

And then… Finch was hit, hard, round the thighs – a full-on rugby tackle. Finch was slammed to the ground. The man was on top of him, trying to spin him over, to snap on the handcuffs.

The presence of a cuff on Finch's left wrist momentarily confused him and gave Finch a precious second. He kicked hard with his right foot. With a sickening crack, Edward's hand-made, ill-fitting shoe connected with the bridge of the copper's nose.

The man rolled over in the mud. Finch couldn't see for a moment, but he was on his knees, dazed, clutching his face, blood dripping between his fingers.

Finch slithered then found his feet. He was off.

'I'll get you, you bastard!'

The indestructible policeman staggered up, caked in brown, and was after him again.

Evasive action…

There were rowing boats in a line at the lake's edge, loosely tethered, abandoned as people sought shelter. It was a gamble. Finch tugged free the rope on the first one, jumped on board and kicked off from the concrete surround. The boat glided out while he rammed the oars into their rowlocks. The boat was already several inches deep in rainwater.

He thought for a second of Nathan Cole and it drove him on. He pulled hard, for all he was worth, getting good traction, churning forcefully, the surface of the lake pitted, as if the heavens were raining stones.

Shit!

But the policeman didn't follow. He was running back over the bridge to cut him off on the other side.

Finch, you idiot.

Facing backwards to row, he could see Sissons and Webb approaching from the rear. A pincer movement. They had him on either bank. But they – *all* of them – had made a strategic error.

He simply jumped overboard. The water was barely up to his thighs. Finch waded the few slimy yards to the far end, furthest from them, where a woman huddling with her sodden poodle merely regarded him with bemusement. He had put distance between himself and his pursuers again, now running back round the waterside paths to catch up.

Yet… as he climbed out through the sludge, he saw the black police Ford now haring over the same small bridge, then down the carriageway, the way that Coates had wanted to go originally. It screeched to a halt.

'*Finch!*' Coates was calling. '*Don't be a fool!*'

The driver, Jennings, got out, flung the door wide and leaned on it. It could only mean…

'*Wait!*' he could hear Coates implore.

But there was an orange flash…

BANG!

…as a police revolver was discharged in his direction.

Shit!

Finch ducked. He could hear the bullet thud into a tree.

BANG!… Another one.

It clanged into a drainpipe on the pavilion.

The low building would give Finch cover. He doubled round behind it, facing back. To his left was the Gothic steeple of the macabre Albert Memorial; across the road from it, the great dome of the Albert Hall.

I need them back in the car, not chasing me on foot.

He couldn't see the others, but they must be there, close. Sure enough, he heard more shouts, more whistles and then… thankfully… the car door slam and the vehicle screech off.

Filled with flashbacks to South Africa, Finch, heart in mouth, turned and charged across the no man's land of the sanded bridleway that ran along the southern edge of Hyde Park. He had underestimated the heavy going, becoming bogged right down in the middle. Had PC Jennings been more patient, Finch would now have been an easy target.

The whistles were getting closer. As he extricated himself, he ran though his options. He could jump on a bus, but it was still too far and would make stops. Or…

The police whistles were nearer still. There would be others on the beat rushing to join in.

And then… a taxicab!

He climbed over the railings, nearly spearing his groin. He made a crazed dash into the road, waving his arms in the air, almost causing the horse to rear up.

'Oi, steady on!'

He tucked the handcuffs away.

'Sloane Square. As fast as you can. Emergency!'

The rain now was so hard, it hurt.

He heard a tinny-sounding bell and the parping of a horn.

'Cor, what's his game?' asked the cabbie.

Finch looked round. The Ford had cleared the park and was less than two hundred yards behind and closing fast. The coppers pursuing on foot were now climbing over the railings after him.

'My horse, mister. I'll do what I can but she don't like the rain.'

'Please, just *go*!'

-

Mordecai waited. Of all the weather conditions, this was the worst. Not just a typical London drizzle, but something biblical. Ominous. On the one hand it would slow his quarry, but it added a whole new dimension to his marksmanship. It would test his skills to the limit.

His heart jumped with every new vehicle that turned the corner into the square heading east. One, two, then three police cars. But he knew his target. It would appear soon. He had studied the vehicle at close quarters through the embassy gates – a shiny red Mercedes-Benz, German of all things. ('We may detest their Kaiser,' the rich man had told him, 'but their motorcars are sublime.') He knew every inch of its shiny metallic form and could pick out the ambassador easily.

But now he understood why the thick-necked Brute was there. He saw him again through the scope. He was nodding. At first he thought that the mission had been aborted. But surely such a decision would have been conveyed to him personally. No, it was something more fundamental. He was telling him that the car was rounding the bend. It was next…

-

'Emergency!' repeated Finch.

'Whatever you say, boss,' shrugged the cabbie and twitched his whip.

Had they seen him?

The forlorn, bedraggled horse trotted on and the cabbie veered right, across Knightsbridge, onto Sloane Street. Away down the Brompton Road stood the honey-hued edifice of the new Harrods department store.

The Ford was honking and ringing its bell. Finch looked back at it through the rectangle cut into the canvas. The rain drummed hard.

The car had some sort of device, a pair of mechanical wiping arms that swept back and forth across the windscreen – but they were beating in vain against this deluge. It splashed through the great puddles that had spread across the tarmacadam, beeping its way, the driver yelling at the horses and carts it was weaving around, hitting them with spray.

They passed the gardens of Cadogan Place.

'Faster!' yelled Finch.

But the driver had now twigged. They were after his passenger.

''Ere. What's going on?' he shouted down. 'I don't want no trouble.'

It was no good. The horse-drawn cab could not outpace the car. It was closing fast, wreaking havoc. And Finch could see… the *second* police car. It, too, was screeching down Sloane Street, gaining.

The first police Ford was now close enough for Finch to see inside. It was just the driver – Jennings – with Coates beside him. Coates was waving his arm, indicating for the cab to slow, to pull in to the kerb.

Within seconds, it had revved hard and drawn alongside the cab on its offside, decelerating slightly to impart a message. Finch ducked down.

'*Pull over!*' demanded an enraged PC Jennings.

That bastard just tried to shoot me.

The confused cabbie, his horse spooked by the motor vehicle, thrown off its stride, shouted for the police car to move out of the way. He couldn't comply otherwise.

Coates leaned over, hoping to be heard.

'*Finch, for God's sake, just stop this nonsense!*'

The police car screamed ahead again and went to cut across the cab, which had begun to slow down anyway. Jennings braked the car hard on a diagonal.

Oncoming carts and wagons swerved out of their way.

The slamming of the brakes made it aquaplane. A number 137 bus, with 'Marble Arch' on the front, travelling in the other direction, coming towards them, was forced into an evasive manoeuvre, its jittered horses wide-eyed with panic.

The bus threw Jennings' concentration. On the wet surface, and with his eye off the ball, he lost control. The car spun a full three hundred and sixty degrees and – with a horrific crump of metal – slammed into a gas lamp, almost folding in two around it.

Amid a wild clatter of hooves, the cabbie hauled in the reins, stopped, and jumped down to help. The bus screeched to a halt, skewing sideways, blocking the road. There was steam hissing from the car's radiator. Jennings was slumped over the steering wheel. He had blood pouring from a head wound. He waved his arm, limply, motioning that he was okay.

They were opposite a Lyons' teahouse, where people had taken refuge. Suddenly there was a blur of folk rushing out… and from the bus, too. For a moment, Finch was of no consequence. He seized his moment, climbed down and ran.

Coates had staggered from the wreckage, Finch saw – and he felt relief at the sight. He was gesturing in vain for his men to follow Finch, who had now turned the corner past the Byzantine-style Cadogan Hall. The detective's other arm hung limply.

The coppers from the second police car gave chase on foot. Again, he heard a chorus of police whistles.

BANG! Another gunshot.

Jesus, the police were supposed to be unarmed. But then these were Special Branch…

BANG! Another.

One of the stained glass windows on the Cadogan Hall became a rainbow shower of crystal.

'*Stop, police!*'

Finch turned a corner and ducked into a doorway, an arched red-brick porch, tucking himself out of sight. For a brief moment, his aches and pains, especially in his knee, erupted in symphonic overload. He held his breath.

Four policemen thundered past, splashing through the wet. They had not seen him.

It was grey, soaking and miserable, and yet he was still aware of some kind of crowd forming, the British public never failing to materialise for an 'occasion'.

He was just a few streets away from the Russian embassy. He recalled the conversation in the police car as it had got stuck in Parliament Square earlier... The ambassador would proceed along Eaton Square... the Palace... the Mall...

He dashed down to the main road. There was a large, empty flat-bed cart clipping along. He ran behind it for a few paces, then launched himself onto the back. The driver didn't notice.

At Eaton Square, just a minute away, he hopped off. The driver saw him this time and yelled: 'What the bloody hell do you think you're doing?!'

But Finch had now pushed into the bodies on the south side of the square, working his way along the railings, behind the folks who had gathered two, three deep back from the roadside. He would have to follow the ambassadorial motorcade, try and keep up. But it was going to be impossible to track it all the way to Whitehall. Maybe he could stop it.

Yes, that's it! He must stop it!

Someone from the embassy, or from the government, had had their publicity people working overtime. Along the line of the route, bedraggled children were waving sodden Union Jacks and Russian tricolours. Though he heard, too, adult mutterings of 'Bloody Russians' and how the 'bastards had got off lightly'.

Behind the children lurked more drenched onlookers, drawn, as ever, towards pomp and spectacle, regardless of the politics behind it.

Think, Finch! Where…?

The next stretch, the route round Buckingham Palace and the Mall, was out in the open – easy for close access if a bomb or grenade were to be hurled at the car, though it would be an imprecise act, without guarantee of success and with no cover for an escape.

By contrast, the last leg of the journey, along Whitehall, had high buildings towering over the road – good sniping positions, better for a precision kill – but it would require considerable hubris on the part of any assassin, right in the very heart of the establishment, in the most secure quarter of the British Empire, a mere stone's throw from Scotland Yard.

If he had to stop the ambassador, it would have to be…

Then, he froze.

Up ahead, he saw him… *Smert.*

He was looking upwards, high, to a building across the square.

Of course. It was perfect!

Finch followed the line of vision. He could barely see it, obscured by the black, wet branches. But there, in an attic window… a small lower pane was missing.

He heard the hubbub of excitement and watched Smert nod in communication as, right now – in this road closed to ordinary traffic – a great red Mercedes-Benz limousine bedecked with ambassadorial regalia was turning the corner.

No sooner had he seen it than he was suddenly, violently wrestled to ground, his face crunching into the slabs of the pavement.

'Dr Ingo Finch… I hereby place you under arrest…'

–

Mordecai turned from the Brute and trained his scope on the western end of the street. In the absence of traffic, the

Mercedes-Benz was travelling faster than anticipated. The question of the road closure still bothered him. There should have been *nothing* left to chance.

And now there was some kind of disturbance, a kerfuffle. The police, several officers, were amongst the crowd, pulling someone to the ground.

Concentrate!

The limousine glided along. The rain had eased off slightly, but it still affected the atmospherics… it could distort the flight of a bullet. Mordecai poised his barrel, ready to shoot slightly ahead.

Up front sat the chauffeur. In the rear, behind a divider, but still with an open top, sat two men, one younger, dark-haired, probably an aide, and then, on the left-hand side, in plain sight, the glum, grey-haired ambassador with his bushy moustache, the same face he had studied in a hundred photographs.

How ridiculously, criminally exposed.

But… an umbrella!

Mordecai got the crosshairs on the man's temple, but his view was then blocked. He moved slightly ahead, along the line of the bridge of the nose, aiming to shoot when he came fully into profile. He eased his breathing. Slowly, gently, he squeezed the trigger. But, again, *the accursed umbrella…*

-

Finch was hauled to his feet. There were four police around him. Limping up behind, clearly struggling, clutching his injured arm, was Coates.

'Finch. This is idiocy!'

'Is it?' said Finch.

With one wild swing, his fist flew through the air and connected with the jaw of the constable restraining him. Free again, with a frantic flailing of his arms, he beat a path through the onlookers, right out into the street, waving urgently at the limousine now bearing down on him.

The vehicle slowed, swerved, but continued past.

There was an audible gasp of shock as it did so and Finch thrust a foot onto the running board on the car's left side…

BANG! The echo of a shot.

…flinging himself right across the ambassador.

Chapter Forty-One

As Mordecai increased the pressure in his trigger finger, the car suddenly lurched, swinging off its course. There was a man…

It was too late.

He snatched up the second bullet, rammed it into the breech and slid the bolt forward.

Be calm, control your breathing.

He squeezed again.

BANG!

But the limousine suddenly stopped dead… There were police… Through his scope, he saw the second shot hole the engine cowling. Frantic, the police waved the car on, urging the driver to accelerate out of the area. It screeched off, tyres skewing in the wet.

And now heads were turning… *Up*…

Mordecai calculated the odds. Time was not on his side. He scooped up the shell casings and threw them into the Gladstone bag. He took the chair off the billiards table and grabbed his jacket, instinctively patting the fat envelope. But there was no time to drag the table back over to the wall. To him it made no difference anyway. There was a window knocked out. That was evidence enough. And any detective worth his salt would be able to detect gunpowder residue. The issue was surely not of *where* the shots had come from but of *who* had pulled the trigger.

He hurried down the stairs, almost tripping as he burst onto the first-floor landing. He flew down past the dead, white-sheeted rooms and the pile of post on the doormat.

As instructed, and as he had practised, he undid the back door and relocked it on the way out. Once down the steps into the garage, he dropped the rifle into the drain, heard it splash, then scraped the heavy iron lid back over, kicking dirt to cover the scuff marks.

Outside, the alley was empty, but he could sense the hubbub of confusion wafting back from the main road, the bafflement palpable. He heard shouts, police whistles.

He turned left out of the alley onto Belgrave Place and then continued straight for two hundred yards without looking around, pulling his collar up against the rain, which was still teeming down. There were a few pedestrians but he didn't make eye contact, just proceeded with purpose – the workman with his tool bag.

He studiously didn't look back. One telltale glance could spell the end. But he could hear no footsteps in pursuit, just that ambient murmur. He imagined people recounting what they had just seen, the facts distorting as the story swept along the pavement. And now the shouts, the whistles… they were fading.

It was starting to get dark, too. Some houses had their lights on – the chandeliers of the wealthy. Whoever was in charge of the embassy's security had been a poor strategist. An assassin should not be able to slip into the blackness. Clearly the rich man… maybe Weathers… had planned this whole thing with the help of those inside.

Up ahead was Belgrave Square. He felt the rain ease off again.

Control your breathing. You have walked this route a dozen times.

He continued as rehearsed. Only now, the motor van was there, waiting on the south-west corner, engine running, just as it was supposed to be. It was high and upright, 'Fidelio's Piano & Tuning' emblazoned in gold lettering on the black gloss paintwork.

The back doors opened and the woman – the 'housekeeper' he had met – was beckoning animatedly, urging him to run. This was not right. They must have new intelligence about the situation on the ground, for it had not been included in the plan. *Not* rushing – or rather, not *panicking* – had been stressed most emphatically.

The vehicle was already starting to pull away when Mordecai threw the bag on board and jumped in, the doors pulled closed behind him.

It was gloomy inside, just a small window above the driver's cab. There were two men in there, men in dark suits. They were young, possibly ex-servicemen, Mordecai thought, probably part of the mission's detail. But he did not like it.

There should no unknown factors. Familiarity – control* – was essential.*

The pair sat on the slatted bench seats which ran the length of the van, facing each other... unsmiling, no eye contact. He couldn't see the driver. Mordecai sat next to one man, the woman next to the other.

'You did your duty?' asked the woman sternly – a statement more than a question.

'I did,' said Mordecai, 'but there is *incident*. Police... Someone in crowd...'

She said nothing.

'And that idiot... the *giant*... He stand there... Give game away—'

'The bag. You have everything inside?' she cut across. 'You cleared up?'

He nodded. She took it off him.

'And the weapon has been disposed of?'

'Yes.'

She threw a glance to the two men.

And then Mordecai knew.

No!

He grabbed for the door handle but he was pulled down onto the boards. He struggled but the men knew what they were doing – men trained in physical combat like himself. They held him fast, arms and legs immobilised.

The woman slid out a surgical knife, curved, with a keen blade. She cut hard and deep into Mordecai's neck, whipping it across the jugular. The beast to the slaughter. The blood spurted viciously and continued to do so, well beyond the last drowning gurgle.

She reached inside his jacket pocket and pulled out the envelope. She wiped it on his trouser leg…

–

Annie stood still in the rain. The small silver automatic pistol was pointed straight at her midriff. She had her boots in her right hand. One swing and she could probably connect. But she was caught in that paralysing limbo between fright and flight. Plus, a sudden move, even if she were successful… Even if she could dash the remaining few yards to the gate… the odds were not in her favour. The weapon was low calibre but, at this range, a single shot would prove fatal.

She looked at her miserable, snivelling, conniving captor with the pathetic trickle of hair dye now beading down his forehead.

The longer he lingered, the more momentum swung her way. He did not look at ease with a gun. If she took one swipe… knocked it out of his hand…

But now he was gesturing… turning…

He put a finger to his lips, indicating silence.

He pointed to the gate. And showed her… He had the key.

He grabbed her by the arm and led her on. He rammed the key in the lock and the gate clanged open.

'God speed,' he said.

And with that she was free.

'But who are…?'

'Just go… *Go!*' he urged.

Annie smiled.

'Thank you.'

'*Please!*' he flapped his arm… motioning her away.

There were people scurrying past under umbrellas. She was in her stockinged feet. There was a silver-haired couple. The woman looked at her askance, then turned back to her husband. Annie heard them say something about a shooting… the Russian ambassador… This building… *This* was where he lived… And the police…

The police. She must find the police.

She spun round, ready to run. She had no idea where she was, but sensed she must go towards the source of the trouble… from where people were now streaming. Unless the lavender man could steer her?

She threw a glance back. She saw the look of panic.

And then…

He stood there, impassive, the great powerful, lumbering hulk. There was not a shred of emotion, no expression. But he had grabbed her arm, *hard*. His hand was so huge it completely enveloped her bicep. He would only have to drag her the few feet back inside… back into the sanctuary of the embassy.

BANG! A shot.

The silver-haired woman screamed.

If the lavender man had hit him, the beast showed no sign. He flicked at his side, as if swiping away a gnat. But it was enough to cause a momentary distraction.

In a blur the lavender man had flown at him, an ineffectual charge, but sufficient, along with the gunshot, to cause him to loosen his grip.

'Go… GO!' she heard him cry.

And she ran.

Smert fixed Vax with black, close-set eyes that spoke of curiosity – possibly, for one fleeting moment, *pity*.

There was an audible gasp. Onlookers stopped dead. Vax struggled, but it was a battle that could not be won. Smert locked Vax's head in the crook of his elbow.

More screams.

With an effortless twist and a crunch, the body flopped to the pavement.

Stooping casually, Smert grabbed Vax's collar and dragged his body back through the gate and himself into immunity.

Annie ran… towards the crowd… towards the police whistles.

She ran and ran and ran…

Chapter Forty-Two

Finch drifted in and out of consciousness. One minute he was on the South African veld, being shot at by Boer marksmen, the next minute he was an inconvenient lump, to be manoeuvred by irritable nurses.

He was loosely aware of light and dark, night and day, but had no measure of time… nor of space. He was with Annie, as real as it could possibly be, watching her sleep in the hotel room on the road out of Stellenbosch, the rays of the morning sun streaming in…

But there was, too, a menace, a sense of an enormous, malevolent presence… one that sent cold fear through him, that choked his breathing and made his heart pound. There was water, rising fast. He was chained to a rock as it climbed, higher and higher.

Finch found himself shouting. The act of it stirred him, brought him nearer to waking, nearer to the surface. He heard a voice… soothing… a female voice.

Annie?

And once more he slipped away.

He was thirsty. He vaguely remembered sipping water. He also heard talk of morphine. He was locked in his dream – cognisant, but unable to grope his way to the exit.

There was a different voice now… *male*… It came and went periodically – someone asking, and stressing the utmost importance of a request to be notified the minute he – Dr Finch – woke up.

'Finch… *Dr Finch*…?'

It was coming back.

'Dr Finch…?'

He heard a female voice again, pleading with the man for patience.

'I understand your position, Miss. But I'm afraid time is not on our side.'

Finch struggled to recognise it, but then he knew… the detective.

'Coates?'

'Nurse, he's awake!'

He felt a hand on his wrist, his pulse. Then he heard the nurse dash off… to fetch a doctor, she said.

'I *am* a doctor.'

She stopped.

'*No*, Doctor… I mean *your* doctor… your physician…'

She spoke in hushed tones.

'Please, Detective. Be gentle with him.'

Finch blinked his eyes open. It was bright but blurred. He could see a clear, blue, early winter sky. And now his head hurt… all over, every patch of his skull. He sensed a fresh bandage round his crown.

'Coates?' he asked again.

'Here, Finch.'

His shape began to form. The detective was standing over him. There was something white. He had his right forearm in a plaster cast.

'Sorry…'

'What?'

'Your arm.'

'Not your fault, Dr Finch. Not directly.'

Croaked Finch: 'You need to get yourself a better driver.'

Coates gave a light laugh.

'Oh no, sorry, I mean… Is *he* okay?'

'Jennings? Was just concussed. He's fine.'

'Ingo?'

There was another voice… male… Scottish.

'*Jilkes?*'

There must have been panic… strain in the way he said it.

'Please, you mustn't go upsetting yourself, Dr Finch,' said Coates.

Jilkes sounded heartbroken.

'Ingo, I'm so sorry…'

'He's been here the whole time,' explained Coates. 'Slept in a chair.'

'How long have I been…?'

The nurse had come back in.

'Two days,' she said.

Finch saw a white coat. The doctor was with her.

'But Jilkes…?'

He could see Jilkes now, too – the worry, the concern etched into his features.

'They leaned on me, Ingo… I couldn't act freely… didn't know what to do…'

Coates came close.

'Bastards threatened his family,' he breathed. 'They're okay now. No danger.'

'Jilkes, no, it was *me*. I should never have dragged you into this whole bloody business.'

He reached out his right hand. He felt Jilkes take it. He realised his wrist was bandaged.

'You were doing what you thought was right,' soothed Jilkes. 'We *both* were.'

'But Agatha, the kids…?'

'They're fine, Ingo. All's well. They send their love.'

Finch tried to smile.

The doctor bustled his way through. He and the nurse eased Finch up slightly. There was a pang, a burn, down the side of Finch's neck. The nurse placed another pillow behind his head.

Finch couldn't gauge distance… depth… but he seemed to be in a private room.

'Right, let's have a look at you,' said the doctor.

The nurse gave him the vitals but Finch couldn't compute them. It was just a string of numbers.

'When will we be able to take a statement?' he heard Coates whisper.

'Hold your horses, Detective. Our patient's been a lucky fellow,' griped the doctor. 'Let's not push it.'

'Sorry. But it's…'

Christ… it was all coming back to him…

'The ambassador!?'

'Please, Dr Finch,' said the doctor. 'Don't exert yourself.'

'Right as rain, Finch,' said Coates. 'You saved his life.'

The movement made his shoulder burn again. He winced.

'Take it easy,' said the nurse.

'Bullet hit you just below the collarbone,' explained the doctor, prodding and poking at him. 'A high-velocity bullet. Clean in, clean out. Just missed the artery. But just a fraction of an inch either way…'

He pronounced it as jollily as if to a child who had just scraped their knee.

'…You're a lucky fellow.'

This doesn't feel like luck.

'A *German* bullet… Mauser… 7 millimetre,' added Coates.

'Oh.'

The doctor and the nurse conferred. Coates whispered so they couldn't hear.

'…And so the plot thickens. We're still piecing it all together. Which is why…'

The doctor threw Coates an admonishing look.

'As I said, Detective, all in good time.'

The doctor got to work on Finch, looking into his eyes, examining his pupils. He was shining a light now, then holding a fountain pen, commanding that Finch follow its line of movement.

'Of course, this is all off the record...' added Coates. 'Nothing in the papers... Stakes too high. The assassination attempt? It never officially happened. Powers that be...'

'I see.'

'Bit of a hero, laddie,' chipped in Jilkes, and the word made Finch think, for a second, of Lulu.

'An Anglo-Russian accord was signed. Problem averted,' declared Coates. 'And for *that*, at the very least, Whitehall will give you some kind of commendation.'

Finch waved it away.

'Ingo...'

It was Jilkes again.

'...There's someone else who wants to see you. She's been here with me for most of it.'

It was the question he'd wanted to ask. He had no idea. But any pain he felt was offset by the warmth now oozing through him. It was more powerful than any drug.

'Annie?'

The silence lingered. Something was amiss.

'No, Ingo,' she said.

When the doctor moved, he saw her, sitting in the corner.

'Maude came here the moment she heard,' offered Jilkes.

Whispered Coates, awkwardly: 'Mrs Pointer's midway across the Atlantic... Safe.'

Now it was Jilkes who was leaning in.

'Just let it go, old boy.'

'Maude... Really... I'm sorry... I...'

And once again Finch hated himself...

-

Finch sat in the open tonneau of the government Wolseley as it turned off Whitehall at the corner of Horse Guards Avenue. There was a distinct chill in the air and he pulled his overcoat around him, careful not to let the heavy serge put pressure on his shoulder. His arm was still in a sling, left hand strapped to his chest, the palm resting on his right clavicle.

It had been ten days since his discharge from the West London Infirmary, three weeks on from Eaton Square. Back home, unfit to work, he had spent his time being indulged by Mrs P-A, to whom he was unable to confide the exact nature of his injuries.

He suspected that inconsistencies in his storytelling were rife and respected her refusal to probe them. There was an upturn in the police presence around the house and about the street, she had noted. He knew, without it ever being spoken, that she understood a fraction about some other life that had been lived – in South Africa, and now here.

He doubted if a return to the old ways would ever be possible. Not now. What could he ever get out of his small-town profession other than frustration and disappointment? Though he had never asked for it, and certainly never expected it, he had been awarded a thousand pounds in compensation by the War Office – not that the word 'compensation' was ever used. The cheque was anonymous. It came with its own unique code... a reference number... He was assured its deposit would never trouble the Board of Inland Revenue.

He would see how long the money lasted... and how long till drink accounted for a chunk of it – though he had not touched a drop since his wounding; he had simply lost the taste. It wouldn't stay this way, he knew... and Christmas was imminent. He vowed in advance to give some money to Mrs P-A and to spend a portion of it on the house.

He had not seen Maude since that day in the hospital, and, pointedly, barely seen Jilkes. He knew that his friend's visit that day was as much about the assuaging of guilt as anything else. He was sure Agatha, quite correctly, would put the security of their family first. And that meant no room for him in their lives.

As the car came to a halt outside the great granite edifice of the War Office, Finch looked up. It was colder but clear, the sky bright blue, the wet and grey of autumn lifting for a more welcome crispness, a purging of the gloom that had inflicted itself upon him, in every sense. His breath came in great billows.

The government chauffeur walked round the car and opened the door. He extended a hand to help Finch down, though pride got the better of him and he struggled by himself, regretting it as a twinge of pain flashed through his shoulder and up his neck. He still couldn't recall the moment of being shot – running towards the ambassador's limousine, yes, but nothing else until the hospital.

'You know where you're going, sir?'

'I do, thank you.'

He had been told the number and been asked not to write it down – room 1571. It seemed an unnecessary affectation.

There were two Horse Guards, one either side of the entrance in their dark blue tunics, red-plumed helmets, white trousers and shiny black riding boots. They sported swords and shoulder braids and gleaming cuirass breastplates. They were unmoved as Finch mounted the steps, his troublesome knee at least benefitting from the enforced rest.

In a circular vestibule was a reception desk at which a khaki-clad NCO requested Finch's name and ticked him off a list. The room was on the first floor.

There was an electronic buzz – a door-release system – and Finch was inside. He could hear the *clack-clack-clack* of typewriters as he went towards the stairs. Up the first flight, he walked along a dark, oak-panelled corridor, his shoes clicking and echoing off the shiny black and white tiles.

The doors were all numbered. There were no names. He found 1571, knocked and heard a muffled, '*Wait.*' There was a chair outside. After five minutes of standing, he then sat in silence for what seemed forever. Eventually the door opened and a small, expressionless man in a winged collar poked his head out.

'Dr Finch?'

'Yes.'

'This way, please.'

The man was slightly stooped. Not old, he just seemed it – as fusty as the civil service he represented. Inside, the office was that of a mandarin – a window onto Whitehall (probably in every sense, mused Finch), an oak desk, leather chair, bookcase, an ornamental globe.

It soon became apparent that it was not *this* fellow's office. A side door opened and in walked a tall man in a morning suit. He had a commanding presence. He was probably in his mid-fifties, was balding, but with an impressive moustache and keen green eyes.

'Allow me to introduce Mr Melville,' said the underling.

'Ah, Dr Finch,' said the incomer, shaking his hand firmly. 'No doubting you're a brave man.'

His accent caught Finch unawares – not the cut glass of the public school, but the cadence of the London streets, tinged with the lilt of Ireland… of its remote, wild west.

'I've read the report, Finch. You're a resourceful chap. Can get yourself out of a pickle… and *into* one, for that matter.'

He motioned to the underling, who picked up a wooden case from the desk. He flipped the lid. Inside, on a white silk lining, lay a silver cross, with a ruby in the centre. It was threaded onto a long, pale-blue and white striped ribbon.

'The King's Gallantry Medal,' said the underling.

He indicated that Finch should bow his head.

Melville took it out and hung it around Finch's neck, arranging it across the sling.

'Although, of course, this is all just *entre nous*,' the underling added. 'Can't let it get out in public.'

Melville harrumphed. The underling scurried out and closed the door. The atmosphere felt flat. Far from a reception for a hero. Not that Finch considered himself such.

'I say *brave*,' said Melville. 'But your actions were also reckless… Nearly blew wide open an operation that Military Intelligence and the Secret Service had been working on for years – and not for the *first* time I might add.'

'But I thought… the ambassador…?'

Melville went to the window and looked out. He had big, square hands. He clasped them behind his back.

'Count Alexander Konstantinovich Benckendorff…'

He uttered the words slowly, deliberately and, fancied Finch, with no small measure of contempt.

'…You think you saved his life?'

'Well, I mean… not that I feel comfortable with the term… but he emerged unscathed, the signing went ahead… the accord between Britain and Russia.'

Melville shook his head. He turned.

'I ask you, Dr Finch – not to judge you, a man is entitled to his opinions – but, in terms of this accord, where do you stand…? Were you a man lusting for Russian blood? Or perhaps one who thought that wiser heads should prevail, and a better solution, a *diplomatic* solution, be sought?'

He sensed Finch's hesitation.

'I think that should be obvious.'

'Obvious? In this department, in our *demi-monde*, nothing is ever as it appears… You may speak freely.'

He produced a worn gold cigarette case and offered it. Finch, unusually, declined.

'Well, sir, I would have to say, much as I share the outrage at what happened in the North Sea, it was not something to go to war over. I've seen war up close. It's not pleasant.'

Melville produced a flint lighter and lit himself a smoke.

'So, in your view – and I'm not putting words in your mouth, you understand – sitting round a table, signing an accord, was an important way of achieving that goal?'

'I've not read the small print, and I'm sure there's some humble pie to be eaten on the part of the Russians, but, essentially… *yes*.'

'His Majesty's government would concur…'

He exhaled upwards, towards the ceiling.

'…In which case, Dr Finch, given the importance of this Anglo-Russian accord, why do you think we would place it in even the slightest jeopardy – at this particularly combustible time – by parading the Russian ambassador, Count Benckendorff, through the streets of London… and in an open-topped car in broad daylight?'

'I'm sorry, I don't follow.'

He tapped the cigarette on a large glass ashtray.

'That man you saved… spared from a Bolshevik bullet… I have to tell you, Finch, that was *not* the ambassador…'

'What?'

'…but an actor posing as him. We switched the two men as the vehicle left the embassy… The real ambassador, the *real* Benckendorff, had already met with our foreign secretary in secret an hour before.'

'Oh.'

The more Melville went on, the more pronounced the Irish.

'What's more, your actions, despite your having been warned to stay away on *several* occasions, I regret to say, resulted in the death of one of our chief assets.'

'A *death*?… Who?'

'You knew him as a private detective.'

'*Vax?!*'

'If that's what you prefer to call him. Though that is immaterial now.'

Finch felt cold, numb, sick to his stomach. His words came hushed, strained, pathetic.

'My God, I had no… I'm so… *so* sorry.'

'A skilled agent who had successfully embedded himself within the Russian diplomatic hierarchy and was our greatest single source of information about the Bolsheviks' dealings in this country, something we could only leverage by drawing their little plot out into the open… This Norfolk business, the assassination attempt, we had it *all* covered…'

Melville must have seen the colour drain from Finch's face.

'…His infiltration had also allowed him to groom a female accomplice, a member of the household staff. Needless to say, we've had to pull her out. Months of work sacrificed.'

He went to the globe. The upper half lifted up as a hinged lid. It was a drinks cabinet. Without even asking, Melville poured two generous measures of single malt Scotch into cut-crystal tumblers. He handed one to Finch. He sipped. It didn't taste how he remembered.

'The problem is, Finch, you are a liability...'

He had offered both a smoke and a drink, but, noted Finch, *not* a seat.

'...You've owed your freedom to the fact that, five years ago, during the South African War, you found yourself sitting on some classified information – information that His Majesty's government hoped would never surface. You then used the existence of this information as a bond... *blackmail*, in another man's language... to guarantee said freedom.'

Finch felt the blood rise.

'Goddammit... South Africa... my life was in danger. Those bastard thugs were about to put a bullet in my head. I had no idea of the context. I was wagering those documents on my life... on *Nurse Jones*' life...'

Melville sat on the edge of his desk. He swirled his glass and examined its contents.

'Don't get me wrong, Finch. You played your hand well. Sometimes people..."outsiders"... ones not straightjacketed by specialist training, can be very – how shall we say? – *creative* in their reasoning... their methods...'

He rested his cigarette in the ashtray.

'...But I regret to inform you that you will shortly be receiving a *communiqué* from a private security bank in Holborn informing you that there has a been a break-in at their establishment and a certain deposit box opened, its contents removed. I think you know to what I'm referring.'

Finch felt the nausea return. He nodded weakly.

'We don't doubt who was behind it either – our friends, the Germans. And in the shadow game of the intelligence war, it's a pretty big stick for them to wield. To use the language of the saloon bar, they've now "got something" on us. And why? Because by poking your head above the parapet, as you were *explicitly* told not to, you drew attention to yourself. In this game, *all* actions have consequences. And they'll come after you, Finch, will want to make you talk. If we had any common sense we'd have liquidated you – you *and* your Australian friend. But she's an untouchable now. And so, by association – and by a whisker – are *you*.'

'Are you seriously suggesting…?!'

'Oh, absolutely. The order was sitting right here, waiting for my signature…'

He waved a hand at his desk blotter, his tone utterly unemotional.

'…In this game one cannot afford to get too – how shall we say? – *sentimental*. Eyes always on the prize.'

'But surely…?' Finch spluttered. 'A bloody war has just been averted…?!'

Melville went to the window again, staring out, hands clasped. He took his time.

'Dr Finch, do you know what's going on here? I mean *really* know what's going on here?'

He turned back again. Finch shrugged.

'You really have no idea, do you?'

Finch shook his head.

'The British and French have already pledged themselves to each other as allies. The *Entente Cordiale*. A thousand years of enmity set aside for a free hand in each other's colonies and a bulwark in Europe against Germany. The last thing we wanted – as you correctly deduced – was to get dragged into an unnecessary sideshow against Russia, be it in the Baltic, the Black Sea, the Pacific… or the bloody North-West Frontier.'

His cigarette had been wisping away, leaving a long stem of ash. He picked it up and resumed smoking.

'As a result of preventing the Eaton Square assassination – which we would have stopped anyway, *without* your help – we are now, too, committed to propping up the King's nephew, Tsar Nicholas II, a pathetic, vain man and his despicable regime, one with which we should have no truck were it not for the fact that befriending Russia provides us with a convenient second front against the Kaiser…

'But he'll not last,' he added. 'We are only staying the Tsar's execution – quite literally. Soon, a mighty revolution will come in which the Communists – those Bolsheviks – will seize power. They will purge the past – daresay brutally – and a new Russia will rise from the ashes.'

'Then why not let the Bolsheviks *succeed* in offing the Tsar?' asked Finch. 'Get it over and done with? From what I understand they shun "imperial wars". They wouldn't have wanted to fight us anyway.'

'Because the timing is not yet *right*, Finch…'

He pondered over his words.

'…We are merely *managing* the situation, biding our time, not for some premature insurrection – something that may happen soon, even within weeks – but for the full, unstoppable force of the genuine thing. And when that happens, the *real* revolution, it will come at a moment, and on terms, of *our* choosing.'

Finch put his glass down. He'd given up on it.

'The Marxists have a saying – the "useful idiot",' Melville continued. 'The evangelical politico, the zealot who espouses their cause, but who is enlisted purely as a means to an end – an expendable soul, there to be sacrificed like a chess player's pawn. Well when the revolution's been won, we will make *them* – the Bolsheviks – *our* useful idiots in a struggle against a greater evil.'

'A greater evil?'

'One way or another, war against Germany will come, Dr Finch. You know it. *Everyone* knows it. It's just a matter of when. The strong will win, the weak will perish, the sick and decadent will be consumed. But our job here is to play the long game. It's what happens when that show's *over* that bothers us, Finch. *After* the chaos. A new order will be on its way – a grand clearing of the decks, a lust for the extermination of degeneracy, for punitive action, for the attribution of blame. It will swell. It will be a new Europe of states built on national vitality and order and discipline and vulgar, populist, vengeful strongmen…'

He let the pause hang.

'…*Our* job is to keep Great Britain out of it, to steer her on her own path.'

He stared intently at Finch.

'Do you know who I am?'

Finch felt ridiculous, standing there with his Boys' Brigade gong hanging round his neck, being lectured by a superior.

'I've heard about you, sir.'

'Some nonsense about Houdini, no doubt?'

'Well I—'

'It's like this, Finch. I was, until recently, the head of Special Branch. What had become patently clear, as this recent affair has just demonstrated, is that when it comes to matters of national security – Parliament, Foreign Office, War Office, Colonial Office, Scotland Yard, the Admiralty – the left hand doesn't know what the right hand is doing. Too many cooks. There have been a number of plots against the Crown, against the Empire, that we've thwarted, some the public will never ever know about…'

Melville stubbed his cigarette out.

'…As a result of which, I now find myself in a curious position – a desk at the War Office, in the employ of the Foreign Office, and, by the gift of the prime minister, somewhere around His Majesty's secretary of state for foreign affairs in terms of rank and access to privileged information… *intelligence*, for want of a better word. I have been charged with bringing these strands together into one agency… what is provisionally known as MO3.'

'I'm not really sure what you are saying.'

'Here, you will *never* be free, never truly safe. There is no life for you in England, Finch. Not at the moment. I suggest you leave, and leave soon.'

'*Leave?*… But *where*?'

Melville smiled to himself.

'I suppose you could say my illusionist associations have borne *some* fruit... First we, MO3, will make you disappear, Finch. And then you can be *our* useful idiot... Somewhere.'

He drained his whisky and slammed the glass down.

'You still carry the rank of captain...'

'I *did*... I mean, in the Medical Corps...'

'That was not a question, Captain Finch. Your commission has been renewed.'

'But I—'

Melville extended his hand to shake.

'We will be in touch. That will be all.'

He left the room by the side door. Finch's time was up.

Outside, Finch stood in the corridor for a moment. He turned the worthless bauble on his chest, with its smug Latin inscription and its Ruritanian pomp and wondered, given all that had just been laid at his feet, what the hell it was all about.

He looped the medal over his head, then hung it on the doorknob. His heels clicked and echoed as he strutted off down the corridor...